Praise for *How Fast Can You Run*

"A book like *How Fast Can You Run* is an eye-opening experience, awakening empathy for a much wider world."

—*prickofthespindle.org*

"Because *How Fast Can You Run* is based on a true saga, the viewpoints and experiences of Kuch come to vivid life and weave a powerful saga of politics, struggle, and survival that's hard to put down. Any reader interested in accounts of the Sudanese war will find this a compelling method of absorbing history at its most meaningful: through the eyes of a young eyewitness who didn't just observe events, but lived through and survived them."

—*Midwest Book Review*

"In *How Fast Can You Run*, Harriet Levin Millan tells the story of one boy's search for a mother's love through almost unimaginable pain and suffering. After being separated from his family at the age of five during Sudan's civil war, Majok and later Mike, the novel's real-life South Sudanese protagonist, braved war, hunger, and desperate illness before arriving in the United States as a refugee. Millan, who met Michael Majok Kuch when her creative writing class interviewed Sudanese immigrants, brilliantly renders the contours of Dinka and refugee life as well as the internal life of a young refugee tormented by the loss of his family and childhood. Congratulations to Millan. *How Fast Can You Run* is a marvelous achievement."

—Deborah Scroggins, author, *Emma's War: A True Story of Love and Death in Sudan*

"*How Fast Can You Run* is the story of the indomitable spirit of a boy who overcomes inconceivable loss and countless instances of physical and emotional danger, exiled from everything he had ever known. Millan's telling of Kuch's story is a refugee's dark odyssey that witnesses the vicious realities of the Sudanese conflict and the power of a single human life to overcome impossible trauma with perseverance, hard-won wisdom, and an unyielding grace. Devastating, moving, full of magical grace."

—Tyler Meier, Executive Director, University of Arizona Poetry Center, former Managing Editor of *The Kenyon Review*

"In Harriet Levin Millan's *How Fast Can You Run*, the poetry of pain and trauma leaps off the page as we follow the extraordinary journey of Michael Majok Kuch from a lost boy to a developing adolescent finding his way. A powerful meditation on love, loss, and triumph of survival. A stunning achievement not to be missed."

—Elizabeth L Silver, author of *The Execution of Noa P. Singleton*

"Harriet Levin Millan has transformed the story of one 'lost boy' into an earthy, grittily told, highly affecting novel. With a poet's piercing eye, attuned ear, and facility for recognizing resonant moments, Millan has written an emotionally rich-veined, dramatically moving and ultimately triumphant story. I emerged from this ingenious, fast-paced novel with the sensation of having been taken along by its protagonist on a poignant, heart-pounding journey, enlarged, and changed."

—Okey Ndibe, author of *Foreign Gods, Inc.*

"The un-imaginable journey of Sudanese refugee Michael Majok Kuch becomes an epic tale through the telling. Genre bursting, this part memoir, part bildungsroman, part adventure tale, and part heart-felt family reunion avoids the pitfalls of many of its predecessors. Full characterization from Sudan to Philadelphia, exacting detail from beginning to end, clearly visualized African landscapes in all their complexity; there are no broad brush strokes of civil war, refugee plight and immigration here. A fuller story than *How Fast Can You Run* cannot have been told of the tragic events of war in Sudan that uproot the young boy from the Dinka plains of Southern Sudan to Kakuma refugee camp to Nairobi and Philadelphia and how he has to fight a different kind of war in America from which he emerges victorious. Epic."

—Billy Kahora, Editor, *Kwani*

"The refugee is the hero of our time, a champion for human survival and freedom. At this hour millions of anonymous men, women and children are fleeing brutal dictatorial regimes, drug cartels, environmental devastation and hopeless poverty. They press up against our fences. With sensitivity, passion and grave reportorial insight, Harriet Levin Millan tells the epic story of a single refugee, the indomitable Michael Majok Kuch, and she gives song to them all."

—Ken Kalfus, author of *Coup De Foudre*

"The best war novel written from a young boy's perspective since Jerzy Kosinski's *The Painted Bird.*"

—Nyuol Lueth Tong, *There is a Country: New Writing from the New Nation of South Sudan*

"With stirring compassion and evocative power, Harriet Levin Millan has recreated the heartbreakingly courageous odyssey of one 'Lost Boy of Sudan,' Michael Majok Kuch, as he escaped the hell of his homeland riven by genocidal conflict to the lonely limbo of a childhood spent in East African refugee and IDP camps...*How Fast Can You Run* is a novel of the moment as it informs and addresses the hardships, tragedies and wonders facing the 65 million refugees currently displaced by regional and international conflict."

—Cheryl Pearl Sucher, author of
The Rescue of Memory

"In *How Fast Can You Run* Harriet Levin Millan turns novel-biography into a genre of its own and shows how empathy can turn into a true solidarity. This is a beautiful and crucial story told by two people, one Sudanese with dreams of independence, the other, an American poet who listens to Michael Majok Kuch through her imagination. For Mike in the United States, Halloween with strange fruit hanging triggers PTSD, ethnicity becomes race, soldiers become white police, tragedy there becomes tragedy here and in the end there is only one life for Mike to live. An enduring image for me—a refugee boy blowing up a discarded bloody surgical glove to make a soccer ball, this bio-novel reminds us that the most human of all activities, the one thing that binds us all is finding beauty even in impossible situations."

—Mukoma Wa Ngugi author of *Nairobi Heat*

"As an eyewitness to the Sudan and South Sudan conflicts, I cherish this book. From the portrait of South Sudanese life to Michael Majok Kuch fleeing for his life to his immigration to the US, *How Fast Can You Run* captures a young person's deepest yearnings. Michael's experience and Millan's precise telling of it help give purpose to the human quest for survival. This book will open your heart. Inspiring and necessary. A testament to the human spirit."

—Valentino Achak Deng, Founder of
the VAD Foundation

How Fast Can You Run

A Novel based on the life of Michael Majok Kuch

Harriet Levin Millan

Harvard Square Editions
New York
2016

The first chapter (under the title, *"Yalla!"*) first
appeared in *The Kenyon Review*, Volume XXXIII,
Number 1, Winter, 2011, reprinted with
permission.

ISBN 978-1-941861-20-2
1. Sudanese—United States—Fiction.
2. Sudan—History—Civil War, 1983-2005—
Fiction. 3. Refugees—Sudan—Fiction.
4. Refugees—United States—Fiction.
5. Sudan_Emigration and immigration—Fiction.
6. United States—Emigration and immigration—
Fiction. I. Title.
Printed in the United States of America
Published in the United States by
Harvard Square Editions
www.harvardsquareeditions.org

"Alas, oh land of whirring wings…"

—*Isaiah 18:1*

"Life in extremity reveals in its movement a definite rhythm of decline and renewal. The state of wakefulness is essential, but in actual experience it is less an unwavering hardness of spirit than a tenuous achievement with periods of weakness and strength. Survivors not only wake, but reawake, fall low and begin to die, and then turn back to life.

—*The Survivor, An Anatomy of Life in the Death Camps,*
Terrence Des Pres

This novel begins with the second Sudanese Civil War. It is based on the experience of the main character, Michael Majok Kuch. We met as part of a One Book, One Philadelphia Writing Project conceived by Marie Field of the Free Library of Philadelphia. The book is based on real historical events. While many of the events capture Michael's experience exactly as he told them to me over a three-year period, time sequences were occasionally altered to make the narrative arc more compelling. In order to respect the privacy of the people in Michael's life, characters, businesses, places, events and incidents are used in a fictitious manner. All the names and identifying details of characters are fictitious except for Michael's and his mother's.

PREFACE BY MICHAEL MAJOK KUCH

This book bears witness to my childhood experience right before I would have undergone initiation, which typically marks the end of childhood in the Dinka Bor cultural heritage. My story begins just as I was about to learn to be, and to grow into, a successful herder. My other responsibilities and hobbies would include chasing birds to keep them from eating our crops, especially our sorghum and maize, going hunting with my uncles, fishing with *bith* and *abuoi*, playing hide-and-seek, and, while gathering wild fruits, imitating clan wars in the bush with other boys.

War interrupted all that. This book describes what followed: my trek all over East Africa by foot to refugee and IDP camps, where I lived for ten years, and my immigration to America. The process of telling my story helped bring me closer to healing from its trauma. All during college, I worked as an East African expert for Global Education Motivators. GEM's President, Wayne Jacoby, trained me to become a skilled speaker. I have told my story to thousands of high school students in person and via video conferences throughout the world.

I met Harriet in my senior year of college through One Book, One Philadelphia. That year, *What is the What*, the story of another so-called 'Lost Boy' of Sudan, was the One Book selection. The program director, Gerri Trooskin, chose Harriet and ten of her creative writing students at Drexel University to interview me and ten other Sudanese immigrants living in Philadelphia for *City Paper*.

I felt that a newspaper article could not convey all that I wanted to share. Besides my experiences in Africa, I wanted to share my experiences in the US. I am very grateful for my chance to receive political asylum in the US, but my experience in the US was not without its share of trauma.

For the next several years, Harriet and I sat side by side on the couch in my apartment, or at her house, or the local Starbucks, or at her office at Drexel University, meeting once or twice a week, while I shared my story with her. We'd talk for hours, relating in a way that soon crossed the cultural divide. Our friendship grew, and together with her family and with the help of many US high school and college students, we started The Reunion Project with the mission of uniting Lost Boys and Girls of Sudan with their mothers living abroad. Harriet and her husband and children traveled to Australia with me to meet my family, and Harriet came to visit me in South Sudan once I returned.

This book is a gift to my mother, Adior Magot Majok, my Mother-in-Chief, and to all my extended family. Finally, I would like to say, *aluta continua* in response to the South Sudanese victorious independence in 2011. After a lifetime that partly matches my own, I wish peace, unity and prosperity, to the world's newest nation-state, the Republic of South Sudan!

INTRODUCTION BY DRAGGAN MIHAILOVICH

It was the picture of the wave and the airplane that caught our eye.

By the spring of 2001, news reports about the 'Lost Boys of Sudan,' as they were dubbed by aid workers, had been surfacing across America. That March, a poignant and perfectly framed photograph appeared in *Newsweek* of a hand in the foreground waving goodbye as a barely aloft plane departed Kenya for the first leg of a long journey to the United States. The Lost Boys were the hope of a desperate people and the picture convinced us at *60 Minutes* to head to Africa to document this most unique of resettlements. Two weeks later we were on a plane.

For nearly a decade, the western world had ignored or was unaware of how tens of thousands of boys orphaned by Sudan's brutal civil war walked barefoot across much of Sudan and parts of Ethiopia, eventually staggering into the relative safety of the desolate Kakuma refugee camp in northern Kenya in 1992. And that's where the boys remained, hopeless for nearly a decade. They couldn't go back to Sudan because of the war and Kenya didn't want them. Finally, the US State Department stepped up and decided to admit nearly 4,000. As the late great *60 Minutes* Correspondent Bob Simon put it, 'If any group could be described as your tired, your poor, your huddled masses yearning to breathe free, it was these lost boys from the south of Sudan."

On the mud walls of their huts at Kakuma they had plastered clippings from American magazines so they could improve their English. One couldn't help wonder how they were going to handle the challenges of America. Most had never seen a light switch, a sink or a television.

The harrowing tales the boys told in the camp of their long march had been similar: how their rural villages were attacked and burned by forces from the north, how they walked east for months at a time in bare feet, how hundreds drowned, were shot or eaten by crocodiles during one horrific river crossing. Once in America, their stories diverged. Some fell victim to drugs and alcohol, others struggled to hold on to the most menial of jobs. More than a few were still haunted by nightmares of the walk. But so many others prospered, becoming doctors, teachers, bankers, social workers and soldiers for the United States Army.

Today there are tens of millions of refugees on the move worldwide, an unsettling number under the age of eighteen. Michael Majok was once among them, a lost boy who managed to survive and endure.

Draggan Mihailovich, CBS News, *60 Minutes*,
September 2016

Part One

Chapter One
Dry Season, October, 1988, Jalle Payam, Southern Sudan

LOUD BOOMING woke him. He thought it was elephants and opened his eyes. The hut was pitch-black. He needed to pee but was too afraid to step down on his wounded heel or crawl on his knees to the door. He was just a tiny boy, about five years old, afraid of scorpions nesting in the roof grass, snakes slithering through cracks and crocodiles scurrying up shallows. Another loud boom. Bursting light. Flames shot up. The thatched roof was on fire. His mother rushed toward him, holding his baby brother in her arms, shouting, *"Kare!* Run!"

He sprang up, but didn't follow her. She was screaming and making him more afraid. He waited for her to come back inside and carry him out. When she didn't come, he waited for one of his relatives who'd gathered in Juet for the harvest festival and camped outside. He heard their screams and he could feel the heat from the flames. Instead of running all the way to the door, he ran on the balls of his feet through a hole in the side thatch, but she wasn't waiting for him there and when he called for her, she didn't answer.

Fiery smoke covered the sky. More huts burning and people screaming. Jeeps pulled up with men in robes leaning out of them, clutching rifles to their chests. He wasn't wearing shoes or clothes. It wasn't raining, but trails of lightning-like flashes left people moaning on the ground, so many bodies. He couldn't tell who they were. Their chests were covered in blood, smeared in such a way that the blood looked like fluffed open birds' feathers. He stopped looking at them, afraid one of them might be his tall, broad father, his forehead cut into six horizontal lines in the Dinka ceremonial pattern, or his small, slender mother, her tongue fluttering between the gap in her two front teeth.

He crouched behind a hut and cried, hoping she wasn't

angry at him for not following her out of the hut.

He heard a man call his name from across the dried-up bog that surrounded his family's compound. He looked up at him. The man pointed and waved for him to run through it. The man looked like a friend of his father's youngest brother named Manyuon. Manyuon's face was still painted in white ash and he was dressed in his brown and white leopard-skin dancer's skirt. Among all the bodies, he looked like a ghost. To follow him meant to not stay and search for his parents among the people on the ground.

What happened next he would take back if he could.

A hot gust rose. It brushed his arms and chest. The hut he was hiding behind exploded into flames. Smoke seared his eyes. He ran as fast as he could, springing out in one long jump after another, past smoldering huts as a sour odor—burning flesh—spread through the air.

The soil he kicked up sprayed his legs. He dipped with the ground and entered the bog. Crocodiles lived in these shallows. Roots punctured the soles of his feet, ripping open the wound in his heel. Splashing his feet and pulling them up through the mud, he ran after Manyuon through water reaching above his ankles, then into bottomless channels, mud clogging up his nostrils and ears and crusting his eyelids, every muscle in his body straining to reach the opposite bank.

"How fast can you run?" his mother had asked, stroking his head and kissing him. She told him that he must run very fast, but she didn't tell him that *Areeb* armed with AK-47s and RPGs would attack their village that very night. They were cattle herders, but he was small enough to slip past them.

It happened on the evening of the harvest festival. His relatives traveled to Juet for the celebration. There were three Dinka *bomas* in Jalle Payam—Juet, Alian and Aboudit—built on coarse mounds of Nile swampland, a few hours' walk from one another—all destroyed now. His relatives came by foot. The men carried dugout canoes on their heads and the women balanced baskets filled with grain or held several chickens upside down in each hand. Some of them came with their cows, lifting gourds of water to their mouths to ease them on.

"God save us," an old, withered uncle had cried, when he arrived with his wives and children, bent over by the weight of the shells and beads around his neck. In the swamp between villages, they had encountered people fleeing who told them with quivering lips that the northern government in Khartoum was conscripting local *Areeb* to search out the leader of the Dinka freedom fighters, John Garang, whom Khartoum believed was hiding among them.

Swamp grass stuck to his skin and hair, drenching him in its smell of decay. His hands became machetes tearing through thickets. He twisted through mangroves so snaky, he thought they were moving, terrified that a python would grab his foot, the sound of splashing and slithering all around him, the black night alive with cries and howls.

Hours passed. Shivering and sweating, he found dry land and stopped to rest. Most likely, Manyuon was ahead of him or behind him, and he waited for him to appear. "Manyuon," he called. No one answered. His breath stopped. Where was Manyuon? He stood there for a long time not daring to move.

If Manyuon hadn't called him, he'd have found somewhere to hide in the village. Now he was all alone in the bush. He'd never been alone at night. He cowered as he imagined the sharp teeth of an evil spirit, a *Nyanjuan*, cutting out one of his eyeballs.

"Majok, Majok," the spirit would call.

He groped for a tree, tall, yet low enough to climb, covered over with leafy vines to hide him. He scrambled upward not even testing his weight as he lifted himself onto the next branch. Perched at the top, he looked out across the swamp. He heard noises borne by the wind—wails, moans, gunshots. He slumped forward and, closing his eyes, pictured the bodies he'd seen lying on the ground. No matter what shape *Nyanjuan* took—an *Areeb's* or his mother's—he convinced himself that up in that tree no one would find him.

Morning. Evening. Morning. A voice through the leaves, cackling in the air, boomeranging between the branches.

"You, you, up there," called a boy more than twice his age, at least thirteen years old, in torn, khaki pants and a black, faded, T-shirt, with a Kalashnikov slung around his shoulders. He looked like a soldier, not a member of the army in Khartoum, but one of the Dinka freedom fighters. He balanced on tiptoe, stretched his neck up through the vines and waved a strip of dry meat to coax Majok out of the tree. When Majok wouldn't come down, the boy passed the meat up through the leaves.

Majok grabbed it from him and bit off a piece. The meat was veined and gristly, too dried out to chew. He rolled it around in his mouth, then spat it out. He wanted to taste his mother's porridge.

"Hey, what are you doing? That's meat!"

He looked down at the boy's rifle glittering in the sunlight. The boy stood there clutching it. Majok tensed and flung his body against the thick limb he was resting on. He now knew what a rifle was for. He was afraid that the boy had used it to shoot Manyuon and was preparing to shoot him, too.

"Heh heh heh," the boy's laughter cackled, "*Nyanjuan*'s smelled meat. She's coming up there to get you." He tilted his head, pressed his rifle to his cheek and aimed. "She thinks she's so smart. I can't shoot her anyway. She's coming for you, but it's not worth the noise. Maybe next time, okay?"

He sprang off and slid down. When he landed on his injured foot, a sound in the grass distracted him and he fell.

"I'm joking," the boy laughed, lowering his rifle. "It's a squirrel. Don't tell me you're afraid of squirrels!"

Majok sat in the grass and held up his foot for the boy to see. Reeds and roots tore the skin raw. The area around the wound swelled into a thick lump crusted with pus.

"You'll have to walk on it," the boy said. He poked through the stalks until he found the greenest one, ripped it and broke it in half. He pinched out the sap and rubbed it on Majok's wound. It bubbled up as if to take away the pain. "See, it's getting better." He asked Majok his name.

Majok squeezed closed his eyes and said, "Majok Kuch Chol-Mang'aai."

"You have the spotted bull's name. Majok, just like me. But I'm not from around here. I'm Akol Majok Akol." He raised his rifle. "Lucky I found you before the *Jallaba*. They'll burn you alive. Let's go! *Yalla!*" he said firmly in Arabic, which wasn't the everyday language of the Dinka in these parts, but they used common phrases. The two syllables in the word struck Majok like a whip. Tears flowed down his face, fast and hard.

Akol ordered him to walk. Majok turned in the direction of the village. Out across the swamp, the village was thick with smoke, gunshots that echoed through the night left an eerie quiet. "Not that way, this way," Akol said and spun him around. "We're going East to Kolnyang Payam, then Upper Deck."

Majok had no idea where those places were. Maybe another village. Later, he found out that Upper Deck was the code name that the freedom fighters used for Ethiopia, but the way Akol said it, it sounded right next door, close enough to walk, when the distance was over a thousand kilometers. He covered his ears with his hands. He refused to budge. "Right now a big lorry is driving your family across the desert. If you want to catch up with it, you need to start walking." Akol said and nodded in the direction of an umbrella tree with leaves sheathing it on every side. "Come on. We can't stay here. If the Jallaba don't kill you, the Murle will find you. They'll kidnap you and sell you somewhere far away, and you'll never get home again."

Exhausted and heartsick, Majok sunk down, burying himself in the coarse grass. He cried for his mother.

"Come on. Just to that tree," Akol said. "Walk to that tree. Every one of your footsteps will bring you closer to your mother."

Sunlight picked through the thickets of grass, marking the distance to the tree. Akol pulled him up and pushed him forward. With every little step, pain shot up his leg and across his spine. Limping round about through the grass and reeds, crying for his mother, he trailed after Akol.

They arrived at the tree. Majok huddled and hid himself in its sheath of vines. Akol paced and sighed. He reached in and shook Majok by the shoulders, then dug his hands under Majok's armpits, his rifle scraping the skin on Majok's legs. Akol didn't apologize. If Akol felt sorry for Majok, he didn't show it. "Turn around. Look over there," he said.

A foot poked out of the thicket on the other side of the tree.

Akol grabbed it. It belonged to a boy. Akol laughed. "Hahahaha! Why do you cry? Don't cry."

The boy was broader than Majok and a little older, naked like Majok, his cropped hair dyed orange and his eyes red from crying. The boy kept looking at Majok as if he was trying to figure out something. The boy sobbed and stared. A muffled, "I know you," came out of him.

"You know who I am?" Majok asked.

The boy stepped forward, pointing to the V-shaped scar on Majok's forehead. The wound wasn't fresh anymore, but its memory was painful and up until the attack, he could think of no greater injustice then the time he had an infection in his eye and his uncle Thontiop held him down while his grandmother Nyankuerdit, a healer, slit his flesh with a razor blade to cure him.

"I saw you at the festival. I wanted to play with you, but my father made me wait and eat with him," the boy said.

The evening of the attack, the dancers wore brown and white skins, their hair dyed orange and their faces painted in ash to look like leopards. They held hands, jammed together in a tight circle and jumped up and down, high in the air, to fast drum beats. Their cows joined in and prize bulls with bells around their necks. Majok, with a pack of boys, snuck off with pieces of cow liver from their mothers' *tukuls* and roasted them over a fire. "You were there?" Majok asked.

"My father was the one who yelled at us for stealing *Mang'ok Juet's* cow liver." Cow livers were reserved for *Mang'ok Juet,* the tribe's ancestral spirit. "It's all because of us," he sobbed.

Majok embraced him. The two boys held each other and wept.

"You must be cousins," Akol said.

The boy lifted his head.

"What are you called?" Akol asked.

"Biar Bol Ajak."

None of their first three names matched. If they were closely related, they'd have those names in common. Majok asked Biar to recite his remaining names, but Biar said he never learned them. Majok prided himself for memorizing the names of his ancestors going back ten generations. "Let me teach you a song to practice for your initiation," his grandmother Nyankuerdit had said, leading him into her hut, after the wound on his forehead healed, "that way you won't embarrass yourself by crying when your father picks up his spear."

"What is your clan?" Majok asked.

"Alian." Biar said.

"My mother's Alian," Majok said, looking for the resemblance. Biar didn't have the smaller, slender features of his mother's family. He didn't believe that they were cousins, except in the general sense of belonging to the same tribe, but he didn't dare to contradict Akol.

Akol turned the back pocket of his shorts inside out, and another small strip of meat tumbled down. "Ahh! Here cuz, here's some deep love for you."

When Biar reached for the meat, his fingers brushed the tip of Akol's rifle.

Akol stiffened and reared his head, "Hey, watch where you put your fingers."

"Sorry."

Akol gripped the trigger, *"Duk yot e rian e ang'auich.* Don't jump on a cat's raft."

"Come on, show me how to shoot."

"Watch it. Do you want to get your head shot off?"

Biar stepped back. "I need to learn."

"Later. Let's get going."

"What do you mean? Where?" Biar asked.

"*Tueng*, forward. Once we get to Upper Deck, you can train to be a soldier," Akol said.

"My father is back in the village."

"No one's back there. Only Jallaba."

Majok's voice stopped in his throat, but Biar's came on with persistence. He took hold of Akol's arm and pulled on it. "No, no, he's looking for me. Please…"

"You trying to take my arm off?"

"I need to go back. Please."

Akol held the rifle across his body. "And what'll you give me, a donkey's salary?" He nodded his head and looked at Biar in the eye, "Trust me, whoever is alive is going to Upper Deck. If your father is alive, you'll find him there. Once we get there, you're going to see him."

Biar sat down on a patch of dry dusty soil and cried. Termites built their nests in seedlings and ants bit people's legs and toes so badly they swelled to twice their size. Biar's orange hair glistened in the sun as he bent forward swatting the mosquitos at his ears. "I'm never going to see my family again," he sobbed.

"You will. You will see them."

"They're dead. I saw them die."

Akol became enraged at this. He said that the longer they stayed, the more chances that the Jallaba would find them and kill them and if they didn't hurry, they wouldn't catch up with the lorry that their parents were traveling on. A bird screeched in the air and another answered. When Akol heard the commotion, he held his rifle to Biar's back and forced him up.

The three boys started out and kept on. The elephant grass gave them cover, yellow and brown in every direction. There were many ways to go, none of them marked. Tall with reeds. Prickly. Sharp with thorns. Inhabited with cries and wails. Twisted with wattle. The wattle was scrawny but tall, and it was coarse but low. More dense the further they walked. But the way could not be back.

Majok stopped walking and stood at the bottom of a tree, pushing through the vines that covered it to look for his mother. He hugged the tree and called for her. He was convinced that his mother had run into the swamp like he did and was hiding somewhere. Akol pried his fingers loose. "Let's go. Keep walking. Hurry! Come on!"

Majok walked, but mostly limped. Occasionally shots rang out. And there were other reasons to be afraid. Akol marked off a few paces, sniffed the air, then walked back to clumps of trampled grass. He buried his nose in a clump to detect whether an animal, most likely a hyena or wild cat, was near, when a different sound—the sound of men's voices—came closer. The boys ducked down in the stalks.

Something green and red flashed—khaki uniforms and red berets—of at least twenty freedom fighters marching in the direction of the village. "Come on, let's follow them. They're headed toward the village!" Biar pointed at them excitedly.

Akol shook his head and waved his hands, signaling for Biar to stay down.

Biar hissed back at him, and Akol rushed over and knocked him into the grass, covering Biar's mouth with his hands.

The freedom fighters appeared, their eyes hidden behind dark pairs of glasses. One of them took out a smelly tobacco cigar from a pack and licked the ends with his tongue. He lit it, took an extra long puff and passed it around. The soldiers sent it back and forth, flicking ashes into the grass. The stalks were so dry that if a blade caught ablaze, it would spread.

The last of the freedom fighters dropped his cigarette behind him. A curl of smoke rose from the tip. Majok was too far from Akol to whisper to him. Keeping his eyes on the stalks near where the freedom fighter flicked his cigarette, he waited until the soldier reached the others in his unit and pushed himself up.

As soon as Akol saw Majok stand up and start inching through the stalks, Akol motioned for him to get down. Majok smelled the stalks smoldering and heard the sound of seed pods snapping, and he recalled the stench of the burning bodies in Juet the night of the attack.

A long moment passed. Two guinea fowls with tufted heads and speckled black feathers scampered out. Majok ran toward the smoke.

"Stay where you are," Akol whispered.

"The grass is on fire," Majok said.

"Get down." Akol said, balling his hands into fists.

"Put it out, put it out!" Majok cried.

"Get down, now!" Akol said. He slunk through the stalks until he reached the ones that were smoldering. He used the bulky part of his rifle to smother the smoke before it grew hot enough to blaze. "Come on," he said. "Let's get out of here. I don't want them to see us."

"Why?" Biar asked. "Aren't you one of them?"

"SPLA? Not yet."

"You have a rifle."

"Yes, and if they saw it, they'd take it from me. Right now, we need to find the lorry to take us to *Upper Deck*. That's the only thing you need to be thinking about."

They continued walking through the grass, looking for jackelberries or *thoc* to eat and listening for the sound of the lorry. Akol had no more meat to offer them. Biar pulled a leaf apart, shredding it into pieces. "I'm hungry," he wailed.

He hacked at a root with his fingers.

The sap that drizzled out stung his tongue. The only berries they found were shriveled and black. Biar and Majok picked them and ate them. Whenever Akol smiled and said he heard a lorry churning through the mud, they didn't know what he was talking about. Majok heard something too, he'd heard it all along, but he knew it as the whirring, whining, clacking, strumming, slithering and hissing of snakes, insects and birds in the grass and reeds. Neither he or Biar knew what a lorry looked like or sounded like. Akol found a tree to climb up and said that he wanted to see where the sound was coming from.

Majok asked Akol to describe it from up in the tree. Akol didn't answer until he climbed down. "Just listen for it," he said, "and when you hear it, you'll know."

"Did you see it?" Majok asked.

"No, but I could hear it. Come on!"

Majok and Biar followed close behind, arriving at a place where the weeds and wattle lay chopped up, and as Akol carefully picked their way through the scattered stalks to find the path, he signaled toward a clearing. The three of them ran toward it.

Sunlight flickered on charred sticks and scorch marks in the grass where, buzzing with flies, bones and skulls lay scattered, looking like they had been there long enough for animals to pick them clean. Whatever Majok imagined as the sound of a lorry faded away, along with the image of his parents suddenly appearing before him. The boys stared in shock, as though, if careful to set their eyes on it, the village would return to life.

Akol backed away and pointed into the distant air. "Come on," he said, holding himself stiffly, waving for the boys to follow him in a different direction.

Toward nightfall, they piled up leaves to make beds. Majok's feet bled, his wound had opened up, throbbing. He was hungry and frightened. Akol gave each of them a chewing brush. Biar hissed at him, "If you think we're so hungry that we have to chew on something, why don't we go catch a fish?"

"Boy, you don't know what you're talking about. The river's way over there on the other side of the swamp."

"No, I can see it."

"Your eyes are playing tricks on you."

"No, there's fish out there. All we have to do is scoop them up in our arms."

He was thinking of the rainy season when the Nile flooded and people waded right in. Akol toyed with his rifle. "Fish? I'm holding out for meat. Wait 'til we get to the Sahara Ajageer. It's a wilderness. You ever taste dik-dik?"

"No."

Akol waved the rifle in the air and raised the barrel to his cheek "Well, you're missing something."

"How come I never tasted it?"

"Where we are going is the land of dik-dik. Tomorrow, if you stop acting like a baby, I'll teach you to shoot one."

Majok was asleep only a short time when he woke to hunger driving in its spike and ripping through his gut at full force. Akol stood over him, sliding a finger across his face and pressing down on his lips, "Shhhhh!" Akol whispered.

Footsteps. The rustle of weeds and the brittle snap of stalks.

"Run," Akol whispered.

In a flash, Majok felt something reel toward him. Rough hands squeezed his chin and pinned back his arms. Bare feet locked him to the spot—a man's. Suddenly, the man pulled back and released him.

Even through the darkness, Majok could see Akol press his rifle right up against the man's neck.

"Don't shoot, don't shoot!" the man pleaded in Dinka. He spoke in the accent of the Koc Ka Agorti Dinka, who lived far away from there.

Akol lowered the gun.

Tears ran down Majok's face. His arms hurt from where the man pinned them back.

In a trembling voice, the man said, "My son..." and in his funny accent, Majok wasn't sure who he meant until he finished the sentence, "...got lost in the attack."

Majok leaned against him and held fast to his hips to feel the warmth of his skin. A few moments earlier, Akol might have shot him. The man hoisted Majok up, and put his arms around his neck, and they hugged and hugged and cried.

The man's first name was Wek. He'd been walking for two months. He told the boys that his wife and daughter were waiting for him with others while he went into the bush to look for vegetables to eat. "Why endanger them all?"

"Did you find any food?" Biar asked.

"No."

Biar sobbed. "Did you see the lorry?"

"What lorry?"

"The one from Jalle Payam with our parents on it."

Wek quieted. "I'm sorry. No lorry. The Jallaba does not spare a single village. All the villages between Agorti Payams and Manyideng will be destroyed. The government will take control of them."

Biar sobbed.

"Listen, you can come with me. I don't want to leave you like this," Wek said.

"You don't need to," Akol said with disdain in his voice.

"I can't leave you all alone here. Do you know what will happen to these boys if Areeb find you? Little boys like this. They'll kill you."

Akol thudded the metal cup on his rifle against the earth. "We're not staying."

"Where are you going?" Wek asked.

"East. Upper Deck."

"Ethiopia? That's a training ground."

Majok squeezed Wek's arm, hoping to get him to stop taunting Akol, but Wek continued. "Do you think Ethiopia is around the bend? This is nonsense. You are children, not soldiers. Ethiopia is too far. It's through the wilderness. You'll never make it. Now listen, follow my family and me to Uganda. We're headed straight for the border. If one of your fathers found my son, he would not leave him here."

All the while, Biar paced. His sobs filled the darkness.

"That's enough now. Stop your crying," Wek said.

"Leave us alone!" Biar wailed.

"Don't disrespect me, child. If it was daytime, I'd whip you with a branch. Now come with me. I will become your father."

Majok felt Biar brush against his legs as he sought Akol. A flurry of movement followed. "Stop it! Get off!" Akol shouted.

Biar screamed.

A rifle shot cracked the air. Majok fell backward and Wek fell with him, covering his body, his body so light. He could feel Wek's bones, lighter than a grown man's, much lighter than his father's.

Biar sobbed louder. Akol shouted and cursed at him.

"I'm ashamed. Ashamed for our tribe. I will remind myself that you are young boys," Wek said.

If Biar fired the rifle, it happened while Akol still held it. Akol was holding it now, thrusting it into Wek's back. "Go. Leave us," Akol said.

Wek rose. Majok clung to him. He did not want Wek to leave. If Areeb were nearby, they'd have heard Akol's rifle go off.

Wek released a groan. He squeezed the back of Majok's neck—a signal for Majok to join him—before he slipped away, and his shadow dissolved into the darkness. Majok recognized it as his only chance. Afterward, he always thought of survival like that, a choice in the pitch blackness. He slunk away, feeling the turns in the path, holding his breath and letting it go, sliding downward, almost like swimming in a current, keeping himself upright until Wek who had been waiting, called out, "Shhh! Here, I'm over here."

Wek led him further, through shadows that looked like animals up on their hind legs, ready to eat him up, until they came to a grass clearing, part of it flattened, almost flat enough for the lorry Akol promised. But instead of a lorry, there were dark clusters of slowly moving people, hundreds of them, retreating to the border under the cover of night, a caravan of men, women and children, mostly naked, their few possessions bundled in goatskins, and boys like himself, boys come out of hiding.

In the moonless night, a strong wind howled. He stood next to Wek with his head rigid and back arched, his ears sharpened to the sound of the howling wind. A chill pricked the back of his head, spread up and down his spine, covered his arms with goose bumps. He stopped walking and listened.

Slowly, he realized the howling wasn't wind. Wind whipped the air and snapped back branches. It ruffled through the feathers on hunters' caps perched on tree branches. This wasn't wind. It was voices, many voices floating through the air. It was the voices of people calling and calling for their loved ones. Those voices were growing louder and more alive. He walked alongside Wek, listening for the sound of his mother's voice or her wooden bracelets clanking softly.

As they approached the mass of people, their murmurs charged the dark sky and their outlines softened. He was about to run toward them at full speed, calling for his mother, when Wek scooped him up in his arms. Wek's fingers, thin-boned and light, clamped his wrists. The feel of them was painful and disappointing. "Tomorrow my wife will lead you to your mother," Wek said.

"You know who she is?" Majok said, staring out at the dark shapes before him.

"Any of these women can be your mother."

Chapter Two
In the Days Before the Attack

TO GO HUNTING with his uncle Thontiop meant to learn to speak in the voices of birds. "Chway, Clee-ip, Cleeer." The sad part is that most of those birds are gone now, war having chased them scattering against gunfire.

Dinka boys begin training for their initiation around five years of age, starting with small hikes and eventually sleeping in the bush alone. That sounds young, but it takes many years. Majok was lucky that he had his father's younger brother, Thontiop, to train him. Thontiop was about eighteen years old, and already a legendary hunter from the time he killed two lions, with a single arrow apiece, that had clawed their way into a tent and attacked an infant. And while a sleeping infant cannot be brought back to life, Thontiop knew where to set his traps. Sleek and shimmering, he quivered when he walked as if he stood between the strings of a bow. His own bow was constructed of wood, leather and the lions' hide. He himself was pursued by many girls who wanted to marry him and sometimes a whole group of them arrived at his mother's compound and whispered the words of a song they composed about him through the thatch. Songs turned up in every aspect of Dinka life. People composed songs to their pestles or cattle or even to the fermented cow urine that they used to dye their hair. Although Thontiop also composed many songs and many girls offered themselves to him in marriage, he returned to sleep in his mother's hut.

"Being free is like the sun rising," Thontiop once explained to the father of one of these girls—a withered chief whose skin was caked in ash to keep mosquitoes from attacking him. Majok's father offered the chief a stool to sit on. His daughter, whose hair was shaved to show off the trident-shaped scars at her temples, stood next to him with her straight shoulders pulled back and her chest garlanded in orange ribbons. The old chief's yellow fingernails, curled like claws, made him look like he was waiting for a chance to scratch at the earth so that he could find peace at last.

Majok stood with his mother and watched. He stared at the chief's spear lying lengthwise across his thighs. He was surprised to see Thontiop standing to one side, ready to dodge it. A part of him wished the chief would hurl his spear at Thontiop and witness Thontiop's remarkable agility. That the chief didn't even try, was an affront to everyone.

Once it became clear that the chief's appearance in the village was mostly show, Majok's father took the opportunity to carry his canoe back to the river and help him into it. His daughter paddled him away, making deep strokes to cut through the tangled water hyacinth on the surface. When the chief left, Majok went back to playing with his half-brother, Chiengkoudit. Majok and Chiengkoudit were born only a few months apart. Chiengkoudit who was older, was born to his father's first wife and Majok to their father's second wife. Their mothers raised them as twins. Chiengkoudit inherited their father's broad face and square frame, Majok his mother's slender features. Both boys dyed their close-cropped hair in cow urine, which turned it orange in the sun, and covered their bodies in ash to keep off mosquitos. Both wore no clothing, which their mothers realized was easier to manage and was a better barrier against the heat than the beaded corsets they had been made to wear as single women.

Both boys worshipped Thontiop and yearned for the day when he would take them hunting. They played under a tree with overhanging vines and pretended it was the shadowy veil of the deep bush where Thontiop peered through at a fleeing hind leg, a patch of yellow fur.

For Majok, playing this game was a mixture of excitement and dread. Majok was afraid of snakes. He could not stop himself from imposing their slithering bodies onto the twisting vines and coiling mangroves, imagining them with such intensity that soon a branch would sway slightly. He pointed to one and screamed, and Chiengkoudit, laughing, reached in with a stick and prodded. Majok ran away and hid, afraid that Chiengkoudit was going to pick up a snake with his stick and throw it on him.

"Snakes are our clan's totem animal," his mother tried to tell him, when he ran to her crying, "A snake will never harm you."

She shook her arm, rattling her thick wooden bracelets, the wide gap in her front two teeth showing as she described to her husband how Majok slumped back checking for pythons in the grass and crocodiles in the reeds, when he was supposed to be helping her gather firewood. She said something like this, "*Wun ee Majok, aya woi ke Majok akor, yengo cin yen pal ee rune ago kang nyich amath,*" which meant he was too much of a baby to begin his training.

She grew up in Alian, a village two hours away, and missed its grassy banks where flamingos gathered. Her gentle round face showed how she liked to hold onto the people she held dear. Majok had been hard to wean. She kept her hair shaved with a knot in the center of her head and she wore a bright yellow cloth tied over one shoulder.

His parents argued throughout the day. His mother ground the grain, lifted the pestle—a four-foot-long branch rubbed smooth—and smashed it down against the grain in the bottom of the mortar with all her weight, breathing heavy and groaning, really making a point to show her husband how she felt.

"Either way, if Majok has so many fears, then he needs to start now. The only way he will stay a baby is if you keep worrying," his father said, opening the drawstring on his leather pouch, pinching some tobacco between his fingers and packing it into his copper smoking pipe.

"Chiengkoudit should train first," she said.

Her husband picked up a stick and held it to the fire to light his pipe with it. "Based on what you're telling me, Chiengkoudit does not need to go as much as Majok does."

The strong, bitter smell of *taap*, the homegrown tobacco that grew wild in the bogs blew into his mother's face, almost as if she had been slapped. She moved away from her pestle and sat down on the ground next to her husband behind her *sufuria*, blackened with use, and out of earshot of his three other wives, who would have opinions of their own. "The bush is not safe," she said. "I've heard rumors. The Anyanya are forming an army. There's going to be war." She'd grown up during the first Sudanese Civil War, which ended in 1972, but the conflict between North and South was not resolved.

"That's happening at the borders. Not here. Majok will be safe with Thontiop."

"Against rifles?"

Her feelings did not triumph. His father gave Majok some arrows to sharpen in preparation for the trip. The next day the hunting trip took place.

His father woke him in the dark and it was still dark. They sat together on stools under a tree. Besides crickets and bird cries, the loudest sound was the kettle banging as the women in the compound heated water for tea.

His mother stirred the porridge over the open fire. Wood smoke burned his eyes. He squeezed the two blue bottle caps his father had brought back for him from Bortown to play with between his eye sockets to stop his eyes from tearing up. It didn't help.

"Tired already?" his father said.

"Tired of waiting."

His father's voice started out soft, telling him that it was a luxury to enjoy the quiet and if they weren't waiting for Thontiop, he'd be loading his dugout canoe with squash, maize and sorghum for the trip to Bor. It took maybe two hours to paddle through sinewy swamp to Bortown to trade. He leaned forward and asked Majok for the arrows he'd given him to sharpen. The whole time they sat waiting, his father ran his fingers over the points and tested them one by one.

"They're not sharp enough," he now said in his harsh voice.

Majok hid his face. It seemed like many years lay ahead of him just like this, him hiding and his father taunting.

The soil grew warm. It smudged Majok's feet. He dug in his toes and watched the dusty specks rush into the holes he made. He kept digging in his feet and watching the holes until he looked up to see that Thontiop had arrived and stood in front of him in a shaft of sunlight, wearing his leopard-skin loincloth and feathered headdress and carrying his long wooden spear. Majok's father looked at his handsome younger brother in the eye. There were at least ten years between them.

Their hunting dogs lifted their heads and wagged their tails.

Thontiop moved forward from under the tree.

The porridge was still too hot to drink. His mother came forward, her body moving beneath her yellow robe, her round face strained, but quiet, as she parted her lips to blow on a cup of the porridge as she poured it back and forth between two cups, winnowing it. Even while she was cooling the porridge, Majok stood up to follow his uncle.

"Majok, *kwarkwar*, sit down. Eat your breakfast!" his mother said.

He took a sip, but refused to drink any more and rushed after Thontiop. His mother caught him and forced him to take another sip, but he refused it. She kissed him on the spindly V-shaped scar on his forehead and on his two cheeks one last time.

Thontiop led Majok to their clan's ceremonial ground at the outskirts of the village. Majok ran to keep up and imitated Thontiop's gentle clacking until they reached *Mang'ok Juet's* shrine. In Jalle Payam, *Mang'ok Juet's* dead spirit was the one to be feared. There was no hunt, no kill that he hadn't been offered. If a tribesman didn't offer up meat, particularly liver, that man and that man's children were cursed. You didn't have to be blood to be expected to share your wealth with *Mang'ok Juet's* spirit. If they trapped an antelope or even a quail, they were expected to bring the liver back for *Mang'ok Juet's* spirit. There was the story of a relative of theirs who had defiantly disregarded this ritual. He felt entitled to keeping the liver for himself because he and his family had never tasted liver. The liver made his family visibly healthier and stronger, and he felt justified in giving them the food usually reserved for *Mang'ok Juet's* spirit, until his tongue fell out. He clawed at his throat. His sons led him to *Mang'ok Juet's* shrine to ask forgiveness. It was like a dog asking forgiveness. He had to get down on his hands and knees and bang his fists on the ground and dig at the soil, hoping *Mang'ok Juet's* spirit, in its beneficence, would hear him.

Thontiop bowed down behind a roasting stick where some dry meat still hung. Majok squinted to shield his eyes from the sun and mimicked Thontiop, bowing his head and singing the prayers when Thontiop tugged him backward and pulled him against his chest. Twenty or so uniformed freedom fighters in red berets were standing in front of them, pointing their rifles. They were SPLA, the army John Garang organized against the North.

To this day, Majok can still hear the captain's whistle. It wasn't a whistle he had heard before. It was sharp and deafening. "*Msijitiin*, come here," the captain said, and without waiting for Thontiop to move toward him, moved in very close, poking his rifle tip through the opening in Thontiop's leopard-skin loincloth and then up at the big feathered cap on his head. "You're coming with us. Go wash yourself in the river and get rid of this and this," he said, referring to Thontiop's loincloth and cap. "If you're a warrior, then you should be hunting down Jallaba, not playing with little girl-boys."

The skin on Majok's cheeks burned. He fought to hold back his tears. He looked down at his feet, but in doing so he looked sideways at Thontiop and noticed that he was supporting himself with the shaft of his spear the way he had seen old village chiefs do to keep themselves from collapsing. Sweat ran down the sides of his uncle's face.

"Of course, listen. I want to fight for the cause," Thontiop said, "but I can't leave the clan without food. And tomorrow is *tem de raap*. What is a celebration without meat?"

"Why are you sweating, man? Relax," the captain said. "We're clansman. The clan need their meat. After the celebration, right here. Don't forget to say goodbye to your wives. A great warrior like you must have many women."

Thontiop stopped leaning on his spear and puffed out his chest. He didn't have any wives, but he couldn't resist the temptation to impress the captain and even sing a few bars of the song the village girls had composed about him. Thontiop had a beautiful voice.

The song went more or less like this:

> *I love you and will wait for you*
> *while you are out at battle with the Murle.*
> *I will wait for you as long as it takes.*
> *I will never marry anyone else*
> *but you, my dear Aguntnyang Chol.*
> *If you don't come to see me,*
> *I won't eat and I won't sleep.*
> *I must not forget to ask you,*
> *which path will you be coming from*
> *so that I can see you tomorrow?*

Thontiop finished singing. "No. I'm not married yet," he said.

The crowd of soldiers laughed. One of them said, "The song you claim to be composed by a girl who fell in love with you is not true. You composed that song yourself. Ha Ha Ha Ha! Not married? That's good. No one to shed tears when we send you to the frontline." The soldier looked at Thontiop and spat. Holding his AK-47 in his hand, he stepped up to Thontiop and banged the barrel against the side of Thontiop's head.

Thontiop dropped to the ground.

The soldier was about eighteen years old himself. Boys who composed songs about their favorite cows whose horns they had learned to braid and protect their hides in ash, now sang about killing the enemy and overtaking the Northern government and building a new Sudan.

The captain pointed his rifle at him. "Get up," he ordered. "Bring the boy to me."

A bump protruded from Thontiop's head. Blood dripped down the side of his face. Despite his injuries, Thontiop planted his two feet forward and stood upright. "This boy?" Thontiop laughed, feigning indifference.

"Yes, this boy."

"Look at him. He's too small to fight in an army."

"Fight? A tiny boy like this? HA HA HA HA HA What good would a tiny boy do me? Look around you, comrade. Look at my Dinka tribesmen. You think we behave like Murle men? Kidnapping little boys?" The captain waved his hand in the air. "Bring the boy to me. That way I'll be sure to see you tomorrow."

The others joined in, clucking their tongues. "Don't treat us the way you treat those village girls! Ha Ha Ha Ha! We won't be waiting here forever."

Thontiop did not move forward. The captain scowled. "*Ya jamana*, you people! We cannot build a new country without loyalty," he said and spat on the ground.

Thontiop stared back into the captain's face. Not yet a soldier, Thontiop challenged a basic rule by looking a superior in the eye. The captain kept his eyes riveted on Thontiop. They each kept themselves perfectly still. Majok noticed the hush that paralyzed everyone as the soldiers focused on either the captain or Thontiop.

Majok stood among them, seeing his way clear. Deep and gnarled, rooted and twisted, the bush lay in front of him with weeds to run through. Bushes to hide behind. Thontiop had opened the way for him. Majok turned and ran. He ran for his life.

He ran and ran. His sides ached, his calves. If he stopped, the soldiers would shoot him. He ran through vines that lay tangled on patches of dry grass and through stands of tall grass, running at full speed, until he heard a gun shot, a single blast, and dived in among the mangroves, terrified that the soldiers had shot Thontiop out in the open under the clear blue sky. He believed it, and didn't believe it and looked around for a sign in the reeds and mud.

He held his body rigid, his muscles tense and tight. Quivering, he tried not to imagine the snaking limbs coming to life and twisting around his legs. It was quiet. Too quiet. The soldiers were looking for him, going to shoot him too, but they didn't know where to find him. To distract himself, he prayed for torrential rain to strike down on the soldiers and force them to end their search.

He heard a rustling that didn't sound like twigs. He heard another sound. Breathing. Someone's breath. Coming closer. Whoever it was wouldn't give him a second chance. He'd aim his gun and shoot. He screamed. A hand clamped down over his mouth.

It was Thontiop's. He buried his face in Thontiop's chest. Thontiop picked him up, slowly carrying him out of the soldiers' range, lengthening his stride, building up speed.

Once they were far enough away, Thontiop put him down, but Thontiop's long legs carried him so fast, Majok ran to keep up with him, catapulting himself over marshy spots onto dry earth. Birds darted ahead to find his uncle, flying faster than Majok could run. Whirling, they flapped around Thontiop, draping him in their smooth silk feathers and folds.

He arrived at a wide channel. He was sure that Thontiop got across it in a single step. He remembered his mother telling him how a *Nyanjuan* scooped out the eyes of a boy jumping across a channel as wide as this one. The boy's wounds blistered and swelled. She'd watched the boy's mother carrying the boy's limp body back to their hut.

Majok took a running start and pushed off. As his toes grabbed the mud on the opposite bank, he felt something sharp. He rolled over. His foot felt like it was on fire. He started to cry, thinking a *Nyanjuan* was attacking him, just like it had attacked the boy his mother told him about. He grabbed at his heel and saw the point of a *nema* thorn sticking through it, deeply lodged. He tried to walk, but it was too painful. He hobbled a bit, then gave up and stopped.

"Thontiop! Thontiop!" he called. Thontiop was too far ahead to hear. With his two thumbs hooked together, he blew into the hollow, imitating the whistle his father taught him in case of a wild animal, because he didn't want to shout Thontiop's name through the bush and alert the soldiers.

Within moments, Thontiop darted out from behind a tree, as if he had been waiting all along. "Where?" Thontiop whispered. He sniffed the air and took a few steps, following his chin. Thontiop knew the bush better than anyone, knew that Majok had whistled blindly.

Thontiop picked up a leaf and rubbed it across the bump on his head. "I'm not going to be able to take you hunting anymore. You're going to have to learn on your own. I don't know how, but you will have to," he said.

Light flickered on the red earth and spread underground.

"Those soldiers are going to come into Juet to look for me and your father. I got away from them this time, but they won't let me escape again. You just have to remember who you are. Alright? You're Majok Kuch Chol-Mang'aai. Don't ever forget!"

Majok could no longer hold back his tears. He could not tolerate the pain the thorn was causing him another moment. He held his foot in the air. Thontiop touched the spot where the skin swelled. "I hope that is a thorn and not a curse," he said and stripped some twigs off a branch to use as twine. Binding the twine to a leaf, he tied it around Majok's foot, attaching it in such a way that he left a space between the part of his foot where the thorn lodged and the leaf. The idea was that as he walked the leaf would push down on the skin around the thorn and dislodge it. "Walk, let's go," Thontiop said, as soon as the bandage was ready. He pushed back some vines and waved for Majok to follow him.

Beyond them, the shining blue river glimmered in the sun. It was filled with hundreds of large pink birds with long black beaks. "*Dierr,*" Thontiop said. Their legs seemed too skinny to hold them up. "We've reached Alian. Your mother's birthplace."

A host of them fluttered their wings, glided through the air, circled, skimmed the water and landed again. Majok took a step forward to get a closer look and pain shot up through his foot. He screamed. The birds screamed back in a loud chorus expressing his pain and fear. He lifted his foot and showed it to Thontiop. The tip of the thorn had come through his skin, dripping blood. Thontiop crouched down on the ground beside him. He held Majok's foot in his hand, pinched the thorn between his fingers and pulled it out.

"Look at what was inside you," he said. The thorn was a half meter long. He held a leaf to Majok's foot and pressed down on it until the blood stopped flowing.

The wound is still there. It has closed over in time and formed a keloid, the skin a little shinier and darker that the skin around it. In a different story, it would be gone completely. But this is not that story.

Chapter Three
Dry Season, October, 1988, Jalle Payam, Sudan
Two Days After the Attack

"MAMA ALIER! Mama Alier!" Wek called. All Dinka women take the names of their firstborn. Majok's mother wouldn't even answer to Adior anymore, only Mama Majok.

It was a wonder anyone could pick out a particular voice from so many others. Before long a woman pushed through. Wek whispered something to her about finding Majok in the bush. The baby she was holding began to cry, and she gave it to him.

"Hush," Wek said.

Wek's wife felt across Majok's nose and cheeks down to his mouth and chin. She pulled away and stepped back. Touching him had given her a shock.

"You promised me my son," she said to Wek, "This is not my son."

"You are not Alier," she said to Majok. "Who are you?" and she began to sob. "Give me your hands," she said and when he did, she squeezed them, wailing "Alier, Alier." Then to Wek, "This boy you brought me is not a substitute."

"Stop!" Wek told her. "What are you doing? He will stay with us until he finds his parents, and if he doesn't, we will fulfill our duty and adopt him. He will become ours. Too many boys are unaccounted for. I cannot bear to think of another one." Wek turned to him. "Cup your hands together," he said, "so that I can put something in them for you. Something to eat. Here. Like this. *akuorachot* seeds." He filled Majok's hands with the seeds. "Try not to eat them all at once. Make them last the night."

Majok popped most of them into his mouth.

"Good?' Wek said.

"Yes."

"They're a blessing. Now stay still. I want to give you something to put over your body." He wrapped a cloth around Majok's chest and tied it over one shoulder. The soft linen swished down to his ankles. His skin was covered with welts and scratches. The insect bites on his scalp itched the most.

"In the morning, everyone will stop to sleep. You can use it to shield your body from the sun," Wek said.

They walked that long night clustered together in the mob of people. The first village they came to was Pathuyith, and it took a lot of walking to reach it. No huts remained. The Jallaba had already raided the village. The next night, they arrived near Manyideng, and as they got closer, they could feel the heat from the fire that spread through the village. They stopped walking and crouched down in the grass, far enough away so that the Jallaba driving in their jeeps wouldn't see them. All at once, swarms of villagers ran out, and Majok and Wek and the people they were walking with ran with them. The lion grass ripped Majok's feet—whipping between his toes and against his legs and arms. He ran back into the bush with bleeding feet, running among roots and stumps.

If he slowed down even a little bit, Wek called him a snail or tree frog and pulled him along. The stars stayed in their places. It would take a month of walking and running to reach Uganda. He prayed that his parents were among the crowd and that the very next morning he'd find them. Then they'd arrive in Uganda together. Wek would help him, believing that helping him would be the same as helping his own son.

Night departed grain by grain. The sky appeared, purple then pink. The earth was awake. All living things could see the daylight. Majok wished he didn't have eyes. Hundreds of people stood in front of him, mostly men, their backs and shoulders bare. A man whose chest was as narrow as a child's stood next to him. His rib cage stuck out. The bones of his face protruded and his skin was stretched so tightly, it looked like it would crack. Could this really be Wek?

Wek's wife cast her eyes sideways. Even during the dry season back in Juet, he never saw a woman so bony from hunger, her arms and legs no thicker than his. She wasn't really walking, but swaying to keep her balance.

He threw off the cloth that Wek had given him. Wek grabbed him with his bony fingers. "Stop. What're you doing? Come over here. Look at what I've found for you," Wek said.

He held four pieces of black fruit, each the size of a swollen finger. "One of these is for you." He stripped back the peel, and an army of dead ants slipped out. "Eat."

Majok's throat tightened.

Wek offered his infant daughter a piece of the fruit and she opened her mouth, flapping her tongue.

"She's choking!" her mother cried.

At first, the motion of swinging her across his chest placated her. Then Wek pounded a fist on the infant's back. "It's okay, it's okay," he said, rocking her while she cried.

Wek reached for Majok's hand. "Over here. Under this tree. Lie down next to my wife. You've walked all evening, now is rest time."

Majok could not hold back his tears. "It's morning. I don't want to sleep."

"This is the time for sleeping. Do you understand? This isn't looking-for-parents time. Everyone will be sleeping. My wife will lead you to your mother when the sun goes down."

Chapter Four
Dry Season, October, 1988, En Route to the Ugandan Border, A Few Days After the Attack

MAJOK'S HEAD THROBBED, he felt dizzy and he was sweating. A woman sauntered toward him who was not his mother. A thin blue cloth hung loosely from one of her shoulders. She touched his head as if to confirm his disappointment.

"You have a fever," she said and took his hand, leading him around the tree to where Wek stood bent over gathering bark and twigs.

"He needs water," she said to Wek.

Wek nodded his head. "Go with my sister. She is helping us care for you."

Majok wondered if her little boy was missing too.

He walked with her around a rock escarpment that separated them from the rest of the walkers. Behind it a hole rippled with watery mud. Animal dung heaped in clusters on the bank, floated in the water. Behind the hole, clumps of weeds marked a path that split off into two different directions.

A crowd of about a hundred different-aged boys sat stretched out on a flat rock rise. The older boys wore the V-shaped scars of initiates on their foreheads. The sight overwhelmed him. He raised himself up on a rock, searching their faces for his half-brother, Chiengkoudit. They looked at him and kept looking at him and at Wek's sister who exchanged glances with them as if she'd already searched for her own son among them when she'd come to the water hole before.

"I'm sorry I don't have clean water for you," she said and dipped in her fingers to moisten his head with runny mud. She bent down and cupped the mud in her hands. She lifted her hands to his face. "Drink," she said.

One of the older boys stepped between them, stopping Majok from drinking the water. The boy's austere bearing matched his grave scholar's face. He spoke soft and slow with measured spaces between his words. "Don't give him any," he said to Wek's sister.

"A small sip," Wek's sister said.

"A small sip is too much."

"I know how to care for a child."

"Listen to me," the boy said to Majok, "Don't drink it. As much as you want to, as thirsty as you are, you can't. You have to wait."

"He is burning up," Wek's sister said.

"This water will not cure him. It will make him sicker. What are you called?" the boy looked past Wek's sister to ask Majok.

"Majok Kuch Chol-Mang'aai."

"Bol Jang Juol," he said. "We're Dinka Malual. You are welcome to walk with us. We're not going Uganda way. We are going east to Ethiopia."

"Ethiopia?"

"Yes, not much further now." A vulture glided in the empty sky. Bol Jang Juol pointed his chin toward it. "They're always close behind," he said.

Majok told Bol Jang Juol that Akol wanted to bring him to Upper Deck.

Bol Jang Juol shrugged. "Ethiopia? And he had a gun? You want to become a soldier, don't you? You should have stayed with him."

Majok wasn't sure if he wanted to become a solider, but he liked Bol Jang Juol and was happy to have found so many boys. He wanted to be with them more than he wanted to be with Wek.

Majok stepped closer, inching toward Bol Jang Juol. For every step toward Bol Jang Juol, he took one backward step toward Wek's sister. Two steps forward and one step back, weighing his decision. If he went to Uganda, Wek would adopt him. How would his mother find him, if he was with another family? If he went east to Ethiopia, he'd be among these boys training to become soldiers.

"What are you doing?" Bol Jang Juol asked him.

"Nothing. I was just——"

"Don't move," Bol Jang Juol said. "Listen."

The noise sounded like laughter. Hyenas.

Wek's sister reached for Majok's hand.

"Don't go anywhere," Bol Jang Juol told her.

"We're too exposed," Wek's sister said.

"Too late, they'll corner you. Stay here."

Fear sharpened her features, glowered in her eyes. Some of the boys collected rocks to throw at the hyenas. Majok bent down to pick up a rock and saw something in the distance— tan fur, thin long legs. He squinted to make out the shapes.

Impala lay in a clump of grass, two calves and a doe, beset by a pack of hyenas ripping their flesh. The doe, still alive, turned her head toward him as one of the hyenas closed its jaw on the doe's neck.

Shots rang out. The hyenas froze. They hadn't been hit, but they were frightened. More shots, this time reaching into their skulls. The hyenas humped down one after the next. Majok's eyes were riveted on the shooter. It was Akol. Biar stood behind him. Majok was afraid and excited to see them.

"Majok!" Biar shouted.

They embraced. A circle formed around Akol. He allowed some of the boys to touch his rifle in a way he wasn't willing to do when it was just him and Biar. The circle of boys laughed, comparing Akol's rifle to the bows and arrows their fathers carried. They vowed revenge against the Jallaba.

Akol lifted him up on his shoulders. "What did I tell you, Majok? You'll get plenty of food and clothing once we reach Upper Deck. The Gilo River's low and you won't need to swim. Wheat and rice. Cattle waiting to be fed. Huts to shield us from the sun. Your family."

Bol Jang Juol jabbed at the doe with a *panga* he'd borrowed from one of the walkers, ripping its rectum and dragging the tip way up to its neck and down inside each leg. He jabbed at ligaments and tendons. Hacking loose the skin, he lifted it back to expose the flayed torso and sockets filled with blood. Once he drained the blood, he hacked apart the ribcage and ripped the meat from the haunches.

The boys gathered sticks for a fire. Dusk fell. After the fire was lit, the boys huddled around it, while Bol Jang Juol roasted the meat. Some of the boys told stories. A boy about three or four years older than Majok, with a pink coin-sized hole in the side of his face, said he was going to tell a *akolkol* tale.

"Which one?" Majok said. "The one about the children who eat their mother?"

"Yes," the boy laughed. "You know the story?"

"Yes, my father told it."

"Help me out then."

"Okay."

The boy rubbed his hands together and cracked his knuckles to get everyone's attention. "This is an ancient event," he began. Most Dinka stories begin with these words. "A woman gives birth to many children and one of them, her youngest, is killed by a lion. The woman mourns for her child so much that she can no longer care for her family. She spends day and night walking around in a trance mourning her dead child. She is so absorbed by her loss that she doesn't look where she is going and she accidentally hits her head on a tree trunk and when she does, a tail comes out from between her buttocks."

Majok leaned forward, waving his hands. "Let me tell the next part," he said.

"Stand up," the boy said, "so everyone can hear you."

Majok wasn't used to speaking in front of this many people, and didn't want to stand, but he wanted to impress Bol Jang Juol with his ability to tell a story. He waited until Bol Jang Juol lifted his head.

"The woman in this story changes into an animal. She grows a mane and fur covers her arms and chest. She eats up small animals, then larger ones. She kills so many animals that she takes all the food and the villagers have no food and her children trap her and eat her." Majok stopped talking and looked at the boy with the wound in his cheek. "Is that how you remember it?" he asked.

"The same way," the boy nodded. The boy turned back toward Bol Jang Juol. "Would you agree?"

"Yes," Bol Jang Juol said, "Majok told it well." The meat was now cooked enough to tear off the carcass. Bol Jang Juol ripped off chunks and passed the warm, smoky pieces around, his hands filling and emptying. When he handed the boy with the hole in his cheek a chunk of meat, the boy blew on it and laughed and said, "The meat of the mother, right?"

Bol Jang Juol handed Wek's sister and Majok some meat. "Yes, the mother," Bol Jang Juol said with a serious look on his face. As Majok put the meat between his lips and bit back on the tender flesh, he was filled with dread that the *akolkol* tale was true, and the doe was once human, a human mother. Nausea overtook him. He gagged. He bent over the ground and vomited the meat.

Other walkers who smelled the meat rushed toward them. They pushed into the boys who were eating, and they wailed. Among them, Majok saw Wek, but Wek's sister didn't see her brother and the crowd was too thick for Wek to spot them. After that, Majok turned his back and kept his head down so that Wek wouldn't suddenly catch sight of him.

Night was approaching. Time to start walking again. Bol Jang Juol rounded up the boys. They fell into a queue, two or three boys across. "Are you coming with us?" Bol Jang Juol asked Majok and waited for him to answer.

He looked into the faces of the other boys. The ones who were standing close enough to hear Bol Jang Juol's question, chirped it back, "Are you? Are you?" Majok reached for Bol Jang Juol's hand and clutched it tightly. Wek's sister locked her arms around his neck, pulling him away from Bol Jang Juol, as if her arms were ropes that were strong enough to drag him by force, and she shouted at him to return with her to Wek.

Majok glanced back at the crowd of people where he had seen Wek appear. It was too dark now to tell anyone apart, and he squirmed out beneath Wek's sister's grasp.

"You can't do this... How will I explain this to my brother?" she reached further for Majok.

"Tell him you understand children," Bol Jang Juol said and blocked her from reaching him.

"No! You will turn these children over to the SPLA. Do you think that is a good idea?"

Bol Jang Juol told her that he didn't know.

"A sick child like this," she said and kept reaching for Majok, while Bol Jang Juol held him away from her, his hands crisscrossed over Majok's chest.

"He will receive clothes and food," Bol Jang Juol said.

"Senseless, senseless."

"Don't you see?" he said, towering above her, as if he stood on an escarpment and she stood below it, when really they were standing side by side on level ground. "It's up to me to save the lives of these children."

"They will not survive it," Wek's sister said, raking her scalp with her fingers and cupping her forehead in her hands.

"Will any of us?"

The boys headed east. They walked in a cluster banded together and soon joined hundreds of fleeing people, carrying plastic chairs, cooking pots, water gourds, goatskin bundles or sticks, and among them were many more boys from all over the Upper Nile, other boys who had been separated from their parents. Majok searched the crowds of people for his mother and brothers. "Chiengkouthii, Chiengkouthii," and "Chiengkoudit, Chiengkoudit," he shouted, until Biar sidled back and dug his sharp fingernails into the skin on his arms.

"Stop it! Stop calling for your brothers," Biar said.

The next day near dusk, Majok watched as a boy as tall as Bol Jang Juol, with a faded red shirt wrapped around his knee, wet blood oozing from the cloth, limped toward him. Majok overheard them whispering together.

"Not far?" Majok heard Bol Jang Juol say, and Bol Jang Juol's hands flew up to his eyes and covered his face. "Why didn't they run?"

"Do you, and I will do me—it is the way of evil," the wounded boy said.

"I escaped with them. I walked two months with them," Bol Jang Juol said, referring to Wek and Mama Alier and Wek's sister and all the other people they had been among. Khartoum bombed them. The earth opened up and swallowed trees and antelopes and people. If Majok had remained with Wek, he'd have been swallowed up, too.

He watched Bol Jang Juol walk off alone, seeing only his back in the darkening air, watching him crouch and stand and crouch again, twisting his body as though dodging a spear, practicing a war dance.

It would soon be dark enough to start walking again. Bol Jang Juol made his way back to the boys. Majok linked his hand in Bol Jang Juol's.

For a moment, the two of them fell silent. Feverish and exhausted, his skin coated with dust and pocked with welts and scratches, Majok relished the warmth of Bol Jang Juol's hand. For that moment, Bol Jang Juol was the person he was closest to, the person who had saved his life, and he was certain he would do so again.

"Let go," Bol Jang Juol said, seizing him by the arm. "Keep your senses about you."

They'd come from villages where no one walked at night for fear of animals. Now they walked only at night, because their fear of men was stronger.

Chapter Five

BIAR SANG THE SONGS his father taught him. Songs about
war. The singing helped him keep pace with the boys in front
of him who were older and walked faster.

Majok tried to keep up with him, to skip along and walk in
rhythm with his steps, to sing the chorus and listen for names
he knew. Biar's voice was loud and shut him out. Soon he
dragged his feet and walked slower instead of faster.

Akol led the way in the front with other boys. Bol Jang
Juol stayed at the rear, keeping watch.

Biar wanted everyone to know his story, its taste bitter and
repugnant. It passed from his lips to the mouths of others,
mostly to Majok's, because he walked with Biar while other
boys walked in front of them or trailed behind them.

"Tonight is the first night of battle!" Biar sang as he
walked with Majok hand in hand. "The seeds of *Jieng* will
flourish. We are the people of the people. We will win!" Biar
dropped his hand and raised his arms over his head, bent at the
elbow, one in front of the other, pretending they were bull's
horns. "We will grow horns and hooves. We will charge against
the enemy," he chanted.

Telling Biar to stop didn't make him stop. His songs had
no end. He'd catch his breath and start up again. Biar knew
what he was doing, just as he knew the bush was ending and
desert wilderness was beginning. The earth kept getting softer.
Where weedy fields had sprouted, there were now clumps;
where clumps rose, there were now strands; where strands
rustled in the wind, there was now barren earth. Biar was
breaking down.

The more songs Biar sang, the more memories came to
Majok's mind. He heard the screams of women and children,
how they ran across the field into gunfire. Majok preferred to
keep his family alive and sing freedom songs about John

Garang or traditional Dinka songs or songs about ladies, not songs that Biar made up as he walked. First Biar sang songs about his brother, then he sang about his parents. If Biar's parents knew he was singing about them, broadcasting their deaths, they'd punish him. Majok hoped that *Mang'ok's* spirit was not planning to punish Biar.

"I'm going to sing another song," Biar said. "Ready?"

"No, stop it, Biar."

Biar ignored Majok and repeated another brother's name. Majok wished he had a way to stop Biar other than to hold his ears, which didn't work. So he began to sing to himself:

John Garang is the only political leader in Sudan.
He will give us freedom and deliver us from Ja'afar Nimeri.
He will return us to our villages.
Our dear leader, you are like the sun,
the moon and stars above us in the sky.

All Biar sang about was death. As Majok heard Biar's songs, he could not fight off the sad feelings. No one in his clan sang about death. Maybe in Alian, where Biar lived, singing about death was common.

Biar sang about how he woke up the night of the attack to find his mother and his brothers lying in pools of blood. His brother who was closest in age, was used to getting all the attention, which sometimes made Biar jealous and caused him to pick fights with this brother. Sometimes out of anger. Sometimes just to play. Once this brother smashed Biar's collection of mud cows. The hind legs broke off and they were too small to be reattached so he had to carve new figures. This brother could also be sweet. It was like that with brothers. One moment they politely asked if they could play with your toys and the next moment they'd fling them. Only this brother bit Biar on his nose. The next morning Biar's nose swelled to the size of a yam. His mother sent him to his father's first wife who knew how to stop the swelling with special soup made from twigs. Sipping the soup made him recover enough to trek with his family to Juet for the celebration.

Biar hissed. Five times he sang out a different brother's name. Five brothers in total. Two from the same mother, two from a senior mother and one from a junior mother. Majok didn't want to know their names. He moved his hands to his ears. This covering his ears was still listening and it used up all his strength, so he whistled into his hands to drown out the sound of Biar's voice. "Tell me my brothers' names," Biar said. "Stop whistling, you have to repeat them back to me."

After hearing the singing and objecting to the singing, Majok waited for Bol Jang Juol to stop Biar. But that didn't happen. Bol Jang Juol said to Majok, "Listen. Listen to Biar. It happened in Juet. You have to know that."

Majok said, "No, no, I don't believe you. It didn't happen."

"Yes, that's exactly what happened. It happened in Alian. It happened in Aboudit. What happened in Aboudit happened in Pathuyith. The same thing happened in Mading Bor. Biar and I have talked. We both talked and agreed that this is how it happened."

"No, it didn't happen like that," Majok said "That is not what I saw. My parents are not dead."

"You didn't see dead people on the ground?"

"No."

"You didn't see your mothers or brothers?"

"No."

"If you won't admit it, then go away. We don't want you with us."

There was nowhere else for Majok to go.

"Are you going to listen?" Bol Jang Juol said.

Majok had no choice but to listen to Biar sing about how he ran out of the hut he was sleeping in. The hut was still standing. It hadn't caught fire yet. His brothers who had fallen asleep around the campfire were outside it, lying on the ground very, very still. They didn't raise their heads to call to him as he got closer.

The bullet holes on their bodies. The six initiation scars on the foreheads of his two older brothers. Biar sang:

When a warrior has died,
the initiation scars on his forehead
have been dug so deep
they can identify his skull.

Majok felt less and less like walking. His legs felt limp. Even if he cleared his mind and concentrated on walking, Biar's voice came through, painting a picture of his brothers' skulls grinning back through the darkness.

"Come on," Biar said, "Let's see who can jump further."

"In the dark?"

"I can see you."

"I'm tired. Leave me alone."

"That's because you know I can jump further."

Thousands of stars glinted in the sky, but Biar was no longer beside him. Majok didn't know where he was. "Biar, where are you?"

"Over here." Biar was whistling, humming, repeating the names of the victors and who their fathers were and where they were born. Bol Jang Juol ordered Biar to come back. Some boys up ahead heard Bol Jang Juol whistling for them to slow down.

Through the darkness, no one could see Biar. They could hear him, and his voice sounded like it was moving further and further away. Akol ordered Biar to return and other boys shouted for him and everyone stopped walking and waited. No one could get Biar to come back.

"Come back and I'll say your brothers' names!" Majok shouted.

And Biar answered. "Promise?"

"Yes! Yes! Yes!" Majok called back.

For Biar to return was to listen. Biar sang about Juet, where there were no survivors. He sang about the Jallaba who stood over Majok's dead family and friends and pushed their spears into the flesh of Majok's mothers and untethered his father's cows and led them out of his village.

Majok screamed. Why was Biar saying these things? What was he trying to do? His singing had turned into his desire to inflict as much misery on Majok as he himself felt.

"Say my brothers' names," Biar demanded.

Majok refused.

Biar pushed him down. Majok sprang free. Biar slapped Majok's face, then held him in a headlock and drummed his palms on his back, ramming his head into Majok's. His fists pounded Majok's face like the ends of a club. The earth became a wrestling arena. The two boys dug their knees into it, into the ground-down earth. Biar was on top of Majok, pushing down on his head. Majok gagged, unable to breathe. Biar's stomach was pressed against Majok's, his sharp bones jabbing into Majok's flesh.

"Learn to keep your promises," Biar said, his hot breath in Majok's ear.

Bol Jang Juol gripped Majok's arms and freed him. "I see that you are a rude boy, Majok. What do you want to do?"

Never had Majok been filled with such hatred. He knew one answer, "Fight."

"Good. Now that you understand our struggle, you will be one of the seeds of Jieng. We will fight our common enemy, the Jallaba, not each other. We are brothers."

Chapter Six
November 1988, Sahara Ajageer

"*YALLA!* FORWARD," Akol shouted over the rising wind. Majok hated the sound of that word. His parents used it when they wanted him to hurry out of the hut, pulling him by the arm toward the door, so that they could leave him with a neighbor or relative instead of taking him where they were going.

"If you stop, even for a minute, you'll get caught in a dust storm. Buddy up. Hold hands. *Yalla! Yalla!*" Akol shouted.

Majok was still wearing the linen cloth Wek gave him. Torn and shredded, it offered him protection against the wind. He prayed for food. Even back in the village, hunger was not new to him. During drought, the Nile flowed to a mere trickle, killing their crops and making it impossible to feed their cattle. When he'd complain of hunger his parents told him a story and he remembered it now: *teny e duel*, body conditioning in preparation for a wrestling match. According to the story, some wrestlers were locked in a hut to fatten up before a fight. The wrestlers gorged on so much food that they got sick in the middle of the night, and with no way to get out of the hut, they relieved themselves on the floor of the hut and died in their own excrement.

Majok followed Akol's orders. He held Biar's hand as he walked and promised not to gorge himself, when he would at last find ripe fruit skins dangling from tree branches.

"Look up. See those dark shapes?" Akol said.

Majok looked up at the sky covered with dark clouds.

"They're hills. Keep walking and we'll reach them by morning."

Maybe Akol was telling the truth. Maybe they were hills. He imagined reaching them and running up their green sides, standing at the very top and looking down through the haze to the valley below, where he'd find his family—his mother, his father, his brothers, his uncles, his grandmother—waving up at him. Akol gave him that hope.

Late in the night, the wind grew stronger. So much dust blew into Majok's eyes, he could not resist rubbing them. Because his cloth protected his face, and Biar didn't have a cloth to cover his, Biar insisted on leaning against his back. He hated Biar for doing that. It made it so much harder for him to walk against the wind. At first, he shrugged Biar off. But Biar said, *Please, Majok,* and he would not move off Majok's back.

"You were the one who kept pushing me down," Majok yelled at Biar, "And now you want to lean on me? Get off! Stop using me for a donkey!"

Biar's weight was so heavy, he pulled Majok down, making it harder for him to trudge through the sand. It was unbearable, the way Biar leaned against his back, Biar's stony weight pressing into him. Majok reached around for Biar through the thick wall of dust. He turned completely around and it felt like Biar was clinging to his back, but Biar wasn't there. The wind bore down with so much force that it felt like Biar, but it was not. Majok did not know how long they'd been separated.

"Biar! Biar! Biar! Biar!" he shouted.

No one answered. Majok whined like a dog trapped in a byre. He was alone. Bol Jang Juol wasn't close behind him anymore. The wind was filled with so much dust that he could not see through it to determine how far back Bol Jang Juol might be standing or how far ahead everyone else had wandered. He didn't know if he still followed Akol anymore. The earth wasn't hard packed the way it was when people have stepped on it. He couldn't see through the gathering of black, thick dust clouds. If he closed his eyes, he would fall asleep. He ached for sleep. But if he stopped moving, the grit would bury him, come in through every pore, in the spaces between his teeth, fill his mouth and suffocate him. He tore the cloth off his body to use it to cover his eyes. Dust and sand pelted his skin, but he believed he would survive as long as he had that scrap of material to protect his eyes with.

If this had been the first day Akol found him, he'd lie on the ground and refuse to walk, crying for his mother. No one knew where he was. His mother had watched his every step. She smelled of porridge. She blew on his porridge until it was cool enough to drink and kissed him on both his cheeks as a way of saying goodbye.

Everyone was so far away, they'd become tiny flecks. And what was worse, they didn't stay in one place. They flew through the air. He couldn't find anyone, see anyone. He barreled through the wind, fighting it to walk in the one direction, not knowing if he had gone off course. Trudging forward in baby steps, he prayed for *Mang'ok Juet* to help him the way he'd once led his father to recover their family's cattle from the Murle tribesmen who raided their herd. *Mang'ok* took his father face to face with those exact men. *Mang'ok* was a spirit who led people who couldn't see where to go. *Mang'ok* was wind blowing. *Mang'ok* was air. *Mang'ok* was a giant dust bowl shrieking, knocking him down.

Daylight. Majok opened his eyes and saw Akol standing over him. Majok shuddered. "I've lost Biar," he said.

Akol grew solemn, "I told you to buddy up."

He rubbed his eyes. It was still painful to keep them open.

"Biar is your brother."

Nausea rose from within him, fear over what he'd done. What mercy did he deserve?

"Come on, get up. We have no time for sleep. Do you want to get caught in another storm?" Akol said. The sand was so hot, Majok screamed. Akol stood behind him shouting, "Don't stop! Keep walking!"

He couldn't possibly walk on earth that hot. He ran, pressing down on his toes. Every step seemed like a punishment for what he had done. A group of about ten or fifteen boys were waiting for him. He felt their eyes on him, fresh torture. He looked at Akol, his rifle slung low across his chest. "Right in front of you."

Majok gasped. It was Biar.

"You see him? He's been with us all night. You're the one we couldn't find."

Chapter Seven

THE FEEL of his own face made him tremble. He stopped touching it and dropped his hand. Only its hollowness. He panicked. The sky looked blurry. He squinted, looking far out in the distance. The land was blurry, so blurry.

The blurry vision was frightening. He felt like he was turning into the old, blind man in Juet. The whites of the blind man's eyes had been filled with blood. A blackfly bit him and gave him river blindness. When he used to rush past the blind man's hut, the man heard him and called his name. The blind man recognized him. He had a different way of seeing.

A yellow plant, there in the distance, a long way off. Majok walked toward it trying to calculate how many more steps. His eyes were playing tricks on him. The closer he walked to the plant, the further it appeared. It didn't bear any seeds or fruit, but could offer *thaac*—sweet dew droplets. *Mang'ok* had answered his prayers. He'd found *thaac*. He would take whatever *Mang'ok* offered him. Even back in the village, boys fought over a sip of *thaac*. The sweetest water he'd ever drink.

He inched in, bent his head over the stalks and ran his hands through them, searching for a drop of sweet, wet *thaac*, when his leg brushed against something hard. He held back the stalks from the bottom to see what he had touched. Lying in the sandy soil between the stalks, a boy's head stared up at him, the eyes fixed on his, the face ashen. Majok turned and ran, screaming.

Bol Jang Juol swooped him up in his arms.

"I can't see, I can't see," Majok screamed, afraid to open his eyes. He'd seen something that wasn't meant for him to see, the way the village women used to turn their backs.

The drop of *thaac* was his to drink, but he wouldn't touch it now.

"You can't leave him here the way he is. You have to bury him," Bol Jang Juol said. "Get Biar to help you. The two of you can work together."

Majok told Bol Jang Juol that he was just a tiny boy, and he could not do such a thing. Boys in their tribe got whisked away when there was talk of death. "No, no!" he screamed.

"Watch." Biar said. "You don't have to help if you don't want to but I can show you how to do it."

Biar didn't dig a hole. He bent down and scooped up some sand and tried to cover the boy with it, but the sand was dry and didn't hold together. Most of the sand Biar gathered slipped through his fingers. A mound stuck to the boy's hair, sprinkled across the nose. Only flecks of sand settled on the cheeks.

Bowing, Majok tried to remember the prayer Thontiop recited outside *Mang'ok Juet's* shrine, but he felt himself sinking deeper. He watched Biar, whose red eyes looked spectral. Biar had no trouble speaking. He recited:

Nhialic ee kwarda, god of his fathers, why is it you do not help your son, that he may regain his strength? You god, have left him behind here for me and I refuse to be infected with his death. For this son has no father to bury him and no mother or brothers, and if we had not come along, he would remain in the open. You, god, you are the great person, father of all people, and if a man has called upon you, you will strengthen his body, that no evil may befall him. It is you of my father, I call you to help me, and you of my mother I call to help me.

Biar put his hand on Majok's shoulder to turn him in the opposite direction. "*Wuuuu!*" Biar shouted and waited for him to make the sound *wuuuu* like the followers of prayer leaders.

"*Wuuuuu!*" Majok shouted.

Biar waited as Majok repeated the phrases after him:

> *I call upon you that you may come*
> *I call upon you that you may come*
> *And look after the people of my father's people*
> *And look after the people of my father's people*
> *Look after them well*
> *Look after them well*

That no evil may overtake us
That no evil may overtake us.

Had the boy reached the *thaac*? What if he had gotten to it first and tasted it, would he have wound up like the boy? Had a *Nyanjuan* set a trap in the *thaac*? Or did the Jallaba find him? He could not stop seeing the boy's eyes fixed on his.

Back in the village, there was so much flooding during the rainy season that Majok's family had to look for a place to camp. His baby brother got tied to his mother's back and she walked with a cooking pot balanced on her head. His father led their cattle. Their neighbors came with them. When they found dry ground, they pitched in and looked for sticks to build huts. He remembered how he walked from stick to stick and collected them. Now, instead of sticks, the boy's image marked his steps.

If walking without Biar was scary, walking with him was worse. The milky whites of Biar's eyes now clouded over his pupils. No longer singing, he spoke in a hoarse whisper one word at a time.

Whenever Akol came back to hurry them on, he told them to keep walking to the next hill or the next bush. He pointed to a tree, one of very few, and told them that Upper Deck or the lorry with their parents on it was close ahead. "Keep walking. Don't stop," Akol would say over and over, as if their walking had an end to it.

Weeks earlier, Wek had expressed his doubts whether the boys would make it through the desert wilderness. Now that Wek was dead, his words seemed more true. Majok saw a tree ahead of him and a cluster of people beneath it. When people stopped to rest, they spread out their belongings alongside of them. These people weren't carrying anything. They were here because they could not walk any further. They were here to die. He was ready. He exchanged a glance with Biar, and, as if on signal, both boys slunk down, ready to become part of the earth.

If the sun had already set, he might not have noticed the woman lying beside him. She was pregnant. He turned on his side to look at her. What was she doing here? She wore only a loincloth, her stomach bare. She had made it this far. How had she kept her baby safe? He watched her arch her neck, stretching a little higher, as if for sweeter air, and she smiled to herself.

This vision could be only one person—his mother. His mother inhabited the pregnant woman's body. He rubbed his hand over his belly button and felt how tight the skin was pulled, as if they were still attached. He was going to be reborn. He was going to survive this and live.

This was what he later came to know:

A Kenyan aid worker with a paunchy belly, dressed in jeans and a blue and white checkered shirt, named Sampson, drove onto the Pochalla-Pibor-Bor Road and rescued him. When Sampson loaded the final yellow, five-gallon plastic jug filled with water onto the back of his lorry, he did not know what awaited him. He steered along the bumpy rust-red road. There was no electricity, no lights along the road, no feeder roads, no pointed thatched roofs of a remote settlement. There were no hospitals, primary health care centers, schools, boreholes, NGO's, UN agencies, evangelists, government buildings, wild fruits, riverbeds, groundnuts or berries to eat— nothing to eat except *olemo*, a round, yellow berry which would give him diarrhea. Sampson drove from Gambela for two hours. Monkeys screeched at him from high up in the trees as he drove northeast. To pass the time, he sucked on a bubble pipe filled with tobacco, imagining his own unborn children and hatching a plan to work in the Gambela National Reserve as a safari guide once the war was over.

Three hours out, Sampson's lorry blew a tire. It was dark and there was no one to help him along the road. He'd forgotten to pack a torch. He kept his motor running and flashed on his brights. He got out and crawled under the flatbed where he stored his spare, barely finding, in the dark, the wing nut to unscrew it. He set up his jack and pumped the lever, singing to himself the melody of a Kiserian song, one he had first heard in church before it got air play, his only ammunition against thieves. This road might be his last. When he finished changing the tire, he wiped the perspiration from his face with his shirt sleeves, sang the words to the same song and continued driving again.

"Wake up!" Sampson whispered, listening to the slow, labored breathing of the people he found. He clapped a hand on Majok's tiny shoulder.

To Majok, Sampson's touch felt so heavy, it hurt. Yet instead of registering pain, he blinked open his eyes in dim recognition of the lorry's rumble. Its vibrations shook the ground where he lay. His heart fluttered in his chest, and he coughed for air.

Sampson whispered gently, his voice made soft by the sight of the people spread out beneath the tree, "I am here to rescue you," he whispered. "I am here to bring you to safety."

Sampson scooped up Majok, and his lorry carried him onward. They arrived in Ethiopia very late at night, Majok fast asleep.

When Majok woke to sunlight beating down on his face, he found himself lying on the mud-caked ground. He rolled over onto his shoulder and, remembering the sound of the lorry that delivered him, he stood up, shouting for his parents.

Chapter Eight
Dry Season, December, 1988, Pinyudu Refugee Camp, Ethiopia

HE GAZED OUT over the field. Thousands of boys stretched end to end. The sun's glare was so strong that it was painful to keep his eyes open. He had expected *tukuls* in a village thick with wood smoke and his mother rushing toward him whistling and shouting, running to pick him up in her arms. His feet were buried in thick mud, and he could barely lift them.

Akol found him staring at the crowds of boys. "See what everyone else is doing?" Akol said. He held a stick, which was as thin as his leg, alongside it to measure the stick's length. "They're building huts. Do you want to be the only boy without one?"

The splintered point of a stick poked up through the mud. Akol reached for it, pulling on the stick, his arm trembling. Freeing it, mud splashed, foul smelling, thick and sludgy, splattering both of them.

"I want to go home," Majok said.

"This is our home."

"I mean Juet."

"Through the desert again? Do you want to die?"

"I want to see my mother. Where is she?"

"She's coming."

"When?"

"Does your mother have another baby?"

"Yes, my baby brother."

"You're not the baby. Stop acting like her baby. She is coming with him." He cupped his hands around Majok's face and squeezed.

"That hurts. Stop!"

Akol dropped his hands and his features went cold. "If I stopped, you would be dead."

"You said I would find my mother."

"I said it for you, but I also said it for me. It's safe here. We don't have to walk anymore." Then he called Majok an *ajongkoor*, a donkey-ass, and said didn't he learn anything walking through the desert about how scarce everything is, even sticks, and if he doesn't hurry and find enough he will have to cross the river and go into the forest where the Anyuak live to find more, and then they'd capture him and use him as a decoy to trap leopards for their skins. "So it's either get busy now or risk the Anyuak attacking you."

He helped Akol peel some of the thinner, green sticks into twine. They broke the sticks into equal lengths and tied them into bundles. They covered the sticks with mud and formed walls. They pulled up grass and weeds and padded them down over the roof. The hut they built was so low to the ground that they had to squat down on all fours and crawl on their stomachs to get in. The roof was a half roof to lie under and escape the sun.

"You'll see, now that you have a hut to sleep in, your mama will be able to find you." Akol said. Majok's arms hung limp at his sides. He couldn't picture his mother crouching down in the mud trying to crawl through the hut's small narrow door, but it was more painful not to believe Akol.

Human excrement indistinguishable from mud. Impossible not to step in it. Boys squatted down to fan fires, warming their bodies near the flames. Other boys were so sick, they couldn't walk to the fires, couldn't move.

Boys scratched their mosquito bites until they bled. The boys with *tuk tuk* bites, broke out in pock marks filled with pus. With no water to keep clean, tiny wounds got infected. When nighttime came, the dark covered the boys who did not survive, and they died in their sleep, shielded from sight.

In the morning, a soldier waved his rifle at Majok and ordered him to help with the burials. "Get a group to help you.

Work together! Find something to dig a hole with," the soldier ordered.

Majok held up a stick notched at the top into two branches. "Good." the soldier shouted and lurched off toward another group of boys.

How was Akol able to summon so much energy, Majok thought, when he felt so weak, he could barely move? For example, late in the afternoon Akol marched up and down a hill out there by himself, practicing. No one else had the energy to move like that. Later in the day, Akol practiced marching up the hill some more again, showing off to anyone who could see. He watched Akol for about an hour until the sun burned with such strength that it looked like there were two of him. Majok closed his eyes, and when he opened them, he hoped that the double vision would disappear. He watched Akol for a long time, not knowing if he was watching him or his ghost.

The next morning, Majok heard boys shouting outside his hut. He looked out and saw the white canvas backs of several lorries. Excited, he ran toward them, imagining them packed with everyone's parents. When he reached them, he took in the long queue of boys. No one's parents stood alongside them. No adults had emerged. None. The backs of the boys linked together and formed a wall. Hot sun beat down on their bodies.

SPLA soldiers and Ethiopian guards patrolled up and down the queue, striking the ground with their whips. Majok noticed the red crosses painted on the doors of the lorries. A soldier told him that a food delivery had arrived and that he needed to join the queue if he wanted to get to the food. He looked around in a daze. Back in the village, children were given special consideration. Here, no one waved him in. As he tried to find a place to squeeze into, boys turned around and shouted at him, "Go to the back!" and with more disdain, "Go to the back!"

He watched a soldier strike a whip against the back of a boy stumbling through the queue of boys. The boy's shoulder blades quivered, but did not collapse as his body bore a second and third strike. "If you continue to push, you'll all be whipped," the soldier shouted, pointing at the boy.

Majok shielded his face with his hands and ran toward the back of the queue, frantic to find Akol. Chills overtook his body, the feverish kind that made him sweat and shiver at the same time. Without Akol to help him, he didn't think he'd be able to get a place in the queue. "Look, look where you're going!" someone called with the screech of a howler monkey.

Desperate to get to the food, the boys packed together so tightly that the slightest movement caused them to fall. All around, boys fell forward, landing on top of each other, the boy on the bottom cursing the boys crushing his back. From beneath a pile of boys, Majok heard Akol's sharp cackle cut through all the others. He descended upon the boys on top, throwing his body in every direction to force them to move off Akol.

He hurled his body from boy to boy. He grabbed one boy's arm, trying to push him away. The boy snickered and bashed his chest into Majok's head, pushing him backward. Majok tumbled and flew into the boy behind him, and that boy rolled forward, each boy taking down two or three others with him. Majok fell onto his shoulder. It hurt so much he screamed. A guard lunged toward him, waving his whip.

"I got him," Akol, now freed, shouted at the guard.

Majok couldn't move his arm. It hung limp by his side. "Take me to see the bone expert," he screamed at Akol. Back in his village, his family would pay with a calf for such services.

Akol laughed. "Are you stupid? No bone expert here."

They left the queue and walked around it to the aid workers' tent. Under a tarp, some Ethiopian aid workers stood at a table. One of them held his hands out to show them that he couldn't offer them any food. Akol pointed to Majok's arm, which was hanging limp by his side. Majok squeezed the hand of his other arm around his wrist and pantomimed how much it hurt when he tried to lift it. As Majok mimed the pain he was in, he stared at the Ethiopian aid worker, at his clothes—tan shorts and orange socks—until the aid worker's expression softened like tarpaulin over the back of one of the lorries. The aid worker motioned for Majok to come forward.

Majok took a small step. The aid worker patted the surface of the table he was standing behind and motioned for Majok to climb onto it. Majok stepped forward and approached the table. When he pressed down on its surface with his good hand in order to swing up on top of it, the aid worker leaned over and grabbed Majok's bad arm below his elbow. It happened in a moment. The aid worker slid Majok's arm upward in such a way that the bone popped back into the joint. Majok screamed, but his pain was gone. He could now move his arm again.

The aid worker smiled and bent down. Majok thought that he was going to reward him with food. But that's not what happened. The aid worker merely wanted to pull up his sock. Majok was happy he could move his arm, but food seemed even further away. The aid worker held out his upturned palm, empty of food. Majok stood across from him and stared until the aid worker couldn't take it any longer. He went into the tent and came out with a small plastic bag filled with grain and dropped it into Majok's hands. Before the aid worker could change his mind and take it away, Majok and Akol ran back to their hut. Not having any pots to cook it in, they pounded it with a stone into smaller pieces, grinding it smaller still, down to such a small bit of food.

Chapter Nine
Dry Season, December, 1988, Pinyudu Refugee Camp, Ethiopia

"Stand at attention!" the head *talimji* ordered, trotting past the row of boys, his red beret tilting forward on his head. He sauntered near the taller boys. "Attention. At ease. March, march, march! About turn! Stop! *Enta, enta.* You, you. *Tahli.* Come with us."

"*SPLA oyee,* Jesh el Amer, *oyee!*" the chosen boys cheered. Besides clothes and shoes, they would be given food. Getting picked was the only way to survive. Majok was a slow grower. Most boys his age were much taller than he was. Dinka are known for their towering height. Many of the soldiers were close to two meters tall. Since boys got picked for their height, Majok realized that he would need to invent a way to quickly grow taller. The next day, he piled up a large mound of soil to stand on. When the *talimji* passed before him, he was practically the same height as the other boys. But he did not get chosen.

The shriek of a whistle. "Jesh el Amer!" a soldier called. The soldier held a rifle in one hand, and with his other, he pushed two plastic jerry cans into Majok's face. "Take these away from me," he ordered. "Water duty."

Majok shuddered. Two days before, when he first arrived at the camp, an officer explained that the river was off-bounds. It separated the boys in the camp from the Anyuak tribe, and the Anyuak considered it their property. The Anyuak tribe lived in *tukal* huts clustered on the banks. Their intact families filled the boys in the camp with envy, although their cattle were much leaner and sparser than the large herds the boys cared for back home. Drought made the Anyuak desperate, pitting the tribes in the area against each other. The neighboring Murle tribe raided the Anyuak tribe's cattle so often, that their herds were reduced to one or two cows per compound. In desperation, once the camp filled up with boys, the Anyuak targeted the boys. Anyuak men wearing loincloths and feathered hats crossed the river, carrying clucking chickens tucked in the crook of their arms, expecting food in exchange. The boys in the camp at first didn't have any food, and when food arrived, they received so little that they had none to barter with. Starting from the day the boys arrived, Anyuak men shot at them or kidnapped them, bringing them to their village to work as slaves.

Majok backed away. Too much could happen to him at that river. A spear thrown in his back. Drowning. He hadn't seen Akol since the night before. Every morning they'd risen together or walked to the queue. Now Akol was not beside him. Majok watched the soldiers march a group of new recruits away. The new recruits were barefoot, but soon the army would be giving them shoes. Had he missed watching Akol march off, his back to him, shoulder to shoulder with the other cadets, his green shorts in shreds? If Akol had been chosen to join the army, those shorts would be replaced with a proper uniform.

Majok reached for the two jerry cans. Now they were empty, but after he'd fill them with water, he'd need all his strength to carry them back.

The soldier spun him around by his shoulders, faced him toward the river and ordered him to march. He shoved his knee into the small of his back and jabbed him a straight cut with his hand, keeping close as he rounded up more of the boys who were not lucky enough to get chosen as cadets. "Shhhhhhh! No talking. Do you want Anyuak men to hear you? Do you want to become an Anyuak slave? Do you want to get shot dead?" the soldier whispered as they marched to the river.

Once they arrived, a thick wall of thorny creepers covered the bank, hiding the river from view. The soldier ordered the boys to climb through the creepers.

"Can we swim in the water?" a boy asked.

"No! No swimming! You want to get shot? It's Anyuak fishing grounds."

"Find a shallow and fill up your cans. Hurry!" the soldier said, ordering the boys to get down on their hands and knees and snake through the wall of creepers notched with sharp pointed thorns.

Majok twisted between the vines, screwing his elbows into the mud to give his torso lift and avoid getting cut. Yet every branch he crawled through pierced his skin. Blood dripped from his wounds as he continued pushing through. There was no time to stop. If an Anyuak man spotted him invading the river, he would kill him. The soldier whispered through the vines, "Faster! Hurry!"

At last they reached the water. Water! Two days ago, he was in the desert, searching for a few droplets of *thaac*. Now he was standing in a river.

His fresh cuts stung. Bearing down on the cans to fill them, he heard the cold, clear water gurgle. He leaned forward, using the cans for floats, and plunged in. The cool of the water made him shiver, and his cuts burned, but he had never felt anything as healing as that river.

He was certain that the soldier couldn't see him. The risk of getting caught was steep. He had witnessed other boys get punished. Whipped with a branch. Or made to kneel on their knees with their hands up. His punishment for swimming might have been for the soldier to order him to crawl across the burning hot earth of the field and say, 'How about this swim, eh, is it hot enough? Are you enjoying yourself now?'

A dark shape moved through the water. Fish! The river was filled with fish! There was not enough food for everyone in the camp, when there were fish here! He bobbed forward, trying to grab one.

He whisper-shouted to the boy standing nearest to him, a boy his age with large, deep-set eyes. "Do you know there are fish here?" He pointed to a ripple and the dark shape gliding beneath it. This boy was not a member of his tribe—Dinka. The boy was Mandari. Back in the village, those two tribes were always fighting, mostly when cattle got loose and ate crops on the other tribe's land.

The Mandari boy gasped. His eyes caught the sunlight, but it would take more than sunlight to bring them back to the surface. "Stop it," the Mandari boy said, "you'll get caught!" All of the boys were terrified of the soldiers. He looked at Majok with his cold, sunken eyes.

"Let's swim out and catch some."

"No, we don't have enough time."

Majok knew that the soldier was not small enough to fit through the narrow openings in the vines. "He won't be able to come after us," he said to the Mandari boy.

The Mandari boy shivered and shook. "On the walk my brother carried me. Do you know where he is?"

"Your brother?"

"Yes."

"Mandari? How would I know? Alright, alright, I'll tell you what. I'll help you look for him if you come back here with me."

"When?"

"Tonight."

What was it to fear the darkness of night, to shiver in the cold water of a hostile tribe or to feel his skin sting with cuts, when he could be feeding and drinking? Dragging the jerry cans filled with water back to the camp, Majok walked slowly enough to memorize the way back to the river. He looked for landmarks the way he'd learned crossing the desert wilderness, counting the steps from one bush or tree to the next. Besides the Mandari boy, he convinced Biar and some other boys to join up with him.

That evening, with Majok in the lead, they walked through the camp bunched together. If soldiers spotted them, the boys could disperse. Then the guard wouldn't know which one of them to follow. When Majok saw the trees that edged the bank, he explained to his friends how to twist through the creepers and climb into the nighttime river.

He inched out and let go, feeling the cold water strike his legs. He put his head under to quickly absorb the chill.

Swimming underwater, he counted five strokes, ten more, and swam further, his breath magnified in his ears. It was a heavy sound, like someone being dragged to burial. The ashen color of their skin.

He stopped swimming and looked around to consider the place of salvation that was water. He dove under again to touch the sandy bottom and to grab a handful of sand to rub against the cuts and bites on his legs. It didn't matter that the skin around his wounds had broken now that he was in the water. Here his wounds would get washed. Back in Juet, his father had burnt cow dung and rubbed the ash on his legs to keep off insects. Majok hadn't liked to help collect the dung from the fields, but it worked to keep insects from biting him. He sprung up by his toes, took a deep breath and popped down again chasing a ripple, ready to seize a fish by its tail.

Another ripple, belonging to a bigger fish, maybe a tilapia so big he'd need help to carry it back. He settled into the quiet despite the charged feeling in his body, this I'm-going-to-find-you-and-grab-you-fish-so-watch-out feeling. He licked the delicious taste of the salty, fishy water from his lips as quiet hovered in among cricket chirps.

First he saw another single ripple. Then another, and another. Rings and rings of water rippling. He heard an explosive, vibrating sound.

All at once everything came to life. It was like the big fishing festivals back in the Sudd near his home, hundreds of men dipping in their poles, only these were boys from the camp scissor-kicking their bodies back to the shore—boys running, slipping and sliding on the slippery mud bank.

Anyuak men armed with rifles chased after them.

Majok dove under with only his eyes and nose sticking out. He clung to this thought: the water will save me. He flapped his feet underneath like 'copter propellers, remembering how 'copters churned through the sky. The first time he saw them, he thought they were the limbs of a god. That's what *Mang'ok* looks like, he thought. And then bombs slipped down, exploding, while he stared up where the sky had been and saw only fire, and his eyes burned and his body trembled.

He swam underwater back to his side of the bank. Hidden in the shallows, cold and shivering, he waited for daybreak. He didn't return to the camp until the sky lightened, arriving in time for the morning queue. He saw the Mandari boy standing near him. "You made it up. You don't have a brother," he shouted at the Mandari boy, suddenly angry, blaming him for the Anyuak attack.

A day went by. Daydreams of returning. Immersing his body and feeling weightless. The vines he sprung off from. The scaly bodies of fish sliding through his hands. The river was life. Replenishment. He was a boy again jumping up and down. Or a baby reaching for his mother. Splashing. Kicking his feet.

"If you keep inciting the Anyuak, hell will break loose," the head officer announced over the mobile loudspeaker microphone. The camp leaders knew that there were boys who went to the river for fish. If they caught them, they'd whip them, even though there was not enough food in the camp, and fishing was the only way for anyone to keep the skin on their bones.

Soon it got to be so easy. Every boy who fished in the river brought back fish to share with ten others. The Ethiopian UN workers distributed hooks and fishing nets. What a difference a net made! He was able to carry back twenty little smelt-like *madesha*.

A friend he'd made on these fishing trips, a Dinka Bor boy called Spirit Free, told him that he remembered him from Bortown. Majok told the boy that he'd never been there. But when Spirit Free insisted, Majok played along with him, until he himself believed it. Then they told everyone that their fathers knew one another in Bortown, and boys began to envy them, believing that their fathers were friends, and that Majok and Spirit Free shared brother love.

Some nights Spirit Free stayed behind and waited for him with a fire going. Majok would return when the sky lightened, a furrow of pink color spreading into a field of pink light to mark the return of day.

Majok lay down on the floor of his hut, got in a few hours sleep, then met Biar and some other boys at the edge of the field, trapping mosquitoes by their wings. More furtive than bats, they walked past the soldiers on guard. Most of the soldiers fell asleep at their post. But tonight, the boys heard the rustle of khakis from behind them.

The boys crouched down in the shadows. It was too dark for the guards to see them. Going to walk right past them cocking their rifles. Make sure the guards didn't turn back. Rap a fist on a boy's head. Majok held his breath as he hid in the darkness. Soon, soon, he told himself. There was no shortage of fish. Under the sickle moon, the soldiers couldn't see him. At best, they could only sense him.

A soldier fired. Majok huddled up into a ball, making himself as small as possible. Thanks to God he hadn't leapt out. The soldier wouldn't have felt any shame if he'd shot him. "Satisfied?" the soldier would've said and left his corpse for the hyenas.

Finally, Majok arrived at the creepers. He twisted through them to the bank. Another boy who was already standing there shouted, "*Bara bara*, get out of the way!"

"Don't just stand there, hurry!" said another, who had also arrived before him.

Majok looked through the darkness to the water. Floating on the surface was a dark shape. It belonged to a boy, floating face up. There were other boys floating face down when they were all good swimmers. A group of older boys rushed to the edge and pulled up a boy splashing in the water, furiously kicking his legs. Majok huddled around him once he was positioned onto the bank. His arm accidentally touched the boy's stomach, wet with blood.

"Ayyyyyeee," Majok screamed.

"Press down, press down," another boy whispered and grabbed Majok's hands and pressed them down onto the boy's stomach to stop the blood.

He felt sharp metal protruding through the boy's skin.

"Pull it out," the other boy whispered to Majok.

Majok pushed upward on his hands, but it was impossible to yank the metal loose. It was lodged too deeply into the boy's skin, "It won't come out," he screamed.

"Shhhh! Shhhh!" the other boy hissed. "Keep pressing, keep pressing."

"What happened?"

"Anyuak booby-traps. They attached fishing hooks to their spears and planted them in the mud to keep us from stealing their fish!"

"No! No!"

"Yes! Yes! Try to stop the bleeding. As long as you hear him breathing. If he stops, you'll know you'll have his death on your hands."

A dream: he was dreaming of drifting on water. He heard screams. He kicked his legs, fighting against the current. He dreamed that he was one of the boys who had swum too far into Anyuak territory and his guts had been ripped out. His hands covered in blood, blood would not stop pouring out of his wounds, and he screamed and screamed.

He woke to real pain—hunger—and to real screaming—roosters. Daylight. He looked down at his body, relieved to not see blood.

A voice thundered over the mobile loudspeaker microphone, shouting the same words he had heard every day since his arrival at the camp.

"Jesh el Amer, today is the big day!"

He ran outside to march and practice singing just in case the Army's Commander-In-Chief, Dr John Garang, decided to visit the camp. Every day since Majok had arrived, he'd woken to the same words, "Jesh el Amer, today is the big day!"

He rushed to the practice grounds where most of the boys had gathered, standing shoulder to shoulder. When he looked at them, he saw the gaps where the murdered boys would have been standing.

A motorcade of jeeps with their roofs cut and mounted with machines guns on top of them, surrounded the boys. The jeeps were filled with soldiers wearing red berets and carrying rifles. "Sing louder! Be thankful. Soon you're going to meet John Garang," the soldiers stationed at the camp shouted.

"What's happening?" Majok asked a boy.

"Diktor John."

"Is he really here?"

"No. Soon."

"Come on, we've heard that for weeks now."

"He's left Pibor-Pochalla. He's on his way. You can start rehearsing what to say to him."

"What are you going to say to him?" Majok asked.

"You think we'll get a chance? He going to stand with his bodyguards and we're going to be far, far away."

"I need to…"

"What?"

"I need to ask him for guns for those Anyuak criminals," Majok said and joined the rows of boys standing head to head with their arms wrapped around each other working their voices into an expression of surging euphoria. John Garang's plan to take over Sudan had brought the boys through the desert to safety. It was the last part in his plan to end the civil war and unite the country. Thousands of boys made a wall of flesh.

The sun heated up the morning sky. The air was quiet and the dry desert wind did not usher in the roar of more jeeps. Hours passed. It got so hot that the group leaders allowed the boys to sit down.

"Let's sneak away and find a better spot," Majok said to a boy standing next to him.

"I don't want to get whipped," the boy said.

"We won't get caught. Come on."

They pushed through the crowd toward one of a few trees at the edge of the field. Boys had already flocked to the higher branches where weaver birds built their nests. Majok climbed to a heavy branch and inched along it. He got so high up, he could see the river. The image of the boys on the bank from the night before was emblazoned in his mind. He yearned to tell Diktor John to seek revenge against the Anyuak.

He pressed his stomach against a branch and crept up to the very tip of it. Cool under the canopy of leaves, he fought off the envious stares of boys from far off.

"Remember, Diktor John has a big belly," an older boy near him said.

"He has a bald head," another boy said.

"Yeah, and he's always carrying a small stick and his pistol, but not a rifle."

The older boy whispered, "Why are you so stupid? Do you think he'll come without bodyguards? His envoy will arrive first, filled with soldiers to protect his movements from the eyes and ears of Khartoum. Khartoum would bomb us if they knew he was coming here." Majok wished that boy didn't know so much. By mid-afternoon they were still waiting. "Do you think he's really coming?" Majok asked the same boy, hoping Diktor John arrived with a Council of Elders, who would slaughter goats and vow revenge in the name of the murdered boys.

"If he doesn't, then I'll never believe another thing they tell us," the boy said.

Several hours later, the roar of motors. The whole field of boys rose and chanted: *Diktor John! Diktor John! John Garang oyee! SPLA oyee!*

Majok imagined the sound of Diktor John's voice, sonorous and deep, his sentences swimming like fish through the skulls of the drowned boys and into the ears of the Anyuak as they flocked on the bank.

The jeeps came to a stop, and a hush fell over the camp. Armed soldiers stepped out to surround Diktor John, a stout, bearded man mounting the steps of a wooden platform. Diktor John turned toward the crowd. All Majok could see from the branch that held him was the side of Diktor John's face, the patch of cheek showing over his beard. Diktor John looked out at the crowd of survivors. Diktor John had been given daily reports. He held up his hands that signed papers and gave orders.

The mobile loudspeaker microphone thundered with Diktor John's voice. "Jesh el Amer! Jesh el Amer, *oyee!*"

The crowd answered with the loudest chant Majok had ever heard. "Diktor John, Diktor John!"

Diktor John's voice roared, "Jesh el Amer, Jesh el Amer, I am happy to be here today to see you. I am happy to see that you have survived your long journey and that you are all doing well. The Northern government has tried to kill you, but they will pay with their blood. Anyone who tries to hurt you will pay. We are doing too well to be stopped! We are doing well in Junub. We have captured Bor from el-Bashir's forces. We've captured Kapoeta, Torit. We are winning and we will win. But we need more brave young men. And you, Jesh el Amer, will liberate Junub Sudan. Soon we will make sure you have schools here, and you will have enough to eat. Some of your family will join you. You are the new Sudan. Yes, Jesh el Amer!"

Shouts rose, reaching across the river. Shouts of, "the NIF is just too deformed to be reformed," and, "*SPLA oyee! SPLA oyee!*"

Majok rubbed his eyes and listened, straining to see Diktor John.

Chapter Ten
Dry Season, December, 1988, Pinyudu Refugee Camp, Ethiopia

A FEW MORNINGS after Diktor John's visit, Majok heard a soldier shake the part of his hut roof adjacent to the wall. This terrified him, because he was afraid that the soldier might shake loose the scorpions that slept in the roof grass. Every evening, he carefully shook out the burlap UN aid bag he slept on and checked inside it for scorpions, shook it some more and furiously, before lying down on top of it. He scampered out the door, rushing past the soldier to the practice ground.

Boys were already assembled. Dressed in civilian clothes—dark trousers and a white button-down shirt—Commander Deng, round and bald, paced in front of them. Surprised to see the commander out of his uniform, Majok hurried to join the row of boys.

"Boy, what are you looking at?" Commander Deng shouted at him as he stood at attention. Besides arriving late, Majok had made the mistake of staring at the commander. The commander stopped in front of him and waited for him to speak.

"Commander, you're not wearing your uniform today," Majok said because he was forced to say something.

Commander Deng winked. "No, not army day. No army." He stood next to another man—a *kawaja*, a white man. This was the first white person Majok had ever seen. He was close enough to see the veins under the white man's skin and the hair on his forearms, and his nose that was so long it looked like he must use it for speaking instead of his mouth. The commander ordered the boys to sing their welcome song to greet the white man:

Welcome, Welcome, Welcome!
Today we are happy to see our visitor and sing
Welcome, Welcome!"

"Today you are going to learn two new words," Commander Deng said when the boys stopped singing. "These words are in another language, *thong de Engilisi*. Are you ready?"

"Yes, comrade!" the boys shouted.

"That's good. Here is the first word: Mister. Repeat it after me: Mister!"

"Mis-ter."

"Again."

"Mis-ter."

"Good. Now, listen very closely, here is the second word: Congressman."

"Cong-ress-man."

"Good, now you must say both of those words together, like this: Mister Congressman."

"Mis-ter Cong-ress-man. Mis-ter Cong-ress-man," the boys repeated.

"Again!"

"Mis-ter Cong-ress-man! Mis-ter Cong-ress-man!"

"Louder!"

"Mis-ter Cong-ress-man! Mis-ter Cong-ress-man. Mis-ter Cong-ress-man!"

Commander Deng grinned. "America is very rich. America will give you milk, biscuits and maize flour to make porridge, but America will only give you these things if you work for them. Are you willing to work? Yes? Then you must do exactly what I say. For example, if I throw a stick in your direction, you must leap forward and pick it up. If I throw maize, you must go after it. You must demonstrate your need for it. Our need for it. Without question! Do you understand? Now repeat after me, Mister Congressman, Mister Congressman!"

To impress the commander, some boys broke out into a marching song. They were older boys, but their voices were high-pitched. It was like they carried the frequency of the war in them. They wouldn't have to speak about what they'd seen for people to know.

"Stop it! Stop singing! No war songs," the commander shouted.

The boys stopped singing and stood at attention.

"Do you want the congressman to go away? Do you want to starve? Don't you want America to give you food?"

With one nod of his head, the congressman could have packed them up in lorries and driven them back home to reunite with their families. Majok practiced saying Mister Congressman. He said it to himself over and over.

Biar, who was standing near enough to Majok to hear him talking to himself said, *"Enta majnuun.* You're an idiot."

"Over here," an official shoved them. "Come on, you're going to be schooled." This wasn't the first time the camp elders had mentioned school. Most of the boys wouldn't have gotten the chance back in the village. School back there was hunting, fishing and learning riddles their fathers taught them after the evening meal.

"It's time for a story. Boys, are you ready to become wise? I have a riddle for you," an elder would say, leaning in and waiting for a boy to perform a mental broad jump and take the riddle apart. One of the most common was the *Foodchain Trap Riddle.* A group of boys would be asked, 'how can a fisherman who needs to take a lion, a goat and a sack of maize to the other side of a river get them across if he has enough room in his boat for only one of them besides himself?'

The boys were told to keep this part of the problem in mind: 'If the lion and the goat are left alone together, the lion will eat the goat; if the goat and the sack of maize are left alone together, the goat will eat the maize.'

Even back then, Majok was the first to figure out the answer to the riddle: "Take the goat and leave the lion on the bank with the sack of maize. You know that the lion won't eat the maize. Then leave the goat on the other side and come back and pick up the lion and leave the sack of maize. Leave the lion on the other side by itself, and take the goat back in its place. Leave the goat on the side where the maize was, then pick up the maize and take it in the boat and bring it back where the lion is. Then go back one more time and pick up the goat."

The commander's second officer gathered the boys under a tree. He passed sticks around and told them to copy the *Dingileese* letters he formed in the dirt. One of the boys refused to pick up a stick. Even with the congressman watching, the officer caned the boy, landing blows across his shoulders.

The boy rolled over on his side, not daring to whimper. The commander stepped forward. Clean-shaven, his skin beamed with light. His pink tongue looked enlarged in his mouth and the red in his eyes glowed. He held a handful of maize, maize they had seen so little of since they arrived at the camp, maize the congressman could supply them with.

"Watch," the Commander said. "I want to show Mister Congressman what good students you are." He stepped forward and threw the maize in the air.

Majok watched the kernels rain down in slow motion. He darted out to catch as much of it as it could. "Baba," he said to himself as if his father could hear him: "I know the answer to the riddle."

Commander Deng jeered at Majok's accomplishment. "Congratulations!" he shouted and pointed at Majok while he spoke and his translator interpreted for the congressman. "Look, that boy over there. Look how much maize that boy's managed to catch. This is the kind of boy we raise here!"

The commander stepped forward and tossed several more handfuls of grain in the air. The boys fought to gather it, getting down on their hands and knees, frenetically zigzagging, Majok thought, like soldier ants detecting crumbs with their feelers. The bodies of the boys were shiny with sweat. The congressman unbuttoned his shirt and clawed at his necktie. He too was perspiring. Majok backed off, afraid that one of the boys might try to grab his fistful of grain. What was to stop them from knocking him down and stealing it? He felt ashamed for clutching the grain in his fists, yet he knew that it would be foolish to give it up. If any one of these boys were in his position, they'd claw and scratch to defend themselves to the death to keep this handful of grain.

The congressman's hair was gray, his eyes blue like water. As Majok stared at the congressman, he saw his eyes grow more and more watery. In Dinka culture, to see a man weep meant that the world was ending.

The commander gave a signal and turned to the boys. "You have done well, boys," he beamed. He put his arm through the congressman's and led him toward their jeep. The boys remained standing at attention, their eyes lowered. The commander and the congressman and their entourage drove off.

Chapter Eleven
Dry Season, December, 1988, Pinyudu Refugee Camp, Ethiopia

THE VERY NEXT MORNING, earth vibrated beneath him, waking him from sleep. Shouts tore the air. Ululations. A convoy of UN lorries churned through the mud, their open backs filled with plastic sheeting over cartons that slid from one side to the other, as their wheels bumped up and down over the ruts in the field.

"Did the congressman send this food?" Majok asked a soldier.

"Mind your own business. Yes, it's *uimix* and *papa*, but it's not ready to be eaten. Go with Group Seven and wait." The soldier pointed to a spot in the distance. "See where that patch is? Group Seven will gather there."

"Can I help unload? Please?"

The soldier showed him his *panga*. "Go, now!"

The convoy made a terrible screeching noise and came to a halt. Ethiopian UN workers climbed out and made a human chain to pass the cartons off the trucks.

Burlap, twine, scoops and oil drums were soon discarded and lay scattered near the convoy. When Majok lived in Juet with his family, his mother cooked grain in a *sufuria*, which was a hollow piece of metal dug into a pit in the ground, that looked something like these oil drums.

He searched for the soldier and found him standing at the back of the truck, overseeing the Ethiopians. Majok convinced the soldier to help him split one of the oil drums in half, so that he could have a pot to cook his grain in. The soldier handed Majok his *panga*. Suddenly, the soldier moved between the oil drum and Majok, challenging Majok to strike him instead.

Majok dropped the *panga*.

"Pick it up, Jesh el Amer, and give it to me."

Majok handed the soldier the *panga*, kneeled on the ground and shielded his face with his arms. There were soldiers who abused their power, soldiers who had lost their minds.

Laughing, the soldier lifted the *panga* into the air. Majok closed his eyes and covered his face with his hands, but the soldier pulled on Majok's arms and moved them away from his face.

"I want you to watch," the soldier said.

Majok kept his head bowed and his eyes on the patch of dry, cracked soil in front of him. If he looked up, the soldier would see that he was weeping for his life. Any show of emotion would only serve to hasten his death. The soldier touched the tip of his blade to the flesh on Majok's neck, forcing him to lift his face. As he did so, Majok heard the metal clang of a lorry door nearby. He heard the aid workers' voices.

He screamed.

The soldier drew back his *panga*, reached across and struck the blade into the oil drum. "What are you so afraid of?" he sneered. "I need a chisel. Go, find me one."

Majok rose and turned around, not daring to look at the soldier, and ran back to his hut for his fishing hook.

"I didn't think you would come back here. I thought I'd have to search you out myself. You're smarter than I thought," the soldier said when Majok returned with the hook. He then used it to chisel little holes in the drum that he joined together with the edge of his *panga*, dragging the blade lengthwise to slice the barrel in half.

"There, now you have a cooking pot," the soldier said. The cooking pot looked very much like the *sufuria* his mother cooked in back in the village, blackened with use, ready to be filled with food. The rations the congressman sent were divided among thousands of people. The soldiers were the first ones to get to them. The new recruits were second. By the time Majok buried his new cooking pot into the earth and gathered sticks to heat it over a fire, all the rations were taken and he had to wait until the following day to receive any. He repeated many curses directed at that soldier. He supposed that the soldier had known that a boy like him wasn't going to receive any food.

Chapter Twelve
Rainy Season, March, 1991, Pinyudu Refugee Camp, Ethiopia

NO RAIN, just the smell of it. Early in the morning. Late at night. Majok closed his eyes and breathed it in, expecting the air to be filled with the chirps of beautiful birds fluttering their wings. He thought of his uncle Thontiop showing him the pink birds of Alian. He imagined them flying into his arms and becoming people he knew from far away, their feathers and voices.

Birds weren't the only animals rain would bring. Rations now arrived every two weeks, but they consisted only of maize, oil and salt—no meat. Everyone was wishing for impala and antelope meat, and the camp became very quiet, as people's mouths watered in anticipation of eating meat.

Finally, the rain arrived. So steady. Its fresh smell kept Majok awake at night. He'd inhale it and feel infused. Some nights screams woke him. The sound of rain entered his deep sleep and he shouted at the people in his nightmares, leaping up at the enemy he saw crouched before him.

Though the rains came, it did not bring any animals. Everyone was so hungry. Since the congressman's visit, the commanders who ran the camp hired local Ethiopians to work as teachers. Classrooms were held under the trees. The boys sat on the ground practicing drawing alphabets in the dirt.

That day the teacher's usually smiling face looked filled with sorrow. He stood in the center of the circle of boys avoiding the eyes of the boys sitting nearest to him and spoke in a deep slow voice. "War is approaching," he said. "This is not your war. It is a war between the Tigray People's Liberation Front and Mengistu. I am sorry that this is happening. Other countries besides Sudan go to war, and although this war does not concern you, it might affect you." For the time being, the TPLF tolerated the presence of the

SPLA, despite the fact that the Jesh El Amer in other regions had already exchanged fire with TPLF soldiers. "Stay calm," the teacher told them. When he finished talking, the boys stared at him in disbelief. The teacher had no more information to give them and said that it was best to hone their minds so that when the time came, they would be clear headed.

The teacher passed around a book and asked Majok to sound out the letters on the page. "What does this say?" the teacher asked, tapping his finger on a word. The teacher's voice was so different than the voices of soldiers. It was not a voice that ordered him to stand up or march. It was a voice that asked him to sit still and think.

Majok looked at the letters. The word began with an H. The other letters crowded around it. He shaped them in his mouth. "H...h...hello," he stuttered.

"Good, Majok."

"G....g....good, M...M...Majok," a voice near him repeated. There was laughter, suppressed beneath hands.

Learning came easy to Majok. He could sound out a word for the first time and remember it when he came across it again. Other boys chided him for it. They envied his abilities and used every small slip up as an opportunity to punish him.

He deafened his ears to the boys' snickering voices and stared at the picture of the family in the primer and wished that his mother's face would appear on the page in front of him.

The primer was called *Hallo Children*. Inside was a picture of a family. Father, mother, daughter and son. The father smoked a pipe. His name was Mr Kamau. The Kamau family lived in Nairobi. They slept in beds and sat on chairs at a table with hot food on their plates. As Majok looked hungrily at the picture, his eyes watered and his throat burned.

The teacher pushed through the circle and yanked a boy by his ear. Though capable of pushing back, the boy stood facing the teacher, as he struck a twig across his up-turned palms.

Watching the boy receive his punishment, Majok felt the life moving through his body with great intensity. At such times, he felt himself being carried far beyond the camp, proving that life awaited him elsewhere.

Many of the boys who chided Majok got chosen for the frontline. The teacher said to the ones who were left behind, "Let the pen be your sword. Use it to defend yourself." In the months to come, he learned how to read Arabic and Swahili but not Dinka, although Dinka was the most common language in the camp, because at that time, the Dinka were the majority. The boys spoke Dinka among themselves without realizing until years and years later that the Dinka they spoke was the five-year-old version.

"YOU KNOW where he got that shirt?" a boy named Marko said, pointing to a boy in a red T-shirt with Coca-Cola written on it. "He got it at the Anyuak market." Marko's father married an Equatorian and he was raised in Kopoeta. Marko still wore a piece of white string around his arm. His right eye looked like it was stitched shut. He'd cut it swimming across the river to the Anyuak camp to steal crops. He healed on his own without stitches or serum, but he couldn't see out of that one eye. "We should go there and barter trade," Marko said.

Any mention of giving up his rations threw Majok into a panic. He rose to his feet. "Are you kidding? We can't go anywhere. There's going to be war."

Marko winked his good eye. "Then we'd better go right away before it happens."

"It's going to happen soon," Majok said, looking up at the sky, expecting it to soon be covered in fiery smoke.

"Didn't your clan barter trade with neighboring tribes?" Marko asked.

"Murle tribe? Nuer? They stole from us," Majok said.

"No, I'm sure it was trading even though you called it stealing. Think of it as one of the black days. You can skip eating for one day. You do it every month," Spirit Free said. Black days were the days when the roads in the camp were too muddy for food trucks to get through and the food delivery was delayed until the roads were navigable.

"Not like a black day," Marko said. He unrolled his burlap UN aid bag, shook it and turned it inside out, checking for scorpions. Satisfied there were none, he balanced himself in a squatted position until the bag was flat on the ground, and he sat on top of it. Like Majok, he slept on a burlap UN aid bag lain out on the dirt in the corner of the hut designated for sleeping. "I have a plan. What we do is, after we get our rations, we go back into a different queue, and this time, we hide our left arms in our T-shirt sleeves like we've just been maimed. Then, the Head Counter won't be able to tell that our fingers have already been dipped in ink and he'll have to dip the finger on our right hand and we'll get a second ration. We can sell it and use the money to buy a shirt."

"If that's so easy, everyone would do it," Spirit said. He skipped meals to save up food. His ration bags doubled the size of everyone else's. He buried his jerry can filled with oil in the ground to hide it from all the starving people in the camp who would covet it.

Two or three scrawny cats skulked near the opening in the door. They stretched their backs for a rub, and a rain of fur came loose. "Scat!" shouted Marko, waving his hands in the air.

"Wish we had something to feed them," Majok said.

"Not worth worrying over when there are so many rats for them to eat," Marko said.

"Then why do they look like they're starving?"

Marko laughed, squinting his good eye. "How do you think you look?"

Mid-afternoon was the quietest time in the camp. Most people needed to conserve their energy. Even with the entire afternoon dedicated to sleep, some people weren't able to wake up. Their immune system weakened, and it was called dying of natural causes. "Marko's right." Spirit said. "It's not just the cats."

Near the end of the next rations cycle, the three boys set out for the Anyuak market. They walked past the Ethiopian aid workers' tents in the UN compound, across paths made through barren bush in between sprigs of bleached-out grass. The skies were empty. The longer Majok walked, the more prickly his face felt. Panic spread across it and infused his body, as he anticipated the warplanes that would soon be flying in the air above them. He tried to convince Marko and Spirit

Free to turn back, but they insisted that because they'd already come this far, they wanted to keep going.

Beyond the rise, crowds of Ethiopian farmers and Anyuak tribesmen gathered, dressed in feathers and tunics. The farmers stood amid tables covered with lanterns, combs, stools, copper trays, cups and cooking utensils. The tribesmen stood amid red and orange and yellow robes and scarves and hats made of feathers hanging from tree branches. Spread out on blankets on the ground, were T-shirts, armbands and neck bands made of beads, feathers and shells, each one fanned out like a separate centerpiece.

Majok saw a shirt that was identical to the one the boy back in the camp had been wearing, a red one with Coca-Cola imprinted on the front. Near it was another T-shirt embroidered with a picture of a man with shoulder-length dreadlocks playing a guitar, and palm trees and a round orange sun. A metal scale stood on a table. An old, lined, Anyuak man paced behind it. He tilted his head toward the boys, leaning forward and waving to them. Marko could not walk fast enough.

Spirit whispered, "Slow down. Don't look so anxious."

The man's head cloth was hung so low, it partly covered his eyes. His *jallabia* was folded in gathers around the rope at his waist.

"*Salaam*," Spirit said to the man, revealing his childish voice.

"*Kaif el halak,*" the Anyuak man said.

They stood facing each other. Another man, not as old, perhaps the man's brother, sat on the ground behind the table. He gathered an empty grain sack in his hands and leaned to one side, rooting among the filled sacks for his rifle.

The old man turned around and said something to the man who looked like his brother, who was now holding the rifle. The brother passed the old man a coin. The old man showed it to Spirit. It was worth two shillings.

Spirit shook his head.

The old man offered Spirit another shilling. He pressed his hand down on the scale and tried to coax Spirit to empty his rations.

Spirit refused. He was unsatisfied with the price. Sighing impatiently, the Anyuak man waved his hands in the air. His brother on the ground rose.

"Come on," Marko said to Spirit Free. "What are you waiting for?"

"Ok, watch," Spirit said. With his thumb as a gauge, Spirit opened his plastic bag to release his rations at the rate of a pinch of grain at a time. The grains poured out so slowly, the Anyuak men laughed. Spirit stopped the flow and held up his finger to indicate that his price would be one shilling more.

The Anyuak man turned to his brother who was now standing beside him and the two laughed together. They drew the attention of other Anyuak men who were armed with rifles and *pangas*. The Anyuak man shoved Spirit's hand away and Spirit's remaining grain spilled out all at once onto the scale. The man quickly unlinked the chain that held the metal plate beneath the scale and poured the grain that had accumulated from Spirit's plastic bag into a sack.

"My rations!" Spirit shouted. "Give me back my rations!" Spirit screamed and cursed.

Majok saw a crowd of people running toward them from across the market. "They have knives. Rifles. They'll kill us. Let's go! Come on, it's a trap," he said. He felt his blood rush to his head as he berated himself for agreeing to go with Spirit and Marko to the market, when he knew that the Anyuak regularly trapped and killed boys.

"What are you still doing here? Do you want to get killed?" shouted a voice behind them. It was a soldier from the camp. Spirit pointed to the Anyuak man. "He stole my rations!"

The old Anyuak man clasped his fingers together, pleading for his life.

"Move out!" the soldier ordered. "Pinyudu Camp is under attack. It's not safe here anymore. Turn around. Look for yourself."

In the distance, planes. Antonovs. Too far away to hear.

"Run! Why are you standing here? What's wrong with you boys? Go! Go!" the soldier shouted, shoving the boys in the direction of the crowd of running people.

The boys ran along with the Anyuak men, clutching their rifles and *pangas*, until they caught up with crowds of boys running, thousands of boys, the entire camp escaping, running away from Pinyudu and away from Ethiopia, away, away, and away, leaving the Anyuak village, its chickens and cows, leaving the cholera-infected fields, lifting their heavy feet as they sank down.

Chapter Fourteen

THE GILO RIVER is a tributary of the Blue Nile. One side is Ethiopia and the other side is Sudan. It is a seasonal river. In the rainy season it floods. When it floods, the crocodiles that make their homes on the lily pads and in the water hyacinth scurry up to the banks. To escape the war that was now surrounding them, the boys needed to cross the Gilo River back into Sudan. Moving targets, they ran three long days to reach the river, the nights cold without food.

No matter what age Majok was, whenever he found himself running, he tried to avoid getting stuck in the back with those too sick to run. When he was five, or six or seven years old, as he was now, those he started out with were other small boys. He outran them and moved as fast as he could and breathed in and out in order not to get a stitch in his side. He knew he could not look back and see the fire where the market stood. He didn't think of what could happen if a stray bullet hit him or if a wild animal, itself fleeing, appeared before him or if a bomb exploded right in front of him. All the while, he heard gunshots and saw the flash of fur and he felt the heat rise across his chest. Knowing what he left behind him, he lifted one foot after the other and concentrated on going forward. That is what kept him believing that he would survive and that he was going to see his cousins and brothers and mother.

They came to a hilly area in the Gambela region of Ethiopia known for its floods. The rain had changed the sloping land into giant mud hills. To step into that mud is to see your feet grow. Boys shouted and yelled as their feet grew with the mud that accumulated around them. And these shouts became part of a game as one by one boys leapt into the air up the steep side of hills, over their tops and down the other sides. As soon as one boy jumped and tumbled, another followed behind him.

It was a game where a lot of boys got their backs rammed into by the boys behind them.

As they ran, the soft, gentle sound of rain dripped between tree branches. Their bodies sodden, the rain amplified the noises of war: kaboom kaboom kaboom. There was no time to stop and sleep. The war was advancing behind them. If they didn't hurry, they'd get caught in the crossfire. Majok could not understand why this was happening to him again, why he was forced to spend so much of his life running.

Fifteen hours later, there it was. His first sight of the Gilo River stretched out before him—glittering and shining. Ringed by mountains and tall, scraggly trees, the river was wide, wider than any he'd ever seen, its current strong. He had no idea how he was going to get across it. On the sand bank lay feathers shed from hundreds of enormous dark brown birds with long skinny necks and legs.

"Ostriches," a soldier told him.

He watched the ostriches run in step like soldiers marching. He remembered the *akolkol* tale about ostriches and how they ran from rain. If rain was coming, they'd run in the opposite direction, rapidly zigzagging their flightless wings.

He remembered another tale about a snake escaping to heaven wrapped around the legs of an ostrich. According to the way his father told it, when heaven first created ostriches, they could fly. Often they'd visit heaven. Heaven greeted all animals except snakes. Snakes crawled on their bellies and flicked their poisonous, forked tongues to prey on other animals. Heaven did not want to become a place for prey and forbade snakes from entering. For this reason, one especially clever snake coiled its body around an ostrich's long legs so tightly that he survived the trip through the air to heaven. As punishment for the ostrich's vulnerability, heaven took away its ability to use its wings to fly.

The ostriches on the bank were tamed. The soldiers stationed on the Gilo bred them for food. Majok couldn't help thinking that he was as artificial as they were, raised in camps, kept from his mother and father. He had become that rare breed, flanking the banks of the river, spread out in every direction.

There was no turning back. The soldiers who came with them from the camp, reported that TPLF soldiers, who at first tolerated their presence, were now charging forward in pursuit of them.

Majok stood on the sand bank, immobile. The river roared wild with current. Besides its imposing width, it was scattered with large rocks. He watched as the rocks rose then glided forward.

"Crocodiles! Crocodiles!" people screamed. The soldiers responded by furiously chopping down trees along the bank and hacking them apart to build dugout canoes.

He heard shelling from behind him and turned around to stare amazed at the TPLF troops moving forward, their uniforms green and tan, splendid in the sun unlike the shoddy and worn out mud-stained fatigues that the SPLA soldiers wore. So many of them were women who, he thought, should have been home, carrying babies on their backs.

He dived into a dip in the ground behind a stand of weeds. Along with many of the boys, some of the ostriches did not get away from the shelling in time. Shrieking, they fell on their backs or wings. The dugouts were not yet water-ready, but the soldiers shoved them into the water. Amid flying bullets, boys ducked low to board the canoes. The boats filled up fast. Spirit refused to get into one. He was terrified of the crocodiles in the river. Instead of stepping into a canoe, he grabbed onto a ropey vine and would not let go of it. Majok struggled to pry his fingers off the vine and pull him into one of the last canoes to fill up with boys. Crouching low, he braced his foot against a rock to pull Spirit loose, but he slipped on the mud and fell. Spirit would not stop clutching the vine. "Leave me! Leave me!" he shouted. But Majok would not leave him, and they missed getting a place in one of the canoes.

Now the only way to get across the river was to swim. Majok kept his eyes on the crocodiles. The water will save me, he repeated to himself. "We can't stay here, we'll get shot!" he screamed at Spirit. "Hold onto me and I'll carry you across."

"No, no!" Spirit sobbed. "Crocodiles!"

"Put your arms around my neck. Don't worry. We'll make it," Majok said in a soft voice—which he now recognized as his father's voice, before his father yelled at him for not making the points on the arrows sharp enough to use on his hunting trip with Thontiop. He heard it again in the water lapping against the bank, promising him it would carry him across. He believed he could do it. "Okay, when I say three, jump in." Majok said and waved his arms in the air and counted.

"Are you ready?" he said to Spirit.

A hand clamped his wrist.

"Spirit! Spirit! Spirit!" Majok shouted, trying to break free of the soldier pulling him. The soldier picked him up and carried him onto a canoe in a seat near the bow.

"Get down, get down!" the soldier shouted.

Bullets kept flying. The soldier pressed down on Majok's back, forcing him to stay down. With the soldier covering him, he couldn't pick up his head to look for Spirit. He was forced to keep his eyes on his feet stuck on the boat's rough, splintered bottom. There was no talking, no asking for Spirit. Water soaked his body. His ears grew deaf from the shots both sides fired. He could feel the canoe's flank brush up against the bodies of the crocodiles, swerving to avoid their snapping jaws and spiny tails. He closed his eyes and shuddered. When the boat thudded against the bank, the soldier pulled him out, and he stepped into the water, if he could still call it water. It had changed color. It was the color of blood, filled with floating bodies, many of them in parts. The soldier dragged him toward the crowd of running boys and SPLA army soldiers, directing them into the bush.

Chapter Fifteen
Running from Gilo to Pochalla, Rainy Season, July 1991

"RUN, RUN!" people shouted.

Two different armies were shooting at each other from across the river, the TPLF and the SPLA. The TLPF had taken over power from Mengistu, who fled the country. The SPLA were no longer welcome in Ethiopia. They now had no choice but to find a base in Sudan. They led the boys, walking for at least a month through Anyuak savannah land to reach the SPLA base in the garrison town of Pochalla. The hot, dry afternoon they arrived there, three planes sputtered in the air above them. Old and lugubrious, the planes flew closer. Majok could make out the letters UN painted on their flanks. He ran toward them and bumped into another boy and fell, both of them shouting obscenities.

"Chohr e raan? Are you blind?"

He could not waste time talking. Every moment that he wasted meant that he would not be the first to receive food, someone else would catch his portion as it fell from the sky. He was sure there would not be enough food to get around.

He noticed a woman dressed in a yellow robe, a woman of about the same age as his mother, staring at him. She radiated the same worry and strain that his mother did the morning he went hunting with Thontiop without finishing his breakfast.

She was small and slender. She cocked her head and turned toward him, smiling, and he was able to see that her front teeth were gapped, just like his mother's. He ran toward her.

The woman lifted her arms.

"Mama Majok, Mama Majok!" he called. At last, at last, at last, he had found her! They stood face-to-face. He could feel her heat. He couldn't breathe. They stared at one another locking eyes, as if they were the only two people in the field.

Tears welled up in the corner of her eyes. He was smiling, but she was crying. She covered her face with her hands and said, "No, I am not Mama Majok," crying so loudly she was all he heard. Her sobs drowned out the dipping churn of the propellers.

He stumbled backward and took off through the mud, mud up to his knees. He was stricken with longing for his mother, but the reality made him even more determined than ever to be among the first to get to the food. He measured the distance with his eyes. He was still quite far from where the sacks fell through the heavens, down through the vastness of space. Miracle manna: one-hundred-pound nylon sacks with blue UNHCR letters written across them. He had wasted precious minutes talking to the woman and now it was going to be harder to get through the crowds to the food.

"Go back! Go back!" people shouted at him.

An older boy caught him and grabbed his arm.

"Let go of me, let go of me!" Majok screamed.

"Stop! Stop running!" the boy shouted.

He pulled himself free of the boy and squeezed through the crowd. In the center, a boy lay on his back, unmoving. Not only this boy, there were more, each surrounded by a circle of people.

The bags were not manna. All ten sacks lay split open on the ground.

Determined, he ran toward the scattered grain. Other boys had the same idea and scooped up handfuls of grain before he could reach it, but most of the people were so horrified that they did not want to touch any of the grain. Majok waited until the boys who were collecting grain turned their backs, and he snatched some grain from their piles. One of them saw what he was doing and yelled, "Thief, thief!"

Majok yelled back at him, *"Cuin ace cuin du te ken en lo ne yi yaac.* Your food is not your food until it's in your stomach."

Later that night, what hadn't slipped between his fingers and spilt onto the ground was his to roast over a fire. The pops were so loud it almost made him believe that he was cooking a real meal when it was just small coarse pieces of grain, hot to the touch. He looked across at the field, the sky black. A boy around his age who was tending the fire asked him if he knew the clan names of the boys who were killed.

"No." Majok said. "Do you?'

"No." The boy touched the end of a stick and the nest of fire shifted. "I don't know who was more stupid, us for running under the sacks or the UN for dropping them onto us," he said.

"I can't figure it out," Majok said.

"What's there to figure out? It's chance." The boy touched another of the sticks and several of them collapsed.

"No, I don't think so. Someone saved me today. I thought she was my mother."

"I always think I'm seeing my mother."

"That's just it. It wasn't, but if she didn't stop to talk to me, maybe I'd have gotten to where the sacks were falling and one of them would have struck me down and killed me.

The boy gasped.

Just then, the voice of the *makuen e gok*, the nighttime crier, shouted over the mobile loudspeaker: "Dig a foxhole. Get down! Get down!"

The two boys left the fire to burn out on its own and ran toward a group of boys scraping the ground with their fishing hooks. That whole night and into the morning, Majok stayed crouched down in the hole with his hands over his ears, not lucky enough to have a mat to cover his head from the roasting hot sun. When the soldiers finally addressed the boys through mobile loudspeakers, they ordered them to climb out and search the holes for the bodies of boys who had died and bury them. Digging them out wasn't necessary. The soldiers ordered the boys to throw dirt over the holes and mark the holes with sticks so that no one would climb in with a corpse when they went back into the foxholes for cover.

The next night Majok had to pee so badly, he climbed out of his foxhole. In the dark, he couldn't find his foxhole again. He felt around on his hands and knees, whispering for the boys he'd been in the hole with. Although the sky was quiet, he lacked cover. It took longer to dig a hole alone, and he fretted over the possibility of a bomb exploding before he finished. The hole he dug wasn't deep enough to cover him, so he crouched down into it as low as he could, all night long terrified of a bomb blowing him apart. That night and day he spent by himself squeezing the heel of his foot against his groin to suppress the sensation to pee. The foxhole he dug looked like a latrine. The foxhole smelled like a latrine, and no one except him would know if he peed in it. But if he did, the soil would turn damp and cold.

On the third morning, a soldier bent down and tapped Majok's head with a stick. "Hurry! Get up, get up!" The soldier pointed toward a clearing. "Go to the end of the field and look for stones, spread them out on the ground, then keep spreading more."

The wind had picked up speed. It swept across the ground. The sun was pale, hidden in smoke. Majok joined other boys working up and down the field, carrying rocks in groups of two or three boys to build an airstrip. When the ground became filled with enough gravel for a plane to land on it, Majok returned to a larger foxhole, grateful to crawl in with others and shut his eyes and sleep.

The next morning, he woke to a soldier rapping his knuckles on his head, "Quick, boy." Majok climbed out to the rumble of lorries. He waited for the soldier to lead him aboard one. Instead, the soldier told him to find a group of boys to walk among. He told Majok that they needed to clear out of Pochalla and begin walking again. He said that he didn't know exactly where they were headed, but he believed that they would be leaving Sudan and crossing into Kenya. With sore muscles from having been cramped in his foxhole for so many days, Majok felt too weak for walking. When the soldier approached another foxhole, Majok pretended he was looking for a group of boys to walk among and squatted behind an oil drum. Exhausted, he couldn't keep his eyes open, and he fell asleep.

A different soldier found him and shook him awake.

"What's going on? What are you doing still here?" The soldier embraced him. He was a boy himself, until he remembered his training. "Go!" he shouted.

Majok was one of the last to leave the camp. He walked with his BP5 biscuits in a basket on his head and his nylon backpack filled with enough rations for a week. And even though he received these rations, the days spent hiding in foxholes left him afraid of being exposed. He gripped his hands across his sweat-soaked chest and shivered. The soldiers ahead of him were waving magnets over the earth to clear the path of land mines. Each time a soldier swept his hands over the ground, Majok felt his breath stop up in his throat.

A week into the trek, he found himself walking through Mogos and Boma, hostile Murle land. Murle tribesmen hid in the vines that covered the umbrella trees and shot at the boys. "Get down!" someone shouted each time a shot exploded.

Terrified and exhausted, he arrived at a water hole. "Fill your containers," a soldier ordered. A herd of gazelles stood on the bank, leaning in and lapping up the water.

"Careful," a soldier shouted into a megaphone, startling the gazelles. "There're tribesmen around the area."

The soldiers spread out to guard the boys, their rifles raised in the air. "Hurry," they shouted. "Go fill your containers."

Majok edged toward the water hole. He'd taken only a few steps when rifle shots blasted through the air. Clods of animal dung exploded.

He covered his face with his backpack and ran.

"Don't run! Don't run!" a soldier shouted. "Ignore the shots and fill your containers!"

A voice through the megaphone: "Time out! Time to cook."

"What? You want to do what? Cook when Murle are shooting at us?"

The soldiers laughed at the expense of the boys. "Ha Ha Ha Ha. What's wrong with you boys, we'll protect you. Go on, go gather sticks and grass for a fire. Spread out, spread out!

What? You refuse to spread out? Okay, if you're too chicken to go by yourself, come with us."

Majok followed some soldiers through a scattering of thorn bushes and down a small hill thick with brush. "Food!" a soldier shouted. "Ha Ha Ha Ha," the soldiers laughed.

Several dead impalas lay humped on top of each another, the ground pooling with their blood. The shots were from the soldiers gathering meat for the boys. That night the soldiers cooked the boys a feast. While the boys split apart tender chunks of fresh smoky meat with their fingers, the soldiers rolled joints and taunted the boys with descriptions of how frightened they had been. In general, the soldiers didn't supply the boys with any information, keeping them in a state of constant anxiety.

Men, women and children were also journeying through the desert route of Magus to Pakok, hundreds of thousands of refugees on the move. While seeing adults was comforting, Majok soon grew exhausted from searching their faces. Whenever he passed a hut, he'd search the openings for his family.

In Magus, groups of women sat spread beneath the shade. When they saw the hordes of boys walking in the distance, they ran to them to search for their sons. Majok squinted and walked, walked and squinted, dazzled by the sight of so many women, many of them Taposa dressed in orange and purple robes, their thick woven necklaces wrapped around their necks and their hair dyed bright orange.

When the women couldn't find their sons, they begged the boys for water. The sun made a haze out of the road and the earth and the weeds. If Majok gave any of these women water, he wouldn't have any for himself.

After a couple of days, scattered huts became actual settlements and towns. At the outskirts of a town called Narus, an old woman recognized him. "Tsk, tsk, tsk," she clucked. She sat on the ground, wearing a black robe tied over a white robe. She held out her hands. This time he was out of water. He had nothing to give her. Despite offering her nothing, she continued to talk to him, "I know you. I know your mother. She was here just a few days ago. She was asking for you."

Stunned, he stared at her.

"What are you doing, child? You're losing time. Hurry, you can still find her."

Narus was smoldering. Majok raced through the streets, desperate to find his mother. Packed with people, the town had the charred look of a garrison with few huts standing, the air filled with the smell of gunpowder. The town had already been captured and the rebel army camped on the roads to plan their retaliation. Boys concealed their injuries and walked up to the commanders and asked to join. For some, joining the army was the only way to feel safe, but Majok had no interest in joining. He wanted only to find his mother. He was so crazed with wanting to find her that each time he saw a woman, he shouted so that she could hear him over the static of the loudspeakers mounted onto lorries driving all over town.

"MAMA MAJOK, MAMA MAJOK" he shouted until his voice grew hoarse. He was so busy shouting that it took him awhile to hear the broadcasts: "Pack your things. You have to leave in thirty minutes. The town has been captured by the enemy. You have to leave." A crackle lit up the sky. Through it he saw the mobs of people rushing out of the town. Now he ran with them, unable to shout loud enough for his mother to hear him call her name.

"Run, if you want to see her," a different woman shouted.

"Is she here?"

"Yes, she is here."

He ran along with this woman, shouting for his mother. They ran through clearings, charred with smoking fires. At last they came to a larger clearing that had the feel of a settlement, the kind of middle-of-nowhere desert settlements where the UN placed refugees. Within the hour, UN lorries appeared.

The Kenyan driver walked to the back of his lorry, pulled away a plastic sheet and revealed the tap on a water tank. He offered Majok and the woman who accompanied him some water.

"Karibuni sana," the driver said to the woman. "Lokichoggio is just a couple hours down the road. Come on. Get in!"

Majok rubbed his swollen big toe where he had kicked a stone. He knew that he would not be able to walk on it for another couple of hours. His feet had taken him this far, but they could not carry him any further. The woman reached for him, and the driver nodded in agreement. First, the driver lifted the woman in, then he lifted Majok in. It was hard for Majok to remove his arms from around the man's neck, he was so grateful.

"Mahbrukh Alehkhum! Congratulations!" the soldiers guarding the checkpoint shouted as the lorry squeaked to a stop.

Lokichoggio, the UN settlement they were headed toward, was a few kilometers down the road. But the camp could not hold the thousands of arriving boys. After two weeks of sleeping in tents and eating UN-rationed food, Majok was separated out again. He said goodbye to the woman and boarded a lorry with other unaccompanied boys. This lorry delivered him to another settlement around a hundred kilometers away called Kakuma.

Chapter Sixteen
Kakuma Refugee Camp, Kenya 1991

MAJOK SAT ON DRY EARTH among thousands of stunned boys and nudged the boy next to him. Fewer trees grew in Kakuma than any other refugee camp that he'd been to. "Come on," he said, "we can't stay here."

"What?" the boy said in the middle of closing his eyes.

"Too much sun. Let's go find shade."

"Not now."

"Why not?"

The boy showed Majok his foot. Majok shuddered and turned away. Covered with thick crust, the skin on the boy's toes was a mass of bubbly scales.

"Maybe when it gets better," Majok said.

The boy's eyes narrowed into slits and his body slumped like a clod of earth. Majok wondered if the boy would make it. Somehow, the boy made it here.

Majok, too—he made it. Not because of chance. He stopped thinking that it was chance. His name, Majok, didn't just mean bull. He was named after the spotted bull, the strongest bull in the herd, a name his mother gave him. He escaped bombs and gunfire, because he knew how to dig a foxhole. He wasn't old enough to be initiated, but he had enough cuts and bruises and scars to decorate the skin on the foreheads of twenty boys. And he also knew that staying alive had something to do with his search for his mother. He narrowed his eyes as if seeing her in the distance. Was it possible? Was she guiding him? He believed she was leading him to her, wherever she was at that moment, and each moment was filled with her.

He dragged himself around the field, sidestepping tippy-toe in and out of groups of boys, balancing over legs and arms and backs. By the time he reached the trees, all the thorn-covered shade acacias were filled. Boys crowded together, fighting for a spot in the shade. To his astonishment, someone shouted his name.

"Majok!"

He turned around. It was one of those moments he experienced a few times in his life when he felt the pulse of the earth slow down and come to a standstill. Spirit Free stood in the center of a group of boys.

"Spirit?" Majok looked him over. He couldn't believe it. "Spirit!"

"See this guy?" Spirit closed his eyes and rotated his head as if evoking deep pain. "This guy was with me at the Gilo. He's not to be trusted. Let's go!"

Majok bowed his head, tears formed in his eyes. He didn't forgive himself for leaving Spirit at the Gilo. Clearly, Spirit wasn't willing to forgive him either.

"I'm joking," Spirit said and embraced him. "Our fathers knew each other, remember? We're brothers."

The taller boy, called Gabriel, whose every feature—nose, mouth, hands, feet—seemed oversized, stepped forward and stooped to shake Majok's hand, though Majok did not feel like he deserved to be welcomed into their group. Not everyone swapped stories. Some boys didn't speak about their experiences, but he was sure that Gabriel was a hero. While Majok allowed himself to be separated from Spirit and lifted onto a boat, he imagined that Gabriel helped younger boys across, his arms long enough to hold three or four boys hanging from his shoulders.

A stern, shrill voice over a loudspeaker interrupted them: "Juet Community! Juet Community!"

"Stay. We don't have to report to them," said the boy called Ayuen. Ayuen wasn't as tall as Gabriel, but he was still taller than Majok by a full head. His far-apart eyes, Majok later learned, made him better at seeing things than most people. Spirit and Majok stayed to guard the tree while Ayuen and Gabriel gathered sticks for building a hut. If they all left at once, their tree would get taken. Teams of boys prowled nearby. Despite the voice that shouted from the mobile loudspeaker, Spirit and Majok hunkered down among the branches to guard the tree.

By midday, Gabriel and Ayuen still hadn't returned. Majok was beginning to wonder if he would ever see them again when several soldiers, sweating in their khakis, their murky eyes filled with blood, marched toward him and Spirit.

"This is a great tree," Spirit said when the soldiers reached them, rapping his knuckles on the trunk. "Look, we're going to attach a wall for our hut right here."

"Ha ha ha. You call this a tree?" the soldiers laughed.

All at once, the soldiers lifted their rifles eye-level with the boys and ordered Spirit and Majok to walk with them across the field and up a small hill.

"This is where you'll build," the soldiers said when they arrived at the top of the hill. "This is the new land of Jalle Payam—Juet, Alian and Aboudit. You will all be living in one zone. Start building your huts."

Gabriel and Ayuen appeared. The soldiers had led them up the hill hours earlier and they were busy building huts. This was the first time since Majok left his village that he lived with his clan. Although it looked nothing like the dry stream beds or rich, green channels floating with hyacinth and water lilies that surrounded the real land of Payam Jalle, Kakuma became his permanent home with all the stations of normal life: Typhus. Malaria. Roundworm. Cholera. Whooping cough. Polio. Measles. Chicken pox. Chronic anemia. Rheumatic fever. Diphtheria.

Huddled in his hut, he waited for evening to come. Hunger pains kept him awake if he didn't eat close to bedtime. His rations were no better here—a two-week portion comprised half a cup of flour, salt, oil and grain. It was barely enough for one meal a day.

More and more people—boys, also entire families— arrived at the camp, stunned and ill, speaking in whispers. In addition to Sudan, they were escaping from Ethiopia, Congo, Somalia, Rwanda and Burundi. Seeing them appear, Majok began to feel hopeful. He no longer remained huddled in his hut, but spent whole days searching the faces of the arriving adults for his parents. He'd get out of his hut and walk around, going up to the women, turning his eyelids inside out, wiggling his ears and stretching his lips, making funny faces, getting them to laugh, so that he could see whether any of them smiled with the gap teeth of his mother. If he could get the women to smile, he could find out if his mother was among them.

So many people arrived that in a very short time, Kakuma looked like a city clustered with pointy roofs on mud huts and a central compound with white, canvas tents where the aid workers lived. The posts outside the aid workers' tents listed the names of the agencies they worked for: Friends from the West, The UN Refugee Agency, The Lutheran World Federation, The World Food Program, Save the Children. Majok memorized the names of each one, thinking that there might be a time when he could seek out help from them. The aid workers built schools, three-walled mud-and-stick structures. Each community and zone had its own school, food distribution center, clinic and NGOs. Even when the boys had been too weak to train, Jesh el Amer commanders forced them to run up and down in the heat of Pochalla, training for the army. At Kakuma, SPLA commanders stood at the water line and pulled out boys and led them to school.

Boys huddled on benches and bent over copybooks, tracing maps to learn the locations of the continents, counting off bundles of sticks in fives. The teacher's voice competed with the clattering of kettles, shuffling of feet and crying babies. As the months passed, Majok became one of the boys who didn't stop raising his hand and volunteering answers even on the days when he was too hungry to concentrate. He became the person who gave up sleeping two extra hours to get into the water line before dawn and arrive at school before anyone else. One day toward the end of middle school when it would soon be time to prepare for high school entrance exams, the teacher stood in front of him.

"If you continue being a top student," the teacher said, "you'll get a high mark on the KCPE exams and you can qualify for a scholarship to attend a Kenyan secondary school in Nairobi. You want to get out of the camp? You want to go home one day? It's your only chance. Don't give up. Keep trying."

He didn't need the teacher to tell him not to give up. He studied every free moment. Since the term started, his brain absorbed more information than a bank saturated with river water. "What do I need to do?" he asked, still countless exams away from applying to a secondary school in Nairobi.

"You need to get your hands on a Top Mark book. No one can excel on the exams without such a book."

"Top Mark?" he hadn't seen one yet.

"There is an aid organization called Friends from the West…"

"Yes, I know Friends from the West," Majok said.

The teacher beamed at him. "How do you know?"

Majok described having seen the name of that organization written on some of the aid workers' tents.

"Good, you know of the work they do. I will get you an application. They will find you a sponsor and your sponsor will send the money for you to buy a Top Mark."

"This is what you will do. You go to Kakuma Town with the money and barter down to fifty shillings. Do you hear me? Fifty shillings, not a shilling more."

Chapter Seventeen

HEAT SLITHERED against his chest, rested in the creases of his neck. Damp heat loosened the binding on his *Top Mark Math Book*. Stored in a box filled with Bibles on the back shelf of a shop in Kakuma Town, not a single page missing or crinkled. He wondered who owned it and kept it in mint condition. Though not new, its yellowing pages smelled slightly of meat—gristle and marrow. Brain foods.

Torn from a discarded UNHCR bag, the brown cardboard cover protected its pages from the stampeding fingers of boys. The boys in Majok's class hovered near his seat on the bench until the teacher entered the room. Even with the teacher watching, the boys surrounding him leaned over or screwed their necks backward or forward to look inside his book. All through the lesson, he cradled it in his hands to keep boys from grabbing it.

When no one was looking, Majok opened the book to page 101 and wrote his initials inside it, shaping them as small and black as the print. No one flipping through the pages would ever know that he'd written his initials in them.

Afterward, Majok wondered if he should pick a different page to write his name in. Maybe, page number 101 was too obvious. All day, every answer to every math problem was the number 101. The teacher said it repeatedly, "There are a hundred and one ways to solve this problem. There are hundred and one ways to pay attention." When the teacher introduced a new subject, he called it Topic 101. The temperature in Fahrenheit. The amount of days until the KCPE exams.

After class, Ayuen studied Majok's face, "You're going to pass out, man. This book is stressing you. Leave it and come swimming." Ayuen and Gabriel planned to go swimming in the flooded volcanic escarpment with Melat and Aamina, two

Ethiopian girls. The escarpment was located on Turkana land in that part of the Great Rift Valley where the camp was located and the Turkana tribe lived.

"Yeah," Gabriel nodded. "You should come."

Melat and Aamina lived in the very next zone and had seen the boys walking by, carrying rations and scraps of brown wrapping paper. They waved to them and begged them to stop. It was too dangerous for girls to go to the escarpment alone. Just gathering firewood, they could get attacked. It was a chance they took every day. Besides fearing the Turkana, the girls feared many of the men in the camp. Many of the men came from places where girls don't walk around by themselves. Not to mention the girls' fear of enemy armies during their walk to Kenya that raped or killed even very young children.

The Ethiopians were the least traditional of all the people in the camp. Part Italian, the girls dressed in short shorts and T-shirts. These girls were a couple of years older than Majok and his friends. The girls had already developed their women's bodies. Gabriel and Ayuen experienced their growth spurts early—they were ten or eleven or twelve years old, like Majok, but he hadn't grown yet. Ayuen and Gabriel had been talking about the girls for days, bragging over which one had a chance with them.

Before leaving for the escarpment, Majok returned to the hut to bury his Top Mark book in the earth to keep it safe. He marked the mound with an X, then he met Ayuen and Gabriel at the girls' hut, and the five of them snuck past the unaccompanied-minors zone across dust fields to a secret trail where Turkana men and their camels had stamped down the weeds. The girls said that they were living on their own just like the boys. Melat said that her mother and father were both dead. Aamina didn't explain about her parents. She said the camp was hard and lonely, staring down at the ground while she walked.

Even though the Turkana were mostly cattle and goat herders, they wore knives wrapped around their wrists. As they walked to the spring, Melat kept turning her head from side to side, flashing her eyes to take in the landscape, listening for the approach of Turkana.

Gabriel pointed to the escarpment up ahead. "I'll run up and make sure no one's on the other side," he said. After a few minutes, he waved his hands for the rest of them to follow.

Clumped everywhere on the bank, sand and rocks, in between stands of marsh grass, was camel dung, it's odor so overpowering Majok pinched his nostrils together until he got used to the bloated, sour smell. Some people believed that the escarpment was part of the Turkana religion and to swim in it was to sacrifice yourself to the Turkana gods. Murmurs went through the camp each time a boy disappeared who was last seen swimming in the spring. If the camp elders knew that the boys planned to swim in the spring, they'd cane them.

"Fresh dung," Gabriel said. "We don't have to worry. No one's coming back until tomorrow." Melat started to say something, but Gabriel stopped her, "Fresh dung means no one's coming back. You don't have to be afraid to go in."

The water in the escarpment glittered, its surface stiller than the sky. Melat walked to the edge. The bottom of Aamina's shirt wet got wet as she sprinkled water on her neck and arms. Melat dipped in her toe.

Ayuen watched them. "*Jemila,* beautiful!" he said of Melat's glittering eyes and Aamina's bright white smile. Before they left for the escarpment, Ayuen told Majok that he liked Aamina. Majok responded by saying that Aamina was too old for him.

"Why? Too old for what?"

Majok didn't want to hurt Ayuen's feelings, so he said Aamina was too old for him to marry.

"To marry? An Ethiopian? I'd never marry someone outside the tribe. Would you?"

"No, of course not."

Ayuen agreed that he wasn't going to marry Aamina.

"What's wrong?" Gabriel asked Melat, who was crying. "What is it?"

"She has her blood," Aamina said, turning around, waving for Melat to follow. "Come on, if it's like mine, it can't be that heavy. Anyway, the water will stop your flow."

"I told you there's nothing to be afraid of," Gabriel said. He stood very quiet. "Listen, the water's whispering your name."

"It is?"

"Listen, it's calling you. Melat…Melat…"

"Stop it. You're scaring me."

She agreed to go in the water only if someone stayed on the bank and kept watch for Turkana. Gabriel grew impatient and said, "Okay, Majok will stay." Majok realized that Gabriel and Ayuen had brought him along, at best, for this. He had done the same thing as a child on the banks of the Nile when his father brought him as far as the shore.

"Majok?" Melat said.

"He won't mind, will you, Majok?" Gabriel said, not taking his eyes off Melat.

Majok kicked up some water. "Why do I have to be the one?"

Melat grinned. "See, he doesn't want to. He wants to play in the water."

She embarrassed him in front of the other boys, talking to him like he was so much younger, when he was nearly their age. He picked up a stone. Melat cocked her head and screwed up her eyes, regarding him. "What are you doing with that stone, Majok? Do you think you can scare away a Turkana man with a stone?"

"He can," Gabriel said to her, coming to Majok's defense. "Majok's a sharp shooter. His aim is better than mine. Isn't that right, Majok?"

Ayuen stretched his arms over his head. He'd always been more of a friend than Gabriel. He turned in Majok's direction, "If you stay here and keep watch, Majok, one of us will replace you after a while."

Majok nodded and sighed. Ayuen and Gabriel ran off splashing into the water, pulling the girls along with them.

Ayuen splashed water in Melat's face and she wriggled away, laughing. He stopped chasing her and splashed Aamina. The way Ayuen went after Aamina, Majok thought, was like a fisherman back in the Sudd where there was more swamp than water and people baited fish with a net that got tangled up in the weeds. Ayuen grabbed her arms and wrapped them around his neck, pulling her with him into the deeper water. She struggled for an instant, then relaxed against his body.

Majok watched Gabriel put his arm around Melat's shoulders and guide her onto her back. "Majok needs a turn. Melat, do you want to be with Majok or would you rather bring one of your girlfriends?" he said loud enough for Majok to hear.

Melat dove under water and kicked water into Gabriel's face.

"I'm just joking. You know I'm just joking," Gabriel said, grabbing her hands and stretching them out in front of her, as if he had at first decided to teach her how to become a better swimmer, then decided against it and pulled her with him into the deep center of the pool.

Majok couldn't look at them or listen to them talking any longer. Gabriel acting like all he had to do was to say he was joking and everything was okay. Majok knew that Gabriel was going to try to kiss Melat against her will and he didn't want to see it happen. He turned away from them to shoo off the damsel flies that buzzed around his head. Every time he swatted at one, another landed on his neck or shoulder. He heard Melat call for him, and he turned back toward the water. Gabriel was nowhere in sight. Melat was treading water, coughing and choking.

Majok prayed that the stories about the Turkana gods weren't real and that Gabriel hadn't disappeared forever. He panicked and jumped in. He reached Melat and wrapped his arms around her body to help her stay afloat.

Gabriel emerged next to Majok, baring his teeth. "What are you doing? You're supposed to be on the bank watching for Turkana!" Pink jagged scars zigzagged Gabriel's shoulders where fishing hooks had ripped his skin. The whites of his eyes were still sprinkled with red from all the dust in the camp. Majok let go of Melat. Gabriel tackled him and pushed him underwater.

"What? What did you think?" Gabriel said to him, releasing him and inching toward Melat like he owned her, crooking her neck in his arm.

"I thought you were in trouble," Majok said.

"Get off, get off of me" Melat screamed at Gabriel. She freed herself and dove underwater, swimming furiously back to the bank. She climbed out, tears rolling down her cheeks, not talking to anyone, not even Aamina who shook the water from her body when she stepped onto the bank to walk with Ayuen through scattered sunlight back to the camp.

Gabriel called for Melat, but she refused to wait for him. When the camp's pointed, thatched roofs came into view, she ran across the field without saying goodbye. Gabriel walked silently with Majok. "I almost had her until you came and ruined it," he said after a while.

The soil was a pale sand color. The sun shone down on it, glazing a pebble lying on the ground. Majok stopped to pick it up and tossed it between his hands, sensing that Gabriel was ready for a fight.

Gabriel stepped forward. Majok threw the pebble. It struck Gabriel's ear.

"Why did you do that?" Gabriel shouted.

Majok frowned, thinking of Melat's desperation, how she scissored her body through the water to get away from Gabriel. Maybe Gabriel would have been a different person if he still lived in the village, someone a girl might want to kiss. "She doesn't even like you," Majok said.

Once Majok returned to his hut, he wanted to start studying to make up for lost time. He dug around for his Top Mark under the X in the spot where he buried it, but he couldn't feel its sharp edges. Hundreds of people passed his hut each hour, each day, each of them eager, he thought, to have his book. He covered his eyes with his hands. His hut lay on the way to a water tap, to Kakuma Town and to the various communities. There was no reason for anyone to wave to him, especially the old chief walking past on bent legs. This chief might have had bad eyes, but Majok couldn't help feeling suspicious of what the chief was doing so close to his hut, as if he was conspiring with the boy who stole Majok's book. Babies were crying, and it seemed like they were trying to tell their mothers who stole it. He thought back to how Ayuen begged him to go to the Turkana spring. 'See what you'd be missing,' Ayuen had said. Majok stamped the ground with his feet. Or maybe Gabriel was trying to get back at him. Would Gabriel have carried things that far? All Majok did was throw a pebble at his ear. Stopped him from trying to take advantage of Melat. He thought back to the last place he saw his Top Mark before he returned with it to the hut. He ran to the schoolhouse, racing past the Ethiopian zone with his hands over his face.

Some of the girls who lived in the zone stood outside their huts grinding grain. One of them called out, "Slow down, boy, where are you going?" Another asked Majok if he wanted a ride on her back, laughing at him, because even though they were close in age, she was so much taller, she could easily carry him. If Melat came out, he'd have no choice but to stop and talk to her, at least to ask if she was okay. If she were ever foolish enough to ask him to take her to the spring again, he'd be sure to say no.

He walked into the empty classroom. The benches slid across the smooth dirt floor. As he pushed them away, he felt beneath them for his Top Mark. The setting sun cast shadows on the walls and on the floor. His friends were back at their huts, preparing the evening meal. Tomorrow would be his turn to cook. Today was Ayuen's turn. Both he and Diktor would gather the water and stir the fire. His hand brushed something hard, not hard like a book. It was crawling. He jumped back. A pair of pincers curved in the air like twin letter Cs, belonging to the scorpion standing in front of him. His hand had just brushed its shell.

"Waaaaaaa," he screamed, wiping his hand on a bench to make sure he hadn't rubbed it against the poison. Maybe the person who stole his book planted it here, baiting him so he would get stung and die, and the thief would get to keep his Top Mark book forever. Frustrated and angry, he watched the scorpion crawl on its top-heavy body, its bug eyes just beginning to sense him as the room darkened.

Back at the hut, Ayuen and Diktor convinced Majok that he must have left his Top Mark somewhere, and if he thought hard enough, he would find it.

"You know that's not true," he said, sniffing the air as if guilt held a scent.

"You don't think one of us took it, do you? We're tight, Majok. You have to know that," Gabriel said.

"Return Majok's Top Mark now," the teacher told the class the following day "and nothing will happen. Return it later and you'll face humiliation."

The teacher interviewed each boy one at a time. None of them confessed.

"Just like that," the teacher said to the class, snapping his fingers so loud there was a hollow blast. "One of you has killed Majok's chance for a sponsor. Just like that!"

A few days later, Majok returned once again to the classroom, hoping the person who took his Top Mark book decided to leave it there. He found a boy sitting on a back bench working out problems in a book covered in UNHCR brown parcel paper that looked like his Top Mark. He never noticed this particular boy before. He belonged to the Nuer tribe, the same tribe as Riek Machar who plotted against John Garang for control of the SPLA. He didn't know what this boy was doing in a Dinka school. Nuer had their own schools.

"Is that your Top Mark?" Majok said to the Nuer tribe boy.

The boy stretched his neck as if trying to relax a kink, "Yes," he said in his Nuer-tribe-accented English.

The boy's long legs stretched under the bench in front of him. On the right side of his cheek was a cyst the size of a half-shilling coin. The boy rubbed it with the fingers of one of his hands without taking his eyes from the book.

Majok's mouth filled with the desire to spit at the boy. "I need to see it," Majok hissed, sucking his saliva back into this throat.

The boy ignored him. Although the boy was so much bigger, Majok walked over and tried to grab the book from the boy's hands, but the boy was quicker and cradled the book against his chest, so that Majok could not get to it. Majok stood over him and reached for the book, but instead of grabbing the cover, he grabbed a page and it ripped. Humiliated, he stared at the ripped piece of paper in his hand that had come loose from his once-perfect book.

"That's my book," Majok shouted. "What are you doing with my book?"

Just then, the teacher appeared at the door.

"That's my book!" Majok shouted again so that the teacher could hear him.

"What are you talking about? You can't accuse every boy with a Top Mark of taking your book. Where did you get this?" the teacher asked the Nuer boy.

"Someone in the market," he said.

"It's mine," Majok shouted. "I can prove it to you. Turn to page 101. I wrote my name there."

"No, it's mine," the Nuer boy said. "I paid with my rations for it."

The teacher sucked in his breath and blew it out sighing. "One of you is lying and must pay the consequences. Majok, being careless with a book will bring upon you its own punishment. If you have lost your book, you will not rank near the top on the exams. But accusing another boy of stealing your book, will bring you lashes. Let me have the book."

The Nuer boy handed the teacher the book. The teacher opened the cover. He flicked the pages with his thumb and the sound washed over the room. Majok waited, the pages flicking, speeding like his pulse. For the first time since he arrived at Kakuma, he had something that could ensure his survival. He could not allow himself to lose it. The book would get him to score higher on the KCPE exams than Ayuen, the highest ranking boy in the class. It could get him a scholarship to a

Kenyan boarding school. It could get him out of the camp and lead him to his parents. He prided himself on being smart enough to have written his initials in the book. His Uncle Thontiop's words echoed in his ear. "Don't ever forget your name Majok. They may come looking for you, but don't ever forget who you are."

The teacher held the book flat in his hands, so that both boys could see it open on page 101. The teacher turned to Majok. "You are lying. I don't see any writing on this page."

Majok stepped forward. "It's there!"

"Are you going to look at me in the face and tell me something that is not true? This is why there is a conflict between our two tribes. It starts here with the accusations of children. Where? There is no writing here."

Majok pointed to the small black letters at the top. "Look!" he tapped the page with his finger. "My initials. 'MMK.' That's who I am."

"I don't see anything," the teacher said. He looked at the empty rows of benches opposite, then back at Majok. "Oh, I thought you'd make it out of here." He spoke one word at a time, not out of anger now but with the astonishment of someone watching a dream implode. The teacher had special plans for Majok and the two of them had talked together many times.

The Nuer boy got up to leave. He held out his hand to claim the book.

"On top of everything else…" The teacher bit his lips and shook his head at Majok, then rocked back on his heels to slant the page toward the light and glance at it a final time while Majok wiped his eyes.

"Ahhhh, I see it," he beamed.

"MMK," Majok shouted.

"Calm down, Majok," the teacher said. "You have your book back."

Chapter Eighteen

"PUT IT TO YOUR MOUTH and blow it up," a Ugandan boy said to Majok, waving a rubber glove, streaked with blood, in front of his face. The boy had fished it out from the garbage pit behind the maternity tent filled with soiled menstrual pads, diapers, syringes and bandages. There were several small hospital tents in the camp. Few sick people who entered ever came out. The rust smell of blood reached Majok, making him feel nauseated.

He looked at the glove and wondered if it held life. The desert wind blew in hot sweeps. Dust stuck to the blood streaking the glove's surface. He didn't even want to touch it. "Why?" he said.

"You want to play football don't you?"

"It's dirty,"

"It's okay. I've done it lots of times."

The two boys were not standing close enough to the tent to see the faces of the women lying on cots inside, only the backs of their heads, some belonging to very young girls. The wind flapped the edges of the tent. Inside, nothing moved. He stole steps toward the tent. A woman in a white medic's gown entered. She led two men carrying a stretcher. They walked toward a cot. Lowering the stretcher to the floor, they loaded it with the body of a woman wrapped in a muslin cloth.

He gasped.

"Majok, where are you going? What's wrong?"

He didn't want to tell the Ugandan boy that he was thinking that the dead woman on the stretcher could be his mother. He would never know whether it was her. He had been too afraid to stop and look at the faces of the villagers lying on the ground the night of the attack on his village. If he'd turned around and looked, even for a moment, he'd know whether his parents were alive.

The Ugandan boy noticed Majok looking at the stretcher. "Jesus, God, come away from there!"

Majok stared at the stretcher, the motionless shape beneath the cloth.

The Ugandan boy led him back to their spot near the pit where he found the glove. The boy stretched the opening where a hand would slide in, then gathered it together and held it in front of Majok's face. "Come on, I thought you wanted to play!"

He closed his eyes to block out the image of the woman on the stretcher and he pushed the glove against his lips.

"Blow into it," the Ugandan boy said.

The rubber tasted bitter. It took all Majok's breath. Bit by bit, the rubber inflated and the glove's five fingers stuck up like the crown on a rooster's head. He felt lightheaded. He sat down on the ground with his arms around his head.

"Breathe normal," the Ugandan boy said. He shook the fingers on the glove. "I bet you've never see anything like this!"

"No, what's it for?"

"Watch."

The boy rooted around in the dirt for two stones, one that was smooth and one with a sharp edge. The boy put the smooth stone inside the glove, knotted it and wrapped it round and round with some plastic twine, the kind of twine UN parcels are wrapped with. He placed it in Majok's hands and went back to the garbage pit and searched through the refuse until he found a sock. It was torn and black with dirt. The boy walked back to him and took the glove from his hands. Then he squeezed the glove through the sock. "Watch," he said, throwing the sock covered balloon on the ground, "now it will bounce." Then the boy kicked the balloon with his toes to see if it would bounce and was hard enough to sustain pressure.

"Tell me the positions," the boy asked him.

"Midfielder, defense, striker and goalie."

"Striker. That's your position. Speed plus determination." The Ugandan boy put the balloon on the ground. "Show me what you've got."

Here's what Majok came to understand. His feet should not have been able to kick the ball very far. They were scorched, blistered, scratched, calloused, swollen and cut. This was what happened. He kicked it across the burning hot ground, further than anyone else in his zone, on the Ugandan team or in the entire camp. It flew over the maternity tent and landed on the other side.

The Ugandan boy grabbed Majok's arm, his hand sticky from the things he'd touched. "Come on, before someone sees and takes it away from us."

Every Saturday from December to February, Majok hiked with a group of Juet and Palek boys to the Turkwel River and down its steep banks to the bottom. The Turkwel River snaked through Kakuma. The river flooded over during the rainy season. It was completely dry those three months, its muddy bottom baking in the sun until it hardened into a perfect playing field. Unless, of course, camels had soiled the ground, and Turkana men stood at the bottom, leading their camels to the river or from the river or riding on top of them. When that happened, Majok rose onto his tip-toes, balancing himself, imagining what it felt like to bounce from side to side so high off the ground.

That day the field was clear. "Let's get this game going," a boy said, appointing himself referee. He picked two captains: a boy named Kuol, who was at least two heads taller than Majok, and whose head had a funny shape to it like the back of a shovel, as captain of the Palek team, and Majok as the Juet captain.

In place of a coin-toss, the referee boy took off his dark blue T-shirt and tossed it in the air, calling the backside of the shirt. His shirt landed on the front side, the side with the writing on it.

"It's not fair," one of the Palek players said. Everyone looked at Majok, the boys on the Juet team and the boys on the Palek team, some of them having shot up over the year, others with the thin, short legs of ten-, eleven- or twelve-year-olds. Majok still didn't own a shirt.

"Kuol," the referee boy shouted, "take off your shirt and give it to Majok."

Kuol's once-white shirt had a picture of a car on it, a side-view showing two wheels and a round top and a square back. Majok looked at the shirt, thinking it could take him somewhere if only he could find a way to open the door and get himself inside.

"Why?" Kuol said. He was anything but friendly. After years of being on their own, most of the boys in the camp had grown suspicious of each other, willing to fight at the slightest provocation. It wasn't safe at Kakuma and the unaccompanied minors didn't have families to protect them. They never saw the faces of the men who set fire to their villages. They still heard cries and smelled the stench of blood.

"It's our turn to be skins," the referee boy said.

"He'll dirty it with his sweat," Kuol said.

"Then turn it inside out. Come on, let's get started."

Kuol moaned. He pulled his shirt over his back. His eyes on Majok, he turned it inside out, then bunched the shirt up into a ball and used it to wipe off the sweat behind his neck and under his arms. Only then did he give it to Majok. "Here, you can have it now," he grinned, handing Majok the shirt streaked with his perspiration.

The referee boy burst out into a fit of laughter. Majok couldn't remember the last time he'd worn a shirt. All he wanted was to feel that shirt on his skin. Boys enlisted in the SPLA just to have that feeling. Majok pulled the shirt over his head. The feel of the material was so soft, he shut out Kuol and the referee boy. It was as if he were sitting in the car seat on the front of Kuol's shirt, safe behind the windows, his eyes free of the dust that irritated everyone's eyes in the camp. Kuol looked at Majok with his shirt on his body. "God won't let you score with that shirt on your back," Kuol said.

Majok rammed into him. He was so much littler, Kuol laughed. The referee boy spat on the ground in front of them. Then the referee boy swayed his shoulders and clapped his hands in two short bursts like a chief back in the village preparing the ground for a ceremony. "Get into position," the referee boy shouted.

Majok played with twice his usual aggression, and he was not the only one. He kicked the ball deep into a corner. Before he could pass it, the Palek boy blocking him got his foot on the ball and kicked it toward the center. The Palek team turned it over and it looked like they were going to score. Ayuen, who was on the Juet team, screamed "Cheat! Cheat!" Ayuen was a sore loser. He sulked off to the side of the field.

The Palek boy who was blocking Ayuen screamed, "No, you cheated."

Another one of the Juet boys shouted, "Cheaters! Cheaters!"

"Your grandfathers steal cows," the Palek blocker sung, knowing how attached Dinka boys are to their cows. "We rescued your cows from the Murle. All the Juet cows are defenseless. The poor sick Juet cows."

Ayuen ran to the Palek blocker and slapped him in the face. They wrestled. Ayuen held the Palek boy on the ground and twisted his arms behind his back. Someone threw a stone and hit Ayuen in his back. Ayuen screamed. It was an unspoken rule not to aim at each other's stomachs, chests, faces, or heads. No one wanted to die of a broken spleen. Above them, there was movement—a group of older boys were beginning their climb down the steep banks of the riverbed.

Majok got back to his position on the field. The older boys had a clear view of them. He imagined how they'd shout: *"Yaa shababb,* if you want to fight, go join the SPLA in the frontlines!"

The referee boy threw the ball into the middle and everyone started to chase it. It was on the opposite side of the field from where Majok stood. He ran toward it, and a Palek boy kicked it forward and it came into Majok's range.

He wished his father was there. Sometimes he felt like his father was in the shadows when people mentioned his name at night around the fire. "Did you see Majok play today? He's going to be a CAF champion one day." He thought he should be playing up. Actually, he wanted to be playing with the older boys, wanted them to see what he could do. If he was ever going to be a champion player, he needed to advance to a more skillful team.

The ball was right in front of him, a direct line to the goal. He felt like he could score. He ran forward. Kuol blocked him. He tried to get past Kuol, when Kuol pushed him, and he turned his ankle and fell. Kuol got to the ball and passed it to someone on his team and the boy scored a goal. The Palek boys jumped up and down and cheered.

The older boys reached the bottom of the bank in time to see the play. They clapped. Sharp pains shot up from Majok's ankle.

Shaking, he stood up. He yelled at Kuol for pushing him down, but the play began again and Majok needed to defend his position, especially since by that time the older boys were watching. Soon the ball was in his range and he went in for the goal. Kuol blocked him again. This time, he was not going to let Kuol play dirty. He straddled his feet around the ball, so that Kuol couldn't get to it. He had under two seconds to kick. He looked for the right angle on the shot. If the ball went too far to the left, it would miss the goal. He lifted his leg to kick the ball and just at that moment Kuol pushed him and his standing leg gave way, and he fell down. This time the other boys saw him fall, but they hadn't seen Kuol push him. The referee boy didn't stop the game. Kuol kicked the ball to one of his teammates to take it to the opposite goal. Instead, the player kicked the ball to the side and it landed into a thorn bush. *Bang!* The ball exploded. No one moved. The noise stayed in the air, reverberating up and down the hollow riverbed.

A Palek boy cheered and the rest of the Palek team joined in. Ayuen ran to Majok. "They're cheaters," he said. "Every time we play them, they cheat. They kicked the ball in the thorns just so that the game would stop while they were ahead."

"That's not all," Majok thought to himself, without mentioning what Kuol had done to him. He couldn't risk getting the reputation of someone who would rat out another boy. He listened to the slaps of the high-fives the older boys gave the Palek team, happy that the game had ended so that they could take over the field. They lined up and picked players. Majok's ankle was swollen. It was sprained. He hoped it was not broken. Sometimes a rounded bulge that looked like a swelling was really the bone about to poke through. He'd seen it on a friend and hoped that wasn't why the skin on his foot felt like it was on fire, while the rest of his body shivered.

He couldn't put any pressure on his foot. He leaned on the arms of his friends and hobbled all the way out to the Turkana spring, brittle *khram-khram* grass whipping the skin between his toes. His friends helped him along, while he tried to ignore the pain he was in. He knew that it was best not to dwell on pain. If he did, it would charge at him. Dig its sharp nails into him. Hold him down and keep him pinned to the ground. Ayuen said that they needed to come up with a plan, so that the Palek boys wouldn't cheat them out of another game. Ayuen was angry. "You're the better player and they know it," he said to Majok, punching the air with his fists.

Diktor said, "Stop blaming them. We don't practice enough. That's a team problem."

"We can't practice now," Gabriel told him. "Majok's ankle is hurt."

"Figures," Ayuen said. "Figures our best player would go down. What happened? You're indestructible, Majok. You never go down."

"What do you mean?" Majok said.

Ayuen stopped walking and with his far-apart eyes stared at Majok. "Wait a second," he said.

"He missed the kick, that's all," Diktor said.

"Twice?"

"Nothing… okay…I wasn't going to tell you. I'm not a hundred percent sure."

"What happened, Majok?"

"Didn't any of you see Kuol push me down?"

"Ha!" Gabriel said. "Is that why you stole his shirt?"

"Stole it?" Majok was still wearing Kuol's shirt.

"Kuol's going to come looking for you," Ayuen said.

Majok's hand quivered as he ran it across the soft fabric. He looked from Ayuen to Gabriel to Diktor and back to Ayuen. Kuol's presence felt close.

A hush fell over them as they listened for footsteps. "Let's go back," Majok said.

"No, let them come get us," Ayuen said as they reached the escarpment.

Gabriel laughed. "I'll tell you what you're going to do. You're going to keep this shirt. Yes, it belongs to Majok now," Gabriel said, then he ran ahead to make sure that Turkana weren't on the other side of the escarpment. After a bit, he waved his hands behind his back for the rest of the boys to follow.

Majok's hands still quivered as he found a clean spot near the water and stretched out, keeping watch for Kuol, picturing the different ways Kuol would try to avenge himself. The hot, dry air singed the tip of his nose. A damsel fly stitched a loop around his knee. Going into the spring was out of the question. The water might have soothed the swelling on his ankle, but the threat of getting trapped in the spring with an injury was too risky.

Gabriel splashed into the water. His strong body appeared and disappeared between breast strokes. He swam back much faster than he swam out. He was always setting records for himself—obstacles, challenges. When Majok first met Gabriel, the day he arrived at Kakuma, burning with fever from having walked months through desert wilderness, Gabriel boasted to him that he could build his hut faster than anyone. "Once I find enough sticks," he said, "watch me." Gabriel worked all day standing deep in mud. Majok would look across the field and get distracted from building his own hut by the crowds of sick, starving boys. He'd lie down on the earth gasping for breath, unable to accept how his life had changed since he'd lived with his parents in Juet. "Why aren't our parents here? Where are they?" he'd cry. Then he'd look at Gabriel working so hard and be inspired to pick up a stick himself. When Gabriel splashed back to the shallows at the side of the bank where Majok was sitting, he stopped to pick up a stone. Majok followed Gabriel's eyes.

Kuol stood on the rise. Majok looked down at the shirt on his body. Kuol stepped forward. Gabriel threw the stone, shouting at Kuol who was now in plain view, his arms loaded with stones.

"Thief!" Kuol shouted and threw a stone at Majok.

The stone hit Majok in the mouth. It didn't hurt, just the force of it, but there was a sting followed by pain. He rubbed his mouth with his hand and felt warm, wet liquid. Blood. "My mouth..." he cried and fell forward.

Chapter Nineteen

HE REGAINED CONSCIOUSNESS as tall strands of grass surrounded him. Sharp throbs of pain kept him lying on his stomach with his head on the earth. Ayuen stood at his side. "Majok, Majok. Let me take a look," Ayuen said. Majok was afraid to move his hand away. Ayuen dragged it from his face. "Aaaaaaagh!" Ayuen whistled. "Your front two teeth are hanging by a thread! "

"My shirt!" Kuol screamed. "Look what you did to my shirt. There's blood all over it!"

"Shut up! You have no right to speak," Gabriel shouted.

"He has got to get his teeth put back in their sockets," Ayuen said. "That's the only way they'll grow back in."

"Then why did our mothers throw our teeth over a roof?" Kuol asked.

"That was milk teeth. These are permanent teeth," Ayuen said.

Majok rolled over onto his back. His eyes and Kuol's eyes met. The pain was tremendous. Blood was pouring out of his mouth. He felt as if his life was leaving him.

"He needs to be taken to the hospital tent," Ayuen said.

"No," Majok cried, finding his voice as he remembered the body of the woman carried out on the stretcher. "I don't want to go there! I don't want to go there!"

He tried to stand, but he felt too weak. Ayuen saw him stumble and held him under his elbows and dragged him up to a standing position. Gabriel reached for his other elbow and with his weight distributed between Ayuen and Gabriel, they walked him forward. His head felt like bombs were exploding inside it, his mouth felt raw and the gap where his teeth had fallen out felt like an open pit roaring with fire. The ground tilted and dipped. He leaned over to vomit.

At the hospital tent, a male medic held a measuring tape around the withered arm of a child balanced on his mother's hip. As the medic saw the boys come in, he rushed toward Majok, waving his hand in front of his mouth to shoo away the flies that swarmed in the blood. Majok saw the medic glance back at the mother and child to determine which emergency came first. Majok stared at the child in his mother's arms and felt himself begin to regress, become smaller and smaller.

"Everyone outside," the medic said to the mob of boys. "Except you," he said to Majok.

Diktor, Ayuen and Gabriel deposited Majok on a low stool. "You're going to be alright," Ayuen said and left the tent. The other boys marched out. Kuol didn't move.

The medic grabbed Kuol by the wrist and led him toward the opening in the tent. "Out! Don't lay a finger on him as long as I'm alive," he said. Leading Majok to the table, he asked him to open his mouth as he reached into a drawer for gauze. Blood was still pouring out. "Open, let me see inside, the medic said. He pushed away Majok's hand, pressed his thumb down on Majok's lip and forced gauze packing beneath his tongue. Reaching into the drawer for a fresh piece of cotton, he swiped Majok's gum sockets with some bitter tasting liquid and jabbed his teeth into place under his gums, applying pressure with his fingers.

Majok screamed. He stared at the woman. She was too absorbed with her own child to feel any sympathy for him.

"This is the amount of pressure you have to apply each day for your teeth to reattach," the medic said. "It's a serious injury and you have to treat it with seriousness." With his free hand, the medic grabbed the handle of a jerry can and filled a cup with water. He reached into a jar filled with salt, pinched some salt between his fingers and sprinkled it into the cup. He handed Majok the cup. "Rinse. Two or three times a day. That's very important."

"Rinse?"

"Yes, the area must stay very clean or else you will get it infected. If it does, you will have to come back here for medicine."

The hospital tent was far away from the block where Majok lived—Jalle Payam. Jalle Payam was located in Zone Six and this clinic was in Zone One. He knew that he wouldn't be able to get back to the clinic on his swollen ankle. That was something the boys on both teams would have agreed on. The woman would also agree. The medic wouldn't. Majok looked down at his hands and at the shirt stained with blood. One thought occurred to him: he needed to get out of there, out of the camp if he was ever going to become whole and stop looking for his mother in the eyes of dead people.

He felt woozy, about to faint. He'd lost too much blood. His teeth tingled and burned in their sockets. He grabbed the medic's arm for support and propped himself up on his good leg the way he had positioned himself in the game, touching his tongue to his teeth, trying to keep himself upright.

"THAT'S TWO WEEKS WORTH. Make it last," a UN aid worker said to Majok, digging a metal scoop into a sack. Another worker punched a hole in his food rations card. Because of his injury, Majok hadn't gone to school. He gripped the ration bags in his hands. The sun was so hot it was melting the nylon. He'd just received his rations and already it felt like they were disappearing.

The only way to make the food last was for his hut-mates to pool their rations together. Even with the six of them sharing rations, there was only enough to eat one meal a day. It was easier to wake up hungry than it was to go to sleep hungry, so they decided to eat their one meal at night. They chose days that each of them would be responsible for fetching the firewood or water from the pump or grinding the grain or pounding it or making the fire or stirring the pot. Whenever one of them got sick and couldn't do his job, the rotation went quicker. Some weeks he felt like all he was doing was fetching water, fetching firewood and cooking.

When Majok arrived back at the hut, Spirit was there, waiting for him, although he should have been in school. Spirit gazed at Majok, then settled on a point in space and wept, pinching a piece of the twine around his neck. His chest heaved up and down. "Can you give me something to eat?"

"You're the one always storing extra food."

"I've gone through it."

The camp quiet—most people rested after the long walk through the heat to the rations station—he waited for Spirit to explain. Spirit showed him the twine around his neck, his rations card no longer attached to it. The cards didn't have people's pictures on them. A lost card was someone else's good fortune. Spirit shrugged and wept.

Majok didn't know what to do. His throat felt dry, his mouth bitter. The burden Spirit put on him felt immense. He didn't have enough food to keep himself alive. How could he spare any for Spirit? Goodbye to the front area of a hut where women sit. Goodbye to the cattle hearth where men sit around a fire. That way of life was gone. What could he do? Sacrifice himself for Spirit? Let Spirit die with no help? Was he the only one who could save Spirit now? Why was it up to him? He spoke to Spirit as if he could make him see that he wasn't the only person who could help him. "I don't have enough," he told Spirit. "If I give you my rations, I will starve myself. It's never up to one person. It takes more. We have to find others who will pitch in."

"You have fresh rations," Spirit wept.

"They're so little. It's just enough for myself! I would like to give you some, but how can I?" He turned away and looked through a hole in the thatch, where he saw a scorpion crawling on the ground. He stepped back in dread of it. Every day or so someone got a scorpion sting and died. Until *Abuna* Phillip arrived with serum, most people with scorpion stings didn't survive even if they made it to the clinic in time.

A few days ago, Majok laughed as he watched a boy throw a torch on a scorpion. The boy heard his laughter and shouted, "Stop it! You're going to bring bad luck!" Was this the reason Spirit lost his card? Did he bring this onto him by laughing at the boy? He didn't really know why he laughed at that boy. At the time, the boy's action seemed senseless when there were so many scorpions nesting in the soil. If you saw one, it meant that others were close by.

He went to the kitchen corner and opened the jerry can where his hut-mates kept their food supply. If his hut-mates saw him disturbing it, they would cover him with punches. Besides which, feeding Spirit was not an easy matter. He would need to fetch water, firewood, grind the grain and cook it for him. It would take time, at least two hours.

Spirit was no longer weeping. He was falling in and out of sleep. Majok shook him awake, but he fell back to sleep again. Seeing Spirit in this state, he saw himself too, a boy all alone.

Now Spirit had given up hope, when hope was the one thing that would keep him alive. Spirit was going to die all because of him. "Spirit, Spirit!" he shouted. "Wake up, I'm going to cook you dinner."

Spirit didn't open his eyes. Majok stomped on the ground to wake him, but it didn't do any good, so he decided to start cooking for him in case Spirit woke up. If his hut-mates came in while he was cooking, he was certain they would understand.

Majok went outside to build the fire. He was busy grinding the grain when Ayuen arrived, followed by Gabriel. "You're cooking now? Is that what you do when we're not here to stop you? Steal our food?" Gabriel shouted.

Majok pointed to Spirit who was slumped over on the ground.

They gasped. Majok told them what happened.

"If we each give up one day's portion..." Majok said.

Ayuen rammed his shoulders into Majok's chest. "One day's portion?" Majok hit a wall and it rattled. "Who made you chief?" Ayuen said. "I am not one to forfeit my portion because of stupidity."

Majok punched Ayuen in the face.

Gabriel laughed. Majok didn't pack a hard enough punch. Like Ayuen, his hands were weaker than his brain.

Spirit moaned. Gabriel wedged his hands under Spirit's armpits and carried him to the wall to prop him up against it. "He should be taken to the clinic," Gabriel said.

"It's too far to walk. He'll never make it there," Majok said.

"Don't force him to eat. He is not ready to eat. Gabriel is right. First, he needs treatment," said Ayuen.

Majok was boiling like the water in the pot, angry at how selfish they'd become. He shouted at them to make them understand that he too had been selfish, but abandoning Spirit when he most needed help was a crime.

"Look at him," Ayuen shouted.

Clearly, Ayuen believed Spirit was dying and didn't want to waste his rations on him.

Majok couldn't hold in his anger. He pulled a stick out of the wall and swung it around, accusing Gabriel and Ayuen of killing Spirit. Spirit was more to him than a friend, he was a part of him. Seeing Spirit suffer was to suffer himself.

Gabriel ran out of the hut to find help for Spirit. Ayuen grabbed the stick from Majok's hands.

"Go to Loki and get Spirit a new rations card," Ayuen said to Majok.

"How am I going to do that?"

"You can get a ride," Ayuen said. A transport goes to Loki once a day. You can ride it there and back."

"For 1000 shillings!"

"Someone will lend you the money. That guy who rents out Phoenix bicycles. That guy built up a business from his rations while we hoarded ours. Acheng Deng. I borrowed money from him once. Yes, he is very generous. He will give you the money."

Majok had never met Acheng Deng before, but he had seen people riding the red Phoenix bicycles he rented. "It will be dark soon. There isn't time."

"You will have to hurry. In Loki, you can ask for news about your parents."

Ayuen was right. He could get that kind of information in Loki. He could write a letter and give it to the Red Cross in Loki and they could put it in the hands of a messenger who might be able to locate his mother.

"Be careful. I haven't heard any gunshots recently, but if the Turkana can kill Pastor Twil of the Episcopal Church of Sudan, they'll kill anyone," Ayuen said.

Gabriel burst into the hut with four other boys, dragging a blanket tied across two long poles. Majok directed Gabriel to where Spirit leaned against the wall. Gabriel thrust his hands under Spirit's body and lifted him onto the blanket and carried him away.

Majok said goodbye to Ayuen, vowing that he would find a way to help Spirit.

"*Lor yin bi biong de mor kony,*" Ayuen said. "Go ahead, may your mother's god protect you."

Chapter Twenty-One

BLEACHED BONES and withered fur. Must have been a rat's carcass. The bottoms of his feet were tough. He didn't always know what he stepped on until the skin broke and he got an infection.

Zones One to Six contained Southern Sudanese communities where 'unaccompanied minors' lived—a name the UN had given them to stop the SPLA from sending them to fight in the bush. Among themselves, they still called each other Jesh el Amer, even those who no longer hoped to get recruited. Zone Seven was where whole families lived: Ethiopians, Burundians, Ugandans, Congolese, Rwandans and Somalis. Majok didn't like to think of the reasons why they were there. Back in Juet, there wasn't a way of asking. People kept their sorrows to themselves. Everyone's hut looked the same—cone shaped.

At Kakuma, especially in the Southern Sudanese zones, each group of huts had a different shaped roof. For instance, the roofs in Group Two were pointed, the roofs in Group Three were flat and the roofs in Group Four were conical. The different shapes made it easier to know where he was and in which direction he was facing.

No material objects went to waste. Sticks, bones, old socks, USAID food bags, tea leaves, smashed plastic bottles, twine, cardboard. The Turkana, who lived on the outskirts of the camp, collected whatever nobody else wanted and used it to build the roofs of their huts. Their roofs looked like garbage piles with pieces of plastic and metal tied down with twine. They didn't have UN support and considered items like smashed plastic bottles a prize.

Majok prayed that one of the zonal leaders wouldn't peer out and ask where he was going. This close to dusk, he couldn't tell anyone he was walking all the way to Zone Six. He wondered if Acheng Deng would lend him the money to travel to Loki. Everyone knew how hard-working Acheng was for building a business in the camp. How could he explain to Acheng that he wasn't there to rent a bicycle, and that he was there only to take Acheng's money. Maybe Acheng would grab his head and wrestle him to the ground. Even if he proved to be the stronger wrestler, Acheng might take the insult to heart and refuse to lend him any money.

But Majok had a secret weapon. Every boy from the villages around Bor held his uncle Thontiop in awe. Although he hadn't seen Thontiop since before the attack on their village and didn't know how to go about finding him, he knew Thontiop was alive. Bor Dinka children heard so many stories about Thontiop's bravery that they shouted, *Thontiop oyee! Thontiop oyee!* whenever there was a victory, as if Thontiop alone was responsible for every victory in every battle. Majok continued walking, convincing himself that even from far away, Thontiop had the power to help him.

A group of boys passed in the opposite direction. "*Salaam,*" one of the boys said and smiled. The others waved.

"*Kaif,*" Majok said.

They were returning to their huts to prepare the meal. Most boys ate after dark. No one wanted a story going around the camp that they'd been seen doing woman's work. The smell of wood smoke reached him as boys began making fires.

He would need to depend on starlight to guide him back. Thanks God that someone had the idea of planting Kakuma trees wherever a trail turned off to the main road. And rocks, heaps of them. He touched the bark of every tree he passed. He wished he could touch their roots and learn to take in from the soil the way trees did. His mother's footsteps, his father's. His baby brother's pitter-patter. His baby brother would have learned how to walk by now, he realized.

Crop seeds grew along the trail of water that trickled from the taps. People scrambled for pieces of land to grow okra, kale, flowers, beans, maize and kedkede tea.

A boy on a Phoenix bicycle turned onto the road and waved. Another boy on a bicycle passed, and Majok realized that he must be near to Acheng's hut. Over the pinging sound of yet another pair of bicycle tires hitting stones, Majok heard someone call his name. It was one of the zonal leaders flagging his hands.

"Boy," the zonal leader shouted. "I'm talking to you! Where are you going in such a hurry?"

Majok turned around.

The zonal leader walked with the help of a cane carved from a tree branch notched at the top, clenching it so that the stub of the missing middle finger on his right hand bumped against the notch. He reached Majok and screwed the tip of his cane into the earth and waited for him to answer.

"I need to see someone."

"Yes, you do. It was the reason I stopped you."

There was less than an hour of daylight. The sun's falling light mixed with the dust from the unpaved roads, covering the air in haze.

"So I have your permission?" Majok said, blinking through the haze.

"Permission? I am here to take you myself. Come with me to my hut."

"I can't go with you." Majok fabricated an answer, giving the only excuse he considered the zonal leader would accept. "The teacher is waiting for me."

"The teacher is waiting for you? Are you sure?"

Majok rubbed his hand across his eyes. "Yes."

The zonal leader leaned on his cane and looked down into Majok's face. As the leader lifted his cane, Majok squatted, shielding his face with his hands to protect himself from the blows.

"Get up. I am not going to cane you." The leader pointed his cane back toward one of the zones and shook it in the air. "You are correct. The teacher is waiting for you, but he is waiting for you in my hut." He tapped his chest with his free hand. "What is wrong with you, boy? Why do you allow yourself to forget the old ways? You could not have known that the teacher was waiting for you. Indeed, you are correct. He is. If you knew he was waiting for you in my hut why are you walking in the opposite direction?"

Majok hung his head.

The leader laughed. "I cannot torture you any longer. Today I will forgive you. Today is the day for which you have been waiting." He stopped talking for a moment to relish the news. "The teacher has found one of your relatives."

Majok stepped forward through the blinding haze. "My mother?" he asked the leader. The air filled with her face. Larger than life, her eyes were open, and her lips curved into a big wide smile that showed her two-gapped teeth.

The leader shook his head. "No. Your cousin. One of your cousins is here. The son of your father's brother, Chol Nihal," he said.

Mama Majok's image disappeared. Majok hid his face in his hands and wept.

"Majok, what are doing? *Yaa walet,* boy, I'm ordering you. Stop crying."

The leader stepped in closer. "Come on, boy. Stop taking a knife to your heart. You live in Kakuma how many years? How long have you been looking for your relatives?" His fingers curled against his stub as he reached for Majok's arm.

"Maybe my cousin is not ready to receive me," Majok said.

"He is waiting for you right now."

Majok's chest heaved with his cries. If he didn't help Spirit, he didn't know how he could live with himself. He would be like one of those boys who jumped from a tree and killed themselves. It happened every week. A boy started asking questions and then he couldn't find the answers and he lost the will to live. "I have to go to Loki," he said.

"Be serious, how would you get to Loki? People are so desperate that they charge you for the trip there and back and take you only in the one direction. They leave you in the middle of the desert, and if you survive, the only way to get back is to walk."

Majok told the leader about Spirit.

"Spirit who?" the leader asked, and Majok told him it was Spirit Free. The leader smiled, "Yes, that Spirit has been taken to the hospital tent. I hear he is getting better."

It was impossible for the leader to know this, although to survive at Kakuma, Majok knew that he couldn't allow himself to think that people were lying to him. He needed to believe that people spoke the truth at all times.

Chapter Twenty-Two

THROWING A STICK between his hands, playing a game to pass his time or calm his nerves, a boy squatted on the ground outside the teacher's hut. Majok never saw him before. The boy must have lived in a different zone, attended a different school. As soon as the boy saw Majok, he sprung forward, rushing toward him, standing so close they could almost touch.

They looked around the same age. Perspiration beaded the boy's lip. A pea-sized scar marked his cheek where a wound had healed. The boy smelled like burnt things, trash heaped in a pile with bits of plastic. Maybe the boy was standing too close for Majok to recognize him.

"Wen walendie?" Majok asked.

"Yes, I am the son of your uncle," the boy said.

His grandmother's compound. He had loved to go there and play. There were always a group of children gathered in her yard, their skin dusty from playing in the dirt. If this cousin had been among them, Majok didn't remember. He forced a smile.

They walked inside the hut where the teacher was waiting for them, the air stale, hot. Besides a stool, there was a bed made of mud and twine. In a kitchen corner, dented tins and plastic bottles hung from pieces of metal shaped into hooks attached to the hut's stick walls.

The teacher clasped Majok's hands. The boy and Majok sat down on the floor.

"I heard about you before the Gilo," the boy said to Majok.

"Way back then? You were there?"

"Yes, how did you get across?"

"Canoe."

"Me too."

"Were you at Pochalla?"

"No, I came to Kakuma through Itang."

"Why didn't you go straight through?"

"I reached Magos at night. I found a ditch to sleep in. Three boys had already claimed it and there wasn't room for all of us. They told me to go away. I had nowhere to sleep except in an open field. A SPLA soldier stood guard. I was too frightened sleeping out in the open like that to fall asleep. After a couple of hours, I heard a shot go off near where I was lying. A Toposa man shot the soldier keeping guard and then he shot the boys sleeping in the ditch. Those boys actually saved my life. If I'd climbed in with them, I'd also be dead. I got up and started to run. The Toposa man fired at me. I was running, running, running. I was sure I was going to be killed, but I was faster than he was and I escaped."

"You were very, very lucky," the teacher told him.

"It was the hand of God."

"Yes," the boy said, "God's hand."

"There is more. Speak," the teacher said to him.

The cousin nodded. "I have something to tell you. Some news."

Majok pushed his foot back and forth across the dirt. He still held the stick in one of his hands. When the boy covered Majok's hand with his, Majok thought that the boy was trying to comfort him. "Stop, I don't want to hear it," Majok said.

"You must."

"No, not if it is bad."

"No, no, no, it is not what you think."

Majok closed his eyes and took a deep breath. He let go of the stick and ran.

"Majok," the teacher called, "Where are you going? Come back!"

Majok skirted a bundle of sticks blocking the path and they caught up with him. "It is not what you think," the cousin shouted.

"What isn't?"

"God is smiling on you."

Majok didn't believe a word of what the cousin said. Since when has God smiled on any of them?

"God has given you a miracle. Your brothers and your sister have been located and they are here."

"What are you telling me?"

"It's taken all this time."

"What?"

"Your brothers and sister are alive. They are here in this camp."

Chapter Twenty-Three

THE TEACHER'S WIFE was grinding grain, bearing down on the pestle that came to her chest with the strength of a woman giving birth. She'd given birth to five children, none of them living in the camp. If they'd survived, her daughters may have been taken as slaves to the same Arab village where her sons in the SPLA were tossing grenades.

"*Salaam,*" she said.

"*Kaif,*" Majok said.

"Too much work without a daughter's help." She pointed toward the door of the hut, "Hurry, boy, they're waiting for you."

Inside the faint light stood two boys. One—his half-brother Chiengkoudit—was only slightly taller than himself. The other, his younger brother Chiengkouthii, looked so different from the baby he remembered. A girl, much taller than all of them, practically full-grown, held her hands over her ears. She seemed very far away, even though he could walk over to her in just a few steps.

"Is it Majok Kuch Chol, *menhkei,* second-born son of my father?" the girl shouted.

Half-shadowed among the shaft of dust motes dancing in the windowless air, her Dinka name entered his brain: Anok. The teacher called her Rebekka. Among themselves, they didn't use their Christian names.

"Yes," he shouted back. She had a different mother than he did and other brothers and sisters, but they shared the same father. Majok watched her face, her large round eyes. They were the eyes of his father attempting to steady him. He rushed toward her and pulled her hands away from her ears. His body swayed as his sister and brothers surrounded him, their arms interweaving like the branches of mangroves. They clutched each other as if rooted in soil.

Majok called his brothers' names the same way he did when he used to look for them walking through the wilderness among hordes of boys, then stopped himself. When he had shouted their Dinka names he never found them. "Ezekial?" he appealed to his step-brother. Before the attack, their mothers had raised them like twins. He hissed to form the letters in his Christian name.

"Yes."

"Young? How did you get through the wilderness? You were just a baby."

"A man carried me."

Rebekka made loud noises. She was sobbing. "Our parents?" she asked.

His breath caught in his throat. It would be better not to admit that he had heard nothing. The last he heard about his mother's whereabouts was in Narus. When the beggar woman said, 'your mother was just here,' he didn't know if she spoke the truth. That town was scorched with smoke, wild with burning sedge. Only Young and he shared the same mother. He had heard no word about their father. Rebekka clutched Majok tightly.

"We'll find them," he said, filled with clarity. "God has given us proof. He is with us. The five of us are alive. If we live, then our father and mothers live."

Twenty-Four
Dry Season, October, 1996

MAJOK HOPPED across a sand patch on the earth floor of the hospital tent. Someone had thrown it there to cover up vomit. Must have been the bare-chested attendant dressed in camouflage shorts sitting on a stool. He waved his hand to stop Majok from continuing down the aisle. "This is not a playing field," he said.

"I'm looking for a friend. Spirit Free," Majok said.

"Don't you know where to look for him?"

"Where?"

"Up in the sky where his Daddy is. In the sky," the attendant said a second time, pointing. "That's where he is."

Majok pictured Spirit Free's body floating in the sky above him, his head resting on a bed of gray clouds. "No," he shouted and bolted, running all the way to the practice grounds. When he arrived there, he saw that a raised platform had been set up. He found Ayuen listening to an officer making an announcement over the mobile loudspeaker. Ayuen cleared a space for Majok to sit beside him on the earth. Majok listened to the officer telling the boys in the camp some startling news. Their leader John Garang met with American officials and signed papers that would allow for many of them to immigrate to America, but not all of them. America could not take all fifteen thousand of them, only four thousand.

"I need to be one of the four thousand," Majok said.

"What's wrong with you? Don't you see?" Ayuen said.

"See what?"

"This will turn boy against boy. John Garang would never make a deal like this. It's a trap."

Majok took hold of a handful of earth and watched the sprinkles fall through his fingers.

"You've seen the jeeps drive through the camp carrying the delegations," Ayuen said. "Have you ever been selected to meet any of them?"

"No."

"You haven't and neither have I."

"I need to find my parents."

"In America? What makes you think they went there?"

"I don't, but America will give me the resources to find them."

"How? It's too far away." Ayuen waved his hands.

"I'll have the use of a telephone."

"True, but your parents won't have one."

"Doesn't matter. Newspapers, computers. Red Cross, Save the Children, UNICEF, they're all based there."

Ayuen's voice shook. "You're wasting your time. This is the worst thing that could happen to us."

Majok looked up at the sky. "Spirit is gone. I don't want to die here."

"No, he's recovering."

"He's gone. I spoke to an attendant at the hospital tent."

Ayuen kicked the dirt with his toes, releasing a cloud of red dust. "If he died, it was because of his stupidity."

"I thought you were his friend. When did you become so cold? How can you blame Spirit? I see what is happening. Yes, if I continue here, I will become the same as you."

"You're a fool if you sacrifice everything you've been working for."

"And what exactly would I be sacrificing?"

"You'll be entering high school. You're one of the top students in the class. You'll get a high score on the KCPE exams and you'll get a scholarship to a boarding school in Nairobi. You'll go to school. To the city. You'll leave the camp!"

"Kenya will never be home. We don't belong here."

"And you think it's America we belong?"

"For the time being."

"Not America. Sudan. We belong in Sudan." Ayuen always said the most obvious things to make people feel like he was the smarter one.

"Yes, when the war's over, and I'll be the first to go back, but it doesn't seem close to ending. We're outsiders in Kenya. You know how they treat us here. Do you want to spend your whole life applying for a Movement Pass each time you want to leave the camp? This isn't living. It's like living in a jail!"

Ayuen sucked in air and released it slowly. "Not if I become a doctor."

"That's a long road."

"Then I'll become an orderly," Ayuen shrugged. "I'll help sick people. It's the least I can do."

"Don't be this way, Ayuen."

"I have to. It's too risky."

"When was the last time you went to Kakuma Town and felt safe?"

"That's not what I mean."

"What do you mean?"

"Khartoum could be behind this. They tell you that you're going to America and really you're getting captured by the enemy."

"What?"

"You mean it's never crossed your mind?"

"Honestly? No."

"Then you're just plain stupid."

"You said so yourself, we never know what's going on, how can you know?"

Chapter Twenty-Five

NO BOY WHO ADMITTED having nightmares would get chosen for America, no boy who harbored revenge or learned to shoot a gun or detonate a bomb. Majok sat on the ground and listened to the camp leaders explain who would get chosen. Every boy who was sitting with him had done or learned some of these things. The worse lie Majok reconciled himself to repeating over and over was that his parents were not alive. Only those without parents would get chosen. He told this lie, but in his heart he knew the truth, that his parents had survived, and he would find them once he got to America—this he promised himself.

After waiting a month, his first interview got postponed two more times. The second round of interviews took several more months and involved verifying his ration card number against his name. Many Dinka people have the same name. There were so many Dinka boys, for example, named Majok, that even if his mother sat outside the gate to the unaccompanied minors zone and called for him, too many boys would answer.

If Spirit survived, he'd be one of the people who did not qualify for this round. Anyone who had lost his ration card had no way of knowing the number that was given to him upon entering Kenya at Lokichoggio. Spirit would be very sad. He'd ask Majok if he remembered the numbers on his card. They'd sit together and try to think of them.

The sky dawned. Someone was striking a hammer onto a piece of metal near Majok's hut. The prayer call sounded from the road for the Somali Muslims to gather at the mosque. Music came out of a boom box. Chanting. But the hammering was louder.

Majok's tossing and turning continued in his mind. All night he had been awake fretting over the fact that US Immigration Services scheduled his interview at the same time as the end-of-year Kenyan Certificate of Primary Education Exams. He'd been preparing for these exams since his first year of school, and there was no make-up test. The problem presented itself in the worse possible way. Once again, he was reminded of himself as a small child fleeing Sudan, choosing which group of people to follow to safety. If he missed his immigration interview, he'd miss his only chance of going to America. His siblings too. They would all be disqualified.

On the floor by the door trying to catch the light, Ayuen was sneaking looks at Majok's Top Mark Math Book. Holding a pencil to a piece of brown parcel bag, Ayuen scribbled down answers.

"You can have it. Take it!" Majok told him.

Ayuen stared at him, uncomprehending.

Majok walked to him on his knees. "Take it. It's yours. I can't take the exams. My UNHCR interview is scheduled for today."

"Are you dumb?"

The other boys in the hut heard them and sat up.

"Diktor, Gabriel! Talk to Majok. Say something!"

Ayuen grabbed Majok by the shoulders. "Don't you see? It's a trap. Don't go! Don't go!"

"Shut up!" Gabriel shouted and turned over. "Go back to sleep."

Ayuen wagged his finger at Majok. "You don't know what you're doing!" Ayuen was top in the class. The exams were the final hurdle. Ayuen had driven Majok to study, conditioned him to crave feeding his brain over his stomach, yet books and school did not prepare Majok for touching his sister's arm and hearing her sob. With that touch, he became the head of a family.

Ayuen picked up his jerry can. Majok grabbed his can and followed Ayuen outside. All along the road to the water tap, Ayuen told Majok how stupid he was and what a big mistake he was making. "It's a trick," Ayuen said, "Can't you see that?"

Majok felt queasy like he was being thrown from side to side in the back of a lorry, his body slamming into metal, the feeling fresh because he rode in one a few days ago—a UN lorry leaving Kakuma Town for the camp. To his disbelief, the driver asked him if he needed a ride. The driver's name was Sampson. Sampson said he was one of the drivers who rescued boys in the desert ten years ago when they walked from Ethiopia back into Sudan.

"You should have seen yourselves," Sampson said. "Walking skeletons. It's amazing any of you survived."

He looked at Sampson, wondering if he owed him his life. He owed a lot of people. How was he supposed to know who they were? When Ayuen and Majok reached the tap, two women were filling their cans. One of them had set out two more cans in addition to the one that she had just filled.

"Mother of a whore, what do you think you're doing?" the first woman said. "Stop! You can't do that!"

"These cans belong to my sisters," the woman filling the cans told her.

The first woman blocked the second, stopping her from approaching the tap to fill her extra cans.

The second woman lifted the filled can onto her head with quiet dignity and walked away holding one unfilled can in each of her hands.

"And you broke the nozzle!" the first woman shouted after her. "Look," she said to the queue of people, "there isn't enough pressure. It's just a trickle."

Water ran from one of eleven boreholes in the camp and if someone broke off a nozzle, the pressure changed, causing an immediate shortage of water.

In the long queue of people ahead of Ayuen and Majok, mothers stood nursing their infants. When the mothers got to the front, they splashed their children with water to wash them free of the dust that stuck to everyone's skin in the camp. By the time Ayuen got to the tap, there was no water left to trickle out. He turned to Majok and cursed.

"Why are you acting like it's my fault?" Majok shouted, disapproving. "I'm not the selfish person who broke the nozzle. Go find that woman and beat her up."

But Majok was the one who would suffer. He couldn't set out for Kakuma Town without water. Ayuen kept a small can of backup water covered with muslin in their hut. "Give me your backup water," Majok said.

"That's emergency water."

"In exchange for my Top Mark."

"No," Ayuen said.

"Take it, Ayuen. Else I have nothing to give you."

"I don't need a thing from you."

"You'll give me your water regardless?"

"No, Majok. Some things just take time. Hope everybody going to enjoy the walk."

Chapter Twenty-Six

"PRESS HARD," the Kenyan UN staff person said through a Dinka translator. "Whatever you write has to go through to the carbon copy." The queue of mostly boys was two-hours deep, all waiting to reach into a little cardboard box for a pencil stub to fill out UNHCR Immigration forms at the center in Kakuma Town.

The UN staff person working the tape recorder, asked Majok to speak slowly. He hoped that when Rebekka, Young, Ezekial and James got called they would remember the answers to the questions they rehearsed with the aid workers at the camp. The slightest slip-up and they would be denied asylum. With so many thousands of boys seeking to immigrate, America could be choosy.

The questions, however, were easier to answer than those he practiced. 'Yes' or 'No' was a sufficient answer, no need to elaborate. He could honestly check the 'No' box next to the questions, 'have you ever been a member of the military? and 'do you know your parents' whereabouts?'

When he handed in his completed form, an immigration officer gave him another piece of paper. It was a medical form with questions he didn't know how to answer. The skin on his arms broke out into pimply shivers. His body swayed. If he wasn't careful he would hit the ground. Ayuen was right. It was a trick. He would never get to America. These were the depths the government in Khartoum took to rid the country of its Africans. He'd misjudged this process.

He was afraid to look at his brothers and especially at Rebekka, who was stuck at least twenty people behind him waiting to receive the medical form. In a matter of time, she would receive one and from what he could tell of the way she reacted to obstacles, she would not be able to keep still. She would chatter with person after person and try to create a crisis. Those in the queue would start shouting and shoving. The officers would not be able to control the crowd and all of them would get disqualified. They would, each of them, Majok thought, die in the camp like Spirit. One from hunger, one from illness, one from despair. He could not let that happen.

He read and reread the questions: 'Please indicate true or false in the spaces on the right: "'Have you ever been treated for any of the following diseases: TB, Polio, Malaria, HIV Aids, Hepatitis, Yellow Fever, Round Worm, Diabetes, Asthma, Heart Murmur, Eczema, Dysentery, Diphtheria, Pneumonia, Stomach Ulcers, Gastritis, Crohn's Disease, Blood Clot Problems, Sleeping Problems, Headaches, Migraines, Depression, Hallucinations, Fainting, Bed Wetting?"'

He balled his fingers into fists, trying to feel the power in his hands. The unsmiling immigration officer showed in his face which boys would be denied asylum. Trifles as small as a runny nose could mean a life-threatening illness.

Rebekka was almost at the front of the queue. Majok watched as a staff person handed her a medical form. She glanced down at the page and raised her head, looking for him with an anguished look on her face. He heard her voice rising in his own throat, the blood in her body rushing into his own head. Her entire future depended on him. How could he fail her?

"Oh no!" Young whispered, as if to further destroy his dreams. "You four go without me."

"What?"

"Yes, I'll never be admitted. I've had all these diseases."

They were five malnourished, bed-wetting, malarial brothers, a cousin, and a sister. But every time Majok looked at them, he knew he must use his powers to give them strength. "I will never allow myself to be separated from you again," he said to Young.

"I don't want to hold you back."

"I mean it, Young. There's another way to look at this. The question isn't which of these illnesses we had, it's which of these we haven't. Check them all, all of them except HIV

AIDS. Maybe they want to discover how we managed to stay alive."

"Stupid! A stupid, foolish plan," Ezekial said, whirling around, fists tightened into hammers.

"What's yours? Do you have one?" Majok asked.

"Give me time to think," Ezekial snapped.

"Time? It's run out. Just two boys ahead of us."

Rebekka arrived panting, pushing through shoulders and backs. "It's a trick. Hopeless!"

Young embraced her.

"Tell him what a fool plan is this," Ezekial said to Rebekka referring to Majok's idea of checking all the boxes on the form.

"Majok is right. God's with us in the truth," Rebekka said.

Ezekial turned away from them, each step away breaking Majok's heart a little more.

"Come on," Majok said to Ezekial. "We're together in this, whether we go or stay. We can give up right now. Whatever you want to do, I'm with you." He often recalled a story Ezekial had told him about fleeing Sudan. Ezekial had seen a group of boys he walked to Kenya among get shot in front of him. The shooters were shouting like crazy: 'Who wants to go next? Which one of you?' Only Ezekial had escaped. One day, after Ezekial had reunited with him, Ezekial stared at a piece of firewood and said, "Ghosts. All I see are ghosts," referring to that incident.

"What's the matter with you?" Rebekka said. "This is it! The only chance."

The immigration officer said something in English and the Dinka translator waved his hand in front of them. "Who is head of this family?"

Ezekial leaned forward. Raised as twins, the years apart had made them into two completely different people.

"I am," Majok said as he stole a look at Ezekial and witnessed his brother's face fall.

"You will take responsibility for this family? If you do, you must never miss an interview or else you and your entire family will be denied asylum. Do you understand? Will you be willing to do that?"

"Yes," Majok said, not daring to look in Ezekial's direction.

On the way back to the camp, Majok continued to avoid Ezekial. Mid-afternoon and the streets were empty. Most people didn't walk around in the heat. White-robed Somali men and women stood in the shade of their shops, leaning over their counters for support. They passed streets lined with tin-roofed shops filled with mangoes, bananas, okra, sweet onions, cassava, kale, fresh brown eggs, huge slabs of meat and cold Miranda soft drinks. They passed shoeshine boys, firewood for sale, blacksmiths and finally shacks that sold torches and radios and batteries. Just once, Majok thought, he would like to stop at a counter and lean over it and present a shilling coin and ask for an orange-flavored Miranda soft drink. He vowed to himself that day and in the following days that a Miranda soft drink would be one of the first drinks he'd taste once he got to America, not knowing that Miranda drinks were generally unavailable in the US.

A beggar woman pushed herself between him and Rebekka. "Grain?" the woman said, her mouth and nose covered with a black veil. Her purple, swollen feet, which blistered with sores, were bare.

Rebekka opened up a small cloth sack tied around her waist. She handed the woman a flap of flatbread.

"That's not enough," the woman said, "Give me more."

"That's everything I have," Rebekka said and turned the cloth inside out for the woman to see. "Please, take it."

They were approaching a small restaurant with a barbecue grill outside it. Smoke rose from a heap of fiery coals. "We told you we don't have anything! Go ask in there," Ezekial said, lashing out, venting his anger toward Majok at the woman.

Majok held onto his sister's hand. He needed to show her that he could be strong. In America, too. He wanted her to be certain that she could depend on him. She would want to go to school, learn English, find a husband and have babies. In the camp, her life was on hold.

"When the war is over," their leaders told her, "when you return to Jalle Payam, when you are reunited with your clan, then you can study to become a teacher."

Rebekka had gnashed her fists at them. "What if I don't want to become a teacher? What if I want to study medicine and become a doctor?"

Everyone wanted to study medicine, even the girls.

Chapter Twenty-Seven
Dry Season, October, 2000

Boys were getting picked. An aid worker would walk out of a tent carrying a single sheet of brown parcel paper and a mob surrounded him, trying to grab the paper out of his hands. Every month or so, a different list got posted. Once an aid worker managed to tack it up onto the back of a tent, other workers blocked the list to keep boys from tearing it down. In an attempt to scatter the crowd, one of them now scanned the list and asked if anyone wanted him to check it for their name.

"*Hehehehehehe Ca miol?* You think we can't read our own names?" a boy in front of Majok yelled. He was called Panther. Panther did chores for people in Kakuma Town. He swept the street in front of a shop or walked around collecting twine, plastic bottles and scraps of paper to barter trade.

"Do you see my name?" Majok yelled from the center of the crowd. No, his name did not appear on the list. The extra burden of disappointing his siblings, especially Ezekial, kept him from going to their huts and hearing them ask, "When, when?" Most days he'd sneak out of the unaccompanied minors zone and play dominoes with old timers who'd have been birthing their herds if they still lived in the village. Instead, they sat on the ground under one of the rare acacia trees growing out of the soil, slapping down tiles and chewing khat, their cheeks bumpy on the side where they bunched the weed. From standing among the group watching the game to being asked to shuffle tiles, he got to understand the game well enough to play.

It wasn't their fault, Majok thought, that the domino players were too old to go to school or join the army. What else could they be doing to pass the time? They didn't talk to him about anything except dominoes. He never ran into any of them with his friends in the unaccompanied minors zones, but when he returned to his tent for the evening meal, Ayuen sniffed and smelled the smoke on his skin and hair, and said "You haven't given up, have you? Please tell me, Majok, that you have not given up. You can go back to school. You can repeat the year again." Ayuen had no idea how dignified people tolerated despair.

"HEY YOU!" Panther shouted at Majok. "*Wen de Kuch*, your father's name is Kuch, right?"

"Yes," Majok said.

"Well, you're going to be showering with mineral water," Panther said and cleared a space through the crowd for Majok to stand in front of the list.

Majok pushed his way through and read the names on the list. He scanned the forty or so names. Half-way down he stopped.

His name! His name! Right in the center, and beneath it, typewritten in bold, the names of his sister, brothers and cousin.

He rushed off to tell them. He knew he'd find them in school. He ran into their different classrooms and called them outside. The five of them held hands and jumped up and down. Their friends watched from inside, but some of them ran out to congratulate Majok and his siblings, hugging them and weeping with smiles on their faces. Ayuen didn't want to hear the news. When Majok found him leaving the classroom with the Top Mark he had given him clutched under his arm, Ayuen didn't say a word to him. Aside from Ayuen's disciplined mind, which helped him excel in school, his stubbornness kept him as hotheaded as the desert heat.

The boys who were selected for immigration ran around saying goodbye to people they wouldn't see again, giving away all their hoarded up possessions—tin cups, jerry cans, bits of brown paper, twine, muslin, animal skins, plastic bottles, slingshots, stones, soap, even food ration cards—that they wouldn't need any more. If Spirit were still alive, Majok would bestow upon him his rations card in case Spirit ever lost his again. Majok was leaving, but Spirit's body would always remain at Kakuma. He wept, furious with himself for the two times that he'd failed Spirit.

Later, Diktor, Ayuen and Gabriel stood in front of the fire outside their hut where a pot of stew boiled over a fire. Of the four of them, Majok was the only one who volunteered for asylum. Diktor's father had escaped to Egypt, but his application to get out of the camp and join his father there was not accepted by the Egyptian government. If he wanted to see his father in Egypt, he would have to escape illegally. That night it was Diktor's turn to cook. Watching him stir the stew, Majok laughed.

"What are you laughing about, Majok?" Diktor said.

"I'm laughing at the way you cook like a woman."

"That's not something to laugh about. Don't laugh about me when you get to America."

"I will. I'll laugh about you stirring beans in a pot."

"Yeah, it's funny," he said. He fell quiet, then lifted his head. "You think you'll be laughing about me stirring beans in this pot? I don't think so. When you get to America, you're going to be so happy you're not here, you're going to be praying to God. You're going to be thanking him for every bite of meat he gives you. Look at this food. Take a good look at what we eat here and don't laugh about me when you get to America, Majok."

Each of the boys who were selected for asylum in America received a tote bag the day they left the camp. In it was a special tape that their leaders made filled with Dinka songs and sayings so that they wouldn't forget their traditions. Majok hadn't listened to it yet, but he looked forward to hearing his elders' voices in America, a place he was anxious to go to, yet he couldn't help worrying whether he'd made the right decision.

The plane, a small Cessna with a red cross painted on its tail, was carrying them to Nairobi. There they were going to receive a brief cultural orientation. After a few days, they would transfer to a KLM jet to Amsterdam, where they would again change planes to arrive, first in New York and then in Philadelphia.

The sting of wood smoke made Majok's eyes water. Wind hit his face, bringing with it the smell of roasting groundnuts—the smell of the earth in Kakuma. He breathed in deeply to fill his lungs, not knowing whether he would ever smell that earth again. He looked across the field and saw two dik-dik bending their long necks over the grass.

"Look," he tapped Ezekial on the shoulder. "Do you see it, dik-dik?"

He wanted to tell Ezekial that the possibility of tasting this animal got him to cooperate with the child soldier who led him out of Sudan, but he did not want to disturb Ezekial's own memories. If he had to catch a glimpse of one last animal before leaving Africa, he was glad it was this one—compact like a toy deer, as if all of it, everything that had happened to him was only his imagination run wild.

They mounted the steps of the moving staircase with a group of other boys who were also traveling to New York or Philadelphia and boarded the Cessna. Ezekial and James took seats in the last row. Young took the seat next to him, and in the row ahead of them, Rebekka, who was taller than they were and needed more leg room, stepped through the aisle to sit in the co-pilot's seat. The pilot handed her a pair of sunglasses identical to his to endow her eyes with a nighthawk's vision.

A rumbling noise vibrated inside the plane. Majok covered his ears. Trapped by the seat in front of him, his legs were shaking. The plane taxied along the gravel, then ascended into empty space. Ezekial recognized one of the boys who boarded with them. "That's Acheng Deng," he pointed. Acheng Deng was the extraordinary boy who had built up the bicycle rental service. Now he was vomiting into his gray United States Refugee Program T-shirt. Majok carried his USRP T-shirt balled up in his fists—something for him to latch onto. Young clenched his arm. Majok didn't say anything to Young. He didn't need to. The outline of Majok's face was reflected in the window, not his features but Young's over his.

Once more, Majok sensed the feeling that if anything bad happened, he'd be responsible. Yet, he convinced himself that his decision was the right one. He would never find his parents if he remained in Kakuma. Leaving the camp was the only way he would ever get any information about them.

Sunlight burned through the windows. The earth tilted. His body began to relax as if being borne aloft had turned him into a bird and he had suddenly grown feathers and wings like a character in a tale.

"America is a magical place," he said to Young. It can make anything happen." His heart pounded, beating with anticipation for his mother. He pictured her cooling a cup of porridge for him, blowing on it with her mouth open, as if to offer the porridge she had cooked for him so long ago. This time he would not refuse it.

In Nairobi, their group stayed for a few days and received cultural orientation. Kenyan aid workers who had lived in the US, taught the group of asylum seekers a little about the history of Philadelphia and showed them a calendar to learn the seasons. On the last day of their orientation, one of the group's orientation leaders baked a big cake with white frosting on it in their honor. He said that this was a birthday cake. Dinka do not celebrate birthdays or mark the day that a child is born. "This will present some difficulties in America," the orientation leader told them. "Many forms you will need to fill out will require the date of your birth. I recommend that you choose January first as your birthday. That way you will remember it and you will celebrate it on the first day of each year that you live in your adopted country. It will become your rebirth."

Majok did not wish to be reborn. He didn't want to forget where he had lived with his mother and father. He yearned to find them and one day be reunited with them. He understood that he would need a birthday if he was going to live in a place where birthdays were important. He believed he was anywhere from fourteen to sixteen years old, but he wasn't exactly sure. He had been slow to grow and was smaller than most Dinka boys close to his age, such as his brother Ezekial. Yet because of his ability to understand things better than other boys and learn to read and write so quickly, he suspected that he might be older.

January first, the day that he chose as his birthday, was still two months away. It felt funny to wait to celebrate his birth, and in a way anticipating it, did feel like he was in the process of being born again.

At airport security, the guards in charge ordered Majok and his siblings to drop their tote bags onto the moveable counter. After the guards patted them down and they walked through the security line, they stood at the counter, waiting for their tote bags to be handed back to them. "What tote bags?" the two security guards manning the counter said.

Majok couldn't understand why the guards denied the existence of their tote bags. The tapes inside them were worthless to anyone outside of their tribe. Why would anyone want them? Yet without their tapes, how would they remind themselves of who they were?

The next plane Majok and his siblings boarded took them to the airport in Amsterdam, where they walked, amazed by all the white people—tall and blonde in sheepskins and leathers. Indoor vehicles, lights and restaurants marked the beginning of their new life and identities as they waited in the Immigration queue to present their I-94 cards.

"Where the hell are we in the world?" Young said, enthralled by the strangeness all around him.

"Amsterdam," announced a voice over a loudspeaker.

Once they boarded the plane and found their seats in row G, an airline host asked Majok if he knew how high the plane was going to fly.

He shook his head.

"Twenty-two thousand meters!" the host said. "Pick up the shade and look out the window. You can watch the takeoff."

He gripped his USRP sweatshirt in case he vomited. He was anxious to get back up into the air. From the earth he had never been able to see up through the clouds to the sky, but from the sky, he could see down through them to the earth. All those times in his life that he wished he could fly, being pursued, running through burning fields. He felt so sorry for the people and the birds that had never experienced this—the ostriches that ran directly into the line of gunfire, because they were afraid of rain.

Part Two

Chapter Twenty-Eight
November 2000, Philadelphia

MAJOK TAPPED REBEKKA'S ARM and pointed out the window. It was after midnight and the city beneath them was lit up like day. It looked like the city was on fire. From so high in the air, he couldn't tell what was happening below, whether tanks and soldiers filled the streets, whether people were fleeing. Ayuen's words came rushing into his brain, 'It's a trick Majok, you're not going to America, you're being brought to the enemy.'

The plane tilted to one side like a camel shifting its weight. It veered along a river. Three different bridges crossed its span. From this height they looked like toys. A baby wailed. Young was still asleep.

Majok clenched his sister's hand. "Phila-del-phee-ahhh," she turned to him and said in a dreamlike voice.

Sitting across from them, James and Ezekial held their heads in their laps, their arms hugging their knees. Majok's ears filled up with pressure. The baby wailed and woke Young.

When the pilot's voice barked through the loudspeaker, Majok's ears were so stuffed up he couldn't make out the words. He copied the other passengers around him, who appeared calm, unbuckling their seat belts, and followed them into the aisle. A young mother sat with the baby that had been wailing close to her chest and talked to the child softly while she waited for everyone else to exit. Meeting her eyes, Majok saw that this was new for her, that she needed more time to adjust.

This time, he didn't exit down a movable staircase and onto tarmac or step down onto the middle of an airfield and fill his lungs with first scents. He and his siblings walked through an enclosed metal ramp into the terminal with no separation between the inside of the plane and the airport, so he still felt like he was flying.

They floated past stands that sold T-shirts, replicas of the Liberty Bell, Phillies shirts, 76ers Allen Iverson basketball jerseys, autographed pictures and balls—corridor after corridor onto a moving staircase so steep they pulled one another on, under a banner that read, 'Mayor John F. Street Welcomes You to Philadelphia, City of Brotherly Love,' which sent a light tickling feeling through their bodies, amazed that the word 'Philadelphia' carried such meaning and that they had been sent to such a place. They reached Baggage Claim, though they didn't have any bags to claim. Their sad USRP T-shirts were wrinkled and worn. The cassette tapes that their elders made for them instructing them not to forget the tribe had been stashed in their tote bags, which the airport guards in Nairobi stole from them when they went through security.

At the bottom of the moving stairs, people stood squeezed together holding up signs. Majok and his siblings walked from one sign to the next, looking for their name, the English lettering barely decipherable. The eyes of the people hurried past their faces, which were blacker and stranger than the relatives they expected. Someone waved, but not at them. Over the din, Majok thought he heard a woman's voice call 'Kuch!'

The five of them floated toward a face belonging to a smiling white woman. She looked like a white version of the mother in *Hallo Children*, the English primer Majok learned to read in Kakuma—her black hair peppered with gray, the skin on her face creasing into folds around her mouth and beneath her eyes, her dark blue slacks and wool coat, her black leather purse slung over one shoulder. Beside the woman, a man dressed in a tweed jacket and khakis smoked a pipe like the father in the book, with white skin and hair and a look-alike teenaged son. Majok could never read *Hallo Children* for long without having to stop and catch his breath each time he opened a page. He'd have to close the book, unable to bear the contrast between the family depicted in those pages and his own existence. The woman, man and their son jumped up and down, waving their hands, shaking a large cardboard sign that read, 'Welcome Kuch Family!'

The woman wrapped her arms around Rebekka. She pressed Majok in close to kiss him Dinka style, one kiss on each cheek, showing him that she knew their customs, the skin on her cheeks damp with tears. She must have been crying because she knew how anxious he was to find his parents, Majok thought.

"Shhhh…It's okay," she said. She kissed his two brothers and his cousin. "I'm Grace," and she stepped aside to make room for her husband and son.

Her husband embraced Majok. "Viktor," he said.

"Mike," Majok said. He decided to use his Christian name.

"Tom," their son said, shaking his hand. The same height as Mike, he had the lean build of a soccer player. Mike wondered if he played.

"Welcome to Philadelphia!" Viktor said. "We know what this must be like for you. We've lived in Sudan."

Mike straightened his back and smiled. "You did?"

"Yes. 1982 to '88. Everything's going to be okay now," Viktor said.

Mike didn't dare to disagree with him. Viktor's voice sounded like thunderclaps. Later, Mike found out that Viktor was a pastor in the Lutheran Church.

The conversation turned to luggage and Young told Viktor and Grace about their stolen tote bags. Viktor touched Young's shoulder and clutched his arm. Grace and Tom led Rebekka, James and Ezekial. "Come on," Viktor said. "You've been traveling how many hours? You must be exhausted. Let's get out of here." He looked at their T-shirts and *mut u keliu* rubber-tire sandals. "A bit of a warning. It's going to be a little cold outside," and he steered them through the crowds.

To let strangers lead him out of an airport and across a paved road to a parking lot was to lose his ability for his two feet to carry him back to the village of his birth. He stood on a stool and shivered. Viktor grabbed him by the wrist to help him step into his silver Lutheran Services van, the words written in black letters across the side door.

Inside the van, Mike felt so cold, he hunched in his seat, the faint smell of petrol leaking into his lungs, and peered out the windows at the lit-up night. First, they drove down through a tunnel and then up over a bridge, all the roadways connecting in wide lanes so that any direction looked possible, listening to the screeching rush of cars. They passed fields filled with mountains of metal—car parts, water taps, crushed up beams.

"Don't judge the city by these junkyards," Grace said. "The rest of the city is beautiful."

Junk? Mike imagined how people in Kakuma would react, observing this abundance.

They drove past big houses and signs until Viktor exited the highway and stopped the van in front of an enormous house, a house even bigger than the President's mansion in Nairobi, which their Cultural Orientation Leaders pointed out to them on their way out of Kenya. Americans lived in such big houses. Mike sat in the back of the car, too amazed to leave.

"This is the rectory," Viktor said. "You'll just be living here a few days until your apartment is ready." They were not the only group of unaccompanied minors coming from Kakuma who would be given their own apartment to live in. Lutheran Family Services supplied apartments to groups who came as siblings as long as at least one of them was over twenty-one. Rebekka was the oldest and she was the reason that they were able to qualify.

Rebekka grabbed Mike's arm. "It's the rectory," she said to him. "Did you think it was a house?"

"Yes, did you?" he said, trying to read her expression.

"Yes, or a king's palace. I am ready, Majok, ready to live like a princess."

Rebekka stepped out. She was so tall she had to duck her head from hitting the roof of the van. Mike followed behind her, only bending his head slightly. They stood together on the pavement laughing excitedly and whispering to each other while Viktor jiggled a key in the lock, trying to open the enormous wooden door decorated with iron bolts spaced evenly apart. Finally, Viktor clutched the release on the handle and pushed the door with his free hand and it creaked open, exposing the dark hall.

Viktor walked in first and as he did, the room filled with light. He motioned for them to follow him in. Mike's eyes roamed up to the light boxes hanging from the vaulted ceiling. No one had prepared him for the shock of seeing this, not their Cultural Orientation Leaders in Nairobi and certainly not the elders at the camp. All their lives they had lived without electricity and had feared the night. Shivering, he rubbed his hands up and down his arms. It felt colder inside the building than outside. How was he going to bear it?

"I'm so sorry," Grace said, her voice slow and soft. "The heat's too low. You know Christians. All that stoicism. We can't help it. Let me look for the thermostat and I'll raise it a few degrees."

Mike, along with his brothers, sister, and cousin stared back at her blankly. Rebekka stayed near Mike's side as they walked up the staircase to the dormitory. It was a giant room of sloped walls and windows lined with metal beds with mattresses and blankets and pillows—the first they'd ever slept on.

"We'll be back in the morning to show you how to use the kitchen and the shower." Grace said. "It's late now. Try and get some sleep."

Rebekka stared at the doorway after Viktor and Grace left and said," Angels. They're angels."

"Ha," Young said, "Heaven's cold."

"It is," Ezekial said.

"I'm going to get into one of those beds and I'm not going to leave it," Mike told them.

That night he slept for what felt like days wrapped in sheets and blankets like a pupa in a cocoon. In the morning, he untangled the sheets from around his legs, got out of bed and looked out the window. Rebekka was already up. She came and stood beside him, her arms spread wide. The two of them stared out. Mike tapped the glass.

So there it was, some hours after sunrise, the sky still filled with color: gold and orange and red. Autumn. The season didn't exist in Northern Kenya.

Mike ran into the hall and looked out more windows. He stood at the top of a staircase so high, his steps trailed the tops of trees. Grabbing the handrail, he skipped down the steps and rushed to the door and outside.

Cold air bit his face and arms. A dog barked, making a far-off hollow sound. When Viktor and Grace arrived, he asked them about the cold. "Is it permanent?" he said, thinking of Kenya's hot weather that never changed.

"This is nothing," they said. "This is only November. Wait until December, January and February."

Grace shepherded them into the kitchen. She gathered them around her to introduce them to the gadgets in the drawers. Can opener! Silverware! Scissors! Only spoons made their way to South Sudan. Otherwise, they ate with their fingers or pieces of bread to scoop up meat.

She placed the can opener in James's hands and helped him practice turning the gear wheel with one hand and piercing a metal lid with the other. Grace equipped Ezekial and Young with potato peelers. Soon, potato skins speckled their fingers. Rebekka, who wanted to explore everything, pulled open the refrigerator door's upper compartment. She hadn't seen ice before. Blasts of cold air leaked out. She ran her hand along the stark white surface inside it.

"Ouch," she said, pulling back her hand. "It's eating my skin."

"That part is the freezer," Viktor said. "This is where you keep things frozen." He squeezed a cube of ice into each of their hands. "Here, try one of these."

Young juggled his ice-cube from hand to hand. He asked what its uses were.

"If you want a cold drink, you can put some ice in it," Viktor said.

Ezekial hissed. He'd worked in an NGO office in the camp, one of the few people who used a computer and looked up information.

"You want to know what it is? It's for food to not spoil and rot. For to cool down a burn on someone's skin when a bomb explodes. To take down swelling if you bleed or broke a bone. Or you know how a dying person says 'water!' and can't take the sip?"

Mike pictured old men and women, infants and young children by the sides of roads and slumped under trees.

"If you have ice, you give it to them and they suck it."

Scraping the sharp edge of a cube of ice against his skin, he inscribed the word WHERE on his forearm. Where were his parents? He had seen boys back at Kakuma scratch this word on their skin with the sharp end of a stick. The letters turned liquid, dripped down his arm.

Grace watched him. She said with an excited look on her face, "Come over here, Mike. There's something I want to show you."

Mike liked to think Grace singled him out because she knew that he wasn't made for the kitchen. His brothers and sister followed him with their eyes as Grace led him into the hall.

"There," she said, and pointed to a black telephone sitting on a desk.

He clapped his hands, the sound of his exaltation coming back to him. Finding his parents was going to be easier than he expected.

"Isn't it incredible!" Grace placed the receiver in his hands. "If Sudan had an infrastructure, you'd have found your parents a long time ago."

"I am quite sure that I will find them now," he told her. He stretched the phone cord to his shoulders and the receiver beeped. He dropped it onto the desk.

Grace laughed. "It's okay. It won't hurt you."

He hovered over the numbers and letters printed on the dial. It was eight hours later in Kenya—too late to call. People at Kakuma didn't leave their huts after dark. It was too dangerous. No one would be available to receive a call at that hour. He lived on the opposite side of the world now. He'd need to stay up all night and wait for daybreak.

"Mike," Grace said, "what's wrong? Don't you want to make a call?"

"Yes."

"Who do you want to call, Mike?"

"Kenya."

"Kenya? No, Mike, you can't use this phone to make international calls."

He lifted the cord from where it had twisted around his neck like a serpent seeking to extract his blood, put the receiver back in its cradle and gripped the desk to ground himself.

"I'm sorry, Mike, sorry I led you on. I was excited to show you the phone and didn't realize that you'd want to call Kenya right away. This phone belongs to the rectory and we can't ring up a bill."

"If I can't call Kenya, then what is the use for it?"

"Local calls. If you call anywhere else, it costs a lot of money." She snapped open her purse and fumbled around in it, finding a pen and tablet to scribble down some numbers. "Here's our number," she said. She tapped her finger against the page she'd written on and tore it off and handed it to him. "You can call Viktor and me whenever you want to talk with us. Alright?"

He stared down at the number. So many years had passed, any further delay might result in not being able to locate his parents. He couldn't stop thinking that something bad would happen to them. To think that they had been alive all this time and that some massacre or illness would suddenly overcome them, made him insane with worry.

"I need to call Kenya in the morning," he said.

Viktor was rounding everyone up for a trip to the mall to buy some warm clothing. Viktor found Grace and Mike in the hallway and shouted, "Are you ready? What's going on?" Viktor saw the grave look on Mike's face and the telephone on the desk between them, its shadow enlarged on the wall.

"I'm trying to explain to Mike that he can't use the rectory phone to make international calls," Grace said.

"Even when you get your own apartment, you should never make international calls without using a prepaid calling card. Otherwise, you won't have enough money to pay your phone bill and your phone will get disconnected. You'll have to wait until you get your monthly check, and then you can go to the store and buy calling cards. They sell them everywhere, drugstores, supermarkets. Right, Viktor?"

"Listen to Grace and you won't go wrong," Viktor said making them both smile, though for different reasons. Grace smiled to show Mike that Viktor agreed with her. Mike smiled because he was familiar with how people talked when other people were nearby. Viktor couldn't really tell Mike what he wanted to in front of Grace, so he spoke in a joking way in hopes that Mike would figure it out. Viktor clanked his keys together and motioned for Grace and Mike to follow him out the door.

"Come on," Grace said.

Mike lagged behind. As he made his way to the others in the van, he said a prayer for his parents' safety.

Viktor showed Rebekka how to move her seat back so that she could have more leg room. She sat in the front next to Viktor, leaning forward in her seat and tapping the glass with her fingertips to point at houses and cars and trees. Young squished his face right up against the window. Ezekial and James turned from side to side not wanting to miss anything. Mike glimpsed out the window to follow with his eyes the miles of telephone wires, the poles that linked them and the birds that roosted on them

"America has the resources to help us find our parents. Wherever our parents are hiding, America will help us find them," he had promised his brother Young back at the camp. He had been dancing in a crowd and he stopped to lead him in a jumping match, bending his knees down low. Better not to worry, Better to renew his vow to him that he would fulfill his promise.

Viktor parked the van near flowers planted in pots and trees and bushes planted on the pavement, colored so deep a red that they looked like burning bushes close to God. Leaves scattered, got swirled in the wind, twirled in little dances round and round.

Viktor stepped on the center of a black mat in front of the door to Walmart, a shop that looked large enough to be a very large school. Without even touching the door, it sprung open.

"Go on, you try it, Viktor said. Mike stood in the center of the mat. Like magic, the door opened on its own.

The shops in Kakuma Town were only big enough for two people standing sideways. Here, four people walked side by side. Viktor led them to the racks of ready-made clothing, which smelled warm and clean and fresh. The scent of sweat and rust had seeped into the fibers of the smallest piece of cloth worn at Kakuma, but these fabrics tantalized him with their clean smell. They walked among the clothing—trousers, jeans, jackets, sweatshirts, dress shirts, and bins and bins filled with sneakers and shoes. All during their journey to Philadelphia they traveled among people whose toes stayed warm in leather shoes and boots and athletic shoes, while theirs stiffened with cold. Mike's feet burned with wanting a pair.

A few of the other customers glanced over and stared at them. A dark-haired woman weighed down her cart as her three small children climbed in and out. An African-American guard in a dark blue uniform. A drunk with a scruffy gray beard who wove among the mixed crowd of black, white and Chinese people pacing before the racks, regarding the ready-mades with the reverence of people in church. Viktor stood off to the side watching. "It's okay," Viktor said. "You can touch the clothing. Go ahead. Pick something out. Try something on."

Mike ran his hands over a row of jackets and picked out a jeans jacket that he had seen Americans wear in the orientation pamphlets he received in Kenya.

Viktor told him to go look at himself in the glass. He stepped up to the full-length three-way mirror, one of the few times he had ever seen his body reflected. With the jacket on his body, he thought he looked like an American teenager. He lifted his arms, he turned around. He laughed.

"A scarf, gloves and a hat," Grace said, her arms filled. "You may not need them yet, but I promise you that you will." She crinkled her nose and shook her head. "Do you want me to show you a real winter jacket? You'll freeze in that thing. Come over here." She led Mike to a rack where she pulled out a bright blue jacket, unzipped it and draped it over his shoulders. He stuck his arms through the sleeves. Once he had it on, she zipped it together to lock him in, fastening the snaps so that it covered his face all the way up to his ears.

The jacket was enormous, big and puffy. He could barely move. His chest felt like it was being constricted. He pined for American clothing, jeans and t-shirts with the names of American sports stars emblazoned across the chest like on UN hand-me-downs. He could almost hear Ayuen hiss at him as he looked at himself in the glass. He ripped off the hood.

"You don't like it?" Grace said. "Okay, when you see snow coming down, you're going to be sorry."

"Mike," Viktor pulled at his arm. "Come over here. Viktor winked and led Mike away. "Grace is very mothering," he said. Blue eyes twinkling, Viktor vainly groped the racks for something less bulky.

Chapter Twenty-Nine

"WHEATIES," VIKTOR SAID, "Breakfast of champions." He rinsed out a bowl and placed it on the table, poured cereal out of a box, milk out of a carton. "I ate this cereal for breakfast every day when I was your age. Tell me what you think of it," he said.

Unaccustomed to eating breakfast, Mike stared down at the bowl wondering why the UN at Kakuma didn't distribute Wheaties instead of raw grain that took all day to grind and cook over a fire.

"Go on, try it," Viktor said. "Don't let it go soggy."

He loaded up the spoon and brought it to his mouth. Brittle and gritty, the flakes tasted like the twigs he ate during the walk to Ethiopia. "It's good," he said, the cereal so dry it wouldn't go down his throat.

"I knew you'd like it," Viktor said. "A lot of the food in America is processed and tastes artificial. Wheaties are pretty good."

Mike and his siblings piled into the van and Viktor drove along Buttonwood Avenue all the way to the east end toward Buttonwood High School. The van bumped over cobblestones as Viktor explained that these streets were paved back in the seventeenth century. They passed houses with colored banners on their lawns printed with the names of famous people who once lived there.

Viktor pointed them out: "That's Beth-El Church," and "Look, that's the Dickinson House. It was one the birthplaces of the anti-slavery movement in America. One of the reasons Grace and I are proud to live in this part of the city."

Buttonwood Avenue stopped being residential and became a shopping district—art galleries, cafes, a cheese shop, florists, a theater, an oriental carpet shop, a Mexican import shop, a children's clothing shop, bookstores, bakeries. Trolley cars slid on iron rails welded onto the cobblestones, their wheels and antennas filling the air with sparks. People walked dogs, a sight he'd never see in Sudan, dogs tethered to leashes like prize bulls.

Across McRobert Street, the neighborhood, which had been elegant and in a good state of repair, changed. The cobblestones gave way to asphalt; paint peeled off pillars and porches; plywood pierced with bullet holes replaced windows and doors. Viktor parked the van in front of an enormous, dull brown-brick building surrounded by a fenced in yard.

"This is it!" Viktor said. "Buttonwood High."

Mike stared at the building while he waited for Viktor to open the van's back door.

The wind blew broken bits of leaves from the street into the yard, carrying with it a smell of decay. The grand front entrance was boarded up with wood spray-painted in black and silver graffiti, the letters so slanted they looked like they were written in Arabic.

Although the school day was beginning, police blocked the entrance, waving magnetic metal detectors. Mike stood still and held out his arms while an officer ran a detector along his body. The students stood around dressed like rap musicians in jeans and hoodies—the very people his elders back in Kakuma warned him against, (and if he still had his cassette tapes he'd play them and remind himself). Those kids were everything Mike assured himself he would never become. A bell rang just as he and his brothers reached the principal's office and hordes of kids, running, pounding, shoving, cursing, trampled out into the halls.

After the principal registered Mike and his brothers for classes, Mike asked if it was possible for them to receive some extra tutoring to help them catch up. He didn't expect the principal to respond the way he did, his head hung low. "Sounds like a good idea, but without funding we couldn't."

"What do you mean?" Mike asked.

"Everything's unionized. We'd have to pay a security guard to man the room, pay custodial to keep it clean. There's a budget crunch. Programs are getting cut, nothing's getting started right now. There's no money. It's very complicated, Michael, the system is failing. The City is looking for a private agency to finance the school system. These might be the final years of the Philadelphia Public School System as we know it."

Outside the principal's office, a girl was propping up a piece of cardboard that read 'Bake Sale' in front of a single cake and a box of cookies on a folding table. Mike walked over to her. Square-shaped with thick dark brown icing and pale pink flowers all along its edges, a cake like this greeted him and his siblings in Nairobi during their stay there.

"Your birthday?" he asked the girl, the concept still new. No one in his village kept birth records. Their ages were merely approximations, most likely off by months or even years. "Birthday cake," his Cultural Orientation leaders explained in Nairobi, when they chose January 1st as their common birthday, although it had been months away.

"No." Along her face was a scar, sideways down her ear.

"This is not birthday cake?"

"No, it's just cake."

He knew nothing. "Sorry," he said.

She asked where he was from.

"Sudan."

Where's that?"

"Africa."

"Africa…" she repeated in a dreamy tone, "what's that like?"

"Great."

"Then what are you doing here?"

"There's war in my country. I got separated from my parents."

"Don't pride yourself. I haven't seen my father in ten years."

"Sorry."

"Sorry yourself," she said.

She lifted a spatula under a slice, slid it onto a paper plate and handed it to him, and he felt what it was to bear something. She nodded for him to try it. He thanked her and took a bite. She didn't know that he'd eaten cake only once before. If he told her, she'd probably make fun of him. Kids streamed in through the double doors, a dull roar heading for the table. Her attention turned to them, and he waved goodbye.

The windows in his homeroom opened only a crack. The permanent locks on them kept kids from sticking their heads out. It was a cold, clear fall day, but the air inside felt like it was steaming out from a swamp. After the bell rang, the teacher didn't begin the lesson. He sat at his desk, occasionally looking up to yell at someone, while the kids in the classroom leaned over each other's desks, talking and cracking chewing gum. Fifteen minutes later, two huge police officers brandishing their sticks walked into the classroom, stood at the front and solemnly called a boy's name.

"Get your things and get up," one of the officers shouted, waving a pair of handcuffs. Both officers rushed forward to surround the boy, glancing at Mike as they approached his desk.

"It was only a paring knife," the boy shouted. The officers locked the cuffs around the boy's wrists and led him out of the classroom. "How am I supposed to eat an apple if I can't slice it up?" the boy continued shouting as the officers dragged him out.

When Viktor pulled up in the van after school, Mike asked him why his son, Tom, a ninth-grader, the same grade as himself, attended a private school instead of Buttonwood High. "For the Christian education," Viktor said. It immediately struck Mike that there were two systems of education in America, public and private, when he thought that everyone got the same.

A trolley car that stopped at the corners to let passengers in or out, blocked the van. Sparks popped off the antennae mounted at the top and attached to the overhead wires. "Damn, trolley," Viktor said. At the red light Viktor came to a full stop. He kept his eyes on the glass windshield, the people and traffic on the other side. Finally, he spoke, "Once your English is up to par, I'm sure you will be recommended for the

Success Academy. It's all ninth graders. You won't have contact with any of the students in the upper grades."

"If we stay in that school, we'll never make the upper grade," Mike told him.

That night, too distressed for sleep, Mike slipped out from between the warmth of the sheets and felt the same fear that waking in the night always gave him, as if expected to walk through it. He found a notebook and sat down at the kitchen table to write a letter to Brother Renee Baccash, the President of Pennwood Prep, the private Catholic school that Viktor's son attended, asking him for scholarships. For a letter to reach Brother Baccash, all he needed to do was to slip it into one of the many blue metal post office receptacles on Buttonwood Avenue. Once he would tell Brother Baccash what good Christians they were, he was convinced that the Brother would grant them scholarships to Pennwood Prep. Mike wrote a sentence, then corrected it, crossing it out and rewriting it several times. It took him until three a.m. to write an acceptable letter to the President of Pennwood Prep to read. He explained how freedom fighters flocked from village to village and forced people to burn their idols—big piles of the wooden idols Loi and Mormit—and pointed their rifles at the crowd and restrained people from diving in to rescue them, shouting, "Now you are Christians!" He described the attack on Juet, the walk to Pinyudu, Pochalla, Kakuma and the years of subsiding on a two-week ration of half a cup of grain, oil and salt. He wrote down the words of the SPLA leader, John Garang, and his teaching, "Education is your mother and your father," so Brother Baccash would know in an instant how much an education at Pennwood Prep meant to him and his siblings. The years they studied with the goal of getting selected for a Kenyan boarding school, the exams, the fevers.

In spite of Mike's faulty English, this letter would have to touch Brother Baccash in ways beyond words. It would have to contain the desert where Biar threw him down and shouted in his ear the names of his brothers and the names of his own brothers who Biar wanted him to believe lay on the ground in a pool of blood. It would have to make Brother Baccash rise up out of his chair and cross into Kenya, sun swelling the fingers on each hand. It would have to hold the smell of sulfur and rust and groundnuts and wood smoke and camel dung and burning flesh and human excrement and stand before the Brother like a Turkana tribesman dressed in an orange robe, an ostrich cap made of brown feathers on his head, holding a curved knife blade in his hands. The Brother would then know what it felt like to drop the firewood he'd gathered at the outskirts of the camp and run over prickly burr grass in desperation, ignoring the burning in his feet and outrunning the tribesman who would spare him no mercy, to flee with his life.

Chapter Thirty
January, 2001

MANY PEOPLE who have lived in refugee camps develop
stomach problems that continue to plague them. Mike
experienced horrible stomach pains at Kakuma when food was
scarce. He didn't think he would still feel this pain in America,
where food was available. On the second day of school, his
stomach flared up. The pain started as an irritated feeling then
grew in intensity until he doubled over, hugging his stomach
against his chest, because his stomach hurt more when he sat
upright.

His Earth Science teacher appeared at his desk. More like a
babysitter than a teacher, he gave pop quizzes to justify
himself. Starting beneath his breastbone, Mike's stomach felt
like an explosion rocked it. "What's wrong, Mike?" his teacher
said. "You look like you're in pain."

His teacher couldn't send him to the nurse's office, he said,
because she wasn't in on that day. The district could only
afford a travel nurse who came in twice a week. Mike passed
the principal's office on the way to the bathroom. The girl and
the cake sale were gone. He spent most of the period in the
bathroom, locked in a stall, vomiting.

That night, he found blood in his stool. Worrying that he
might die, Rebekka called Grace and Viktor. At Kakuma,
stomach pain medicine didn't exist and he suffered through it.
He'd lie on the floor of his hut and rock his legs back and forth
trying to soothe himself. He did the same thing now, waiting
for Viktor and Grace to come for him in the van and drive him
to a medical office in West Calvary. The doctor, Dr Alan
Stivers, who volunteered to treat Mike, belonged to their
church, "Let me hear you breathe," Dr Stivers said and pressed
a cold medal stethoscope against Mike's back. "Take a deep
breath. Okay, Michael, you can let it out. Tell me, when you

lived in Kenya, did you often swim in rivers?"

"Not rivers that many. Water holes, and of course, journeying to Ethiopia and also Kenya, where I saw water in a pool or a hole, I bathed or drank."

"Okay, Michael. I'm going to take blood samples just to be sure it isn't something more serious. "Don't worry," he said. "If it is, you'll get treated."

Mike never thought he'd be saying this, but he dreaded going back to school. The police at the entrance checked his backpack, opening the zippered compartment where he kept his identity card. Walking through the halls set off his stomach. It hurt so much he took baby steps the way he trudged through the sand and wind en route to Ethiopia. The kids were like soldiers who it was forbidden to look in the eye. Even glimpsing sideways at one of them was enough for them to call him names or pick a fight. Survival meant pretending he didn't know anything. The teachers didn't teach, the kids leaned over each other's desks talking and blowing chewing gum bubbles, and the building was in such great need of repair that no matter where he sat, plaster rained down on his head, making his hair look like it had turned white.

He stayed out of school until his blood work came back. When it did, Dr Stivers called him to his office and told him that he didn't have schistosomiasis—a chronic illness spread by snails in riverbeds—but that he did have a stomach ulcer called H. pylori. "I'm worried about you, Michael. Did you ever talk with a therapist?"

He smiled up at Dr Stivers from the examination table. The paper sheet crinkled as he crossed his legs.

"I'd like you to talk with someone," Dr Stivers said.

"I'm sorry. That's not something I can do."

"Why not?"

"Culturally, I cannot do that."

"Culturally? I think you're experiencing trauma, Michael. We have a name for it. Post Traumatic Shock Syndrome. You might not get well without intervention." Dr Stivers filled a vial with orange pills and handed him the bottle. "Swallow them with a meal or else they'll upset your stomach. Take them three times a day," he said.

"Don't let anyone see you taking a pill at school," Grace warned, "or they'll get confiscated."

"I'll write you a note and you'll keep them in the nurse's office," Dr Stivers said. He didn't know about the travel nurse.

"What if someone gets hurt?" Grace said after Mike explained that the school didn't have its own nurse. "What if there's an emergency? These kids are so fragile."

"Philadelphia School District," Viktor shrugged his shoulders.

Dr Stivers retracted the ballpoint on his pen. "No need for a note then, is there?"

Dr Stivers did write a note, or make a phone call, or travel to Pennwood Prep in person to contact Brother Baccash. The very next day, Brother Baccash contacted Viktor and Grace and they invited him to their home to meet with Mike and his siblings. "No need to prepare anything,' Grace repeated the Brother's words to Rebekka, Young, Ezekial, James and Mike as they gathered around her while she arranged chunks of cheese with crackers on a white plate.

"Dig in," she said. "Try a piece. This cheese comes straight from the heartland. Wisconsin. Wisconsin Cheddar, a food I really missed when we lived in Sudan."

"Heartland," Young said, and laughed. He bit into the cheese and crunched into a cracker.

Brother Baccash, a tall elderly white-haired, white man, walked through the covered porch into the foyer. Grace helped him off with his overcoat. Beneath his coat he wore a black clerical collar and a white clergy shirt. Grace introduced them, and the Brother shook their hands. Besides cheese and crackers, Grace had placed a tray on the coffee table filled with a stack of cups and saucers, a canister of hot water, tea bags, sugar, spoons and milk.

Brother Baccash sat down and poured a stream of hot steaming water into a cup. In his large, prayerful hands, the cup looked like a holy chalice. He raised it to his lips. He took three small sips and placed the cup back in its saucer. In the silence, it clattered against the table's glass surface.

Brother Baccash shook his head. "I have to tell you, I have never received a letter like this. When I first received it, Michael, I asked myself why? And then I realized, you are the survivors. You are the ones who have survived. If anyone can prosper in an environment like Buttonwood High School, I have no doubt that you are the ones to do it."

Didn't Brother Baccash come to Viktor and Grace's to personally deliver scholarships? Young slunk into the sofa cushions. Rebekka sipped her tea and met Mike's eyes, plying him to do something.

Brother Baccash removed his spectacles from the flat black leather holder in his back trouser pocket and crossed over to the opposite wall. It was covered with framed photographs, mostly of Sudan. While the Brother moved from one photograph to the next, Viktor looked over his shoulder, offering a running commentary.

Behind their turned backs, Grace waved her hand, encouraging Mike and his siblings to stand with them. Rebekka went first and the rest of them followed. They crowded behind Viktor, who stepped forward so that they could all squeeze in.

"I took most of them myself," Viktor said, "with the Canon AE-1. Juba's only 300 miles from the equator. Can you imagine how bright the light was? Most of the time you're battling sun exposure." He pointed to one of the photographs. "That one's at the Oasis Hotel. See how bright the sun was? There were palm trees on the grounds of the hotel, very small ones, not like you'd imagine growing on the banks of a river as grand as the Nile."

"I've never been," the Brother said, "so I wouldn't know."

"Yes, but you must have imagined?"

"I see what you mean."

"See this picture?" he said and pointed to the one beside it. "These boys floating down the Nile? They're floating on garbage bags. We saw them walking around the hotel and filling up plastic bags with garbage. We thought they were working for the Oasis. Next we see them paddling down the river on them."

"Clever."

"Yes, but dire."

Viktor pointed to a picture of himself in shorts and rubber *mut u keliu* sandals, the kind made out of old tires. Young laughed and explained for the benefit of the Brother: "The sandals Viktor is wearing have a name in Arabic that means, 'Die and leave them'. They last forever. They will last longer than humans."

Brother Baccash smiled.

They all laughed.

In the picture, Viktor cemented cinderblocks on a church wall, and standing beside him, Grace held a carton filled with Bibles.

"Your mission?" Brother Baccash said to Viktor.

"The Evangelical Church of Sudan. Chevron was pulling out. It was getting too dangerous to stay."

"Is that right?"

"Yes," said Viktor. "We left Juba in '88. We couldn't remain. There wasn't a single road in use, and Juba was once considered a transportation hub. The fighting was everywhere, destroying everything."

The Brother motioned toward a picture of Viktor, Grace and their son Tom riding camels in a caravan led by Toposa tribesman wearing orange robes, the sand flattened out with tire ruts, a rose of Sharon in full bloom. "What's it like riding a camel?"

"Not too bad. The Toposa treat their camels like babies. They keep talking to them the whole ride. The camels were so tame, we fed them straw out of our hands."

"What were they like in the wild?"

"They were pretty temperamental animals. You don't realize how big they are until you're standing in front of one of them."

Brother Baccash pointed his chin at a picture of Tom on a soccer field. It looked like it was taken in America. It was before his growth spurt. Straw colored bangs stuck out from beneath his cap. He wore a red jersey, red socks and white shorts, squinting to block the sun.

"I'm sorry Tom stopped playing. We could've used him last month," Brother Baccash said.

Mike took a step forward. "I can play soccer," he said.

Brother Baccash shot him a glance.

"If I go to Pennwood, I promise you I'll become a member of the team."

"That's a pretty hefty statement, Michael. What makes you so sure?"

"I played soccer in Kenya. Soccer was more than a game for me. I played it to keep alive."

"What do you mean?"

"When I play, I forget where I am. If I score a goal, I can actually hear my father congratulate me."

"What position do you play?"

"Striker," he smiled like a champion and made the condition with himself that he would only accept a scholarship if his brothers, cousin and sister were also offered scholarships, all five of them, their little clan.

Brother Baccash reached into the side pocket in his trousers and produced a handkerchief. He removed his spectacles, wiped them and cleared his throat. Even before he spoke, the words stuck in Mike's throat like the breakfast cereal Viktor gave him to eat.

"We are dire for education," Mike said, repeating the word that Viktor used to describe the boys floating down the Nile on garbage bags.

"The kind of scholarship money we're talking about here is hundreds of thousands of dollars," Brother Baccash replied.

Mike asked Brother Baccash if they could work in exchange for the money, but Brother Baccash said that there were no jobs for students at the school, "If we sponsor you, we don't just pay for tuition, we pay for everything—books, uniforms—everything. All I can tell you right now is that God is present within you. Keep your faith, and it will be granted."

Was this a bad joke of God's? "Oh," Mike said, "I will never lose my faith. It's my mother and father I'm afraid to lose."

"What do you mean?"

"They're somewhere in Sudan, Ethiopia, Uganda or Kenya."

"How do you know?"

"I don't. But the more education my siblings and I receive, the more ways we will discover of searching for them."

"I would like to help you, Michael, all of you, but now isn't the right time. I'm afraid soccer season is almost over. After Christmas break, the season resumes in March. I can try talking to one of our donors. The team could really use someone who's learned to play soccer in a country where people have more passion for the sport. It's our loss, but even if I can't find a place for you at Pennwood, you have nothing to worry about. You are going to shine at Buttonwood High. You will, you absolutely will." He fixed his eyes on Viktor.

Viktor picked up the cue. "That's right," Viktor said, without acknowledging that Buttonwood High didn't have a soccer team.

Chapter Thirty-One

MIKE KNEW HOW PASSIONATE people felt about soccer. It was only a couple of months until March. From having lived in Kakuma, a place where time clunked along on its head instead of flowing forward, he was practiced in waiting.

From his spot behind the driver's partition, the windows white with morning fog, the aisle filled with standing people, he scanned a poster advertising 'The Newcomer Learning Academy.'

That afternoon, he noticed the same poster on his return trip home. Once he arrived, he called Viktor. Though temporary, Viktor agreed that The Newcomer Learning Academy, located in an annex of South Philadelphia High School, seemed more appealing than Buttonwood High. Instead of going to school with disenchanted American students, dulled by the unchallenging curricula, Mike and his siblings could study at the Academy where they could improve their English and be among other immigrants, as eager to learn as themselves.

On one of his very first days at the Academy, he accidentally turned through the cinderblock hall that belonged to the high school instead of walking through the Academy's new plasterboard annex. He noticed a door with the words 'Computer Lab' written on a piece of cardboard taped up behind a broken glass pane. A teacher opened the door, then slipped inside. When Mike knocked, the teacher didn't answer right away, but he was persistent. Finally, the teacher opened the door a crack.

Mike put his head through.

"Stand back," the teacher said. He gestured at the cardboard. "Can't you see someone tried to break in? This room is off limits to students."

In his best imitation of an American accent, Mike tried to get the teacher to change his mind. "I've been told computers have finding skills. Please, can I use one?"

The teacher heard his accent, looked at his face, saw that Mike was not from around there. "Are you a student here?" the teacher asked.

"I am a student at The Newcomer Academy," Mike told him.

His eyes settled on the scar on Mike's forehead. Most people noticed it right away, the V-shape spindly, too faint to resemble the mark of a warrior. "Finding skills," he said. "That's a good one. What're you trying to find?"

"My parents. I hope my parents got to a refugee camp in Kenya, Uganda or Sudan. I lost them in the war. I have not heard anything from them in ten years."

"Jesus Christ," the teacher muttered under his breath. "I don't have time for this." He opened the door just wide enough to let Mike in. It was one of this teacher's qualities, Mike was to discover, how he said he didn't have time to waste on students, but was willing to make an exception. The teacher pointed to a computer at one of the desks and went back to his task of chaining down the computers and attaching combination locks against student theft. The only way the chains could come free would be to use a metal cutter, which would never get past the police checking the students for weapons at the entrance to the high school. The teacher grunted and mumbled as he moved from desk to desk.

Mike had never touched a keyboard before, unlike Ezekial who worked in an office in the camp. He couldn't figure out how to turn it on. The teacher flicked the switch on the back. "You weren't kidding, were you?" He placed Mike's fingers in position on the keyboard. Mike marveled at the stars shining out from the dark blue screen. The password he chose was his mother's name. It had the power to burst through the sky and make the search bar appear. He typed in other names that were dear to him, such as Juet, Jonglei and Dinka—the names of his village and province and tribe. Mike asked the teacher if he always stayed this late in the afternoon, and when he said that he did, Mike asked him if he could use the computers again to Google search for news of his country.

News of Sudan was scarce in America, yet the very first article on Sudan.net sent Mike reeling: CEASEFIRE! Swarms of refugees were leaving the camps and returning to southern Sudan. The new arrivals included two thousand women and children abductees whom an independent committee freed from their Arab captors. For the first time since the start of the war in 1983, the fighting had stopped.

The blank screens surrounded him like a mass of unknown faces. He got out of his seat and kneeled down on the floor. He began praying, crying.

Everything was different now. MAMA MAJOK! MAMA MAJOK! he had called through the streets of Narus. If his mother was grinding grain outside a hut in Sudan, the ceasefire would now make it possible for him to find her. The postal system might be functioning, and travel would again be possible and agencies like the Red Cross would be able to communicate with their field workers. Messages would travel to Bortown and to IDP camps. He could email the Red Cross chapter in Philadelphia with his "I am Alive!" message and grant permission for their representatives to contact the UNHCR offices of the camps in Uganda, Kenya, Ethiopia and Congo, asking if his parents lived there.

Among the members of his community, they joked that American news reporters would not have been able to call them Lost Boys if the war had not interrupted the postal service. Word-of-mouth news sat on someone's dry, swollen tongue. It was swallowed in the final exhalation of the bearer.

He imagined how they might have walked together—his mother, his father's three other wives, perhaps with his grandmother Nyankuerdit—on the ground-down earth, carrying cooking pots and water jugs on their heads. Until dawn they'd walk, always in darkness, never quite sure that they would arrive safe. Walking for months, they'd come upon acacia trees, vine trees, mud hills, stony hills, wild animals (mostly impala), hostile tribesmen, soldiers, water holes and fruit trees, stopping to load up their arms before walking on with the jackelberries they'd find on the trees, sweet ripe fruits giving them hope.

Chapter Thirty-Two

DEAR MAMA,

If you received my letters you would know that this isn't the first letter I've written to you. Most of them in my head. I've written you so many letters, that if each word were a blade of grass they would fill an entire field. I didn't have pencil and paper. Actually, I didn't know how to write, but once I learned the letters, I wrote your name with a stick in the earth so many times that if I were digging a hole, I'd have found water. The reason I keep writing to you and what I want you to know is that I believe you are alive. I have never given up that hope, and it has kept me alive, too. We may have been in some places at the same time. Like Narus. Were you there? I always think that to find you, all I have to do is ask a woman to smile and I'll recognize you by the gap in your two front teeth. So, if you see a boy who you think might be me, though I'm much older now—fourteen years old on America's record, but I'm probably two or three years older—don't forget to smile at him.

Your loving son,

Majok Kuch Chol

Chapter Thirty-Three

HE PUNCHED in the 'secret' code on a prepaid international calling card that Viktor and Grace bought him for Christmas. He hadn't given up trying to reach Kakuma by telephone, imagining sound waves sloshing through wires and cables waiting to be connected.

Nothing happened. Static. Beeps. Dead silence.

"Precious time you should be spending asleep," Rebekka shouted. She continued to rant about how tired he looked with circles under his eyes and that his lack of sleep made him grumpy, and if he didn't start taking care of himself, she was not going to cook for him anymore. She was a high school student herself and had her own need for sleep.

Then the others chimed in. Young slapped Ezekial's shoulders and nabbed him around the neck, and Ezekial punched Young, and Young tackled him to the floor.

Rebekka shouted at Young to take his hands off Ezekial. Young insisted on lying on Ezekial's back and pinning him to the ground. Because Rebekka knew Young was going to wind up getting hurt, she pried his fingers off one by one from Ezekial's neck. Then Rebekka blamed Mike for getting everyone excited with the hope of finding their parents when the task was impossible.

A narrow walled-in alley had become Saint Vincent de Paul Church's only working entrance, a chain and lock permanently fixed through the grand front door handles. Mike smiled and waved to parishioners who recognized him from previous Sundays.

That morning he saw a familiar face, sitting in a corner pew, mouthing the English words. Their eyes met, and he recognized the kind face of Acheng Deng, who rode on the small aircraft they took together out of Kakuma. Mike was overjoyed to see

Acheng. Soon after that day, Acheng, who was in contact with several more members of their community, brought Mike to gatherings at these friends' apartments. About seven years older than Mike, Acheng didn't feel comfortable sitting in a classroom with students so much younger, and instead studied at home for the GED. Mike began to time him on practice tests in exchange for rides in his taxi cab and dinners at Kaffa's Crossing, an Ethiopian restaurant in West Philly where Acheng fed his *alicha* craving.

That morning at church, Mike asked Acheng if he'd ever used an international calling card. Acheng smiled. He clicked the ballpoint he kept in the breast pocket of his tailored white shirt. "Try dialing 254 before you dial your number," Acheng said. "It's the country code for Kenya."

Grace and Viktor, who had both lived abroad, somehow overlooked informing Mike that he needed to use a country code when dialing outside the States. Holding the receiver pressed to his ear so hard it shook, he punched in the numbers. A pre-recorded message told him how much time he had left on the card. At last, he got this thing to work. He heard the phone ringing on his end. Another person needed to hear it on the Kakuma end. If a soldier heard it, he might not have picked it up. Why complete a chore no one ordered him to do? But if an aid worker heard it, or a refugee with missing family of his own, that person would jump.

Sweat formed around the earpiece, making the plastic feel hot and slippery. No one picked up. Mike called the camp several times to the same effect. At this rate, he'd use up the forty minutes on the calling card in one night. He decided to go to sleep and try the next day, hoping that there was still someone back in the village who might think of him and sacrifice a goat in his name.

He discovered that minutes do not get depleted if no one picked up on the other end. To let the phone ring cost nothing. Praising Comcast, he called Kakuma night after night, counting twenty, thirty, fifty, a hundred rings. The ringing that sounded so close to his ear and filled with so much alarm brought to mind the sounds of war that he would have liked to forget. Standing alone in the kitchen late at night listening and remembering, he was grateful that his brothers and sister and cousin were not also listening.

One evening, Ezekial and Mike sat at the kitchen table together doing their homework when Ezekial questioned him, "Are you sure you're using the correct number?"

Mike blinked, fumbled with the cap on the highlighter in his hand. "Of course."

Ezekial zipped open a pocket on his backpack, removed a paperback, eyed him suspiciously. "What number *is* it?"

Mike recited the number he'd memorized.

"That's wrong," Ezekial shouted. "Fool. It's 254 not 245." Ezekial's mind was so sharp that he didn't even need to curl his fingers into a fist to execute a punch.

Mike stood up to leave the room, but he tripped over Ezekial's brown loafers and fell between his chair and the garbage pail. The garbage pail toppled over. "Look at the mess you made," Ezekial said. Mike held in his response, gathered up the rinds and eggshells, dropped them into the pail and scrambled into his bedroom.

A few evenings later, the telephone rang. Both Ezekial and Mike had been sitting at the table again, but in the moment when the phone rang, Ezekial had been filling a glass with water, so Mike got to it first. Through the static, he heard a male voice with the familiar softness of people back home.

"*Salaam,*" this voice said.

"*Salaam!*" he said.

No answer.

SALAAMSALAAMSALAAM

Mike banged the receiver against the counter. He punched in the code to try again and all he heard was the dial tone, then beeping. He rattled the receiver, slammed it against the counter once more.

With breathless determination, Ezekial turned off the faucet, moved out from behind the sink and grabbed the receiver. He held it up for Mike to hear the operator's robotic voice, "Your call cannot be completed as dialed, please hang up and try again or dial zero for the Operator."

Ezekial pushed the button labeled OPER and another prerecorded voice said, "Welcome to Comcast. To charge this to your calling card, enter your calling card number." He grabbed Mike's calling card from his hand and entered the number on the card and the voice continued, "The number as dialed is not valid. Your call cannot be completed as dialed. Thank you for choosing Comcast."

The kitchen's probing white light hurt Mike's eyes. The next day, Grace and Viktor sat down with Mike and Ezekial and explained step by step how to use the card. For Grace and Viktor, these steps were intuitive.

"Good luck," Grace said when she had first presented Mike with the card, fully believing that it would enable him to reach his parents. "Say hello to your mother for me."

In a dream, he heard the shrill peals of the bell around a goat's neck. He tried to get up, but a hyena was digging its teeth into the goat's hind leg. He couldn't free himself and the pain was sharp. He managed to open his eyes. The apartment was silent. The red letters on the digital alarm clock read four a.m.

He skipped across Young's bed, which was closest to the door, and slid onto the rug in the hall, then tiptoed across the hardwood floor to the kitchen. It was ten a.m. in the camp. People in America might have been sleeping, but in Kenya, people were up and about. He dialed the number he'd memorized, believing it to be the correct one, and this time someone picked up. Through the static, it was hard to hear.

"*Salaam,*" the voice of a man said. Instead of answering *kaif,* Mike answered *hello* and told the man that he was calling from America. The man sounded excited. "America?" When he told the man that he needed help locating his parents, the man explained what a good time this was to look for missing relatives because the cease-fire had changed everything. "No more checkpoints. No more roadblocks. Everyone is free to travel from north to south. Do you want me to look for them?"

"Can you?"

The man told him that he would charge him a very fair price: three hundred dollars. Mike needed to wire the money before the man started his search.

He hadn't realized he would need to pay someone to find his parents for him. He'd assumed that someone would do it out of a common need. Acheng had told him about other members of their community who have had luck locating their families and never mentioned a fee.

No sooner did Mike end the conversation than the telephone rang again. The previous caller must have hurried and told someone to try and prod him for money. Over the next few days, runners, who made money connecting lost relatives, called from Ethiopia, Uganda and Egypt. One called from Khartoum. He knew he must not be rash. Not all of them were well-wishers. Some of the runners were so needy they might tell him that they couldn't find his parents, when in reality, the runner might have never left his hut. Others would set out for the village without the special characteristics—enthusiasm, energy, a sharp mind—that would be essential in tracing his family. If a runner asked too many questions, people in the villages would think he was a government informant and command their most ferocious bulls to charge at him.

It was evening. Mike was about to eat his evening meal. He still ate one meal a day. Besides lingering gastrointestinal issues, he hoarded his monthly check. Regardless, the food on the supermarket shelves didn't look edible. He'd never seen so much food, rows and rows, mostly boxes and cans, nothing fresh. Americans didn't farm in their back yards, didn't eat homegrown foods.

The telephone rang. He picked it up. Another runner. Word traveled fast among the members of his small community. Dinka families were so large that they had many blood relatives. With dozens of cousins, uncles and aunts, someone was bound to make contact with someone related to him and might deliver word of his parents.

From his seat at the kitchen table, he excitedly stomped his feet on the floor. The runner on the other end told him that while some people would remain in camps during the ceasefire, others who had never left the Upper Nile River Basin would remain in hiding in its swamps. The runner called himself Lago Biar Acheng.

"I know the Sudd better than anyone," Lago said. "I am a master navigator." He convinced Mike of the possibility that his parents had been hiding all this time. The vast swamplands stretched thousands of miles. Unlike the other runners who had called, Lago said that Mike didn't have to pay him upfront. When he gave Lago the go ahead to start the search for his parents, he also told him how his friend Acheng needed someone to search for his family. One day at church, after watching Acheng cross himself and weep through most of the prayers, Mike leaned over the row to promise Acheng that he would do everything in his power to help him.

"I don't believe it," Rebekka said after Mike hung up from speaking with Lago. She carried a bubbling pot of stew to the table, "Khartoum's army will hunt them from the air."

"That's right," Ezekial said, "Whoever tells you Baba and his wives are safe in the swamp is a liar. You're too trusting. And that's what is going to get you into trouble. Ask us first before you agree to anything."

"Yes, you need to ask," Rebekka said. "Remember Grace told us that after two months we're going to be on our own? Our assistance money is going to run out. We're not working. How will we pay this guy? Even if Grace and Viktor help us out, there won't be enough for this. You promised this guy money we don't have. We're not ready."

Ezekial and Young ripped off pieces of flat *kisra* bread that Rebekka had kneaded and baked to fold into envelopes for sopping up meat and rice.

Mike broke off a piece of bread to load it with chunks of meat, but he'd lost his appetite.

"What's wrong, is the meat too tough?" Rebekka asked.

"No," he said.

"Next time you cook! I'm sorry there is not champagne on the menu."

He cracked a smile.

"It is my responsibility to feed you," she said, her voice on the verge of tears. "Anything happens to you and I suffer." She tore off a piece of bread and grabbed at it, breaking it into little pieces that fell to the table.

"It's not your cooking. I've been sick all day."

"Me too," Young said, barely having touched his food.

"You have to eat." Rebekka sat down. "You have to get used to having food in your stomach."

"I can't eat, I can't think, I can't do anything until we find Mama and Baba," Mike kicked out his chair. "In March, the peace negotiations will begin. If the sides argue, another war will break out and we'll lose this opportunity."

Rebekka swung her arms down on the table and leaned forward on them to balance while she stood up. Practically six feet tall, Rebekka looked very imposing in her traditional Sudanese robe that covered her from her shoulders to ankles. "Tell me something," she said. "What is so special about us? Why are we the lucky ones?" She brushed the pieces of bread on the table into one of her hands and walked to the garbage pail.

He followed her, and they stood inches apart.

She tossed the bread in the pail, an action neither of them ever dreamed they'd be doing, throwing away food, even the littlest crumb. She closed her eyes and tilted forward, rocking on her toes.

"Bad news will kill me," she said.

Ezekial wiped his mouth with the back of his hand before speaking.

"Shhhh!" Rebekka said. "All of you."

Then—and for a long time afterward he would remember this—during the days they waited for the call: "If it's bad news, if anything bad happened to them," she said, "it's going to be all your fault. You started this. You're going to have to help me handle it."

Chapter Thirty-Four

HE WAITED. He sat at the kitchen table spooning sugar into his cup of steaming tea and stared at the telephone, willing it to ring. "You'll see," he said to his sister and brothers, "Lago's going to find everyone. Have patience."

Viktor called most nights to ask for news. Despite not receiving any, he retained his cheer. Next to Rebekka, Ezekial was the most skeptical. For the next few months, Ezekial made sure he beat Mike to the telephone, surging toward it and grabbing it on the first ring. So, Ezekial was first to hear the news when Brother Baccash called welcoming the four boys to Pennwood Prep, and Rebekka to Little Sharon, Pennwood's sister school.

"Can you repeat what you've just told me?" Ezekial said into the phone, then held the receiver in the air for Mike to also hear.

"Congratulations," Brother Baccash said. "You've been accepted into Pennwood Prep. The O'Mallory Family Foundation is sponsoring your scholarships. You and Mike will both enter ninth grade. Young will enter seventh, and James will enter tenth. Rebekka will be attending school at Little Sharon."

After Ezekial hung up, he wrapped his arms around Mike, "I'm sorry," he said. The night before, Ezekial had punched Mike in the arm when he opened a letter from The Newcomer Learning Academy inquiring what their plans were for the upcoming term. The bruise felt tender. "Maybe next time you'll learn to trust me," Mike said.

An hour later, Viktor showed up. "Hallelujah," he shouted through the buzzer.

The next day, Mike, James, Ezekial and Young ran their hands over the creases in their new tan khakis and starched white shirts that Viktor had helped them buy. Rebekka unwrapped the tissue paper from the new navy blue skirt and white shirt she'd wear on her first day at Little Sharon. In the van, Mike leaned forward in his seat and grabbed the hand straps, too excited to sit still.

Once they arrived at Pennwood Prep, Viktor insisted on walking them inside. Viktor counted many of the families connected with Pennwood Prep among his congregation. He wanted to greet Brother Baccash and thank him for sponsoring Mike and his brothers.

When Mike walked through the grand wooden doors into Pennwood Prep's main lobby, no policemen stood waving a metal detector over his body. Plaster did not rain down on his head. The walls, paneled in mahogany, were covered with black and white photographs of early American battles, with their titles written in gold leaf on the frames: 'Washington Crosses the Delaware; Valley Forge'.

Brother Baccash introduced Mike to Kathy Duda, who stood in the hallway, waiting for the Kuch's to arrive, as if they were her only concern in the world. Kathy explained that she would meet them at that very spot everyday after their classes.

"Well, I won't be standing here the whole time," she said, as she watched Mike's eyes gaze up at the clock mounted on the wall above her. She and her husband drove an hour from their home in Wyncote to stuff Mike and his siblings with ham and cheese sandwiches. The sandwiches made Mike's stomach ache, but he was too grateful to refuse. Overjoyed, he learned that Kathy would help him to speak without the inflections that Americans had such difficulty understanding—especially the silent way he pronounced the 'h' at the beginning of the word 'honor.' Without Kathy Duda's help, he'd have never received the grades he did and passed each year and graduated.

Then there was Coach. The first thing Coach did was to test Mike's running speed with a Super Quality All-in-One Outdoor Exercise Data Wristwatch. The team welcomed him: such lush green fields, real balls, uniforms, cleats, jock straps, Gatorade, score boards, trophies.

"Take off the shoes, Kuch," Coach said when Mike stepped on the scale for his weigh-in. It wasn't like he was trying to add on extra pounds. He was wet from showering and cold air lingered in the basement locker room. "You need to catch up, Kuch. I want you to reach one hundred and thirty pounds. And I don't mean filling yourself up with Butterscotch Crumpets. I want you to hit the gym," Coach said.

When Mike put on his jersey, the shirt drooped down over his shoulders and the shorts slipped off his hips. He realized that Coach was trying to protect him from getting hurt, but he felt like Coach thought he was small enough for a hawk-eagle, if one should swoop down on the field, to carry him off.

In the mornings, while it was still dark, Mike, always the first to arrive for practice, would find Coach sitting in his car with his headlights on, staring at the empty field covered in mist, at home in the quiet. Deer sometimes gathered to nibble on the bushes, leaving mounds of scat on the grass. Coach arrived early to chase them away. He looked out for all the boys, but especially for Mike.

He lined up scouts to watch Mike play. He'd raise his clipboard, scribble something with his ballpoint, tap the page with his index finger. "Lehigh College, Kuch. I've handpicked that school for you myself. You're a first-rate player and this school is first rate." He'd repeat this interaction several more times, rattling off the names of Christian colleges, once Mike told him that he wanted to continue his education at a Christian school.

Coach had it all figured out. Soccer scholarship. "By the start of junior year," he told Mike, "you'll have signed your letter." Mike didn't even know if he wanted to play in college. If he wasn't going to be a professional player, why would he put that much time into it? He'd much rather spend his time reading and learning. In Kenya books got censored. Everything he learned was from a Kenyan perspective. He was beginning to realize that now. He didn't realize it when he lived in Kenya.

"I take particular pleasure in placing my players," Coach beamed. "What you're lacking on offense, you can make up on defense. All you have to do is play your heart out and let me handle the rest."

On the weekends, to better his game, Mike showed up at the Greater Philadelphia African League game in West Philadelphia. African immigrants from all over the continent converged on that field. Besides sharp reflexes, the game demanded stamina, and he knew that he'd improve more playing on that team than with Pennwood Prep's team. To get to the field, he trailed the rowers on Boat House Row who walked toward the river with their canoes upside-down on their heads, until the street widened and he jogged past them. He'd forgotten that a river cut through the city. A reporter, who had come to Pennwood Prep to write a story about him, once asked him, what was the worst ordeal he'd experienced?

"Crossing the Gilo River filled with crocodiles in a poorly built dug-out canoe while being fired at by two different armies and seeing the river turn red with blood from thousands of floating bodies, many of them my friends," he said. "Nothing can match that."

The reporter stopped his tape recorder and asked Mike what he could do to help other Lost Boys living in the U.S.

"You can write more articles about South Sudan. Educate more people about what's going on there. It's a genocide and a lot of people don't know that."

Whenever he geared up in his Pennwood Prep jersey for an important game, he knew that a recruiter might drop by to watch him play. The mothers of the kids on his team pressed together in a conversation that never seemed to end, on the bleachers or on the sidelines, hooking their fingers into the fence wire. He looked over at them from time to time, superimposing his mother's features until the game or the practice ended and his teammates' mothers walked against the wind to meet their sons in the parking lot.

After practice one day, rain came down in fast fat splashes. The mothers who hadn't made it to their cars, ran toward them, clicking the remote controls on their key chains. The sound of car alarms beeping and car doors opening and closing collided with the sound of rain hitting asphalt. Most of the boys jumped into a warm minivan or station wagon, where their mothers waited with the heat turned on high and wipers at full speed. At each practice, the mother of a different teammate brought a plastic tub filled with oranges cut up into slices for the team. Because of the rain, the boys didn't get a chance to eat any orange slices. The boy whose mother prepared the oranges on that particular day sat in the front seat of his car next to his mother, with the tub of oranges on his lap. He had all the cut-up slices for himself. Mike envied that boy snapping open the lid on the fruit and filling his mouth with cold, sweet juice.

Mike's jersey soaked through to his skin, rain dripping off his hair, he waited for the bus. It arrived trailing black exhaust. He entered and stood in the front fumbling through the wet books and papers in his backpack for his bus pass. Shivering, he remembered all the times in the dust and the heat of Kakuma that he wished for rain. If he'd known that he'd get drenched in a downpour on a street in suburban Philadelphia, he'd have laughed.

It was rush hour, the bus filled with the damp smell of clothing, the windows too steamed up to see out. Every seat taken, he stood in the aisle clutching the handrail. A passenger sitting near him cleared a section of the window with her hand. Through it, he glimpsed the big milk bottle on the billboard advertising Harbison's Diary. It was an enormous white bottle made out of plastic—ten or even fifteen feet tall—mounted onto the top of the billboard. Milk was wonderful fresh from the cow. Nothing like it. As a boy, he had loved every single cow in his family's herd, especially the calves. When one of his uncles, not Thontiop, but another one of his father's brothers, took him to Jalle Payam's cattle camp, it was his job to watch over the calves. His uncle watched the cows and he watched the calves. Between them the herd numbered several hundred. They sat and watched the cattle graze keeping their own cattle separate from the other villagers' that shared the grazing lands.

One day in particular came back to him. The day was hot and long. In every direction the view was tall grass growing out of bogs. It was hard to see very far over the cattle's thick backs and their curved horns and the mist and the dust. At first the loud screeching noises he heard sounded like elephants, the dust rising the way it did when beasts that big were near. Sometimes elephants wandered into the village, and his mother would pull him inside and tell him to stay there, but he had never heard them from this close. Neither had his uncle.

The screeching noises grew more mechanical. It didn't sound like animals anymore. The other villagers watching their cattle began to run. He and his uncle ran with them. Their only thought was to run to the closest *boma*. That's when they saw fire in the air. It didn't strike down the huts in the village they were running toward, but flew over them. It was tank fire, something neither he nor his uncle had seen before, and didn't recognize as a warning.

They arrived at the village. The huts remained standing, but all the people who lived in them had fled. Everyone was gone. Outside a hut, he saw a *puur*, which was a garden tool with a wide metal blade and a wooden handle, lying on the ground. He picked it up and ran with it, following his uncle through the muddy channel that surrounded the village and further into the swamp, seeking cover.

His uncle thought that the people who had deserted the village would also be hiding in the swamp. The others who had been watching their herds with him and his uncle ran with them into the swamp looking for their families and friends and called for them. Then the noise of all the people calling the names of those they expected to find, began to grow dim as rain started. Hidden in the tall reeds and grass, he used the *puur* to make troughs in the mud to keep dry. He curled up next to his uncle and fell asleep. In the morning, his uncle took him back to Juet.

The rain caused this memory to pour out of him. As the memory loosened, he felt the relief it brought. His mind was like a big tree that held itself rigid while he perched at the top and only now when he was no longer in danger and no longer needed to hide from anyone, did it bend for him to climb down. Had his parents known about the tank fire? What if his parents had heeded that warning? What if they'd left Juet that night, would they all be together now?

The Harbison's milk bottle was so huge that he could still see it out the bus window a mile down the road. Most Americans hadn't tasted milk fresh from the cow. They drank watery liquid out of a carton. They didn't know what they were missing. He knew what fresh milk tasted like—thick and rich—and he knew what he was missing, and he became incredibly thirsty for it.

He should have called his sister from school to tell her that he'd be getting home late. She didn't like him out alone after dark. Unable to accept that Philadelphia was a city filled with crime, she checked and rechecked the locks on the windows and doors before they left the apartment or went to sleep. He would have to tell her that he forgot to call, and she would again remind him of his obligations. Perhaps she would even rebuke him for not calling to ask what he could pick up at the market on his way home from school. Certainly, she would have wanted milk.

He got off at his stop on Cobbs Creek Parkway, the sky black, rain falling even harder than when he boarded the bus, raining so hard that if the streets were the mud-red paths of Kakuma, they'd swell to the size of rivers. Incredibly thirsty, he felt like he was returning from his desert journey. His life happened in miniscule on that journey—birth and death and being reborn. In rain that filled the cracks on the sidewalks and splashed into the potholes on the street and rushed along the gutters, he opened his mouth to fill it.

Chapter Thirty-Five

"SO...CAN ANYONE TELL me about the importance of the beast in *Lord of the Flies*," Brother Daniel asked.

A hand shot up. "It's to show the forces of evil."

"What else?"

"It gives Jack a chance to be powerful."

"Good. Anyone else what to try?"

More hands shot up. Brother Daniel called on an obese boy wearing black spectacles. He looked just like Piggy in the book. "It's allegorical. Its purpose is to show that everyone has a beast inside them," the boy said.

"Very good, that's a major theme. I'm glad you see it," Brother Daniel told the class.

Kids nodded in agreement. Brother Daniel opened his book to begin discussing the next chapter. Mike didn't turn the page. He usually didn't participate in class. He was too unsure of himself. What if he'd misunderstood the context? He wouldn't want to risk the teacher thinking his English was poor. He shot up his hand. Brother Daniel called on him, "Yes, Michael?"

"I d...don't agree. I come from a situation like this and from my experiences everyone work together. Everyone c...cooperates. If they do not, they will lack water and food. In a situation like this one, everyone depend on everyone else."

Brother Daniel tapped the piece of chalk in his hand against the desk. "So, what you're saying is, you think people are inherently good?"

Mike squinted to keep the hard stares of the boys on either side of him from scattering his thoughts. "Yes."

"You come from a cooperative society. *Lord of the Flies* is based on the British, a competitive society. There's a difference."

Shaking his head, Mike defended his point of view. It surprised him, that as a man of faith, Brother Daniel wouldn't agree. "I don't think that," Mike said. "This book is a novel. It isn't real. In the real situation, everyone will put the efforts into helping everyone else."

"Aaaaaah, we're in deep stuff here," Brother Daniel said, as he rubbed his palms together and moved out from behind his desk. "Would you be willing to prepare a talk Michael? I'm not sure if everyone in the class is familiar with your story."

He was right, Mike thought. There was an awkwardness on both sides. Nobody except Coach and the guys on his team had ever asked about his background.

"It will be a little bit of extra work, Michael. But I'd be happy to put it toward your participation grade."

Mike thought back to Sampson, the driver at Kakuma who said that he had looked like a walking skeleton. He summoned Spirit for help. How could he describe his experiences to a room filled with American school boys?

For the remainder of the class, he sat thinking, trying to organize the years into coherency. When the bell rang and the other kids closed their books, he rushed up to Brother Daniel.

"Brother Daniel?"

"Yes, Michael?"

"I'm sorry, but I do not feel prepared to talk about my experiences in front of the class."

"Forgive me, Michael. I've put you on the spot."

Mike paused. He needed time to consider his reaction. "It's complicated."

"I wouldn't have asked you, Michael, if I didn't believe you could handle it. But maybe I'm wrong. Here's an idea. What if you spoke to our human rights club? Our school and Plymouth Whitemarsh. There's a joint meeting coming up. I could put you on the agenda."

Talking to a club sounded less threatening. "Okay," he said.

"You might need practice. I have a friend who heads a nonprofit. What if I ask him to practice your talk with you? Sound good?"

"Okay," he nodded.

The following week Brother Daniel arranged a meeting between Mike and his friend Ryan Teagle. Mike rode the bus to Ryan's office in the basement of a large stone building at West Calvary College.

"It might be painful, Mike," Ryan Teagle said, standing in front of a tall, metal file cabinet, the concern in Ryan's blue eyes belying the stoicism in his tightly drawn jaw. "I don't think you realize it, Mike," Ryan continued, "once you start talking about your experiences, they're going to cause you trauma. Have you ever been treated by a therapist or social worker?"

"No. Why?"

"I see certain signs in you. For example, you were willing to come here today. If you had been less traumatized by your experiences, you wouldn't have sought me out."

"No, that's not true. Brother Daniel started this. It was his idea."

"And you agreed."

"Not at first."

"And now?"

"I want to tell people the events that happened to me."

"That's what I mean. You're looking for an explanation. I don't have to tell you the feelings of guilt and shame that you must be experiencing."

"How do you know?"

"This is what I do. I work with survivors." He opened a drawer in the file cabinet and pulled out a folder filled with photographs. "Let me show you something. Take a look at these pictures."

Mike stared at the black and white prints, unable to take his eyes off the pictures of unclothed children with tight round stomachs and skin hanging off their bones. His lips felt dry, his throat sore, knowing what it was to have been among them.

"Mike? Are you okay?"

He nodded, searching for his face among the children in the pictures. "Where did you get these?"

"UN archives."

"I was there."

"I know Mike. These pictures were taken in Ethiopia in 1990."

"Do you have more?"

"Not here, but I can get more. Why?"

"I want to find myself."

"This is what I'm talking about, Mike. Healing. Bearing witness. That's what you'll be doing. If showing pictures like this and talking about them doesn't offend you, you'll get the chance to tell people about what you've experienced and spread awareness, maybe even make some changes. The work inspires people. I think it will inspire you, give you a reason for having survived all this."

Ryan unwrapped the cellophane on a fresh tape cassette and jammed it into a small tape player. He plugged an external microphone into the side of the machine, placed the microphone in Mike's hands and asked him to say his name into it.

Echoes of Thontiop's warning came back, *don't ever forget who you are,* as Mike spoke his full name into the tape player, speaking louder than he was comfortable speaking and still Ryan asked him to speak louder and repeat words and to bring his mouth closer to the microphone. Ryan hit the stop button, then the rewind. When Mike heard his voice, he cringed. His sentences had grammar mistakes in them. His accent still sounded foreign, his voice softer than most Americans, so soft Ryan turned up the volume to full capacity. Ryan lifted the cassette machine off the leather pad on top of his desk and placed it into Mike's hands, telling him to practice at home.

He met with Ryan several more times. Ryan practiced grammatical constructions with him until his speech was perfect. Ryan helped him fill in the dates of the battles he knew and got him to memorize the casualty numbers.

"Being a good speaker takes a certain amount of courage. You have to believe in your own experience—that it's worth sharing. But you have to share it in a way that's open and generous and attracts other people. You have to be unrelenting," Ryan said, "with the permission you give yourself to speak and bear witness."

Mike walked up the steps to the stage and looked back at the students. An after school event, parents and alumni sat scattered among the rows. Behind them stood the large glass window that formed the back wall. Early November, and the first snowstorm of the season was predicted. There was word of Mike's talk being cancelled.

The air felt ominous, a chilly, damp ghost-like confluence of humidity and eerie quiet. Just that morning after brushing his teeth, his mouth fresh with mint Crest, he read an internet article about a raid on Kakuma. The teacher who first helped him get his Top Mark, who had been both father and mentor to him, was killed overnight in a Turkana raid. Turkana men came and slashed his throat, killing him and his entire family while they slept.

The combination of the eerie chill in the air outside and the overheated air inside the auditorium felt combustive. Mike felt sure that the ghosts of his teacher, Spirit Free, as well as people he'd never met like Lago who tried to help him, would be listening. They would want to insert their own versions of the story and discredit him. Be quiet, this is my story, he said to them. Though you will have a place in it, I want to tell it from my point of view.

Slowly he took his place behind the microphone, testing it with his hand before he spoke from the speech he memorized. He started with the evening of the attack, emphasizing how afraid he was to stop and look among the bodies on the ground for his parents. "If I did, I'd know whether they were still alive. My mother's final word to me was 'run!' I was five years old. Afraid. Obedient."

The auditorium was hushed and silent. His father had been an orator. Perhaps he'd inherited his father's skills. He continued to describe how fast he ran toward the bush, the sounds of gunfire, the walk across the wilderness, arriving at Pinyudu and Kakuma. His mouth grew dry, his body still remembering. He stopped talking and reached for the glass of water that had been provided for him. His hand shaking, he gasped.

Snowflakes! Whenever he saw snow falling, he felt like he was witnessing a miracle. The PA system crackled with Brother Baccash's voice announcing that the assembly was going to end and all after school programs would be cancelled, "Your parents have been notified and your buses will be waiting for you in the bus circle."

A snow-closing that day might mean no school the next. Although Mike wasn't finished talking, a cheer rose from the back row. A boy sitting in the center clapped his hands. Mike didn't know whether the boy was clapping because of the school closing or because of Mike's talk. Maybe a little bit of both. Another boy joined him. It was contagious. One by one, the students in the auditorium stood up and their applause grew thunderous, gaining momentum in his ears. Every out-of-control student was on his feet, every kid in the auditorium standing, cheering and clapping, the teachers given up trying to get them to sit down.

All at once, a group of kids flocked up the steps to the stage to surround Mike, thanking him for his talk. The roar of applause followed him out the heavy steel doors where Acheng stood waiting. One thought dominated him: why didn't Acheng come in?

"Khartoum's going to find you and hunt you down," Acheng said.

Mike pictured Acheng vomiting into his T-shirt during the flight to America, unable to settle his nerves. Fear to speak, fear to tell, fear this, fear that.

"Is that why you didn't come in?"

"What does this have to do with me?"

"Everything. You've never shared your story."

"You know it. It's the same as yours."

"No, it's not. I'd like to hear it some day."

They walked to Acheng's taxi in silence. Tiny white crystals topped their heads. The schoolyard was filled with the hum of bus engines idling while students boarded.

"Michael!" a man called. Strands of his reddish-brown hair

fell forward into his eyes as he extended one freckled hand, then the other, clasping his hands in both of Mike's to thank him for his talk. "Is college in your future?" the man said.

"Yes, college will be part of my plan."

"I always have one eye out for young people like you. Call me when you're ready." He handed Mike his card: 'Phillip Armstrong, American Insurance Company.'

"Thank you, Mr Armstrong," Mike said, tucking the card inside his wallet.

Mike waited until after soccer season was over to call Phillip Armstrong. Phillip hired him over the phone, and a few days later Mike had a job at American Insurance Company. Now he dragged black plastic trash bags that were as silent as corpses to the dumpster in the parking lot. The first time he plugged the Hoover into the wall and it roared, he ran to the other side of the room, expecting an explosion.

"It's white noise. After a while you won't hear it any more," Phillip said.

"White people noise?"

Phillip laughed. "Yes, it recedes into the background."

While Mike swept the carpets, the Hoover's white noise pushed him deep into his private world. He fantasized about Lago finding his parents tucked inside an impenetrable swamp where *toc* grass formed grazing areas at the edge of the Nile. He pictured every detail, from Lago hacking apart a mahogany tree's twisted limbs and building himself a dugout canoe to rowing the Nile's hyacinth waters in search of encampments. He imagined how Lago would sniff out the scent of smoldering campfires, strain his ears for the weighted creak of roots and enter upon a group of villagers bathing or cooking or just looking up at the stars. He imagined how the quiet would stir in Lago, infiltrate his veins and fill him with a sense of duty, imagining his thoughts: if he could find the parents of one boy then all was not lost. He imagined how Lago would quiet his oars as he approached or else the villagers would think he was the enemy and shoot at him with AK-47s they had found on the bodies of soldiers or bartered off enlisted men in exchange for meat.

Lago would understand, Mike imagined, the heart belonging to a mother who had not looked upon her sons' faces for ten years. How desperate she'd be to settle her eyes upon them once again. Idling his oars, he'd stalk the musk of cattle, crouch in shallows, wait. He might think about whistling, blowing through his teeth to make the sound to alert others of danger, a forceful blow of air followed by short chirps, but he'd reject that idea. If he alarmed the villagers, they would mistake him for a cattle rustler. They must remain open to him, willing to accept his mission and the message he carried. Next time he'd bring dried meat to offer them. Instead, he hacked away at weeds to make navigable channels. Legs sprawled over the sides of his canoe, belly up on the bottom, he hacked away with his *panga*.

Philips' employees gone for the day, their desks cleared of papers and files and message reminders, Phillip called Mike into his office to ask him if he had good computer skills. Phillip pulled out a cushy leather conference chair and placed it in front of his desk. A clean glass ashtray lay on the coffee table and pictures hung on the walls. Mike straightened his back and cleared his throat, as he looked into his own face through the glass frame protecting Phillip's college diploma.

In the months to come and in the following year, Mike became Phillip's surrogate son. Their relationship was so warm, so close, that Phillip's wife, Sue, cooked extra portions of food for Phillip to take to the office for him. After Mike won a game or earned an A on a paper, he called them and boasted. If a week went by and he didn't have any news to tell them, they'd call and ask about his grades or games. Yes, their conversations were one sided, because Phillip and Sue were so interested in Mike, they usually bombarded him with questions about himself. "Of all the Lost Boys," Phillip told him, "you're the one who is going to make it big one day. I wouldn't be surprised if you became a world leader, if not here, then back in Sudan."

Phillip asked what he could do to help him find his parents. He told Phillip he could write letters to INS lawyers. "Sometimes lawyers visit the camps. Perhaps the ones you write to will bear your letter."

"Hold on," Phillip said. "What are you saying? Are you saying that my letter will get to the camps or it won't? Help me, I can't wrap my mind around what you're saying."

"People do not have telephones. The postal service doesn't function. The newspapers are suspended. Most people do not have access to a computer," Mike said.

Phillip shook his head.

"It is because of war."

"Then it doesn't seem very likely that my letter will reach anyone."

"However unlikely it may seem, it is the only possibility."

The telephone on Phillip's desk rang, erupting into the silent room. Phillip didn't take the call. "This is when a cigarette would come in handy," Phillip said.

Mike nodded, the emptied ashtray in view. "In the camp, desperate people chew khat."

"Khat? What is that?"

"Very addictive. It's a combination of tobacco and drugs."

"You didn't?"

Afternoons spent playing dominos flashed back to him. "Noooo..." Mike said. "If I did, I would not be sitting here with you. I'd be back in the camp, nodding in the sun, dreaming about a trip to the moon."

Chapter Thirty-Six

"WHAT ARE YOU DOING HERE?" Mike asked Acheng, who was hunched down on the square of green *Welcome* outside his door.

Acheng shrugged, shook his head, unable to answer. Mike didn't press him. Instead, he went back inside to tell Rebekka that Acheng would drive him to school.

The preternaturally dark eyes in Acheng's driver's license mounted on the dashboard of his taxi cab matched his actual eyes as he turned the key in the ignition. "Lago can no longer help us," Acheng said.

"Why not?"

"The news is unfortunate. I am sorry to bear it to you. A tribal war. A few days ago. Nuer against Dinka. Lago is one who did not survive."

It didn't take Mike long to find the internet article. This was why the killing started: the police station in Jonglei, a crumbling barracks that was once a teacher's mess hall, held broken, rusted AK-47s left on the ground from previous battles. Mobile phone networks nonexistent, people could be reached only by satellite telephone. A group of young men, initiates of the Nuer tribe, led the cows which once belonged to their fathers, toward the river. They saw Lago from a distance and believed he was not alone. They mistook him for a cattle rustler and shot him. Soldiers had trained these boys to shoot. They were surefire hunters of men and of hippos, both in and out of the water. Unlike the feast that followed a successful hunt, Lago's body was left on the red earth under the scalding sun.

Blood money. It usually got paid in cows to compensate for loss. Or in installments according to an agreement drawn up by the two parties. Mike recognized that he and Acheng each owed Lago's family members three hundred dollars, the money that Lago died trying to make, the money Mike did not have. He would never learn how much progress Lago had made in trying to find his parents. Whoever else he hired would need to start from scratch. Maybe the fares and tips Acheng earned would provide him with the money to hire another runner or compensate Lago's family, but Mike held his breath every time the telephone rang, expecting to hear a voice introducing himself as one of Lago's brothers or sons requesting their due.

Mike asked his sister to sit with him on the couch. Ezekial, James and Young were preparing for bed. The bathroom door opened and closed as they took turns at the toilet and sink. Outside the brick walls of the apartment building, the enormous pine trees clustered on the lawn grew so close together, they etched secret words and letters onto the glass.

Rebekka sat down on the edge.

"Something has happened that you probably will not want to hear," he said.

"Then don't tell me."

"I have to."

"Why are you always giving me bad news?"

"Lago has been killed."

"The runner?"

Mike nodded.

"What did I tell you? I told you not to hire him," she shouted.

"We are not to blame."

He watched her face grow cold as he fired one offensive after the other: "What good is being in America if we don't use its resources? What if the ceasefire ends and war breaks out and we miss our one chance? What if our parents need our help and we don't know that it's up to us to help them?"

She rose and walked toward her bedroom.

"Isn't that why we came here?" he called after her.

"No, not for me," she turned back to say. "I'm trying to get on with my life and you are trying to prohibit me from doing it."

Chapter Thirty-Seven

MIKE DIDN'T HEAR the shower or toilet. He listened for footsteps. He looked at the clock on his bedside table. Ten thirty. He overslept and now it was too late to go to school. Why hadn't Rebekka woken him? Except for his asylum interviews, he never missed a day of school at Kakuma even when burning with malarial fever. Now he could not deny the refrigerator's hum and his deep conviction that the soul of Spirit Free had found him. Maybe Spirit communicated with Lago, the two of them hovering over the Nile, blaming him for their deaths.

He dialed Acheng's number. "Hey, *Mony loi ye deeh?*"

"*En piol,* what are you doing home? Are you okay?"

He was relieved when Acheng came to get him in his red and white Capitol cab. Mike rode in the front seat next to Acheng while he raced to the University of Pennsylvania Hospital to pick up an elderly white lady and drive her forty-five minutes to Berwyn.

The traffic was bumper to bumper. Outside the windows of the cab, the trees were still bare, their branches twisting, finding a path to the sun. Mike didn't feel any less haunted than he did back in the apartment.

"Oh no, oh no," the woman muttered from the back seat. "I'm not going to get home in time to take my pills."

"The lady is talking to you," he said to Acheng. He didn't know why, but it felt very important to him for her to take her medicine on time. Ahead of them on the right was a Wawa. On the left was one of the brick academic buildings belonging to Drexel University, bunches of students standing outside smoking. Mike pointed to the Wawa, and Acheng pulled into the parking lot. He stopped the cab.

"Where is this? Where are you taking me?" she shouted, obviously frightened.

Mike turned around to the woman. "To buy you some

water so you can take your pills," he told her.

After they dropped off the lady, they went to see some friends from Kakuma who lived nearby. Two of them had flown on the same Cessna out of Kakuma with Mike and Acheng, and the two others moved to Philadelphia from Kansas City. Another friend, whose name was Abraham, arrived from Kakuma half a year before. A top student, a Franciscan nun was able to get him a visa to study in the US. After arriving in Philadelphia, he stayed at the apartment of another member of their community while his roommate was out of town. This friend had a reputation for being disturbed—the result of war—but war could not be blamed entirely. This friend had told Abraham that he could live in his apartment as long as his roommate was away. One night, Abraham sat on the black leather couch, his feet stretched out on the coffee table, while he watched TV, when his friend told him to take his feet off the table. Abraham did as he was told and went back to watching TV. The friend continued shouting at Abraham about his lack of respect for the furniture in the house. Abraham realized he had overstayed his visit. It was too late at night for him to leave immediately, but he planned to do so the next morning. Abraham returned to watching TV, but his so-called friend lifted a hammer into the air and brought it down on Abraham's head, splitting his skull open. A neighbor who lived next door heard the commotion and called the police.

Now, wrapped in a long, blue wool coat, Abraham huddled around the open flaming barbecue grill. He turned his head to see Mike and Acheng walk up the steps to the patio and came forward to embrace them. Another friend, Pankar, stood in front of the grill, shouting a greeting. Pankar wore an oven mitt on his hand and an apron tied over his T-shirt. Demonstrating how he still cooked *Riing Chi* barbecue the same makeshift way that he did at Kakuma, he stirred the coals with a stick. Mike hovered near the bowl on the ledge, inhaling the fruity scent of the marinade.

"How about a beer?" Pankar asked, embracing them. Pankar reached into a metal chest packed with ice and handed them each a cold can of Coors. "Mikey Kuch..." Pankar said. "Why don't you come around more?"

"School...you know."

"Yeah..."

"And after that?"

"I got a letter from West Calvary College. If I keep up my grades the rest of this year and next, that's where I'm going."

"Wow, you've been accepted to college?"

"Soccer scholarship." Ryan Teagle had brought the Athletic Director of West Calvary College to Pennwood Prep to watch Mike play. It was a Division II school. "A compromise," Coach said, "but if they want you and you'll be happy, I'd accept that."

"Way to go Mikey Kuch!"

"Congratulations, man," Abraham said, adding that he was thinking of applying to Widener. He searched under a newspaper on one of the green nylon lawn chairs for a folder containing the application and when he found it, he passed it to Mike.

"You want me to help you with this?" Mike asked, moving closer to the ventilation holes in the sides of the grill in order to read by the firelight. He opened the folder. Behind the application was a printout of a news article Abraham had copied off the internet from *Sudan Today*.

"If it's not too much to ask?" Abraham said. His voice quiet, still the soft speech of people back home. Or maybe after the hammer incident, which fractured his skull and led to the incarceration of his previous roommate, he vowed never to raise his voice again.

Mike held the printout in his hands, looking right at it. The headline in bold: **Khartoum to Sign Comprehensive Peace Agreement with South**. At the bottom was a photograph of the SPLA leader, the future Vice-President of Sudan, John Garang, alongside some of his Army officers. He stared at the photograph.

Acheng noticed his startled expression. "What? What is it?" Acheng asked, reaching for the article.

Mike clutched the edges of the folder. His eyes flicked to

the photograph and back to Acheng.

Pankar opened the lid on the grill to baste the meat with a brush. "Perfect! Going to be cooked just right," he said, closing the lid.

Mike's eyes grew teary from the smoke, but he stayed positioned near where the flames shone through the ventilation holes to study the photograph. The face of the man sitting beside Diktor John was not the young face of an army officer in Juba, not the shimmering face he remembered—it was becoming recognizable. Now middle-aged, older and rounder, he bore the shimmering resemblance to his uncle Thontiop.

Pankar flung open the lid on the grill. Flames flared up and he slammed the lid down over them to contain the fire. "Move back!" he shouted.

"Thontiop!" Mike stammered. "It's my Uncle Thontiop in this picture."

Pankar's mouth gaped open.

"It's him!" Mike said, his lungs scorched from the flames burning inside the grill, deeper and deeper inside.

"Your uncle—?"

When Mike burst through the door, Rebekka rushed toward it to greet him. Dressed in her long black robe, she'd replaced her colorful Sudanese dresses with all black ones, mourning the death of Lago. She wanted to bring Lago's body back to Kakuma. Without a proper burial, she felt responsible, fearing his spirit would haunt them. In the days that had passed, Mike found Rebekka standing in the kitchen unable to finish cutting a green pepper for her famous stew, praying: "May God provide strength, comfort, love and guidance to Lago's family, extended family, community and to all Dinka and friends of Dinka everywhere at this very sad time and for the difficult days ahead."

Now, as she rushed toward the door, her robe caught on her shoe buckle. She flung off her clunky high heels. They spun in the air and slid across the hardwood floor, hitting the wall "Where were you?" she asked Mike, her face tear stained.

"The peace initiative is real. Sudan is changing. John Garang spoke about this ten years ago and it's finally going to happen!" Mike waved the news article with the photograph of Diktor John and Thontiop.

"Take it away, Majok. I don't want to read about Sudan."

He trailed behind her into the kitchen ranting and raving as she opened the refrigerator. Crying with her head hidden inside it, she searched the shelves until she found a plastic container filled with the remains of that evening's stew.

He jumped out from behind her. "I've eaten. If I have to eat again, my insides will burst."

She hesitated before putting the container back on the shelf. "Don't ever do that again," she said in a voice that he'd heard before. She closed the refrigerator and walked to the sink and turned on the spigot. She picked up the sponge.

He reached around her and turned off the spigot. Young, Ezekial and James were in bed. They'd left their books and papers spread open on the table. Maybe she didn't remember Thontiop. He was his *awalen*, not hers. The day Thontiop came for him in the late morning hours to take him hunting, Rebekka was sleeping, pale light sprinkling the holes in the thatch roof hut that she shared with her mother and sisters.

"Put the spigot on," she said.

"No, not until you look at this."

She turned around and reached for the folder.

He opened the folder slowly in her hands. With the pages between them, she seemed to soften.

"Look at the man next to Diktor John. It's Baba's brother. Look! Thontiop! You do remember Thontiop?"

"Of course. He was so handsome," she said, studying the picture.

"It's him, I tell you."

"Thontiop?" She laughed. "And what if it is? Do you want him to tell us that our parents have met Lago's fate? I don't."

"They haven't."

"Don't do this to yourself, Majok."

"Do what?"

"It's our parents or it's Thontiop. You prop yourself up with these expectations. When are you going to accept what has happened?"

Chapter Thirty-Eight

BY THE TIME the receptionist called Mike's number and a Red Cross caseworker came out to greet him, it was nearly noon. Mike removed Thontiop's photograph from his backpack. His uncle had grown to become magisterial, resting against a piece of canvas slung around the back of a chair, his legs crossed at the knees. Mike never dreamt of Thontiop—which he took to mean that Thontiop was alive. He'd dreamt of Spirit Free many times. The last time, Spirit was sitting behind the steering wheel of a car, wearing a white goatskin jacket, which was especially bizarre because Spirit never wore any clothing besides a torn, oversized T-shirt and he never learned to drive.

The caseworker, a thin African-American man with a black crocheted skullcap on his head, led him to a chair in a cubicle. He showed the caseworker the photograph of Thontiop. The caseworker leaned over to peer at the picture, not daring to pry it from Mike's hands, risk the air squirming it away.

"You might get lucky," the caseworker said.

"Everyone knows this guy. He's a legend. There are songs written about him."

"Alright then, let's give it a shot. I've seen it happen before." The caseworker produced a sheet of paper. It was a list of twenty or so internet agencies that specialized in the reunification of relatives. The Red Cross's 'I am Alive' program topped the list. Mike told the caseworker that he applied to that program years ago. "Have you ever conducted a search aimed specifically for your uncle?" the caseworker asked.

"No."

"That's the way we'll conduct this search," the caseworker said.

They slogged through the list together. Most were federal agencies and required DNA samples for proof. The caseworker told Mike that he would first try the agencies that didn't ask for samples or payment.

"It's good you came in. Most people try to navigate these sites on their own. One agency at a time, that's how they do it. Then they find out that the government's shut down that particular agency and they give up their search, when all they have to do is try another agency." The caseworker extended his hand. "Good luck," he said. They quickly shook while the words were fresh.

On the filled-to-standing bus back to Cobbs Creek, Mike grabbed the cold metal rail near where a young mother had just finished tying the string on her toddler's hood into a bow. When she lifted the baby, he prided himself on finding an empty spot, wistfully believing that his mother had been responsible for the seat's sudden appearance. He never stopped believing that his mother connected with him through other women. She didn't stand before him, but she manifested herself through others. Maybe. Just maybe.

Chapter Thirty-Nine

THE EMAIL ARRIVED on his server bundled in junk mail and utility bills. Cleaning his inbox, he almost deleted it. He saw the words, American Red Cross, at the bottom of the page and he stared at the address, breathing heavily. Thontiop was his childhood hero. Thontiop was still his hero. He clicked on the letter.

The very first sentence made him gasp. He tilted back in his chair, his Algebra textbook open on the table in front of him. He leaned back too far and toppled over and fell. He started to right himself, then gave up.

He was already familiar with the events of the Bor Massacre that occurred on August 29th, 1991. Thousands of Dinka people got killed that day, thousands on the roads with their cows and thousands more in the swamps. The email he was reading contained the information that all four of his father's wives had been presumed among the dead—Ezekial's mother, who was his father's senior wife; his mother and Young's mother, who was his father's junior wife; Rebekka's mother, who was his father's more junior wife; and his father's fourth wife, who did not have any children. The email also contained the information that his father was killed earlier, in Juet, during the attack in 1988 that he and his siblings escaped.

Ezekial, Young and James wedged themselves in to read the screen, but he did not want them to see it. Filled with black type, the white screen grinned like a skull appearing out of roadside rubble. He closed the lid on the computer and pushed them away, ramming into them with his shoulders. Ezekial fought back and Mike wrapped him in his arms, pulling him onto the couch, away from the screen and its wild, menacing grin.

Rebekka came through the door after eleven p.m. Once she stopped mourning Lago, her smile was wide again, her voice so full of power. But when she saw Mike, James, Young and Ezekial sitting together on the couch, neither one of them watching TV or studying, her face fell. "Majok, what's going on?" she said.

Before answering her, he made her wait while he went into the kitchen for some water. He needed another moment to himself. He filled a glass, then walked back very slowly, carrying it between his hands to keep the water jumping against the sides from spilling, and gave the glass to Rebekka. "Drink," he said.

She waved her hands in front of her face. "What are you doing? I don't want that. Take that away!"

"You need a sip."

"No, I am not a child. Tell me what's going on."

He put the glass on the coffee table and stood opposite her, his voice soft.

"The Red Cross sent an email today."

Rebekka closed her eyes, squeezed them shut.

The room was as quiet and as still as the water in the glass. Young buried his head in his hands. Mike felt like he was back in a place where mortars fell and banged the earth on impact as he told Rebekka that their father and their mothers were presumed dead.

"I told you, Majok, not to pursue this." Rebekka said.

Mike grabbed her hands. The steam in the radiator beneath the window began to sizzle. Rebekka stood up, looked into his face, then turned away. "You started this, Majok! You think you know everything, but you do not. I've known all along. I couldn't bear to tell you."

"What?"

"They were shot in the back, in the village when they saw their huts burning and woke us."

"Why didn't you tell me?"

"You were too young."

"For what?"

"To give up hope."

He understood that Rebekka wanted to get on with her life, that she could not spend every waking moment searching for their parents. She wanted closure. She fought hard to begin her life in Philadelphia. She was the first to drop her anglicized accent. She learned how to fry hamburgers and indulged him with late-night pizzas.

He believed in the meaning of the word 'presumed,' or else why would the Red Cross have included it? More proof that his parents were alive and that Rebekka was wrong.

"I will never stop searching for my mother or for Baba," he told her. "It is my obligation. I am their son."

Often in the presence of women he encountered on the street walking with their children, he sensed his mother. Women wheeling baby strollers. Another squeezing the hands of her two boys as she held them close, crossing an intersection. The smiles on those women's faces gave him courage.

"You fill yourself with this false hope," Rebekka said. She reached for the water and sipped. "Okay, you can believe it if you want to."

"Nothing's confirmed," he said.

"In the letter, maybe, but I know the truth," she said.

"Thontiop is alive. I'm trying to contact him."

"Well, has he even responded?"

He would have liked to knock the glass out of her hands, but there was more water running down her face than could fit in a glass.

"You're lying!" he shouted. "I don't believe you!" The radiator seemed to shout at her, too. The steam backed up and swelled in the pipe, screeching with sudden force.

He rushed into his bedroom and slammed the door to make the walls thunder and the glass to go smashing and the water to spill.

He couldn't wait to graduate high school and move out of the apartment. He went through the motions of those last few months feeling only half alive. The sweltering, sunlit afternoon he walked onto the stage and received his diploma, he waved it in the air, as if to somehow materialize it where his parents could see it. He forced himself to smile when Viktor Figgins rushed into the aisle and snapped his picture. Seeing his brother Ezekial walk up the steps of that same stage was his only moment of happiness.

At the party the Figgins threw for the two of them, Mike clung to a glass of Coke and sipped, talking in a soft voice to the smiling people who congratulated him.

Part Three

Chapter Forty
October, 2005
West Calvary College, Pennsylvania

WALKING TO SISTER MARY'S European Studies seminar, he passed skeletons hanging in windows; pumpkins carved like human heads; sheets draped over lampposts. Unprepared, his collar turned up against the wind, he huddled in his jacket, a jean jacket, when he wished he'd grabbed something warmer.

Some events triggered memories. Halloween was one of them. Every year, Halloween seemed to come faster, last longer. He'd witnessed six Halloweens since he'd arrived in America and each time he felt transported back to Narus, which was one hour from the Kenyan border, but so many people never got across it. Bodies and skulls marked the charred field surrounding the town.

Unlike his sister, he hadn't decided to stop searching for his parents when he started college. The four of them each went to different colleges and commuted from their apartment on Cobbs Creek. He was the only one of them who received a sports scholarship and a chance to live on campus. His siblings would need to one day repay their loans. For now, he was rising at five every morning for practice, but he recognized how his soccer scholarship granted him a miraculous opportunity. He hadn't stopped searching for his parents, he merely put his search for his parents on hold to allow himself to recover from the shock of hearing they had died. It was hard being around his sister. For a long time, he couldn't bear to even hear her voice. If, walking to class or riding the bus to work, he found himself replaying her words, ("I know what presumed means") he'd dig his fingernails into his leg until the pain numbed him.

He passed the sagging crepe-paper ribbons festooning Zapatos, a well-known Mexican import store on Buttonwood Avenue, when he felt a light touch on his shoulder and sprang back. It was the young woman he'd met in line at Java Cup just a few days ago. They'd talked waiting for their drinks, and after he told her a little bit about himself, she said that she'd dated all three of the African-American students in her high school, which, she said, set her apart from the other white girls who only dated white boys. "No inner light, no mojo," she told him. She offered to buy him a cup, and he told her that he didn't drink coffee, only *chai*. "Tea? Please let me buy you one," she said, as if he were still in dire need. Now as they stood together on the street, she thrust an envelope between his fingers.

"This is for you," she said and handed it to him. She had glued down the flap instead of merely tucking it inside. He worried about what it might hold. He opened it too slowly for her, careful not to rip it. She laughed, which caused him to stop midway. She didn't know that her laughter echoed inside his head, mocked him with the voices of all the people who warned him against the futility of coming to this country to look for his parents from here instead of remaining in Africa.

He removed a notecard. It was an invitation to a Halloween party, printed on orange paper. Skulls edged the borders. He tried to stop his hands from shaking. She had no idea how deeply this distressed him. He tried to cover up by smiling, but when he did, he became aware that the bloodstain on his front tooth showed from where Kuol had thrown a rock at him back at Kakuma.

"Do you have a costume?" she said. She put down the bright red Zapatos bag she was carrying, heavy with purchases. Her blue eyes settled on his face.

He pointed to his chest. "This is my costume."

She laughed. It may have sounded like a joke to her, but he had spoken the truth. He had not been his real self since the destruction of his village. He nodded only to end the conversation. He had no intention of attending her party.

A few days later he ran into her again, not in front of Zapatos or in line at Java Cup but on the street nearby with two of her friends, the three of them dressed in office clothing, trousers with jackets. He'd been on his way to class and didn't want to be late. She and her friends surrounded him.

"Mike," she said, "do you still have contacts at the refugee camp where you lived? We're interested in volunteering."

He threw her a puzzled look, which neither she nor her friends seemed to catch. They nodded and smiled.

The other blond-haired one extended her hand. She wore her hair loose in wisps around her face. The smell of her perfume cut suddenly into the damp October air.

"Hi," the third one said. "Glad to meet you." She had the kind of smooth porcelain skin people back in the village would want to touch to determine whether she was real. He was too polite to ask her if she was Chinese, but he sensed the question and told him her parents were from South Korea, emphasizing the South. "No small difference," she said, "same as you being from *South* Sudan." She was taller than he was, but maybe it was because she wore heels. Her thumb had a chunky silver ring on it. Her earlobe had four or five piercings.

He could feel his body heating up, his blood racing with the heat of Kakuma's desert sun. No one went there by choice. He had lived there, survived an adolescence watching Turkana men carrying knives and spears as they passed through the dry, cracked plain he used as a soccer field. Their camels' dung soiled the earth and left a sour smell.

The street grew quiet. He said he'd be late and said goodbye. When he entered the seminar room, the words, 'THE KOSOVO WAR' were written across the blackboard. He supported his feet on the slat of the chair in front of him, trying to pinpoint where he was in 1991 at that exact moment in time. He flipped through the textbook. In a picture, some young men stood behind a barbed-wire fence, that, except for the snow, looked straight out of Kakuma. Bare-chested, their rib cages stuck out. His stomach hurt, his mouth felt dry.

He glanced out the window. The only trees with leaves on them were the evergreens. Even in winter, he couldn't walk past them without stopping. It was too much to say they reminded him of home—trees like this didn't grow in Sudan— but they made him feel relieved that he could look out the window and see something that belonged in this landscape. It was morning, although the light did not appear to be growing stronger. He watched the pale light and the clouds.

Music reached him in his single bed against the wall with breathy, sweaty beats. Music vibrated up and down his spine as he lay under his heavy winter quilt trying to sleep, the window panes rattling each time the door opened and closed in the suite next door. He tossed and turned for about an hour. His head ached. His throat felt sore. He felt feverish. He tried picturing his mother's gap-toothed smile to relax himself, but the image only served to make him more frustrated. It wasn't even ten o'clock. His anxiety at its peak, he kicked off the covers, convinced that he needed sedation—a beer or two might do the trick. In any case, he couldn't lie there another minute sweating under his blanket.

He glanced at the invitation on his nightstand and read the address. The party was only a couple of blocks away from his dorm on a street at the edge of town. He remembered the woman turning onto it, when they walked a few blocks back from Java Cup together.

He slipped on his jeans, a shirt, grabbed a sweatshirt and walked out. The streets were still fluttering with Halloween crepe paper and party goers, most of the windows lit up, music ping-ponging, blaring from different loudspeakers.

He found the address on the card of a red-brick apartment building, pumpkins and scarecrows set up on the balconies, and searched the doors for A103. When he knocked, a guy answered, dressed in a black robe and holding a red Solo cup filled with beer. Mike liked how he didn't ask who he was, just waved him in, as if he already belonged. The crowd looked slightly older than he was, maybe one or two years, already working their first jobs. Scattered on the couches, a few of them coupled together, kissing as if they were alone. A swarm in costumes, including one guy tall enough to have been on a basketball team who wore a green toga with leaves stuck on it, and his hair, face and skin painted green, crowded around a beer keg.

Mike stood in the keg line beside the fold-up table.

"Mike!" someone shouted and hugged him. It was the woman from Java Cup. She was dressed as a nurse, a kind he'd never seen in a hospital, her skirt too short and the top of her shirt too low, her hair bleached white.

"Hi."

"Can you hand me a cup?" she slurred and tried to reach across him to the fold-up table. "I'm so glad you came to my party." Then she turned in the direction of the guy who answered the door and the two other guys standing near him, as they let out a cheer. Mike watched them rush forward to pick up another guy by his feet, carry him to the beer keg and turn him upside-down by his legs. The guy grabbed the handles to stay suspended in the air with his lips on the valve release. Mike had never seen anything like it. Not in Sudan, where people leaped four feet high in the air during tribal dances and not in Kakuma where boys tried to keep alive the old ways.

She remained standing next to him, clapping her hands, watching the spectacle. "How does he do it?" Mike asked her.

"Fifteen seconds is the limit," someone answered over his shoulder, then joined the chant with his fist raised, counting how many seconds the guy could chug down beer until he ran out of breath. As Mike watched, he could feel his own stomach grow bloated. At fifteen, another guy shoved in front with some others, grabbed the guy's legs and pulled him upright.

Mike stepped forward. "Ready?" someone called, and in the moment before he could ask, "For what?" the guy waved at his friends, pointed at Mike, and shouted, "AF-RI-CA! AF-RI-CA! AF-RI-CA!" They charged at Mike and reached for his arms, knocking over the cups and the folding table.

He resisted and pulled back, but he wasn't strong enough. He shouted for them to get off of him. They either didn't hear or ignored him. One of them positioned his hands. Three or four of them lifted his legs in the air, guided him up and held him straight. Someone turned the valve on the pump and sprayed beer into Mike's mouth.

The beer rushed down his throat. If he didn't take big gulps of it, he wouldn't be able to breathe. Five seconds passed. Ten more separated him from the ground. He continued to gulp the beer for what seemed like a very long time, but lost count, as the beer backed up in his mouth and dribbled down his shirt.

He furiously kicked his legs in the air. It took a few more seconds before they pulled him down. Once he touched ground, he was so dizzy, he grabbed onto the couch to steady himself. He inched his way along it until he found a free spot and plopped into it.

"Congratulations! You just did your first keg stand," someone slapped him on the back. It was the closest he'd ever come to getting initiated.

The woman found him and blotted his shirt with a paper towel, talking to him in a soft, slow voice, like she thought his English was poor. "That was so great," she said, slapping him playfully on the shoulders. Her friends were there too, though he hadn't noticed them until they appeared from behind her. The three of them squeezed in to surround him and talk over the music into his ears, their breath tingling all the way down through his spine.

One of them leaned her head on his shoulder. "Where you grew up was there anything like Halloween?" she said.

"Sure. Evil spirits. *Nyanjuans.*"

"What's that?"

"Evil creatures that take the shape of humans."

At first, the beer relaxed him, made him feel mellow. Coach had driven him hard today, practicing strategies and positioning him on the field, over and over until his last assist, when he went down again on his right ankle, the same one that had given him so much trouble back at Kakuma. Much as he numbed himself to the pain of those years, his ankle betrayed him. The slightest fall caused it to throb and swell.

The woman squinted and stared at him like she knew something. "I read an article about you."

Mike leaned back. He smiled. "Yeah, there have been a few articles."

"Ha, ha. Honestly, Mike, I've never met anyone like you before. Do you mind being called a Lost Boy?" She puffed on a cigarette, pretending that it was lit. She sucked in air and blew out the breath. Her lips held a kiss.

He had never thought of himself as lost. In fact, he was a person filled with hope, the hope that he would one day find his parents. "When my friends and I speak about each other, we say, 'a member of our community.'"

"You were called a Lost Boy in that newspaper article."

He hoped she'd read the one that blamed the men backed by Omer el-Bashir for attacking his village and not the one that focused on boys getting eaten by lions as they fled through the bush from Sudan to Ethiopia. Those descriptions were terrifying, but they didn't shed light on the conflict between North and South. "Which one?"

"I don't know. It was a couple of months ago, but I never forgot it. Remember when I met you at Java Cup, I kinda put two and two together and figured out who you were before you told me. I was so happy to meet you. You're amazing."

Thoughts of his parents and friends back in Kakuma rushed into his head. "Not really."

"Yes, you are. Look at what you've survived!"

His parents were missing since he got separated from them in 1988. Finding them became less and less likely. With Sudan still under siege, the only people who occupied the capital were soldiers who pitched tents in the rubble. He scoured CNN for news, but the world picked and chose which countries they supported. She didn't know the first thing about him. She didn't know how dark his thoughts would become if he allowed them to surface and how strongly he fought to suppress them. The memories inside him. A river he still waded through as it turned red with the blood of his friends—boys seven and eight years old. He closed his eyes for a moment and when he opened them the room was spinning. He clenched his fingers into two fists and pressed them against the couch, shaking from the effort.

"Mike, Mike," the three of them called, trying to get his attention. The other blonde-haired one spoke first. "You're on your own now, right?" he thought he heard her say.

He leaned back and rested his head against the wall. He told them how Lutheran Services arranged for the Figgins to take care of him and explained that the only reason he was able to go to college was through their help.

She flicked her hair. "I meant, like, if you had a girlfriend or, you know, involved with anyone."

"I wish I did. If I lived in Sudan, I'd be married by now, but the only Sudanese girl I know here is my sister," he said, noticing the expressions on their faces.

"So they have to be Sudanese, huh?" she asked.

He'd had one American girlfriend, Thea. He'd wanted to take her to his senior prom, but she'd already made plans to interview at a college in New Hampshire. He took her sister instead and rode with her in the enormous limo with other couples from his high school soccer team and danced and laughed, but it wasn't the same as being with Thea.

Except for Thea, he'd been saving himself for a girl he would meet back in Sudan or Kenya, once he located his parents, but he couldn't tell them that. He felt their eyes on him. The eyes of the other people in the room. Maybe just another moment left to make up his mind and reach for someone's hand in the moments before nightfall, the river flickering, half hidden in shadow. "No, they don't have to be Sudanese," he said fabricating an answer, in an effort to stay on the surface, "but it's hard to get to know people in America."

She perked up. She arched her back. "So if you don't have parents, who pays for your college?" she said.

"I do. I have a soccer scholarship and some loans and I work nights and weekends at a part-time job. Actually, two jobs."

"Where do you work?"

"At an insurance firm."

"For real? My father sells insurance."

"I just take out trash and vacuum the carpet."

"Is that all?"

"That's a big deal for me. When I first started, I was afraid to plug the vacuum cleaner cord into the wall. I didn't grow up with electricity. I thought I'd get electrocuted."

She laughed. She stretched her legs out in front of her. "What's your other job?"

"I speak at schools and do video conferences about Africa for Model UN."

Every time he did a presentation for Model UN, he felt that first flush of relief followed by dread as he searched the faces in the pictures he exhibited for traces of himself or his parents. 'The worst humanitarian crisis in the 21st century,' a caption read. He felt like he was going to pass out, not from the beer, but from the way they looked at him and fired question after question.

She shook her head and her hair flew into his face. He inhaled the strong scent of her shampoo. He breathed it in deeper and deeper, the way he'd been asked to breathe at medical exams so that the doctor could listen to his heart.

"What are you doing? Are you alright?" she said and the other two repeated the question.

"It's your hair," he said, trying to pull himself out of it.

They laughed.

She rose off the couch. "It's Herbal Essences. I've been using it since I've been a little girl. You've never smelled it before?"

"No."

She loosened her ponytail and her shiny blonde hair tumbled down. She shifted her gaze toward him and smiled, "Lean over."

He bent over her hair and inhaled.

It was the smell of the forest, of earth between his toes, but also a fluttering feeling that he kept buried. He didn't want to feel it. He leaned back away from her, then forward over the edge of the couch and put his head down between his knees. A smashed beer can glinted up at him from the carpet.

"What's wrong? What are you doing?" she laughed, "Is it some kind of ritual?"

He felt like he was going to vomit. He pushed himself off the couch. One of them jumped up and helped him to the bathroom. He was not even sure which one, because envisaging his father's eyes on him, he stopped looking into their faces.

Chapter Forty-One

HE OVERSLEPT. His hair smelled like vomit and stale beer. Orange candy was smashed onto the carpet in the hallway. He opened the lavatory door and gagged. The sinks were filled with beer, beer cans stopped up over the drains. Vomit fermented in the toilet basins. He turned away from the mirrors, refusing to look at himself. His hallmates had also been up celebrating, but there was no comfort in that.

He could already hear Coach shaming him. 'I had high expectations for this game, Kuch,' and 'Every time you walk past the Pilgrim Arena, remember you're walking past the wall where our banner should be hanging.' Even if he sprinted to the soccer fields he'd get docked. Besides, missing practice so close to the qualifier for the semi-finals, Coach might decide to keep on a substitute player.

He felt too ill to study so he decided to clock some hours at American Insurance Company. He sat on the bench in the bus shelter, nodding asleep until he heard an engine whirring. The bus stopped and he boarded, finding a seat in the back where he could sprawl out. He looked out the window as the bus exited the tree-lined paths of West Calvary's wooded campus, zipped through the sharp turns and rattled along the cobblestone pavement on Buttonwood Avenue. The window he sat beneath got scraped against a tree branch and he ducked his head as if to avoid being caned, the voices of Kakuma elders once again shouting in his ears. An overcast sky hid the sun. It was cold by the window. He shivered. Soon he was shaking.

He exited at an earlier stop, hoping that food would revive his body. He went into Russo's to order takeout, hamburger and fries. As he was leaving the restaurant, he heard someone shouting, "*Janjaweed, Janjaweed!*" The lunch-hour businessmen stopped walking and stared. Young women wheeling baby strollers and older women holding shopping bags slowed down and turned their heads.

Janjaweed was the word the Sudanese who lived in Darfur used for the Arabs backed by Omer el-Bashir who raided their villages. 'Now I'm hearing voices?' he thought to himself. 'What's wrong with me? Kids at West Calvary go to drinking parties every weekend and bounce back just fine.' With each step he took, he heard this voice in his ears shouting, "*Janjaweed*," or was it just wind howling? He sensed a swagger, some lingering human trace and clutched his takeout bag close to his chest and sprinted the final block to American Insurance Company and pulled open the door.

"Why were you so out of breath?" Tess, the receptionist, asked, fanning her hair. Mike deliberately slowed down as he passed her desk, his heart racing and his palms sweating.

Tess followed him to his cubbyhole where he tried to inconspicuously move the edges of the shade to see out the window. She stepped in front of him and pulled down on the handle. The shade fluttered to midway. The bright light hurt his eyes. "Who were you looking for?"

He didn't know.

"I'm going to call the police!"

"No, no."

"Something's got you spooked. Ok, whatever it is, I don't want it to be there when I walk out tonight. Is it someone you know, a friend?"

"It's no one."

"As long as it's not my ex-husband…"

He sat down, the ketchup on his burger leaking through the bag.

"Everyone should get buzzed in," Tess said. "I'm going to talk with Phillip about it."

After work, Mike decided to walk back to campus. The idea of being trapped in a bus with thirty or forty strangers made him break out into a sweat. When he was a small child in Sudan, he'd heard stories of a cultural practice now considered barbaric—burying an old man alive. An elder, usually a chief, would announce that his time had come. A ceremonial would be held, the last one in his honor. Then the chief climbed into a hole in the ground and got covered over with soil. Those assembled held staunch without shouting for his release. Whenever Mike thought about this practice, he felt lightheaded or had trouble breathing. When that happened back in high school, the Figgins would take him to see Dr Stivers. Dr Stivers was the first to warn Mike that his trauma wouldn't go away on its own. He told Mike that he needed treatment. But Dr Stivers never warned him that drinking alcohol would cause it to resurface.

Mike stopped at the flower stall at the park entrance to Cresham Valley Road to gaze at the bright spring flowers. It never ceased to amaze him how spring flowers could appear in this city in the middle of winter. A line of four or five cars waited for their turn. One by one, each driver passed money to a man in an apron making change who handed back a bouquet so large they had to hold it sideways through their car windows. More cars arrived at the flower stall. A steady stream of cars pulled over, idled, and the people inside them chose which flowers to buy.

From behind the wheel of his black Audi, Phillip beeped his horn, his all-weather coat buttoned over his suit jacket and tie. Mike walked over and Phillip opened the door, waving him in. "Hey, Mike," Phillip said.

Mike got into the car and sat on the seat beside him. Phillip cast a worried look in his direction. "What's going on? I've never seen you like this. Tess said you were scaring her."

"It's in my head," Mike told him.

"That's even more disconcerting. You're hearing voices?"

"No, I didn't mean it literally."

"Because if you are, that's very serious. I can give you the name of a doctor. Someone to talk to."

"No, I'm okay. I feel a little light-headed."

"Why's that?"

"I went to a party last night, had some beers."

"I thought you told me you didn't go to parties."

"It was a party in town. The kids were a little older."

Phillip smiled. "It's called a hangover, Michael."

"I know what a hangover is. I've had beers before."

"Not this many, obviously. Well, that explains it."

Inside the car, the heat was blasting so high Mike felt it sizzling on his skin. With sunlight pouring in through the windshield, it felt like the middle of summer. "My head is pounding," he said to Phillip.

"Alcohol poisoning. It messes with your brain."

Perhaps it was the beer, or the kids dressed in costumes, or the fact that he wasn't wearing one and neither were the girls he was talking with, unless they were in costume—dressed as human when it was really a *Nyanjuan*. He chided himself over the pull the superstition still exerted.

"We've gone through this, Mike. I know it's hard to bear. You have to move on. Remember our talk about Law School? Have you given it any more thought?"

Mike was sweating, sweat pooling beneath his arms.

"Why not? It will give you a leg up." Phillip said as they reached the front of the line. Phillip rolled down his window and told the vendor that he'd like gladiolas. "Those purple ones," he said, pointing to a bucket filled with tall blooms. "Don't get me wrong," Phillip said, turning back to Mike, "I love this country, but I don't have to tell you that there's a racial divide."

Mike watched the man in the apron cut off a piece of cellophane from a roll and wrap it around Phillip's flowers. How it was possible that these flowers were alive and his parents were dead? The incongruity churned in his stomach, enraging him. "I don't believe my parents were killed," he said. "I feel them. I don't feel their ghosts."

Phillip faced him. "Okay, I understand. I know what you mean. I think that's a good thing. When my grandfather died, I had so many dreams about him…became so aware of his…*presence*…"

The vendor passed the flowers to Phillip, who placed them on the seat between them. The stems released droplets, wetting Mike's legs. "No," Mike said, brushing his hand over the cold wet drops. "They're alive. I don't dream about them. I know what it is like to feel the presence of someone dead. This is different."

"Okay, Michael. Calm down. I'm here to help you." Phillip reached across the flowers to squeeze Mike's arm. "So you think there's been a mistake?"

"Yes."

"Are there any more web sites you can try?"

"There are always new sites, but they share resources. I'll get the exact same letter next time."

Phillip returned his hands to the wheel. He inched the car into the driving lane. "What else can you do, Mike?"

"Nothing, I've exhausted everything. Do you know people warned me not to come to the US?"

"Yes, you've told me that."

Mike placed his hands on the flowers. The cellophane rustled like wind knocking him to his knees. "I'm grateful for the incredible opportunities I've received. I'm a different person than I was. But where has it led? I'm no closer to finding my parents. Seven years since I left Kenya. I can never buy back the time."

Chapter Forty-Two

WHEN HE ENTERED his dorm room and opened his computer, he found a message from the woman from town. She sent him a link to a page, asking him to join. It took him to a site where she posted some pictures of herself from the party sitting next to him on the couch in her nurse costume. She cropped the pictures to make it look like just the two of them. Her girlfriends weren't in the picture. Anyone who looked at them would think that they were alone together instead of in a crowded room.

Ezekial came to visit him that same day, as he often did when he was in the neighborhood, sometimes spending the night, and, without asking, pulled open the lid on Mike's laptop. Too late Mike realized he'd left the pictures on the screen.

"It's not what you think." Mike laughed, trying to make light of the situation.

"Then what are these pictures doing here?" Ezekial asked, shoving the laptop onto Mike's lap. "Get rid of them."

He clicked the delete button and watched the images dissolve.

He kept running into her, near Java Cup mostly. They'd talk if he had some free time. Sometimes one of them didn't and they'd make sure to say catch you later. Once, they walked out together to the little square on the sunlit side of the street and sat on a bench. A familiarity engulfed her, a friendliness—maybe reserved for someone else, not him who she hardly knew—which put him in the mind of the village or Kakuma even, where people stopped each other all day long and chatted. He didn't know many people in downtown West Calvary besides Phillip. He rarely shopped in the stores or ate in the restaurants, besides an occasional take-out when his meal plan didn't cover him, and he'd only recently discovered the chai at Java.

The third or fourth time he ran into her there she invited him to her apartment. "Come on," she said. "I'll make you tea. It's cheaper than buying it here."

"Sorry, I have soccer practice."

"Couldn't you skip it?"

"Skip practice?"

The whole college was soccer crazy, especially the Dean, who would give up matins for a home game on a Saturday morning. Just last week, she came down to the field to watch practice and afterward she said, "I feel it in my bones, Mike. This is the year the Pilgrims win the Men's Northeastern Division." He needed to gear up for the big game over Thanksgiving. No, he could not skip practice.

Her eyes looked watery, her voice strained but shaky, on the verge of tears. "What are you doing today after your practice?" she asked.

"I have to go to work. I won't have a lot of time."

"OK, come straight from practice."

She greeted him at the door to her apartment, wearing a bathrobe, her hair wrapped in a towel. She unwrapped the towel and her wet, blonde hair tumbled down, the air filling with the woodsy smell of her shampoo. She shifted her gaze to the mud on his clothes and shook her head in disapproval.

"Would you mind taking them off?" she said, and at first he had no idea what she was talking about.

"My cleats? Sure," he said.

"I mean your uniform. There's mud on it."

A flush of shame came over him. "My uniform?"

"Sure, why not?"

"I don't have anything to change into."

"You're wearing boxers, weren't you?"

"Jockey shorts."

"Same thing." She turned around, walked to bedroom, waved for him to follow, stood in front of the mirror and plugged her blow dryer into the wall outlet. The sound blasted through the room, making it impossible to talk.

Her request wasn't that unusual, he decided, considering how clean she kept her apartment, unlike the students on his hall who threw their clothes and books and papers on the floor. They squashed beer cans and flung them around. Above her bed hung a poster of Van Gogh's Sunflowers and a book shelf stacked with magazines.

If he really did practice Christian values, he told himself, he should be doing penance for feeling ashamed of his body when he'd finally attained the weight of the other members of his team, unlike those early months in high school when his soccer shorts hung down his hips.

Between watching her scrunch her hair with gel and shake her head from side to side, he saw her look back at him through the mirror and point at his clothes as if to say, why are you still wearing them? He scrutinized the titles on her magazines, mostly fashion, to give himself something to focus on as he slipped out of his shorts.

She turned off the dryer. The room was restored to silence. She sat down on her bed, close to the headboard, and he sat down near the foot end. Some music wafted in, a woman's voice that sounded like Alicia Keyes. "My next door neighbors have been listening to this song nonstop. You a fan?" she said, tilting her face toward him and moving her shoulders to the beat.

"It's alright, not really my type of music though."

"Really?" she said, quieting her body. "This album went platinum. Well, what's your type?"

"Usually music from home." She was nothing like his sister and she certainly was nothing like Thea or the daughters of the Figgins' friends, daughters of Christian pastors, who were all very intellectual, very serious. He tried to think of something to say. He felt her eyes on him, the softness of her bed. He inhaled the strong scent of her shampoo.

"What are you doing? Are you alright?" she asked.

"It's your hair again."

She laughed at this and leaned toward him, her bathrobe coming undone. She wasn't wearing anything underneath. She looked at him, her features softening. "Don't worry, I'm on the pill," she said, and he became aware of the drawn curtain on the window, and though the window was propped up with some magazines, the shade was pulled down too. Shadows crept across. He looked away to the wall when a flicker across it made him jump.

"Hey, it's okay," she said, guiding him down onto the bed. She rubbed her hands along his shoulders and down his arms to stop them from shaking. "Relax."

His head touched her pillow. It was very soft, almost too soft.

"W…what are you doing?"

"Shhhhh," she whispered. "Come on, you can't be that nervous. Relax. Close your eyes." Her lips reached his. She got on top of him. She put her hands on either side of his face.

He needed to leave for work. It would take him forty minutes to get there by bus.

"What is it?" she said, "because no one's ever acted like this with me. No one."

He sat up. She was still straddling him, holding onto his shoulders. All he could think to say was that he didn't like women this aggressive and that if it was the other way around, she'd be accusing him of date rape, but he didn't say all that. "It's not you," he offered.

She went silent.

He could tell she didn't believe him. Not much had happened yet and he didn't think he owed her an explanation, but she kept pressing him. "I don't think you'd understand," he said.

"Try me."

"I'm worried about my parents."

"Oh," she laughed, "is that all? I used to do the same thing." Then she told him about the first time she was ever with a boy and how she ruined it by picturing her father yelling at her for taking her shirt off and letting him touch her chest. She stopped talking and looked into Mike's face, resting her eyes beyond the surface of his skin, searching for someplace deeper. She pressed against him so hard he could feel her body tremble, her arms gripping the sheets, stretched out to either side.

To his surprise, she was crying. He knew she tended to be dramatic, but this somehow seemed real. Her tears fell onto his face, wetting his cheeks—he had not realized that blue eyes could grow so bright. Her long blonde lashes stuck together. He had not desired her in any way, but seeing her cry convinced him that she was genuine. She was lonely too, he considered. Lost like he was. She kissed him with her tongue. She called his name. The room filled with the deep forest scent of her Herbal Essence, a scent he'd been looking for since he arrived at West Calvary, trying to find it among the evergreens.

All he knew was beginning to change. Maybe a part of him believed that she was beyond him and he would have never considered dating her and maybe that was the real reason he judged her for wanting to go to Kakuma when really he wouldn't be here, wouldn't be alive if not for Save the Children and UNICEF and Friends from the West. Those organizations had fed and clothed him. When he thought about the aid workers who fed him water in the desert, he knew who and what she could become. He owed her his thanks. He berated himself for judging her.

He stroked her back. He had the impression of health and increasing clarity, recognizing that she was making something possible, even going this far, saying, "Touch me here," and as he did, as he made contact with her, feeling with his hands, one thought popped into his mind: the Red Cross letter was real. Everyone else knew it except for him. His parents were dead. No one was waiting for him in Sudan, not his parents, not his future wife. His life was here. There would be no negotiations over a dowry. He would not get called into his future father-in-law's hut. She clutched him tight. She wrapped her legs around him.

He ran his hands down her legs and discovered she was wet. He put his hands on each side of her buttocks and drew himself up through the slit in his Jockey shorts. He no longer needed to save himself for a girl back home. She told him there were some Trojans in the night table next to her bed.

They kissed a little more and he reached into the drawer and felt around for the box. Her drawer was jammed with objects. He touched something with sharp edges and pulled it out, thinking it was the box of Trojans, but it was not. It was a photograph in a cardboard frame. He turned it over in his hands.

"Who's this?" he said.

She didn't answer.

He waited.

"It's my husband," she said. "I guess I should have told you right away."

He slid out from under her, jumped off the bed and switched on the overhead light. She shielded her eyes. "You're joking, right?" he said. Backfire from a truck outside on the street boomed through the open window. The bookshelf rattled. The top corner of her sunflower poster flapped, the tape too loose to hold it up. It inched down the wall. "Why didn't you tell me?"

"What difference would it make?"

"I wouldn't have gone this far."

"Where is he? Is he going to come home?"

"No, silly, he's on a business trip."

Mike leapt out of bed.

"Stop it. You're doing this on purpose, Michael, to invalidate what just happened between us. This has nothing to do with my husband. This is about you and me." She looked frightened. "Are you going to tell him?"

"I don't even know who he is. Why didn't you tell me?"

"No reason."

"No? It's just common courtesy. I'm right. Aren't I? Don't you think I'm right?"

"Why did you take off your clothes?"

"Why did you ask me to?"

"Because they were dirty."

He stomped toward the door and picked up his jersey. Mud from his cleats had flaked off onto the floor. He flung back the door. The knob hit the wall with enough force to make her sunflower poster drop. Her magazines opened on their spines. He saw all these objects fall to pieces before his eyes—if they weren't actually falling then, they would fall later, the paper disintegrating along with the words themselves as a result of an incomprehensible injustice that she herself had created, when she forced him to touch her: his life was here. His parents were dead. They were shot in the back the night of the attack on his village the way his sister imagined it, but he hadn't been ready to believe. He'd deluded himself, because the truth was too painful. He looked back at her.

She told him not to be angry. "Call me when you get back from your game," she said.

"Why?" he asked.

"Because I want to help you," she answered.

Chapter Forty-Three

EVERY BIT OF SPACE on the stainless steel bench against the walls of the cell was taken. The docket numbers of six men were called before it was Mike's turn. He was led out of the cell to a separate room where he was photographed and fingerprinted and handed a towelette to wipe the ink off his hands, an odd act of etiquette, so unexpected.

Twelve hours passed before his docket number was called again. A toilet sat in the center of the room. The air swelled with the stink of urine and sweat. He thought he'd lose his mind if anyone mounted the toilet and defecated. The only benefit in not having been offered anything to drink or eat in twelve hours was that he had nothing to vomit up.

At last, a guard summoned him out for his arraignment. The guard handcuffed him again and led him to a room with a blank TV monitor. The guard picked up the remote control, faced the screen and without even a glance in his direction, explained that if the judge did not post bail, he would be transferred to the county prison and held there until his trial.

He gasped upon hearing that he might be jailed until his trial. Even so, he experienced, for a brief moment, the calm that watching television gave him—all the television he'd watched throughout high school trying to perfect his English. As the guard flipped through the channels, "The Commonwealth vs Michael Choul" appeared in bold, black letters on the screen—a misspelling. "It's C...C...C... H-O-L," Mike said. He asked the officer if the change could be made, and the guard finally turned around to look at him, glowering, emphasizing that the change could not be made, implying that Mike's great-grandfather's name was of no importance in matters of justice.

"Do you understand English well enough to have these proceedings continue?" the guard asked him.

"Y...yes," Mike said.

"Are you certain, Mr Choul? Because if you are not, the Court is mandated to supply you with a translator."

"My English is f...fluent."

The judge appeared on the screen. "Mr Choul?"

"Yes."

"Are you ready for these proceedings?"

"Yes, your honor."

The judge read from a document on his desk. "Let it be known that in the case of the Commonwealth vs Michael Choul the charges submitted by this court of law are as follows: Three Counts of Aggravated Indecent Assault, Four Counts of Indecent Assault and One Count of Restrained Assault. Bail is set at ten thousand dollars."

Seven years ago at his cultural orientation in Nairobi, a few days before his departure for the US, the instructor said, "Remember, you are not acting on your own. You are representing a nation. You must always set a good example for your people."

"How do you plead, Guilty or Not Guilty?" the judge asked.

"Not Guilty." Mike said. But the judge's face told everybody in the room—himself, the officer working the remote, and two other guards—that he regarded Mike's lack of guilt to be highly unlikely.

Chapter Forty-Four

HE CLENCHED his stomach to stop it from burning. The smell of urine and disinfectant seeped in through the pores in his skin. He bent over the cracked cement floor and gagged, coughing up bile, embarrassed in front of the other men in the cell watching him. Some of them stared, but others laughed, when a boy about Mike's age, his feet encased in clean, white basketball sneakers jerked backward against the wall.

A guard called his name and led him out of the cell a second time, but did not remove his cuffs. The guard led him to an office and told him to sit down on a chair facing a lieutenant. The guard remained at the door. The chair was wobbly and Mike needed to sit back with his legs straddled to keep from tipping over. The lieutenant told him that the woman was at the hospital getting a rape check. He pulled out a pad of printed forms from a drawer, clicked open a pen and asked Mike his country of origin.

"Sudan," Mike said

"Sudan?" the lieutenant shook his head and released the clicking mechanism on his pen.

"It's next to Egypt. In The Horn of Africa."

"You're from the Horn," he laughed. "Very fitting for a crime of this nature. Your name?"

Mike said all five of his names, Michael Majok Kuch Chol-Mang'aai, so as not to dishonor a single one of his ancestors. He didn't dare chance insulting any of them or they'd put a curse on him.

"Whoa! Stop! Just give me your first name, middle initial and family name."

Mike tried to explain about the misspelling of his name, but the lieutenant waved his hands and moved on to the next question. "Citizenship status?"

"I'm a permanent resident. I have a green card." He never

carried it. The reason he kept it buried under his socks in a dresser drawer was because it took years to get it and if he should have lost it or if someone stole it from him, he didn't even know how he could get it replaced. The lieutenant stared at Mike's face, moving his eyes down his body. Mike told the lieutenant that he had been granted political asylum in the US, but the lieutenant screwed up his eyes and shook his head with a look of disdain.

Mike felt unsteady with his hands cuffed together. His eyes had not yet adjusted to the harsh light in the room.

"I'm going to have to check this with INS," the lieutenant said.

Mike shifted back in the chair and slipped off, collapsing onto the floor. The lieutenant caught sight of him just as he started to fall. The lieutenant leaned over the table, mouth agape, holding his breath, eyes bulging. The guard grabbed the chair Mike had been sitting on, righted it, then reached for Mike's elbow and pulled him up back onto the seat. The lieutenant waved his pen in the air, "What the hell just happened? What the hell were you trying to do?"

Mike was shaking.

"Sexual assault is a serious crime. If convicted, you could get up to ten years. Don't pull a stunt like this again," the lieutenant said. He clicked open his pen, bent over his tablet and scribbled something, shaping the words with his lips as he wrote them down, his pen as noiseless as the sleek noses of bomber jets from a distance. "It is not recommended that you represent yourself in a court of law. Is there someone who can represent you or do you wish to use a court appointed lawyer?"

Mike's knees ached, bruised under the skin. "If I use a c...court a...ppointed law...yer," he stammered, "will...I...g..get a fair trial?" The lieutenant clicked his pen and laughed. "Ever hear of OJ Simpson? Do you think OJ would be a free man if he'd had a court appointed lawyer? No, I don't think so. Al Dershowitz defended OJ."

Twenty-four hours later, an officer summoned Mike out of his cell and down the stairs to an anteroom where Ryan, who put up bail, was waiting. Mike spotted Ryan first and got to see how very sad he looked. Mike's cuffs unclasped, his hands unfettered, for now, he was free to go.

He sat beside Ryan in his Subaru in the parking lot, surrounded by a fleet of empty patrol cars. The light through the windshield exploded off the glass. He told Ryan that he would find a way to repay him for posting his bail.

"It's the least I can do," Ryan said, "after all the money you've brought in, all the students whose lives you've touched. I've worked with a lot of speakers, Mike, but you're one of the few who inspires people."

Facing the gray cinderblock building, he suggested—hoping to further show his gratitude—that he could repay Ryan by speaking at more schools. Ryan sighed. "That won't be possible. I'm sorry, Mike. Until you're cleared, that is."

"I don't understand," Mike said.

"Dean Eunice made it very clear. You need clearance to work with school children."

I-76 was jammed with trucks, big semis floating behind them and in front of them. Ryan wanted to take Mike home with him, but Mike declined. He didn't want to ruin Ryan's Thanksgiving holiday.

"I'm not seeing my familly until tomorrow," Ryan said. Ryan switched to the left lane to escape the truck in front of them driving at twenty miles per hour with its flashers blinking.

"No, no." Mike said.

"Then I'll take you to the Figgins."

"No," Mike said, sitting tensely alert as Ryan sped past the truck, noticing dangers he'd never paid attention to in the past. "I don't want the Figgins to know yet." Mike turned to look at Ryan. Ryan drove with his right hand. With his left, he rubbed his cheekbone, something Mike noticed him do when he was confused.

"Viktor? He's a pastor. He's the least judgmental person I know."

"No, I should be with my brothers and sister. Can you take me to Cobbs Creek?"

"Of course. You do whatever you need to, Mike." Ryan nodded, "but we should stop and get you something to eat first."

"That's okay, there'll be some food in the apartment."

"Are you sure?"

"Yes, if Rebekka has cooked something, or there will be pizza or Chinese in the fridge."

"Styrofoam containers ferment pretty quickly, Mike. Come on, let's stop somewhere."

"Okay, you can drop me off at Kaffa's Crossing."

"Ethiopian?" asked Ryan.

He nodded. In his last year of high school, he worked at an Ethiopian restaurant on weekends and Caruso's during the week until he met Phillip and started working at American Insurance Company.

"Do you want me to come in with you?" Ryan asked.

"And eat Ethiopian? No, I don't think so," he said, remembering Ryan's experience eating with his hands.

When they got to Kaffa's, Ryan leaned over and embraced him, and he thought of all the times Ryan beamed at him from across a table during video conferences for Model UN. They sat together in silence for a moment until Mike opened the car door. When he did, he was forced to sidestep the man standing on the curb with his big shaggy dog, barely making room for him to walk past. Mike turned back to wave, sensing Ryan's reluctance to leave him alone.

Chapter Forty-Five

KAFFA'S, LIKE OTHER Ethiopian restaurants he'd been to in America, was located on the outskirts of a college campus. Thousands of students from around the world paid a fortune to attend a school in a neighborhood where rain-damaged plywood replaced the glass panes on windows and doors for entire blocks. Kaffa's owners did not know there would be homicides. Its owners did not know that they'd be clipping mace canisters to their key rings, screwing burglar alarms into their walls, posting video cameras in their kitchens, hiring as servers U Penn students in jeans and T-shirts who had never learned to walk on tip toe across the scorching earth of a dry season, but were used to clutching their purses or wallets tight against their hips with their heads turned over a shoulder, suspicious of the sulk of sneaker soles on the pavement behind them.

After a short wait, a blonde waitress in black jeans came toward the hostess station. She consulted a paper filled with table diagrams that made Mike think of Coach consulting his playbook. He frowned at the irony of his situation.

"Mind sitting in the back?" she asked.

Was it that apparent that he'd spent the night locked in a jail?

She led him to a table for two and as he sat down, she removed the place setting on the other side. She asked what he'd like to drink.

"Ethiopian spiced tea. A small tea, please." Tea from Ethiopia, his first refuge.

"Are you ready to order your meal?" she said.

He glanced at the Amharic, looking for the dishes that he used to serve at the Ethiopian restaurant where he worked back in high school: *kitfo, doro, alicha, injera* and *timatim firfir*. Most people who came in were unfamiliar with the food. He gave them recommendations, and he was always thankful for the handful of regulars. Sitting on small stools made of carved wood surrounding a green and yellow woven *mesob* table with an opening in the center where the trays of food would get placed, sat two white women talking loud enough for him to hear.

The younger one caught his eye and he quickly looked away. He'd never look at another girl in this country. The waitress brought the women a tray of flat *injera*, spread, pureed vegetables and lamb ground into a thick paste with pureed onions and peas. They picked at the *injera* and before long, they were opening the wraps on their dry wipes without having touched their food.

One of the owners appeared, a beautiful Ethiopian woman with large, deep-set eyes, dressed in a *gabi*, her black hair slicked back into a bun. She must have been watching from the kitchen, because when she came up to the women's table, she asked them if there was anything wrong with the food. The older woman said that it was their first time and they didn't know how to eat the food without utensils.

"Didn't you ask for a demonstration?"

"It's not only that. It's the consistency of the food. It's too mushy. I guess we should have ordered the grilled lamb."

The waitress came to their table carrying another tray of food. "No, bring it back to the kitchen," the owner said to her. The waitress returned to the kitchen, the aroma of *doro* trailing her so fresh it made Mike's mouth water.

"If you're unhappy we don't want you to pay for the food," the owner said with the hospitality characteristic of Ethiopians. "We care very much about our food and want you to come back."

"No, no, we insist," the older woman said.

"No, I insist," the owner said, tearing up their check. She returned to Mike's table. As the two women gathered their coats and walked toward the door, the owner smiled. "Americans like to try things, but they don't have the stomach. You know what I mean?"

He nodded.

"You look tired, Mike. What is it?"

"Nothing," he said. If she knew he was being charged with sexual assault, she'd refuse to serve him. If she knew where he'd spent the night, she'd order him out of her restaurant.

"Come on, Mike, I know something's... Oh," she laughed, "I got it. Your chin. Growing a beard?"

He touched his chin. He'd never been able to grow a beard, barely needed to shave. Before he had a chance to answer, she saw a customer waving his hand and excused herself. After taking the customer's order, the owner called to Mike on her way into the kitchen, "I'll be right back." Through the gap in the swinging doors, the kitchen staff's bleached white uniforms appeared and reappeared. The doors opened just enough for Mike to see the cooktop's steel edge, the gray floor tile.

He slumped down in his chair. Printed on the menu's back was the familiar story of how 'Kaffa's Crossing' began. The owner's husband had been a doctor in Addis, but was not permitted to practice in the States and now preparing food for people was the closest he could get to healing them.

"If I stayed in Addis even one more night, I'd have been murdered in my sleep," the owner's husband once told him. Mike had visited them at their home, a large stone house on the Main Line. When they showed it to him, they walked from room to room, turned on lights and opened closet doors saying, "This is a *tukul* compared to the American dream your college education is going to give you one day, Michael."

The owner returned to set a china cup filled with hot tea on the table in front of him. The cup was green and yellow and white and filled with steaming liquid. She slid a silver tray filled with ground cinnamon, chocolate shavings and sugar onto the table.

"Drink it," she said. "It will soothe you. I keep this on the top shelf and only bring it out for friends and family. Tea. From Addis. You and your brothers, you have our respect. You are always in our hearts."

He slumped over the table. Hot steam rushed from the cup into his eyes. He blinked them open and closed.

"Michael," she said, "What's wrong?"

The tea was so hot it burnt his tongue. He swallowed. "It's the steam. It's making my eyes water."

Chapter Forty-Six

THE BUS, IDLING, blew black exhaust as he approached. Coach stood near the door, his eyes lingering on Mike's face. The rest of the team had already boarded. They turned absentmindedly toward the front of the bus as Coach held his arm in the air to bar Mike from entering.

"Kuch, the athletic director wants to see you," It came out sounding like a position change on the field, Coach's clipboard at his chest.

"Why?"

"Why? I have no idea why people do the things they do. Go ask the Director," Coach said, motioning toward a man standing on the curb. "I had high expectations for this team, Kuch."

Mike stormed off the bus.

"I'm docked?" he asked the Director.

"Maybe you can catch up with the team later on."

"I can't miss this game!"

Mike punched his fists in the air as he followed the Director up the hill to the dean's office.

Barred from soccer, cut off from his life at West Calvary, the tan sofa enveloped him. Bright sunlight came in through the windows and warmed the room. The sofa cushions held the shape his body made as he sunk lower and lower.

He didn't move from the couch all weekend.

"Why are you still sleeping?" Ezekial asked Mike on the Monday after Thanksgiving break.

His first reaction was laughter, although he didn't laugh out loud or throw back his head. It was a reaction to seeing the absurdity of the situation—the kind of laughter that made him cross his arms over his chest to hide the stain on his jersey, when the police had summoned him downtown to say that he was being charged with a very serious crime. "A crime? What crime?"

He mostly played soccer, cleaned offices at American Insurance Company, spoke to students as an East African expert for Model UN and attended classes. He was one of the few Africans in a mostly white school, so few that there weren't enough to form a student club, though the campus did sponsor a Save Darfur chapter that he attended once or twice. He had so little time between studying, playing soccer and working two jobs. He didn't go to late night bars in the city or hang out with people who got arrested. He got separated from his parents in Sudan when he was five years old. He'd spent ten years living in a refugee camp for unaccompanied minors in Northern Kenya. The one reason he applied for political asylum to the US was to have the resources—newspapers, telephones, computers—to find them. He'd been writing them letters, applying to reunification sites for seven years, living with the uncertainty, yet it fed him in a way that loss never could. Searching for them had become a survival tactic, an activity, relentless in its pursuit. It made him feel like he was living for a purpose, not just to get an education or a good job, though he wanted those things too. It made him feel like he was still their son, still fulfilling his obligations. Dean Eunice knew him. She was always rooting for him, following behind him after matins on game day, shouting, "Go Pilgrims"

He turned toward Ezekial and noticing his reflection on the blank TV screen, he considered the skin on his face. He saw himself the way other people did, a black man attending a mostly white college. What was he doing there? He'd had the same thought the first time he visited West Calvary, and ironically, that's what drew him to the school—its whiteness. He found it amusing, picturing some of his friends in Kakuma and how they'd laugh and how excited it would make them feel.

It was a new term—his junior year. He'd begun to notice that the college was getting more integrated. Instead of being the only black person in his classes, now there were one or two besides him. They naturally gravitated toward each other. It was comforting to no longer be the only one with a point of view on race relations. He'd started to loosen up a little, started feeling less excluded, arriving in the cafeteria later instead of making sure he got there way before everyone else to lean over the counter, squirt mustard on his sandwich or fill his plate with pasta.

Was this about being black? He didn't like to think so, but that was nothing uncommon. At first, he felt like a guest in this country, the people polite but at the same time friendly. They didn't say hello when they passed him in the street the way of people back home, but he wasn't under attack, his life wasn't being threatened for being different the way it was in Sudan and Kakuma. Yet, the more years he stayed and the more adventurous he became, walking the upscale streets of downtown West Calvary, he'd grown used to police stalking him. He'd never forget the time police harassed him outside a McDonald's where he was waiting for a friend. They actually made him sit down on the curb while they checked his identity. He'd heard stories about very upstanding citizens who the police handcuffed and held in jail for hours because they fit the description of a tall black man. The woman had been nervous about her husband finding out Mike had been with her. Maybe her husband did find out and he'd hurt her and she didn't want him to get into trouble, and she knew people would believe her more easily if she accused Mike.

"Is she okay?" Mike had asked the police.

"No, she is not okay," an officer told him. "She won't sleep in her own apartment. She says that's where you attacked her and she's afraid to go in there."

His cleats had made a terrible screeching noise as he rubbed them back and forth and they skidded against the station's polished wooden floor. Running had saved him since his mother instructed him, as a very small child, to flee their burning village, but it also separated him from everyone and everything he loved. He remained standing in front of the officer, telling him that this had to be a mistake. It wasn't just the police. Americans were always mistaking him, especially since he grew out his hair. One of his teammates only last week said, 'What's up, Kuchy Mon?' mistaking him for Jamaican despite the fact that Dinka people look different from everyone. At five foot eleven, he was above average height for an American, but short for a Dinka. Dinka are thinner, taller, their skin about ten shades darker. "Attacked her? I'm telling you, that's not how it happened!"

As a Sudanese refugee, he was the most celebrated person on campus. Dean Eunice featured him in the college catalog, listed his achievements—star soccer player, honor roll student—as nothing short of extraordinary. She presented him as someone who had realized a beautiful dream. Someone who came so far in life, someone who once lacked basic human needs and overcame hurdles. Someone who did not take his acceptance to West Calvary College for granted. As a Catholic college, West Calvary's mission was humanistic. He was an emblem of the kind of help they gave. She had already invited him to be the student speaker at his graduation next spring, had offered to nominate him for a Soros Fellowship to attend graduate school. His chest felt like it had just been slammed against a wall.

In the village where he was born, news got relayed and stories got told around an open fire. The heat of the flames warmed him. The softness of the earth comforted him. He'd feel drowsy. His mother would carry him back inside their hut to sleep on sheepskin beside her. That stopped when attackers razed their village in 1988. It was the middle of the night. He ran. His family became separated.

Ezekial stood in front of the couch, towering over Mike until he bent down level with his face to ask why he hadn't moved from the couch in two days. The last thing Mike was in the mood to hear from him was a lecture on becoming too Americanized. For going to the woman's apartment in the first place. For having anything to do with her.

"Mike! Mike! What's going on?"

Mike stared at Ezekial with defiance in his eyes. "Leave me."

"Don't you have school?"

"Go to class. I can handle it."

The tea kettle shrieked over a kitchen burner's raging flame.

Mike sat up, pulling the blanket with him.

"Whatever has happened doesn't just concern you. It concerns all of us. If you tell me, Majok, I can help you. But if you don't, there's nothing I can do."

"Turn off the kettle."

"After you tell me."

"You're going to burn the kettle," Mike said, leaning his head against the headrest and rubbing his eyes.

Ezekial rose, walked into the kitchen, turned off the kettle then returned to the couch, settling into the sloping seat. "Is it anything to do with school?"

"A couple weeks ago, I went to a party in town…" Mike watched Ezekial's face grow stern. "This is why I didn't want to tell you."

"Go on, I'm listening."

Mike tried to set him straight, get him to see that he'd been falsely accused. "This woman is accusing me of a crime."

"Woman? How old is she?"

"Only a year or two. I mean, she's not a student. She works in the town."

"Who is she?"

"I don't know. I met her downtown."

"What kind of crime?"

"Sexual assault."

"Rape?"

"No, and don't use that word. You're making it worse than it already is. She's crazy. She was coming on to me."

"Why did you let this happen?"

"There you go again. I told you. She seduced me."

"How are you going to get out of this?"

"I don't know." He reached for Ezekial's laptop.

"What are you doing?"

"I need to check my email," he said and opened Ezekial's computer. "Remember those pictures you saw on my screen?"

"Of course."

"That's her."

"What?"

"Yes. My case would be much easier to clear up if I hadn't deleted them from my email. Then I could prove how crazy she is."

Ezekial crowded next to Mike in front of the screen. "Check your deleted files. Maybe they're still there."

"They're gone."

"Check junk mail," Ezekial said. "Check spam."

"No, no, I deleted it. Even the history."

"Did anyone else know?"

"Just you."

Mike logged out and closed the lid on Ezekial's computer. All the incredible opportunities that he had been given were about to vanish, the entire magical journey from Kakuma to America.

"You've been falsely accused. Why did she do this to you? What does she want? Does Phillip know?"

"No," Mike said. He was afraid to tell Phillip.

Ezekial, however, didn't agree. "Why would Phillip take the side of a person he doesn't even know?"

"You did."

"No, I didn't. Are you crazy?" Ezekial said and dialed Phillip on his tiny Nokia cell phone and palmed it in front of Mike's face like a mirror.

Mike grabbed the phone.

Phillip answered it on the second ring.

"Hello?" Mike said.

"Mike?"

"Yes." Mike said, then he explained what happened. In the hush that followed, he felt relieved that he hadn't told Phillip in person and seen the disappointment on Phillip's face.

"Did you do it?" Phillip asked.

Humiliated, Mike didn't answer.

"I'm just going to ask you this once. I'd appreciate hearing the truth."

"What do you think?" Mike said. Nothing before this had been as humiliating. Not the early days of working for Phillip when he didn't trust Mike with his financial records out on the desk or when he was certain that Mike's accent was too thick for him to handle phone calls.

"I'm sorry, Mike. I had to ask."

"I understand."

"But what kind of a girl is this? Why is she doing this to you, Mike?"

"I don't know. I wish I did. I guess she was afraid her husband would find out."

"She has a husband?"

"I didn't know right away."

"Look, that's awfully generous of you. I don't want to get you even more depressed. America has the most democratic system in the world, but that doesn't mean that people aren't falsely accused all the time. That's what worries me, Mike. You need a lawyer."

"I can't afford a lawyer."

"Money's not the issue right now. I know someone who will take care of you. Practices right here in West Calvary."

"It's not what you think. It's no different in America than anywhere else. You weren't there. You don't know how the police treated me. They think I'm a terrorist because Osama bin Laden is hiding in North Sudan. They don't know anything about the region. They think the North is the same as the South. They don't know that the government in the North was committing massacres against us."

"Which is why you need a lawyer."

Chapter Forty-Seven

"IT'S FORTUNATE you're not a public figure, Michael," said Glenn Steele. To Mike he looked like a gladiator, his black hair slicked back, his chest broad and muscular under his three-piece suit. "A case like this would be given a lot of airplay. Everybody loves a sex scandal. Remember Kobe Bryant?"

Mike relaxed in his chair. He'd forgotten that Kobe was also accused of sexual assault.

"Kobe was found to be innocent. But there's a big difference between you and Kobe, and I don't mean because he's a superstar. Michael, are your parents alive?"

Mike told Glenn about the Red Cross letter.

"I'm sorry," Glenn nodded. "The reason I asked you about your family is because this is a crime of moral turpitude. As I've said, you're not a public figure, so I don't think it's going to appear on the evening news, but I don't want anyone in Sudan to hear about it. Last week, when I spoke to you over the phone, I hadn't received the investigation report yet. The officer who questioned you, Lt. Fitzgerald, forwarded the information to Immigration. If you are convicted of this crime, Michael, you will be jailed and then deported. I don't know enough about Sudan to know what they do to the people or to the families of the people who get convicted of sexual assault. But I do know that Sudan is Islamist and hostile to the US and not likely to be welcoming if you go back."

Mike sprang forward in his seat. "INS is involved?"

"I'm sorry, Michael."

"I'm a Permanent Resident."

"Not if you get convicted. Do you know what a jury does in sexual assault cases, Michael?"

"No."

"They side with the woman. Five or ten years ago, they'd have blamed the victim, but it's not like that today. Back then they'd have said she was asking for it. Do you realize what women have had to endure? Women have fought hard for the right to convict a man of sexual assault."

Mike was perplexed. This guy was supposed to be defending him.

"You're a Political Science major. Do you know what a waiver trial is?"

"I'm not sure."

"It means that instead of a jury deciding your fate, we're going to leave it up to the judge. Any judge is going to be less prejudiced than people off the street, especially women. There are too many strikes against you. You are not an American citizen, you are from a country that is in the news right now for harboring Osama bin Laden, and you've been accused of sexual assault. You've got the racial issue, you've got the gender issue, and you've got the terrorist issue, so I don't think you'd have a chance. Do you agree with me, Michael?"

"Do you know who the judge will be?"

"No, not yet."

"When will you know?"

"Closer to the trial," Glenn said. "Try to stay calm."

His insides were churning. His skin was on fire. He felt like he'd been bit by something and that his face was starting to swell.

Glenn smiled. "I've looked at all the evidence you've given me. I've talked to people about you. Phillip thinks the world of you. So does Dean Eunice. You're an A student. You've brought the College dignity. You've never done anything wrong. I've been at this job a long time, Michael, and I know when someone's been accused unfairly. I believe you are innocent and I will do everything in my power to prove it.

Glenn rose, extending his hand. "Thank you, Michael."

"You're thanking me?"

"This case didn't just come to me by chance. This is a case I've been waiting for. It's my case too, Michael. I'm going to do my best, and I expect you to help me with that."

The next day, Mike spent his lunch break walking the half mile down Buttonwood Avenue to Glenn's office to drop off his list of character witnesses. Glenn had told Mike that his case was no different from any case where the plaintiff and defendant have different stories. His job, Glenn said, was for the judge to believe that Mike's version was the truthful one. His list included Phillip and Sue, Ryan, Selina Bell, the administrative assistant for Model UN, Wayne Chen, a friend from high school, the accounts director at Pennwood Prep School, Viktor, Grace, Ezekial and Rebekka.

That night, Viktor and Grace told Mike they'd be happy to serve as witnesses. "Well, maybe happy is the wrong word," Viktor said, "but you know you can count on us."

"Have you spoken with your list of witnesses?" Glenn asked him over the telephone a few days later. "Have they all agreed to testify?"

"Yes. When do you think we go to trial?" Mike said. "I'm anxious to get back to school."

"Figure on ten to twelve months from now."

"Ten to twelve months?" Ten to twelve months meant that he wouldn't be able to graduate on time. He'd have missed an entire year. Maybe he'd lose his scholarship. It would cost more money than he could possibly make to finish up at another school. He wanted to play soccer and graduate from West Calvary.

"I'm sorry, Michael, the courts are overcrowded. Sometimes it takes more than a year. Phillip told me you're working for him full-time now."

Yes, he was making good money.

"That's wonderful, Mike. And a promotion. What is your title?"

"Data entry."

"No more maintenance."

"Correct."

"That's wonderful. See, that's what I'm talking about. This is only one example. The most important thing for you right now is not to crumble."

Chapter Forty-Eight

BARRED FROM THE DORMS, cut off from his life at West Calvary, he was grateful his old room at Cobbs Creek, although he couldn't bring himself to enter it and camped out on the living room couch instead.

Ezekial came home from school, opening the front door and spilling yellow light onto Mike's face. Ezekial stamped the snow off the bottom of his shoes, thudded his backpack filled with textbooks onto the coffee table and shouted, "Majok! Majok!" When Mike didn't stir, Ezekial marched into the kitchen and returned with a glass of water and spilled it over Mike's face.

Mike jumped up. "Hey! I'm sleeping," he shouted.

"Why are you sleeping? It's not even seven o'clock! Now you're going to be up all night again."

"Look what you did! The couch is wet."

"I don't care! I hear you in here, and then I can't sleep. Could you please try keeping normal hours?"

"Normal?" Mike said. He peeled off his shirt and reached into his suitcase on the floor to pick out a dry T-shirt, one of two that were still clean. Mike flicked on the TV and turned the volume up extra loud. "Normal?" he repeated and moved to the dry side of the couch.

"Answer your phone," Ezekial said.

"What?"

"Your cell is ringing."

From under the pile of greasy Wawa wrappings and McDonald's cartons, napkins and fry bags on the coffee table, Mike traced his cell to its muffled Xylophone ringtone.

"So you're not taking phone calls now?" Ezekial said. "There was a time when you lived for the phone. At least you can extend the courtesy of seeing who is trying to reach you."

"No, I can't talk to anyone," Mike said and closed his eyes.

"Stop it! Just stop it! Stop the self-pity." Ezekial stormed off into the kitchen where he clattered plate on plate, fighting Mike without making contact, then he stomped into his bedroom and slammed the door.

Hours later, Mike woke up in darkness. The glowing red letters on his digital alarm clock on the floor next to the couch read 1:47 a.m. in air cold enough for breath clouds to come out of his mouth. He pulled the blanket up to his chin. To save money on Ezekial's PECO bill, he turned the thermostat to below sixty at night. Without the constant sizzle of the radiator pipes, the apartment was quiet.

The click of a door against the jamb, then the creak of floorboards. Even in high school, Ezekial never slept through the night. He didn't think of closing the bathroom door behind him while he spilled his stream of urine into the toilet bowl, followed by the loud noise of the flush. Instead of going back to his room, he found his way into the living room and sat down on the couch by Mike's feet.

"You awake?" Ezekial said and pulled on the blanket, just like he did when they shared a blanket on the dirt floor in a hut in Kakuma the week after they found each other, only half-believing the miracle.

"Uh huh."

"I can't sleep. I'm sorry. It just hurts to see you like this."

"I know."

"You can't let yourself slip."

"I'm not."

"You are."

"Leave me alone. I kept myself going because I believed that Mama and Baba were still alive, but I see now my folly. They are dead and no one can bring them back. It's the worst year of my life. How many times can I sit here and tell myself that this isn't happening?"

"I'm telling myself the same thing."

"I understand that it's affecting you, don't think I'm unaware, but not as intensely as it's affecting me."

"That's not true. My happiness depends upon your happiness. You're closing yourself off. People have told me that they are trying to get in touch with you. They're calling you and leaving you messages. They're reaching out, man, and you're not letting them in."

"I can't talk to anyone."

"Thanks for the backhanded compliment."

"Don't you understand? People can't find out. Why am I telling this to you?"

"Have you even checked your voicemail?"

Mike thrust his hand under the pile of food wrappings, swiped them to the floor and grabbed his phone. He hadn't checked his messages since the beginning of the week. Among the six or seven callers whose names and return phone numbers were listed were Ryan, Phillip and Acheng, each having called repeatedly.

"Bad news?" said Ezekial.

Mike ignored him.

The next number he checked wasn't one he recognized and the caller's identity was not listed, but there was a voicemail. It was from a friend of a cousin's who had just arrived in Philadelphia from Kakuma. A mutual friend had given him Mike's number. The caller didn't know if he had reached the Majok he was looking for, but he decided to try: *Sorry I miss you. It is urgent to return this call. I carry a letter to you from your mother,* the caller's message said.

Mike gasped.

"Who was it?" Ezekial asked.

"A mistake."

"What kind?"

When Mike didn't answer him, Ezekial grabbed the phone and rushed into the bathroom with it.

"Suit yourself!" Mike shouted, unconvinced. "They're dead," he called into the darkness. Even if his parents were alive—remote as he regarded that chance—he wouldn't be able to make contact with them now. If they were alive and found out that he was being accused of a crime, he'd feel too much shame to ever speak with them.

Angered by Ezekial's impetuousness, he rushed after him. He opened the door. The bathroom floor tile was cold against his feet. Blasts of air leaked out from the gap beneath the window sill. At first he didn't see Ezekial, and he swept his eyes across the pane. Street lamps lit up the yard next door. Behind it was a shed. The cement beneath the shed was breaking under the pressure of tree roots. The ground beneath a rickety wooden jungle gym made from thin planks of wood was also starting to crack into his ear when Ezekial popped open the shower door, where he had been standing in the quiet, and held up Mike's cell and replayed the message. Mike flicked on the light.

"*Nhialic, Nhialic Nhialic,* My God, My God, My God!" Ezekial shouted. Ezekial locked his hands together behind his neck and stomped in place, slapping the outside of his thighs. He was so loud, he woke Rebekka, Young and James. They came running out.

Mike steadied himself against the sink. "Now look what you've done. You don't even know if this is for real. You've woken up everyone," he shouted at Ezekial, watching Rebekka, Young and James gather around them.

Chapter Forty-Nine

THE TRAFFIC was bumper to bumper. Ezekial's brakes squealed each time he bore down on them, crawling past Jamaican, Korean, and Chinese grocery stores, takeout restaurants and beauty shops. A giant Foreman Mills stood on an entire block, its lot strung up with carpets for sale and stacked with chairs and sofas wrapped in plastic.

They arrived at 7186 Olney Avenue and parked along the curb. A small African-American boy was riding a red tricycle in front of the steps to the house next door, the boy's mother standing beside him. Mike couldn't help thinking of himself at that age and believing that his mother was communicating with him once again. He grabbed the black handrail and mounted the steps.

Garelnabi, a tall, dark man in his early thirties, horizontal tribal scars cut into his forehead, answered the door. He pulled Mike and his siblings inside and embraced them one by one. Covering his face in his hands, Garelnabi spoke so softly Mike had to lean in to hear. Garelnabi told them that just that morning, he'd received word of an attack on his village in Darfur in which his wife's uncle was slaughtered. Garelnabi himself had fled Sudan shortly after he'd witnessed his brother getting riddled with bullets for selling Bibles on the steps of the University of Khartoum. Garelnabi wanted to know if Mike had any contacts with the press. He told Mike that the Red Cross had gotten him out of Sudan to work for Amnesty International in the US with one purpose, to tell the world about what was happening in Darfur.

Mike said that he'd saved the numbers of the reporters who interviewed him for *The Pilgrim News* and for the *West Calvary Journal*, and he texted Garelnabi his contacts.

"They're local papers, but we can start with them," Mike said.

"Okay," Garelnabi said and handed Mike a thin airmail envelope.

Mike held it in his hand. "How did you find me?" Mike asked him.

"Two ways. A relative of yours."

"Who?"

"I believe someone saying that he is your uncle."

Mike gasped. Thontiop?

"And also Lutheran Family Services."

"What do you mean?"

"Your name is on a surveillance list. What did you do?"

Mike clasped his hand to his mouth. This was no coincidence. The only reason his mother found him was because he'd been accused of a crime. Must God continually use the most horrible, shameful experiences for his good?

"Open it," Ezekial said.

Mike turned the envelope around and saw blue ink lines through the paper. Careful not to rip it, he unsealed the flap, the envelope so thin his thumb's pressure made a tear:

Dear Majok, *Kwarkwar,*

My nightmare is over. You are alive! This is how I found out that you are alive: "Stop! Stop running," I shouted to Baba. It was the middle of the afternoon. No one runs in Kakuma if they can avoid it. Even in that heat, Baba crossed over in a flash and reached me. He was afraid of what would happen to me if I heard it from someone else.

As it was, I covered my ears, covered my eyes.

You had flown off to America. This is what he told me: "You were living at Kakuma, then you left. You crossed a body of water so vast that a bird would be unable to cross its expanse without dying." *Abab dit,* a river with no shore.

"No, no, no!" I screamed. My breasts were engorged with milk, yes, I was expecting again, and the milk was leaking. I closed my eyes, blaming myself, milk dripping from my breasts, going sour.

I'd have stood by the gates of the children's zone calling your name. All that time I wasted. Five years you were here with me. You were alive when I thought you were dead. Will you ever forgive me? It was because I saw earth rise. I believed it swallowed you the night of the attack. We'd been running and a bomb opened up in the air where you had stood, you Majok, with all your milk teeth in your mouth and you Young with your teeth still coming in.

Who would allow a child with milk teeth in his mouth to die in a war? I didn't know. I didn't know. I kept asking myself that question. I asked it over and over. Now I have a new question to ask. I might have seen you in the camp, but would I recognize my grown child?

I'd been cooking grain and I placed my foot too close to the pot. Baba saw my foot drop over the pot and he pushed it away, but it got a little burnt. I didn't tell Baba this, but I was happy for that pain. If I didn't feel that pain, I'd have to pull my hair out or cut my arms with a *panga* to distract myself. I don't know what made me think of this—the blue bottle caps that you used to jingle in your hands, left in the dust back in Juet. I yearned for you to play with them once again, as I sobbed, and Baba rubbed salve on my foot.

Soon, people gathered around us, people who had seen Baba running, who heard my screams. Now everyone knew you had left the camp and I had lost you again. Oh no, oh no, oh no! My brother, Achier, the bravest man I know, could barely speak to me above a whisper. My mother, your grandmother, Nyankuerdit, nearly eighty years of age, who made the months' long walk with us from Juet to Kenya, went silent.

I looked at all of them, feeling my milk come in.

"Now you know they are alive!" one of the camp elders boomed. "Rejoice!"

It was true. It was true. You are alive.

Later, the plane that carried you to Nairobi roared in the sky and landed back in Kakuma's tiny airfield. At one point, Baba and I tried to get inside it, walking up the mobile steps to the door, looking inside at the empty seats, walking around them like idiots looking for a crumb.

Please do not disappoint me or Baba! You can imagine my shock when I found out you were gone. I did not think I would survive, which is why I am trying to find you. Please call the number you will receive as soon as possible and leave a message when we can call you back. Please give us notice, as we do not want to miss your call.

Your loving mother, Adior Magot Majok

Mike clasped the letter to his chest, thin as it was. Mama had been with him in Kakuma! She had lived there for five of his ten years without him knowing it. He may have even seen her. He could have been standing right next to her in a food line. She may have seen him too, but because he had grown so much, how would she recognize her grown son?

He couldn't possibly have asked every single woman in the camp if she was his mother. There were tens of thousands of women in the camp. So many of them looked the way he remembered her to look. Yet, how could he have recognized her when, surely, over the years, her face had aged.

Mike looked out the window for the woman on the pavement with her little boy. It was true. He'd never stopped receiving his mother's love. Now he could say with complete affirmation that the messages he'd received all those years were real.

Seventeen years had passed without a trace.

How long ago had his mother written this letter? When had she given it to Garelnabi and how long was he carrying it around? Was she still alive? She could have written this letter years ago and it had only found him now. And did his mother think that he was alive or dead? The result of Mike's letter writing was to learn that his parents had died. Had they received the same result? Did they believe that he had died?

His parents didn't have a cell phone. How many traders did they bribe over the years to give them a ride to Lokichoggio to use a telephone in the town? How many seats did they hide under, muffling their breathing when they reached the checkpoints? Lacking papers, how many times did they risk getting sent back to Sudan or shot on the spot?

If Lutheran Family Services put his name on a list, did that mean that people in Sudan and Kakuma knew that he was being accused of a crime? Maybe the elders of Kakuma had been notified and were deciding what to do with him when he returned. Now he could never return to Sudan, or at least not until his name was cleared. Even Glenn knew the consequences of a sexual assault charge back in Sudan. What was going to happen to him? His dream was to go home one day once the war ended. He finally got word from his parents and now he was afraid to contact them. If they found out that he was being accused of a crime, they would never forgive him. They didn't know anything about him and they'd think America had corrupted him. Or, they'd blame themselves, especially his mother, and think that being separated from her had made him into a bad person.

Seventeen years without a trace.

Two days later, his tiny Nokia vibrated. "Hello?" Mike said.

A man's voice speaking in Dinka, both soft and harsh at the same time.

Mike signaled to his brother to lower the volume on the TV, waved him close and held the cell phone between them.

"Baba?" Mike shouted.

Seventeen years.

"Majok?"

"Yes, Baba!"

"Chiengkoudit?"

"Baba! Baba!"

Baba said he had only another minute to talk and had something important to tell them.

"Yes?"

Something was wrong with his heart. He was dying. He couldn't get to the hospital, didn't have the money to buy a Movement Pass to travel out of the camp. He told Mike and Ezekial this instead of passing the phone to Mike's mother. Both boys promised they would send him the money. They told him they would do everything in their power to help him. Mike didn't get the chance to speak with his mother. The line crackled with static, and when Mike called for his father, he didn't answer. Their call was over. Their connection used up.

Mike and Ezekial raced down to the Superfresh on Cobbs Creek Parkway to wire Baba the money by Western Union to buy a Movement Pass. Baba was alive! Baba was alive and he was going to be saved! With this money, he would be able to find treatment in Nairobi.

Two days later, Mike sat on the couch with Rebekka, looking at photographs in *Vogue* magazine of Alex Wek, a south Sudanese model. It wasn't unusual for a Dinka woman to be six feet tall. Mike had heard rumors that modeling agents were on the lookout for Dinka girls. If a girl was lucky, she could get spotted in a supermarket or a department store and be turned into a superstar overnight. His Nokia rang. He flicked open the lid to the voice of a woman speaking to him in Dinka.

"Majok, kwarkwar?" she said over the line in the voice of a woman that had changed more than he'd expected. She was crying.

"Mama?" Mike said.

He realized that his voice sounded different to her, too. She'd known his tiny boy's voice. She didn't know what his grown voice sounded like.

"Majok, Majok," she said through sobs, unable to take him into her arms. "I have to tell you."

"What, Mama?"

"Baba. He didn't make it."

"What?"

"His heart collapsed."

Mike's head filled with images of Baba lying in a cot in one of the medical tents in the camp. In a US hospital bed, he'd have been saved. It was not a complicated problem: a leaking valve. At Kakuma he couldn't get the proper attention.

"It was too late," she sobbed. "The transport was not going out until a few more days. No time. Even if he managed to get on, Baba died before he had a chance."

The phone burned against Mike's ear. "Mama, Mama," he sobbed. He had kept himself alive imagining the sound of his mother's voice. The split seconds he did think he found her back in Pinyudu and Kakuma were the happiest moments he'd experienced. And he'd always regarded those moments as signs.

What is the truth after all? In Pinyudu, a man named Ajak Abregem burned with fever. He became so hot that when he died, a story started getting told that he went to the sun and never came back. He often showed himself, his face rounder and fuller from years of glowing with light. Someone would see him and point him out and the second person would believe the first. One time a whole group of people—adults and children—said they were staring right at him. Mike crawled out of his hut and stood on the field with them and stared until sunspots appeared in front of his eyes. He had to stop looking. He was afraid that if he continued staring at the sun, he would go blind.

"I need to see you," he said. "I need to find a way to get back to Kakuma. I know people who can help. I don't want you to be alone."

"I'm leaving Kakuma. I'm going to Australia. My brother Achier has sent for me. We have been offered political asylum there."

"Australia?"

"I'm sorry," she sobbed. "It took me a long time to get used to the idea. I didn't know if you were alive. What was I supposed to do? I can't stay in the camp. This isn't life. You know that. There are other Dinka people in Australia. Baba's third wife is there."

Mike looked at his sister. "Rebekka's mother?"

"Yes."

"She's alive?"

Rebekka trilled her tongue to form the ululating sound that women make when their emotions cannot be put into words.

"She is."

"My God, my God, my God."

Rebekka grabbed the phone. "Mama Majok?" she said.

Mike squeezed his sister's arms and held her to keep her from falling.

After his sister handed back the phone, his mother told him that she'd given birth to three more children after he disappeared. "Yes. Two boys and a girl," she said. "I have to think of them, too. Australia will take care of us. It is a socialist country. We won't be as miserable there."

Chapter Fifty
August, 2006

THE TUESDAY AFTER the Fourth of July weekend, Mike watched a thick yellow envelope being slipped through his mail slot. Waiting for his court date to arrive was like staring at an open cupboard filled with snakes. He rarely ate, rarely slept. He tore open the envelope, no longer able to delay the inevitable: August 2nd, 2006 was printed in black type. He started to weep. "Only children weep," he told himself, remembering the title of the book he'd read back in middle school in Kenya.

He called Glenn Steele. "Is something going to happen to my mother?" he asked.

"What do you mean, Michael?"

"I told you where she is. It's not safe there. Her brother is helping her get out, but it's going to take some time. What will happen to her if we lose?"

"I've never lost a case yet, Michael, and I don't plan on losing this one."

"I want to wear a suit to court," Mike said. Glenn had advised him to dress like a student.

"No. I know what's important. Trust me on this," Glenn answered.

Wind woke him, sirens blaring. Mike opened the curtains. It wasn't raining, the sky was bright, but not with white light. Instead, it was a kind of ultraviolet haze. Hurricane Chris. The tail end of a hurricane reached land on the very day of his trial. It must have hit during the night. Traffic was blocked up in both directions. Branches from the oak trees in the park across the street had crashed down onto the road, some of them so large that cars needed to go around them to pass.

The summer had been hot and humid, one with little rain. He rushed to get dressed. With one leg sticking through his chinos, he pulled them off and searched his closet for his suit instead. He didn't care what Glenn said. He was going to wear a suit. Phillip had bought him this suit for his college interviews. He felt good in it. The jacket was a little tight, but if he kept it unbuttoned, no one would know any different.

All through his drive along Cobbs Creek Parkway, he skirted fallen branches. The wind lashed against his car windows, pulling him toward the white line dividing the road. Once he exited the Parkway, he kept turning onto closed roads. If a tree wasn't blocking the road, a line of cars stretched from end to end. On Lancaster Avenue, where few trees grew, only papers and leaves had been blown onto the street. A woman walking her small dog across the intersection wasn't taking any chances and he watched as she bent down to pick up her tiny dog and tuck it under her coat to protect it against the wind.

There were two types of men walking the streets near the Municipal Court House at 13th and Filbert, hunching their shoulders and covering their heads with their hands as the wind blew. There were the ones who looked like lawyers and the ones who looked like criminals. The lawyers wore three-piece suits and the criminals wore T-shirts and jeans. He congratulated himself for going with his gut feeling and dressing in a suit.

Despite his suit, however, he didn't need to wonder which group he belonged to when the middle-aged African-American guard stopped him as he walked toward the Figgins, Ryan, and Phillip. They sat on a bench outside courtroom 405, Grace's head turned toward the elevators, waiting for him to emerge.

"Stop, defendants don't enter through this door. Go in through the door opposite the lawyers' lounge," the guard said and pointed past the water fountain to a door on the left.

Mike glanced down at his tie to make sure it was not wrinkled or soup stained, otherwise how did the guard know that he was the defendant? He had tried not to doubt Glenn Steele and his ability to defend him from November 25th when he got out of jail to August 2nd, the date of the trial, and all the hours between eleven and two a.m. while he lay on the couch looking up at the flies trapped inside the plate-glass mount over the light bulb on the ceiling, wondering what it was about the light that attracted them and why they swarmed close to it when they could feel its heat at a distance.

"Of course people will want to help you. These are people who are a part of your life. The last thing they want is for you to cook in jail to pay for a crime you didn't commit," Glenn said the day he asked Mike to assemble his character witnesses.

He remembered the Bible verse that he learned in church. Viktor shouted it from the pulpit, fiery as a prophet himself—Matthew or Luke—and at the time it had meant his whole life and he could not have foreseen its meaning now. It had to do with trampling on snakes or was it scorpions? Yes, that was it. Trampling on scorpions and overcoming all the power of the enemy. *Nothing will harm you*, those were the very words.

Phillip was easy to spot because of his red hair. He sat next to his wife Sue and squeezed her hand. The freckles fixed on his face mimicked his stiff expression, like moving in any one direction might trip a wire and set off a bomb. He didn't smile at Mike or turn to glimpse at him as he walked past.

Rebekka sat in her chair and openly wept. Mike could read his sister's mind. She believed that God was punishing her for leaving Sudan and coming to America. "Why are we the ones who deserve to be saved?" she asked countless times after hearing about another of Omer el-Bashir's atrocities. He saw how she kept turning her head toward the back of the room, as if expecting disaster to follow her in, even after the courtroom doors stopped opening.

At first Glenn subpoenaed the woman's two friends. But in the end, he decided that the hazy recollections derived from girls drinking alcohol at a Halloween party carried no weight. They both told Glenn how they remembered Mike being lifted up onto the keg and the woman saying, "Oh my God! It's Mike. Here's our chance."

"I know she's inappropriate sometimes," they told Glenn, "but she's our friend and we have fun together. We will always be friends."

Glenn did not subpoena Coach. When Dean Eunice told Glenn that if the media picked up the story, the entire soccer team would face attack, Mike stood in front of her desk, eye-level with the cross on the wall behind her, injured, hurt, breathing hard out of his nostrils.

She rose, walked in front of her desk and stood beside him. She wrapped her arms around him the way Grace Figgins often did, warm and mothering. She spoke in a very quiet voice, apologizing. "I'll do what I can. And I'll pray for you," she said.

The journalists who had interviewed him in the past, showed him their compassion. Their voices grew soft as they turned off their tape players and asked him what they could do to help people from Sudan here and abroad. If both sides were permitted to be heard, wouldn't the truth come out and lead to his vindication?

Despite Mike's desire to tell his side of the story to the press, Glenn agreed with Dean Eunice. "If the media steps in," he told Mike, "people will take sides. Most will support a woman, because she's white and female, against you."

"She's lying," Mike said.

"Doesn't matter."

In the room's arrangement, typical to a court of law, Mike sat across from the plaintiff. It was the first time he'd seen her since November. She sat back against her chair, her lips outlined in the bright red lipstick she'd worn on Halloween. He noticed the leopard print on her vest. Why was she wearing leopard print, when he was the Dinka warrior? She was openly attacking him. Why was she doing this? She'd said she wanted to go to Kakuma and help people.

A side door opened. Glenn had told Mike that he'd find out a few days before the trial would begin who the judge would be, and once he knew, he could fashion his arguments accordingly. Yet, he never did tell Mike who the judge was. Now Mike knew why.

The judge, a gray-haired African-American woman, entered. No wonder Glenn didn't pass on the information.

Watching the judge peer at him through her spectacles put him back into a hut at Kakuma, trying to escape the harsh light of the sun. Sandra H. Greenwich was not the judge he expected. He cursed himself for agreeing to a bench trial. Everything depended on this judge. Despite her skin color, wouldn't a woman side with another woman? All along, Glenn's tactic had been to tell him not to worry. Surely, Glenn said this to comfort him, but now he saw that it reflected Glenn's laid back style. Doused in cologne and with his black hair slicked back, Mike had regarded Glenn as reassuringly assertive. His stomach churned and his heart pounded, now knowing he'd misread him.

Judge Greenwich was only five feet tall, yet everyone stood when her entrance commanded the room. Mike caught a look at Phillip, who rose from his seat with his mouth wide open. Seeing Phillip's reaction to the female judge filled Mike with despair. Judge Greenwich banged her gavel on her desk, and her voice called for silence in such a sharp hiss, it was as if a swarm of bees had been released into the room to rule over the proceedings.

The trial took two days. One by one, Mike's witnesses were called to the stand. "I can describe Mike in one word," Phillip said after Judge Greenwich swore him in, "and I don't use this word lightly. The word I would use to describe Mike is noble."

"Why is that Mr Armstrong?" the judge asked.

"If you had an opportunity to meet him, you would know that he is concerned with other people, loves other people. He is an incredible person to be around. People who know him see it right away. I've given him access to my financial records, my files, all my confidential papers pertaining to my company. That's how much I trust him. He has never asked for anything in return. The truth is, he is the first person from Africa I have ever gotten close to and I did not know what to expect. Now I do. Michael has made me a more tolerant person. I've seen Michael interact with all kinds of people. My wife, my children, the college-age children of my friends. He has shown everyone the greatest respect."

Viktor followed. As a pastor, he was accustomed to speaking in front of a crowd, and he commanded the room. Although he was made to sit down while he spoke, his voice thundered. He didn't just say that Mike was noble, but that Mike's nobility showed itself in everything that he did—bringing his family to the US, getting them scholarships to attend a private high school and going to college. "And what is a noble person? Viktor asked. "Is it an encourager? Michael is that. Is it a justice seeker? Michael is that. Is it a leader? Michael is that. You see I could go on and on listing Michael's attributes."

When Ryan took the stand, he presented documentation—a file folder filled with letters that teachers and schoolchildren wrote to Mike after hearing him talk about his life at Model UN presentations. "He's not just a gifted speaker," Ryan said, "but someone who is compelled to tell others what he has witnessed. His experiences have made a difference in people's lives. He had the courage to start life over. He bears testimony that cannot be duplicated. No cemetery holds his dead. No memorials. Michael has learned the hard way what it is to be human. He inspires people."

Grace blinked back tears. She sat before the judge, waiting to be called upon to speak. After she swore to tell the truth, she told the court about the day she first met Mike, describing the rubber sandals on his feet. "Although the air that day was cold—it was November—Mike's feet had trekked thousands of miles across desert wilderness without shoes of any kind. He's become a second son to me. He's given me a fuller, richer life. I love him with all my heart."

Judge Greenwich thanked Grace and she returned to her seat, glancing at Mike with her sparkling eyes. Next was Rebekka. The judge called her name. "Rebekka Kuch. Rebekka Kuch, please take the stand."

Rebekka bent her head to hide her tears.

"Ms Kuch," Judge Greenwich said, "can you continue or do you need a few minutes to collect yourself?"

Shaking, Rebekka apologized for her English and asked the judge to excuse her because this is the best she can do on a day like today:

"For me, the only way to live these long days one after the other, starting from when I was a child fleeing Sudan, was to tell myself that my parents died in that war. I convinced myself that I saw someone shoot them. I played this trick with myself because it is the only way for me to be alive and not suffer in my heart. Our father always tell us that Mike have special qualities, and I know that. The reason I tell this today is because Mike will never tell you. Mike is a hero. He help hold me up. He gave me our father and mothers. He believed our parents are alive. I learned from him what faith is. No matter how many times I yelled at him 'our parents are dead,' he never gave up. He showed me, no matter how impossible the situation seems to be. He searched and searched and just one month ago, after seventeen years of searching, he found our father. Even though our father was far away living in Kenya, we got to speak with him on the telephone for couple minutes. Our father was very ill. This was our final chance to speak with him before God took him up in his arms. Now my heart is very big. Would I have made it here without Mike? Made it through all these years? My answer is simple. No, I would not. I would not have made it without Mike."

No one dared to break Rebekka's spell over the room and even Judge Greenwich observed the silence that followed. "Thank you for your cooperation and your service as a witness. You can sit down now," she waited to say. Rebekka turned away, looking for Mike. He locked eyes with her. Judge Greenwich called Ezekial, and Rebekka sat down.

Ezekial walked toward the bench. "I am my father's first-born son," Ezekial began. "Mike is second, born only months apart. Our father had four wives. This is the way of Dinka people. Mike and I are each first-born sons. We each have a different mother. My siblings and I got separated in the war. I believed they were dead. The day we found each other was a miracle. From that day on, a struggle started between Mike and me. Who would be head of our family? I search my heart and found there one answer. Mike. Why did I let him have it? There is one reason. I was too selfish. We were all trying to survive, but in that place, I was concerned only with taking care of myself. It was a place where you could not depend on having food or water. Every day was struggle. It wasn't that way for Mike. He put the welfare of our sister, younger brother, cousin and myself first. He would walk barefoot through desert wilderness without water when the ponds had gone dry. Here in this country, he supports our family with having two jobs, even as an A student and star athlete. Always putting everyone else first. Never himself."

Mike rose. He nearly stumbled. He repeated the statement to tell nothing but the truth. It was happening. Once again, events were changing the course of his life. His path was being diverted, but this time he was going to stay, here in full view of everyone. This time he would not run.

As Glenn interrogated him, everything stood out clearly in his mind, from their meeting in line that very first time at Java Cup, to the Halloween party—her blonde hair bleached to look white—to the moment when she opened her bathrobe and kissed him.

He took his place at the stand and sat straight and tall, his feet on the floor, his hands in his lap. He summoned his mother in an effort to calm himself. When he was a child he had listened to his father mediate complaints within the clan. And the elders had carried on the tradition in Kakuma. This was the moment he'd been waiting for since his arrest, the moment to present the truth. Glenn approached.

"Michael, can you tell us how you met the plaintiff?"

"We met in line at a coffee shop in downtown West Calvary."

"Just once?"

"No, after that first meeting we ran into each other several times and stayed and talked."

"Why did you appear at the plaintiff's apartment?"

"She invited me for tea."

"Had you been to her apartment before?"

"Yes, she invited me to a Halloween Party." He glanced at Phillip.

"So, it did not appear unusual in any way that she invited you to her home?"

"No."

"And you believed you would be drinking tea and talking together?"

"Yes, that was what I did expect."

"And when she answered the door to let you in, what was she wearing?"

"A bathrobe."

"And did you in any way force her into the bedroom as she claimed?"

"No, she waved her hand for me to follow her."

"After you went into the bedroom, what happened?"

"She kissed me."

"Did you kiss her back?"

"Yes."

"And when you kissed her, as she testified, did she object?"

"No, she did not."

"When you put your hands on her and touched her, as she testified, did you do so without her consent?"

All along he had expected her to retract her accusations against him, leap out of her chair, confess she had not told the truth and stop the proceedings. This could not be the version of justice he had fantasized about in Kakuma, believing he'd find it, once he received the glorious good fortune to live in the States. He could feel Rebekka's eyes on him, welled with tears. "No, I did not," he said.

"Michael, did you in any way force yourself on her, or did she tell you that you did not have her permission or consent to touch her?"

"No, sir."

"Did you against her will kiss or touch her breasts?"

"No, at all times she initiated all the processes we went through, all the activity. At no time did I force her. At no time did I do anything against her will."

"Did she indicate at any point that you did not have her permission or consent?"

"No," he said.

"I don't have any further questions."

Lieutenant Fitzgerald told the court that when he heard Mike was Sudanese, his first thought was to question his status and contact Immigration to determine whether he was legal.

"Did he volunteer any information?"

"What do you mean?"

"Did he tell you that he had lived in a refugee camp?"

"No."

"Did he tell you that he had been granted political asylum?"

"No."

"When you met with Michael, did you advise him of the fact that you had contacted INS?"

"Yes. I did."

"And how was Michael that night? What state of mind was he in?"

"He was shaking and stuttering. He fell off a chair. I couldn't get him to calm down."

"Because you told him that you could get him deported to Sudan. Is that correct?"

"Yes."

"And did he tell you what he was thinking?"

"No. What do you mean? I don't understand."

"He didn't tell you that a charge like this could threaten his life and the well-being of his family?"

"No, he didn't tell me that."

During the testimonies, the courtroom was quiet, but now everyone was speaking at the same time. People didn't even bother to whisper. They turned around to the people on all sides of them to voice their opinions. If Mike got sentenced, then people could talk all they wanted. He wouldn't hear them. He'd be sitting in a holding cell with handcuffs shackled to his wrists, waiting for a plane to Juba.

What made him think that he could escape Khartoum and find refuge in a new country? He looked down at his shoes. If he was deported to Sudan, he would pack the shoes he wore in his suitcase and give them to the first beggar on the street. His shoes would be useless to him, along with his suit.

Glenn thanked Judge Greenwich and listed the consequences of the case. "Number one, a guilty sentence could mean Mike's deportation. Number two, it could mean his death. Third, it could mean the arrest or death of his family in Sudan, those who he had left behind, exposing them to a situation more brutal for its untruth.

Think about it, Judge, and determine whether Michael based on what he has told you today engaged in nonconsensual relations or whether this was a consensual event between two young people. Consider Michael's conduct, the extent of his life experiences and his current interactions and friendships, how he is in many ways, a symbol of honor and fortitude, amazing values that have inspired countless people, as his witnesses expressed. You and I have heard or read accounts of people who have survived wars. We have heard or read about their traumas. The trauma of war is not easy to overcome. War denies the most beautiful aspects of life. Michael's ordeal might have turned some people into child soldiers. It might have made him bitter and angry, isolated from other people. But Michael sought a support system to sustain him. Surviving turned Michael into a person of strength and integrity with support and love from all those he has come in contact with. The people who have come to court today to give their testimonies have described to us Michael's qualities. The word noble has been used repeatedly to describe him. He was invited to a woman's apartment for tea. He expected tea and conversation. What happened next was agreed upon between the two of them. Today we have heard testimony from people describing Michael. Each individual we heard emphasized the integrity and respect for life that Michael holds dear. I have seen this today, Judge, and so have you—no greater offering of evidence of innocence in this very court than I have seen as a lawyer in my twenty years."

After a brief recess, Judge Greenwich announced that she had reached her verdict. She called Mike to step forward. He stood in judgment, bowing his head, remembering the many times when his professors said, "We have a special person among us, a person who will truly inspire you," and the entire class turned in their seats to gaze at him.

He felt for the snake fang necklace around his neck. A magician had given it to him at Kakuma. He didn't wear it often, but he remembered to wear it this morning. He rubbed it between his fingers summoning the snake that shed it. "Don't be afraid. A snake will never bite you," his mother had said to him when he was five years old, pointing to the glittering copper skin curled up in a corner of their hut's dirt floor. "Snakes are our clan's totem animal. You are guarded. You have no reason to be afraid." He hid his face in her lap and cried. She picked up a piece of firewood with which to shoo the snake out the door and the snake's long body furled open, its weight shifting inch by inch while he snarled at her, *hurry!*

"In the matter of Commonwealth versus Michael Choul," Judge Greenwich said, "the court having heard the testimony of all parties and having listened carefully to the arguments of counsel, enters the following verdict:

As to the charge of Aggravated Indecent Assault, the court enters a verdict of not guilty. As to the charge of Unlawful Restraint, the court, having granted the motion for judgment of acquittal, enters a verdict of not guilty. All parties in this matter may be excused. We are adjourned. You may adjourn the court," she said and struck her gavel down on her desk.

Rebekka rushed into Mike's arms. He held her and hugged her like the day they first met in the camp. Ezekial, James and Young joined their embrace. Mike looked up to see Grace wipe her eyes with the sleeves of her dress. He reached for her and embraced her and Viktor, then Phillip, Sue and Ryan Teagle. His friends. His heart was filled to breaking. Even Judge Greenwich stayed to enjoy Mike's triumph.

Glenn's voice boomed. "Congratulations, Mike." They embraced.

Behind Glenn's shoulder stood the woman. She said something to her lawyer, then tried to walk out the juror's door, but the guard waved his finger at her and forced her to circle back.

Ryan Teagle stepped toward her. She lowered her eyes, rushed past.

The next day Dean Eunice called Mike to personally welcome him back to West Calvary College.

He didn't move back to his room in the dorms. He rented an apartment with another member of his community five miles from downtown West Calvary and just a block away from the Schuylkill River where all year long colored lights were strung up on the boat houses stretching half a mile down the bank, decorated for victory, painted yellow and orange and crimson.

Chapter Fifty-One

MIKE WAVED TO Grace, Viktor and Tom inside the doorway at the Starbucks on U Penn's campus. They found an empty table, and Viktor unloaded the cardboard carrying tray filled with coffees for him and Grace, and teas for Tom and Mike.

"We are here for you, Mike," Grace said. Viktor nodded.

Mike looked down at the amber-colored liquid inside his cup.

Viktor took a sip. "How can we help you, Mike?"

Mike used to think that Viktor resembled his father. Thoughts of never seeing his father again highlighted their differences. He blamed himself. He dragged his brothers and sister here, making them travel through the air and experience what it felt like to have wings, when the entire time they were strapped down in their seats. "I need to be with my mother," he said.

Grace caught Viktor's eyes and leaned over. "We're here for you Mike, but I'm sorry, we can't send you to Australia. I'm so sorry. I wish we could be the ones to send you there. I feel horrible. I've looked up the cost of the ticket. Twenty-two-hundred dollars. It's just not in the budget. We can't afford it right now."

"I couldn't go anyway, I don't even have an American passport," Mike laughed it off. "Traveling on a permanent identity card is like wiring yourself with explosives and expecting to walk through security."

He looked around at the women in the café, talking together at nearby tables. A woman's hand gripped her baby's carriage, slowly rocking the sleeping infant. Another woman, tall and blonde, in neon blue running sneakers, stood in line, talking on her cell phone. His yearning to see his mother made his hands shake, his head burn.

He noticed Viktor turned in his direction, watching him.

"You formed my inward parts; you knitted me together in my mother's womb," Viktor recited, as if reading Mike's mind, knowing him well enough to hear his innermost thoughts.

"What's that?" Tom asked.

"Scripture. Psalm 139," Viktor told him.

Tom shook his head excitedly. He pushed his hands against the table, and his cup wobbled.

"Watch it," Viktor said.

Tom glanced from one of them to the other. "I know how to get the money, Mom," he said. He waved his arms around and shouted and laughed, "Why didn't I think of this before?"

"How?" Grace asked.

He told them about his friend's mother, Dr Kim O'Day, a teacher at Harriton High. She advised an afterschool human rights club that held all kinds of fundraisers. Walkathons. Hunger Banquets. She raised thousands of dollars. His friend, Josh O'Day would want to help out too.

"Hunger Banquet?" Grace said. "Sounds like a contradiction."

Mike's heart raced while he gulped his tea. He'd met so many high school students over the years, spoken at so many assemblies. He glanced up at the people coming in and out of the door. His body felt light, making room for them.

A week later, he met Dr Kim O'Day outside the Starbucks. She wore a bright blue, puffy down jacket like the one Grace had wanted him to wear when he first came to Philadelphia. Her wavy, long brown hair reached her shoulders. She smiled at him and he saw that her eyes were green. When they walked inside the Starbucks, she flung open the big glass door so hard it hit the wall. Some people sitting at the tables looked up. She pointed to an empty table.

"We don't have much time," she repeated two or three times. "I have to pick up my son soon, then my husband's coming home from work, so let's get started."

She was a mother of two children, a boy and a girl, one in college and one in high school. She ran her hand through her

hair and grabbed a chunk of it close to her head and said that
this was a trying time for her, "...very emotional, you know the
whole mothering thing. In another year, neither of them will
live at home." She told him that if the students in her human
rights club were going to sponsor him, they'd have to learn
more about who he was. And she wanted some time to get to
know him, too. "Can I have your permission to record this
conversation?" she said. She kept jamming in the cassette. She
had forgotten to bring the microphone. "The tape player
belongs to my son. Do you know how to work it?" she asked
him. He showed her how to slide in the tape, how to turn on
the machine. Because this was their first meeting, she only
asked him about his life in the US, what his first days were like.
He told her about Grace and Viktor Figgins and Phillip and
Ryan and how Rebekka called the Figgins 'angels' when they
appeared at the airport in their silver Lutheran Services van.
She played back the tape just to make sure it was recording
properly. Mike heard his voice and cringed. His accent still
sounded foreign, his voice softer than most Americans, so soft
that she turned up the volume to its full range.

The next time she visited him at his apartment. He overslept.
She pounded on the door and called his cell phone to wake
him, then waited outside on the steps until he showered and
dressed. She said that while she was waiting, the trees were
filled with sparrows. "What kind of birds flew about your
village?" she asked.

"*Dierr*, but I don't know what they're called in English.
Actually, they didn't fly in my village. I saw these birds once
with my uncle near my mother's village. Sorry and sorry again
for oversleeping."

"That's okay. You're like any other college student."

"No, I wasn't out partying. It's taken me many years to fall
asleep without the experience of a nightmare. Now I sleep as
much as I am able."

"Let's start there," she said, walking inside and setting up
the tape player. "What kind of nightmares did you have?"

"It wasn't only me. Most boys experienced nightmares."

"How do you know?"

"At the camp, I'd wake up because I heard boys screaming."

"When did you stop having them?"

"A few years ago. After high school. But I could have them again. I could still be having them."

His apartment liked her motherly presence. Her energy was boundless. She could talk for hours. She liked to cook. She often came to see him with the plastic handles of two grocery bags wrapped around the fingers of each hand, struggling to carry them up the steps to his apartment. First she brought him fruits and vegetables, then she researched Sudan and discovered that his diet was more meat-based and unwrapped the cellophane packaging from beef and chicken. When the friends he introduced her to invited her to their barbecues, she learned the recipes for their marinades. He taught her verbs in Dinka, drove her to social events in the basement of the First Mennonite Church in Strasbourg, where she often clutched his hands and together they danced and sang.

She learned to make sorghum porridge, read Francis Mading's *The Dinka and their Songs*, attended lectures on Sudan at U Penn, traveled to DC to participate in Darfur rallies, watched Mike play soccer with the African League, visited West Calvary College, volunteered at Model UN, watched films with him about the genocides in Armenia, Bosnia, Darfur, Rwanda, and the Holocaust. She talked with him about the refugee crisis today and how little had changed since her grandparents fled from pogroms in Eastern Europe. O'Day was her married name. She was raised Jewish.

"Aren't you angry at them for using you?" she said to him one day. They'd been talking for hours, sitting beside one another on the couch, their shoulders touching, the afternoon light changing to dusk.

"Who?"

"The SPLA. Or what you've been calling them, 'Freedom Fighters'."

"What?"

"Why do you think you weren't getting enough food? Did you know the rebels wouldn't let UNHCR into the camps after dark? That the food intended for refugees was used to feed SPLA officers?"

"Where are you getting this information?"

"I'm reading books."

"It isn't that simple. You can't get this from books."

Kim invited him for dinner at her home. She wanted him to meet her husband and children. She lured him there with the promise of hanging out watching TV and playing video games with her son, an eleventh grade student. While they were waiting for her son to get home from soccer practice and her husband to return from his office, she hooked her dog's leash to his collar and dragged him out of his cage. He was a big, sleepy dog and liked to lie down on the soft, white fleece on the floor of his cage. "Come on, Rocky," she said, pulling her dog by the neck. "Time to go out."

"Would you like to come with me?" she asked Mike.

He nodded.

She offered him a pair of her husband's ski gloves. She went outside without wearing any, one hand hidden in her pocket, the other exposed, clutching the leash. They stopped in front of the driveway to a mansion with turrets on the roof and its own entrance gate. "Mtumbo used to live here," she said, "when he played for the Sixers" and she pointed down the driveway to the oversized door, large enough for a seven feet, two inches tall ball player to walk through without having to bend his head.

"Really?" Mike said.

"Yes, in 2001. My kids were invited to his children's Halloween party."

"That's amazing."

"Yes, my children were five and seven. They sat on Mtumbo's knee and we took a picture of them."

"Did you ever meet Manute Bol?" he asked.

"No, but I saw him play. He didn't live around here when he played with the Sixers. He lived in New Jersey."

Mike told her that Bol had visited Kakuma. Mike didn't get to talk to him, but he was in the crowd of boys surrounding him and calling his name.

"Was he Dinka?" she said.

"Yes. Now he's ill."

"I didn't know that," she said

"Yes. He's been giving away all his millions to Sudan. He started a hospital. That's something I'd like to do one day. Start a foundation back home."

"A hospital?"

"A school. I came here to achieve things and to help people back home."

They fell into a sudden silence until they reached her driveway. Her garage door had been left open, and when they returned, they walked into the den to find her son sitting on their brown wraparound sofa.

"You didn't close the garage," she said to him. "You're letting in cold air." She looked at Mike and rolled her eyes, as if he were the authority on not wasting energy. "I'd like you to meet Michael," she said to her son.

Her son, Josh, dressed in his high school soccer uniform, red and white with 'Harriton High School' spelled across the front and his number, 15, on the back, kicked off his cleats. Mike's nose twitched from the familiar locker room smell. After Josh showered and changed, he handed Mike a controller, inviting him to play *Madden 2010* with him. Kim went upstairs to prepare dinner. After a round, Josh stopped the game, "My Mom has been sharing a lot of your stories with me," he said. "Can I ask you something?"

"Sure."

"How did you do it? What kept you going?"

"Searching for my parents, especially my mother. Seeing her again was my one hope."

"Have you?" Josh said.

Mike sucked in air, released a slow exhale. He saw Kim at the top of the stairs and watched her run down. He waited for her to reach them before he answered. "I know where my mother is. She's in a refugee camp in Kenya. It's the same one I lived in, but I didn't know we were there at the same time."

"What?" Kim said, taking a seat next to him on the arm rest.

"Yes, we lived there together five years. We might have seen each other but did not know. There are tens of thousands of people in the camp. Of course, I was looking completely different. The last time I saw her I was five years old. She probably was looking different too. She found out about me the day after I left for the US."

Josh crouched forward. "You mean she found out that you were living in the camp the day after you left?"

"Yes," Mike sighed. "My mother had been trying to find me. My younger brother too. She must have believed we were dead. She only now received political asylum in Australia, and she is going to arrive there in a couple of months."

"Why Australia? Why not America?"

"My brother and I would have embarked to bring her here, but her application to Australia got accepted first."

"So she can't live here with you?"

"No."

"That's terrible!"

"It's okay. She'll be better off in Australia. They offer more services than the US."

"You should go over there and see her," Josh said.

"I don't have that kind of money. It's not possible."

"You won't need money. Once I tell my school. He looked at Kim. "Isn't that what you want to do, Mom? It will be easy to raise the money, right Mom?" Kim nodded. Josh continued talking. "I'm in this special program. Challenge. It's for gifted students. It's not like I'm smarter than anyone, my grades aren't that great or anything, but the teachers are more open-minded. My mother teaches in it too. She's going to bring you to our human rights club, right? We're supposed to find a project to work on. I can work on sending you to Australia."

Josh picked up his controller, as if everything were already settled.

"I didn't even have to give him driving lessons," Kim smiled. "All he did was get behind the wheel. It came natural after all those hours playing video games."

"A friend of mine isn't going back to school," Josh snapped back at her. "He's going to rehab."

"Is that what you're trying to tell me?" she asked him, "that you're not a drug addict?"

"It could be worse, Mom."

The next time Kim came to Mike's apartment, she told him that after he left her house the week before, her son came upstairs and hugged her, then spoke to her in a low voice, squeezing her tightly. "He told me that he couldn't imagine being separated from me the way you were from your mother. You hit a nerve."

Mike nodded.

"He usually doesn't talk that way. Mostly he takes me for granted. You've inspired him. I can't begin to tell you how much this means to me. I'm losing him. He's going off to college. Just one more year."

Mike pulled out a chair for her to sit down, but she continued to stand. "I'm so happy it happened this way. I was going to ask him to work with me to fundraise for you and then he came up with the idea on his own. My son is serious about starting a campaign to reunite you with your mother. She shook her head. "I feel like he can do this. I'll work with him, of course. We wouldn't make a promise to you that we couldn't keep. What do you think about that?"

Mike didn't know what to think. Mostly he was afraid of what the other members of his community would think. They'll wonder why she'd singled him out for help. Some of them would get jealous. "Maybe this doesn't have to stop with me," he said.

"There are friends of yours who haven't seen their mothers?"

"None of us have."

Kim helped Josh organize an OXFAM Hunger Banquet at Harriton High School to raise the money to reunite Mike with his mother in Australia. Besides the Hunger Banquet, they sponsored a Read-A-Thon, a book club event, and Kim's husband organized a benefit dinner at Tastee D's restaurant near his office on South Street. "And just in case we don't raise enough money through those events," Josh told Mike, "my cousins are going to help and one of them is going to use it for his Bar Mitzvah project, and my grandfather is going to help me send out an email with a PayPal account link where all the people we know can contribute right online."

The book club was held in a mansion hidden behind a forest of giant evergreen trees. Audis, Mercedes and Lexuses filled the driveway. A maid answered the door and led Mike and Josh through the wood-paneled entryway to the room where the woman who owned the house sat curled up on a couch. Her blonde hair cut short, her blue eyes dusky from picking up the sun-warmed covers of hardbacks, she said, "Welcome to my home." But this was not a home. Homes do not have stacks of books piled three feet high in every corner and peacocks painted on the ceilings in gold leaf. Food was laid out on a banquet table, the ladies reaching for chunks of cheese to spread on slices of black bread, crisp chilled vegetables, smoked fish. They drank champagne out of glass goblets. In that house, it felt meaningless to talk about the ten years he suffered in food lines at Kakuma to cook coarse grain over a woodpile, but before long, each lady in the club took out her checkbook and leaned it across her knees and bore down on the ballpoint pen in her hands to link together the letters in their names.

The day of Harriton High School's OXFAM Hunger Banquet, different colored tickets got randomly assigned, each representing a different income group. The people with blue tickets arrived hungry. After all, they'd paid an entrance fee to attend a *banquet* and expected to be served delicious foods to eat, but they received only rice.

A man and woman sat on a blanket on the floor, each holding a bowl of rice, looking on with watering mouths to watch the people given yellow tickets eat soup, roast chicken, potatoes and salad. A girl with long brown hair swinging across her shoulders carried a tray filled with chocolate cakes to the yellow ticket-holders, the fresh scent of the chocolate left a sweet trail. In earshot of the girl, the man shouted, "Rice, we just get rice?"

Kim laughed.

"It was funnier in the camp," Mike said.

"Right," Kim said as she stopped laughing.

Mike did not mean to stop her laughter. Instead, he wanted to catch it. He wanted it to infuse his veins and be carried to his heart. This was a happy occasion. The invitation had read, "We believe our efforts can end poverty and injustice. We invite you to join us."

At the end of the night, Kim laid the money they raised on a table and counted it. The total amount that Kim and Josh and the Harriton students had collected came to four thousand dollars. It was more than enough. Kim led Mike to a computer that stood on a desk in the back of the room. They searched Google Maps for 1449 Moggill Road, the address to his mother's home in Brisbane, Australia. It was located in a suburb, about twelve miles from the downtown region of the city, across the street from a Lexus dealer. Mike smiled at the incongruity. He hoped that she hadn't traded one form of imprisonment for another.

Grace Figgins walked to the back of the room where Mike stood with Kim. She pointed to herself and to Kim. "Michael, look at us. Look at our faces. We're the same age as your mother. Fifty. We were once young and beautiful. This is how we look now. This is what your mother will look like. Are you ready?"

Chapter Fifty-Two

HE HAD NEVER seen a river so clear or blue. Skyscrapers flanked its banks on either side. All those windows staring down at him.

In Juet, the opening to their hut was made of air, not glass. Before the attack, he had walked through it without inflicting a single injury. Now he must regard how he will enter his mother's home. He shook his head. At the time of their separation, he'd been five years old, afraid to run after her.

"I love you," he yearned to hear her say.

"Do you forgive me?" he longed to say, as he sat in the back of the cab, his seat buckle tightened against his hips. Despite his nearness to her, he felt an overwhelming sense of loss.

The driver veered off the exit ramp and rode along the river until he turned at a rotary onto Fig Pocket Road. The next turn was Moggill Road. They passed a sign that read, 'Brisbane Koala Sanctuary.' The Sanctuary was only another kilometer up the road. How did a place become a sanctuary? Three months ago, his mother lived in a mud-and-stick hut in Kakuma. Now the Australian government had temporarily given her a house in a suburban community. Kakuma had sheltered her, but did not offer sanctuary. In comparison, this new place would be better, despite how long it would take her to adjust. Soon they passed the big blue Lexus sign that he had seen on Google Maps before he left for Australia, and the lot filled with shiny new cars.

The driver circled around another rotary to turn at Moggill Road, but missed it and went around again, the way Mike had rushed from place to place, forward around the globe from Sudan to Ethiopia to Kenya to America searching for his mother, arriving in Brisbane. He was unable to guide the driver, dizzy at the thought of making a left turn from the right-hand lane, unaccustomed to the driver's seat in Australia being on the right-hand side of the road. The ride seemed endless, circling infinitely. *Hurry, hurry,* he repeated to himself.

The driver took the correct turn this time and Mike found himself on Moggill Road, searching for 1449. The driver pulled up a narrow cement parking ramp lined with trees. He stopped the cab and parked in front of an eight-foot-high wooden fence, the house behind it hidden.

"This is it," the driver said and turned off the engine.

Mike hobbled out. He had torn his ACL playing soccer in West Philadelphia three weeks before the trip. It happened on his right leg, the same one with the weak ankle that started when Kuol pushed him down in Kakuma. His right foot was the one that a thorn had punctured when he was in the bush with his uncle Thontiop in the days before the attack. That leg had given him so much trouble, it was only fitting that it should be acting up now. Last week, he saw a doctor at U Penn, who told him that it needed an operation. The rip in his muscle would not repair itself. Mike hoped Mama didn't feel ashamed when she saw how he limped.

He hid the crutches behind a bush. For her he needed to be whole. If his Mama saw him holding crutches, she'd think that his leg was permanently damaged. He stood behind the fence and called her on his cell. Someone answered. "Mama...!" he shouted.

She released a sob. When he called from the airport, she'd been weeping, too. She told him that she had expected him to come the day before. He'd confused the time. Traveling to Australia from the US, he crossed the International Date Line and lost a day and got confused. She'd been waiting nearly two decades for him, but this final day caused her more grief than those years combined. She'd kept his siblings home from school. They waited for him the entire afternoon and evening, refusing to go to sleep.

"I'm here. Outside the gate to your house," he said into his cell, words he'd yearned to say all this time. There was no landscape in which he had not imagined saying those words. He thought he'd have the opportunity to say them in Ethiopia or in the streets of Narus, the smoke in the air hastening his mother's arrival, the roads mud-splattered, rutted with jeep wheels and tank treads, leading all the way out to the desert where crowds of people were also running. Her absence had made those landscapes all the more desolate.

"Mama," he repeated. "Come outside. I'm here!"

The driver positioned the camcorder, just as Mike requested. He promised Kim and Josh and the students at Harriton that he'd record his reunion. Those high school kids raised enough money for his ticket and leftover money to lavish on his mother and siblings.

A tall tree with glossy green leaves grew in front of the gate. On one of its branches a bird perched—a cockatoo—one large black eye on each side of its curved bill. It opened its mouth, its cry harsh.

He heard steps, not like the slap of bare feet against soil back in the village where he last saw her, but the crunch of shoe soles stepping onto grass and leaves. Weeping, then a metal clang, and the gate opened.

Two boys emerged. They looked like two different versions of himself. They rushed forward. A little one around the same age he was when he left home, and a teenager, bearing more confidence, taller, dressed in denim shorts and a crisp white T-shirt. They barreled into him and spun him around.

A woman rushed toward him. Still young, she looked exactly the same as she did the last time he saw her, young and beautiful, her skin holding the sun's light. He smiled at her in a kind of dream, as if no time had passed, not a single year.

The air grew blurry with the soft, wood clanking of bracelets. Another woman, her shoulders hunched, her skin no longer radiant, rushed out from behind the gate. She wore a blue and yellow dress, a shawl around her head, and her gapped teeth showed through the part in her lips as screams escaped her. His eyes were playing tricks on him. Now he was looking at the two versions of her, the younger and the older. She lunged forward. Sobbing, she reached him, pressed her head to his chest and clutched his body to hers, under a foreign sky among the harsh cries of a cockatoo, in a country, which his hundred generations of ancestors did not even know existed.

THE END

Acknowledgments

This book's journey began the day that One Book, One Philadelphia's Gerri Trooskin called me in my office at Drexel University and asked me to select ten undergraduate creative writing students to interview ten Sudanese immigrants for *Philadelphia City Paper*. The author and Michael would like to thank One Book, One Philadelphia for choosing *What is the What: the Autobiography of Valentino Achak Deng* by Dave Eggers for their 2008 selection and transforming the City of Philadelphia into a celebration of Sudanese people here and abroad. Michael dedicates this book to the following people: Chol Kuch-plus, Nhial Kuch-plus, Adior Kuch-plus, Awel Kuch-plus, Adior Magot Majok, Museme Munira and the entire Kuch Chol Mang'aai family in South Sudan, Kenya, the United States, Canada and Australia; Mary Akuot Ayom, Jong Adiang, Riak Akech, Manyok Ayuen, Alakiir Makuac Bona Bith, Chol Majok, Chol Akuok, Ngor Chol, Deng Kuol, Mayom Makuach, Malual Nhial, Machar Yuot, Peter Biar Ajak, Aboor Ayii, Ayuen Kuol, Abraham A. Kuol, Garang Kuach; Carl Yusavitz and Mary Tanney; Brien and Jen Tilley, Wayne Jacoby and Global Education Motivators, Gerry Trooskin, Anastasia Shown, David and Karis Yusavitz; Al Puntels, Mike Dolan, Dennis Bloh, Betty Field, Mary Jo Smith, Bro. Rene Sterner, Warren Haffar & Angela Kachuyevski, Selina Coleman, Jacqueline Reich, Sister Cecelia Cavanaugh, Jimmy Lyons ESQ, Sara Kitchen JD, Sister Carol Jean Vale SSJ, Filmon Membrahtu, Lago Gatjal Riaka, David Gatjang, Boutros Kuony, Akuol Aleu, Mabior Ajak, Mabior Malith, Mabior Atem, Ayuen Kuol, James Khot Deng, Ayuen Garang Ajok, Thiong Aker and the Rosehill Street Guys.

Many thanks to anthropologist Brendan Tuttle, for his fastidious fact checking; Patrick Rapa and *Philadelphia City Paper* and the original students and interviewees: Deborah Yarchun, Garelnabi Abusikin, Ahmed Elmardi, Sarah Mason, Fatima

Haroun, Nyoun Yok Gargik, Titus Codjoe, Amira Tibin, Shazia Mehmood, Monica Singh, Amy Brammell, James Lual, Gilbert Flores, Marisa McStravick, Dr Abelgabar Adam, Isaiah Kuch. Thanks to the following people for their help and support: Anastasia Shown and the University of Pennsylvania Africa Center; Dr Terry O'Conner and the Challenge Program at Harriton High School; Drexel University Honors College, Center for Civic Engagement, Kali Gross and Drexel Africana Studies Department, Dean Donna Marusko and Drexel College of Arts and Sciences, Drexel Amnesty International and Justin Bradley; Sheila Watts, Brett Haymaker, Lea Burns, Bill Zorzi, Drexel STAND, Stephanie Lucas, Mia Di Pasquale, Linda and Jake Karlsruher, Troy Iskarpatyoti, Debbie and Steve Wigrizer, Ellen and Larry Cohan, Ellen Frazer, Ellen Sklar, Beth Hartman, Amy Nislow; my parents, Ed and Marilyn Levin, Fran Gloger, ardent listener, Mark Gloger, Matthew Gloger, Jessica Gloger, Cheryl Levin, Aidan Phillips, Emma Phillips; Rigbergs, Rappaports and Millans, David Lynn, Dawn McDougall, Summer Literary Seminars Kenya, Lou Ann Merkle, Angela Vieira, Nyuol Lueth Tong, James Deng, Ayuen Garang, Mary Ayom, Elizabeth Kuch, Elizabeth Silver, Kate Sontag, Cheryl Sucher, Jill Bialosky, Natasha Alexis, Maureen Brady, Jason Wilson, Dan Driscoll, Farrah Rahaman. The Tuscon Festival of the Book Literary Competition, *The Dinka and their Songs* and the *Dinka of the Sudan* by Francis Mading Deng; *Divinity and Experience: The Religion of the Dinka* by Godfrey Lienhardt; *God Grew Tired of Us* by John Bul Dau; *They Poured Fire on Us From the Sky* by Benjamin Ajok, Benson Deng, Alephonsion Deng, and Judy A. Bernstein; *Emma's War* by Deborah Scroggins. Extra thanks to Simone Weingarten of HSE, to my students, everyone who contributed to the Reunion Project—Josh for taking it on, Rick, the visionary who made it happen and, with Teddi, who listened to countless revisions, huge love.

ABOUT MICHAEL MAJOK KUCH

Michael Majok Kuch returned to his homeland of South Sudan in 2010 after attending high school, college and graduate school in Philadelphia. He graduated at the top of his class and was chosen to represent the student body in a commencement speech at his college graduation. During his college years he worked as an East African expert for the NGO Global Education Motivators, speaking at the United Nations on human rights, where he shared the stage with Olara Otunnu and Elie Wiesel. He was a featured Lost Boy of Sudan in the PBS Documentary *Dinka Diaries* and a Fulbright-Hays Group Project Abroad participant. He currently works for the government of the Republic of South Sudan, where he is an advisor in Research and Policy in the Office of the President.

ABOUT HARRIET LEVIN MILLAN

Harriet Levin Millan's debut poetry book, *The Christmas Show*, was awarded the Barnard New Women Poets Prize and the Poetry Society of America's Alice Fay di Castagnola Award. Her second book, *Girl in Cap and Gown*, was a National Poetry Series finalist. She has written for *The Smart Set*, *PEN America* and her poetry has been published in journals such as *Ploughshares*, *The Iowa Review*, *The Kenyon Review*, *The Harvard Review* and *Prairie Schooner*. She holds a MFA in Creative Writing from the Iowa Writers Workshop and directs The Certificate Program in Writing and Publishing at Drexel University. She traveled to South Sudan in 2011, seventeen days before its independence. She and her family founded the Reunion Project, and led by her son, with the participation of Philadelphia-area high school and college students, helped reunite several Lost Boys and Girls of Sudan with their mothers living abroad.

More books from Harvard Square Editions:

CPSIA information can be obtained
at www.ICGtesting.com
Printed in the USA
LVOW12s1712190117
521537LV00003B/587/P